# Highland Rake

## TERRY SPEAR

ISBN: 1480259039
ISBN-13: 978-1480259034

# DEDICATION

Thanks to Vonda Sinclair who talked me into visiting Scotland and shared a fun-filled experience of a lifetime as we set off the alarm at a Wal-Mart equivalent store, drank Irish Cream in Scotland, drove on the wrong side of the road—on occasion—and loved every bit of the dining, bread and breakfasts, and the beautiful castles, friendly people, and fantastic scenery.

Thanks, Vonda, the trip and your friendship mean the world to me!

*-Winning the Highlander's Heart*: "Treachery stalks them at every turn as jealous suitors and scheming family set to destroy a love blossoming under the harshest of conditions." –Coffee Time Romance

*-The Accidental Highland Hero*: "Breathtaking settings, a sword-wielding, sexy Scottish highlander, a great plot, and as an added bonus, a happily-ever-after."—Love Romance Passion

*-Lady Caroline and the Egotistical Earl:* "I got so caught up in the excitement and love story that I could barely put it down. I would highly recommend this one."—Clean Romance Reviews

*-A Ghost of a Chance at Love:* "Murder, Mystery, a ghost and a handsome cowboy...A time travel adventure you'll not forget."—PNR, Paranormal Romance Reviews

*-Highland Rake:* "A fun entertaining Highland adventure. This story was wonderfully humorous but also touching and emotional. Plenty of action, mystery and intrigue make it a page turner. I loved it!" Vonda Sinclair, *My Brave Highlander*

*-Highland Rake:* "Loved the twists and surprises incorporated into the plot--amazing. Kept me turning the pages!" Judy Gilbert

# Prologue

From the moment Alana Cameron and her clansmen had ridden into the mixed pine and oak forest that fall day, she felt uneasy.

The air was cool and wet, gray clouds covering the whole sky as Alana quickly lost sight of her da and the rest of the men racing after the stag somewhere hidden in the dense woods. At nine summers, no matter how hard she tried, she could not keep up with the Highland warriors.

One of the lads stayed with her, eager to be with the men instead of watching her. Landon was five and ten summers like her brother, only Connell had been caught stealing a loaf of bread from the kitchen that morn and their da had punished him by making him stay at the keep.

*Poor Connell.* She knew he had only taken the bread to give to a family living beyond the curtain wall who had not enough food to feed their family. Her da had not been pleased with two of their nearly grown lads who had caused trouble with the MacNeill clan bordering their own lands when her da had not approved it.

But now the sense of foreboding she'd been feeling intensified. At first, all she heard was the sound of the men's horses running through the woods, but then men's shouts filled the air. Cries of warning. Angry words. Curses—the like she'd never heard of before.

The sound of swords clanked against each other as if the men were practicing their sword skills out in the woods now instead of in the inner baily. *That* had her heart pounding furiously. She knew they had to be fighting somebody, and she'd never been in the middle of a skirmish before. She trembled, unable to help herself.

The lad staying with her appeared uncertain. He ran the strips of leather through his fingers as he stared in the direction the fighting took place, hidden from their view. She knew he wanted to see what the matter was. She knew he hadn't wanted to sit watching her if the rest of the men needed him to help them fight off whoever had attacked them.

Yet she was certain her da would have wanted Landon to stay with her.

"Stay here," Landon finally said, his voice hard and a command.

She nodded.

He swallowed hard as he studied her for a moment, looking as though he was uncertain if he should leave her alone. Would he get into trouble if he did?

Then he took a deep breath and frowned at her, his brown eyes narrowed. "Stay. I will be right back." He sounded like a lad trying to be a man.

She wanted to tell him to stay with her. That she was afraid for him and afraid for herself. But she couldn't. He was older and in training as a warrior. He knew what was best. She couldn't help wanting him to remain with her though.

Landon rode toward the fighting and like the rest, disappeared in the thick woods. She sucked in a deep breath, trying to settle her fright. She sat quietly on her horse, grateful Lettie was staying put, not shying away and not making a sound. For the first time ever that she'd gone to the forest, Alana felt scared, the chill in the air seeping into her bones despite the warm green and dun wool cloak draped over her shoulders and the hood pulled up over her head. The fighting continued and she knew they were nearby, but she'd never felt so all alone in her life.

Startling her, she saw her da suddenly ride through the pines, the stark terror in his expression revealing all was not well. He looked angry about the fight and regretful mayhap that she had been with them. She wanted so for him to tell her that all was right and that he was returning her home at once. She wanted to ask where Landon was and why he had not returned the lad to watch over her.

Instead, her da shouted, "Dismount, Alana! Hide yourself, lass!" Then before she was ready to face the uncertainty alone, he turned and rode back into the forest, vanishing in the greenery.

Terrified, she didn't want him to abandon her now. Her heart in her throat and her body trembling, she jumped down from her horse, not wanting to desert her. She was almost certain if she tried to ride toward the safety of the keep— though she didn't know the way as she'd never been this far away from the castle or this deep in the woods—someone could hear her. Her da must have known she could not ride away fast enough to save herself.

Tears threatened to spill as her body shook so hard, she was having a difficult time trying to decide where to hide. She quickly found a fallen tree to use as a makeshift wall on one side of her, wishing she was home, safe inside their stone fortress. She gathered leaves about her and piled more of the rest of them on top of her as if they had blown that way against the log. Some of them had and she hoped the rest didn't look too out of place. They were wet and smelled of mold and decay and made her want to sneeze.

She'd done this countless times before, following her brother and his friends into the woods nearer their home, burying herself so she could listen to the tales they told without them knowing, their bragging about what they would do in the future, how brave they were, and how they had kissed the lasses. She wasn't sure about the other lads, but she knew her brother didn't lie about his own conquests. Partly because he was the laird's son and partly because the lasses found him charming and irresistible, he had no trouble finding plenty of young lasses willing to kiss him back.

She was glad he was not here now or he would have ridden off with his friend, Landon, and they could both be killed. Thank the heavens she had worn her brown *léine* instead of the green one this morn. And her green and dun plaid brat was the one she always wore on a hunt. She hoped she blended in with the dead leaves.

With the dead tree beside her, she felt somewhat protected, and then felt foolish. What if no one was even looking for her?

The shouts and curses of the men in the woods, the clanking of swords and even the neighing and snorting of horses faded away until there was only the sound of the wind ruffling the pines and other trees' branches.

She barely breathed, trying desperately to slow her racing heart, listening for any sound that told her someone was coming. The absence of sounds was more frightening than all the noise before.

No one came. Not a word was spoken as if the battle had been fought and everyone had gone home and forgotten her, leaving her behind.

A million thoughts raced through her mind— of wanting to unbury herself from her leafy blanket, of wanting to find the others.

Then she heard boots walking toward her, crunching on leaves and twigs, snapping them in two.

No voices. No one calling her name. No one speaking to anyone else. Why was no one saying anything?

More boots clomped through the forest and the sound of horses' hooves tromping on the ground. Why wasn't anyone speaking?

A pair of boots drew closer. Too close. She held her breath. The leather of his boot brushed her arm. She choked back a cry of distress.

Was it one of her men? She didn't think so. If it was one of her men, he would call out for her. Did these men know she was here?

If they had found her horse, they would know

a girl had been riding it. She pressed her fingers against the hilt of her dirk, the dagger sheathed at her waist. Her bow and quiver of arrows were with her horse, but these men would know by the size of her bow, that it had been made for a child.

Where was her da? The others?

"She is here," the man whispered. "Somewhere, hiding."

She felt her skin tingle with fresh dread.

Another nearby said in just as hushed a voice, "Keep searching. He wants her found."

*Who* wanted her and did they mean to search for Alana? That they knew who *she* was?

She didn't recognize the men's voices. They continued to look for her farther away now, while dark shadowy fingers stretched into the forest as the day began to fade into evening.

As the sun began to set in the night sky, the rich greens and browns of the forest turned to shades of gray. She shivered from the cold, her wool cloak and linen *léine* no longer warm enough. They were still searching for her, though she wondered if they were using torches now to locate her, when she heard more riders.

These men were speaking, and she thought they couldn't be with the others because they were not as sneaky and had newly arrived and had come from the direction of the MacNeill's land, not the same as the others.

"I heard sword fighting this way, James," a lad said.

"Aye, Dougald, and 'tis no' our concern. If Cameron has a fight on his hands, he can deal with it. These woods are no' our own. And he would be vexed if he were to learn we were here as strained as our relations are."

The MacNeill? James, the laird, and Dougald? The younger brother who was much like her own brother, a rake, even at his youthful age. She wanted to call out to them, but then again, they were the enemies of her clan. What would they do with her, if they got their hands on her?

Another spoke, "Dougald, James, 'tis no' good. I have ill tidings. Over here."

"Malcolm, what have you...God's knees." James quit speaking.

She banked the tears fighting to be released. She didn't want to know what the MacNeill brothers had found. She didn't want to hear the news.

"Come, lass," Alana's da said, giving her a fright, seeming to appear out of nowhere, and she had to cover her mouth to muffle the shriek that tried to escape.

That *did* escape. Muffled, aye, but still she'd made an unnatural sound that was sure to give her away.

The MacNeills grew quiet.

How had her da found her still buried in the leaves now that it was growing so dark? Where were the rest of their men? The lad, Landon?

"Let us go home now," her da said, his voice gentle but insistent as if he was attempting not to frighten her any more than she already was.

She stood, brushing off the leaves that had caught on her woolen cloak and opened her mouth to speak.

"Nay, dinna speak, lass. Dinna say a word. 'Tis no' safe here for you."

Nor for him. Why was he speaking aloud when she couldn't even whisper a word?

"Did you hear it?" Dougald asked. "In the woods some distance away. Over there?"

Panic rose inside her as her da said in a rush, "Hurry, Alana, come this way."

She tried to follow him without tripping over the hem of her tunic or brat or roots or dead branches. She attempted to make the least amount of noise as her boots hurried over the uneven terrain, crunching on the fallen leaves, but not as loudly as the men had done since she was so much lighter in weight. She wanted to ask her da where his horse was and where hers was. Couldn't they ride faster if they were together? Or if she rode with him?

But her da was leading the way and she barely could see anything but him striding quickly ahead of her. She dared not disobey him for he knew the way of warriors and what to do to survive. She dared not lose sight of him, either.

"Over here," Dougald said. "'Tis a young lass's horse. Dinna you think?"

"Lady Alana's horse?" James asked. "She would be the only young lass who would own a horse on the Cameron's lands."

She turned to head back that way—the horse was hers and she wanted her. *Lettie.* What would they do to her? She wanted to protect her.

"Nay," her da warned, his voice rough and

edged with concern. "Dinna look back. We are going home, Alana. The others are still searching for you."

*The others.* She should have asked who he meant, but her thoughts were still on her horse and what the MacNeills would do with it. 'Twas her horse!

"I have searched, but I have no' found any sign of the lass's body with the others," Dougald said. "Niall, look over there."

"I have searched. Gunnolf and Angus are sweeping the area south."

"Riders!" someone shouted in the distance, and she thought they were some of the men who had attacked hers.

A chill swept up Alana's spine as she continued to hurry after her da and the other riders headed away from the MacNeills and away from her and her da.

Her da urged, "Hurry, Alana. We must hurry before any of them find you."

Any of them—the others and the MacNeills?

# Chapter 1

*Ten years later, Braniff Castle, Cameron Stronghold*

With thoughts of preparing for the coming winter and any sickness that might befall the clan, Alana Cameron was snipping medicinal herbs in the garden when she saw movement on the path and looked up, barely managing to stifle a scream. She had not seen her dead brother in several days, believing he had finally passed to whatever world he belonged after he'd died.

She couldn't believe he was here. *Again.*

He'd never visited her in the gardens before, her place of sanctuary. Why couldn't he find his proper resting place and leave her be? Not that she didn't love him, but half the time his sudden appearance came as such a shock, she feared screaming out and her clansmen would believe she was possessed.

Standing tall, his arms crossed over his chest, an imperious look on his face, Connell scowled at her. Earlier this morn, she'd gathered blaeberries, bog myrtle, and butterwort from the moorlands. Why had her brother not visited her there where not a soul had been about? Not that there was anyone in the herb garden at this very moment, either, but there could have been and someone could still show up at any time.

"Go away," she whispered, making shooing motions, only because she was alone or she would have to feign he didn't exist. Which he didn't. At least to anyone else.

Why did she have to be plagued with spirits of those who died a violent death and couldn't seem to find their way to the next world? Thankfully, most did, but a few, like her brother, were the exception. She needed only *one* to make her nearly expire on the spot with his or her sudden appearance.

"You didna warn me the lass's husband was returning," Connell growled.

She couldn't believe how real he looked, standing there in his plaid, his blond hair several shades darker than hers, brushing his shoulders, his blue eyes hard with condemnation. She frowned back at him, having had this discussion right after the Highlander had killed her brother.

The fault was not her own! How could he not see that he should take full responsibility for the calamity that had befallen him? Mayhap that was why he was still hanging around her. He needed to accept his complicity in the matter before he found peace.

"I told you," she whispered in an annoyed voice. "I warned you the lass you were dallying with would be your downfall. That her husband wasna one to challenge."

She loved her brother, but no amount of warning him of his folly would have changed his course. When he wanted a lass and she was willing, that's all that needed to be said. The wee matter of a husband would not have stood in Connell's way.

"My lady," a maid said, joining Alana on the stone path in the herb garden.

Heart pounding, Alana whipped about so suddenly, she startled Pelly, a maid who helped Cook in the kitchen. The maid gasped, then quickly curtseyed, her raven-colored hair plaited tight against her head, her soft blue eyes glancing nervously about as if she might have thought Alana *wasn't* alone. But then seeing no one about, she most likely feared Alana was speaking to something or someone no one else could see.

Alana shielded her eyes from the early morning sun, as she stared at the girl, her pulse racing, afraid the servant had overheard Alana speaking to her dead brother and spied her motioning for him to go away. They'd had no rain for days. She'd had to carry water to her special garden just to keep the plants from burning up, and now she was even hotter than before, her skin freckled with perspiration from worry.

"Annoying flies," Alana said, trying to explain why she had been waving her hand in the air and shooing her ghostly brother away. If the girl had heard the rest of her conversation though…

Pelly quickly lowered her lashes, hiding her eyes and whispered, "A lad came by to tell Laird Cameron that Odara, the shepherdess living near the border between our land and that of the MacNeill's, is ill."

Frowning, Alana rubbed her hands together vigorously to brush off the dirt. "My uncle has been gone three days. Has she been ill all this time and no one has told me?" She tried to keep the bite out of her words, but she should have seen to the shepherdess three days ago!

The woman gnawed on her lower lip, then shook her head. "I…I overheard the lad tell your uncle, my lady. I thought he would advise you of the matter. But…but then you never left to see the shepherdess, and I know you *would* have. I…I thought you should know the way of it." She quickly lowered her gaze again.

"All right," Alana said, trying to be consoling. The girl was not at fault for her uncle's omission. Had he forgotten to tell her in his haste to depart for his destination—that was supposed to be unknown to her, though she'd heard rumors that he'd gone to see the MacDonalds?

"I…I overheard him say he was angry the shepherdess had refused to wed a widowed clansman that had offered for her twice, so she could suffer her illness on her own for all he cared," Pelly finally said, breaking into Alana's thoughts. "So when you did not go to her, I thought mayhap you didna hear about it."

Staring at the girl, Alana realized her mouth gaped and she quickly closed it. How could her uncle be so cruel? He normally wasn't like that, she didn't think. Unless he was aggravated about the shepherdess for some other reason as well. Or mayhap his travel objective had made him cross.

Alana was a healer, her mission being to ease the suffering of others as much as she was able. She didn't pick and choose who she would aid in his or her time of need. Odara was Alana's age and pretty with sparkling blue eyes and light red hair, and had played with her when they were little when Odara's mother used to bring sheep to the castle to sell. She was the only girl Alana had ever confided fully in about her secret. Odara had not feared Alana for her oddity, but instead had been fascinated. Even now that they were grown, whenever Odara brought sheep to the castle, Alana always went to see her and wish her well. Though because of Alana's position, Odara was shy around her whenever others were about.

Pelly dropped her gaze to the ground again.

"Thank you, Pelly. That will be all."

The girl curtsied and moved out of her way on the narrow garden path lined with stones.

Alana hurried past her and headed for the servants' entrance, hoping that if her brother had still been standing behind her, he stayed in the garden and wouldn't follow her. Her uncle would have a fit if he knew she used the servants' passage, but it was quicker to reach from the gardens, and the servants were used to seeing her entering it.

Besides, he wasn't there to say anything about it anyway.

Furious he hadn't told her that the woman was ill, now knowing he had done so on purpose and it wasn't an oversight on his part, she wouldn't delay leaving to see to her. What if Odara were to die? Or had died? Alana shook her head at the thought.

It did no good to consider the possibility.

She rushed through the great hall and noticed a few servants glancing in her direction. Her uncle's advisor, Turi, was speaking to one of the men who would be serving guard duty while a young girl was carrying in fresh rushes and spreading them on the floor.

If her uncle had told his advisor that she was not to leave the castle to see to the shepherdess's health should she get word of it, she feared he might try to stop her. She would use the servants' stairs to the floors below hers when she was ready to leave.

In her bedchamber, she hastily packed herbs in a leather pouch, then quickly exchanged her crimson and blue brat for the pale blue and green plaid wool one. If it had not been so far, she would have walked, but she would have to take her horse, so it would be impossible to leave without some noticing.

She might not have any say in what their people did, but being the niece of the clan chief made her more visible just the same.

She covered her plaited locks with a blue veil, the pale color of her hair a curse. In the full light of the moon, she was certain her hair could be seen from a mile away across the glen.

"Where are you going?" her brother asked, and this time she gasped.

Turning, she glowered at him. Why couldn't he be like a misty version of himself at least, and not so solid she felt she could touch his skin and feel the warmth there still. "Connell, go away! Do whatever you are supposed to do to find peace and leave me alone!" she whispered harshly.

"I canna. 'Tis no' my fault. 'Tis yours."

Annoyed with him that he would find fault with her for his own rash actions, she knew he'd say that again. For whatever reason, he truly believed she was keeping him here, when she had naught to do with it!

"I suspect that our uncle is hoping for an alliance with the MacDonalds," Connell said, changing the subject. "Which means you will most likely be marrying one of the MacDonalds. The middle brother, Hoel, I would think."

She wasn't happy about it, not that she expected to be delighted about any marriage her uncle arranged for her. "Did you overhear him speaking with Turi or someone else about it?" She should have thought to ask her brother. Then again, it would not make any difference as to her fate.

"Aye, I did. I didna wish to speak of it because I didna think you would wish to hear of it."

She'd only seen Hoel once years ago when he was bullying another lad. She'd had to remind herself that he was a warrior, and they all fought and tried to come out on top like a pack of wolves. The weakest didn't stand a chance. With her, he'd treat her as a lady. That's what she told herself. She was only nine at the time, and he, four and ten, so he had only given her a cursory disgruntled glance, his older brother a couple of years older, teasing him mercilessly about marrying the fae wench.

*Fae.* A derogatory slight because they must have heard the rumors she spoke to the fae. Or mayhap it was because of her hair that some said was so unnaturally light it shown like a soft moon's glow. Didn't that make her one of *them*?

"What do you know about him?" she asked.

"He is strange. Mayhap as much as you?"

She glanced up at her brother, not understanding his meaning. He smiled at her, warmly, in a genuinely affectionate way.

Many years ago during the ambush of their father, the Cameron clan chief and his men while she had been riding with the hunting party, and at her father's urging, she had hidden in the woods as he and the rest of his men fought valiantly to the last man. The overwhelming numbers had been too much, and her father and the rest of her clansmen had been murdered.

Although, she did not believe her father had been. Not when he stayed with her to ensure she'd find her way home. It wasn't until she'd reached the walls surrounding her castle two days later that she'd learned her father had died in the forest with the rest of his men and that he *hadn't* been with her at the gatehouse. When her people had fussed over her so and hadn't spoken a word to her father, she'd turned to look and see why he was not shouting orders. He had vanished.

Her uncle had ridden out with an army of men and brought back her father and their clansmen's bodies, but she wouldn't believe her father had not brought her home. That's when her kin really began to worry she was touched by the fae. From then on, she had learned to keep the truth from her people and pretend she was like everyone else who couldn't see or hear the dead. She wished it had been true.

If her brother was here like her father had been, why would Connell remain behind? To see to her welfare? But she was home, safe. No one to harm her here.

"What do you mean that he is strange, Connell?" She grabbed her leather pouch of herbs and hurried out of her chamber.

"I am no' certain. But others say he is different."

"Mad?" she asked. That's all she would need was to be married to a madman.

Once she reached the corridor to the servants' quarters, she moved quickly down the narrow winding stone stairs and was soon at the landing. She glanced back, saw no sign of her pesky brother, and stalked toward the kitchen where she pilfered a loaf of bread and filled her flask with mead. Then she left through the servants' door that led outside. Everyone was busy with their daily chores, so none seemed to notice her as she made her way across the inner bailey. The greatest difficulty would be taking her horse from the stable.

She hoped if anyone had been watching her, they would only think she was drying herbs and plants for future use, stocking up for the winter to come. It wasn't unusual for her to do so, although it was a wee bit early for gathering all the herbs.

As soon as she entered the stable, she smiled brightly at one of the lads grooming a horse. "Can you saddle my horse for me?"

He bowed quickly, stammered an, "Aye," with a belated, "my lady." He began to ready her horse.

As quickly as he could, he had her horse saddled and offered to help her mount.

"Thank you," she said sweetly, climbing onto the saddle, then kneed her horse toward the gates.

She walked her, afraid to stir much interest as a group of men was moving toward the gates, either going to the village or working their fields. A man driving a wagonload of barrels headed out also. Outside the curtain wall, several men were working on repairs to the stone barrier. Guards were always posted along the wall walk, and she was certain they'd watch her as she headed beyond the outer curtain wall and see which direction she was going.

She wanted to head straight for the shepherdess's croft, but there were no plants she could harvest to use to heal the sick or wounded in that direction, so the guards might wonder where she was going and someone might try to stop her. Instead, she took a round-about way to the forest where she would normally collect plants. By then she was too far out of the guards' view for them to see where she was truly headed.

Since her uncle would be away for several more

days, Alana would have no trouble seeing to the woman and returning before he knew any better. If her uncle had been in residence at the castle at the time, the guards might not have made the mistake.

Fearing her uncle might learn of Alana's defiance, she did not take a maid with her. She was afraid he would punish a maid accompanying her as well. Besides, her favorite maid, Turi's daughter, Brighid, was ill this morning. Alana hadn't been able to determine what ailed her. She hoped that whatever she had was not something that was catching among their people. Still, she couldn't imagine how Odara and the maid would have come into contact since they lived so far apart, and she didn't remember seeing the shepherdess at the keep recently.

She had nearly reached the woods that fringed a blue loch when she saw a lad racing across the glen. "Hey, you, Kerwin! What are you about?" she called out, thinking the boy might be able to help her since he did not appear to be helping anyone else.

The boy stopped, turned, and gaped at her, his strawberry curls touching his shoulders, his brown eyes wide.

If Odara could not tend to her sheep, mayhap the lad could, if he was not needed for chores. Since he did not seem to be doing them anyway…

The lad ran toward her then. "My lady," he said, then gave her a clumsy bow.

"Are you done with your chores?" She was surprised that someone as old as he, looking to be about eight, would be through with them this early, and was more than likely avoiding them.

He frowned, flushed a nice shade of red, and said

in a low mumble, "I was helping my brothers, but one shoved me in the pig's pen. They threatened to toss me in the loch to clean me up after they finished the chores."

He did smell like he had been wallowing in the pig's pen, ripe with the stench. "Would you come with me and help the shepherdess, Odara, tend her sheep if she is too ill?"

"Oh, aye, my lady." He gave her a big grin, his face as dirty as the rest of him.

He could have used a good dunking in the loch. It certainly was warm enough.

"Will your mother be worried about you if you dinna tell her where you are going?"

"Nay. There are six of us and she is happiest when some of us dinna come home to eat." He looked up at her as if he was hopeful she would provide him a meal.

"I will see to it that you eat. You may have to stay for a couple of days."

He grinned more broadly.

She sighed. "'Tis too far for you to walk, but my horse willna take you unless you are clean."

His eyes grew wide, and he glanced back at the loch.

A deep voice said behind her, "What trick is this you play on the lad. I didna think you had it in you, Alana."

She felt her skin prickle with heat. She did not turn to see her brother and instead said to the boy, "Do you know how to swim?"

"Aye."

"I will take you with me if you swim a little in the loch and wash off some of the dirt."

"Aye," he said, beaming, and turned, then ran for the loch.

She thought he'd remove his clothes, which wouldn't have made much difference since they were so filthy. Instead, he dove right in, clothes and all. She hoped he'd be cleaner and not just muddy after his swim.

Her brother chuckled. This time, since the boy was not close by to witness it, she turned and found her brother seated upon a horse. Her mouth gaped. "Where did you get the horse?" she whispered.

"He hasna found a way to leave here either, it seems. So I take care of him when I'm roaming the moors. Why are you going to Odara's croft without an escort? A maid?"

"Turi's daughter is ill this morn. Beyond that, I dinna need one to accompany me."

Her brother's serious expression didn't change. He shook his head. "You always need protection."

"I have never had any trouble, Connell. You know that."

"Aye, some say you have a guardian angel who looks out for you. Why are you going to see Odara? You didna give a reason."

As if she owed her brother an explanation. "Our uncle received word Odara is sick. He didna wish me to see to her because she refuses to wed Gilleasbuig." She watched the lad swimming, then turned to her brother. "Had you heard of this?"

"Nay."

"Well, I canna imagine why Gilleasbuig has asked for the shepherdess's hand in marriage. He is not a farmer at heart, and if Odara does not love him, why does she have to wed him?"

Connell shook his head. "Naught something that would concern me."

"Aye, because you intended to marry no one." She cast him an irritated look.

He raised his brows at her.

She continued speaking, glad she at least had her brother to talk to about this travesty. No one else would have cared. "It is not like my own situation as far as marriage is concerned. Our uncle will use me to secure concessions from another clan for an alliance, as disagreeable as the notion is, but I have no' choice. It is my duty to the clan to do as our uncle bids. I have been raised with the knowledge and so have accepted my place in life." As much as she could.

"But Odara. Well, she is just one of our clanswomen, not of any real importance to the clan as far as marriages go. She should be able to wed someone she cares for. When she is ill, she should be seen to, not left to her own devices, sick and unable to work, just because our uncle would have her punished for her disobedience."

He watched the boy splashing in the loch. "Da really did bring you home from the woods the day he died, did he no'?"

She realized then her brother had *not* been listening to her, lost in his own world of memories.

She let out her breath. "Aye, just as I said he had." Her brother had been one of the ones who had been her biggest skeptic. She couldn't help the tears that filled her eyes. It didn't matter how much time had passed, she still loved her father for having brought her home safely.

"I should have been there. I should have killed the brigands," Connell said.

"You were only six summers older than me. They would have murdered you also." She squeezed her eyes shut for a moment, to attempt to forget the events of that day and what took place after. She took in a deep breath and opened her eyes. Instead of dying back then, her brother had gotten himself slain only a fortnight ago.

He snorted. "Because I stole a loaf of bread from the kitchen, Da wouldna let me leave the keep that day to hunt. Do you know who murdered them? Some still say you would know the men who slaughtered them if you saw them again."

She shook her head. "I was hiding too well. I had buried myself in the undergrowth of the forest and fallen leaves. I dared no' leave my hiding place while the swords clashed against each other. When all was quiet, I knew Da would come for me. And he finally did."

Only she had believed him to be alive. That was why he had spoken to her the way he had. Not in a hushed voice like she thought he should have, but out loud because no one else could hear him. Had he even been alive when he came to her the first time and warned her to hide?

That would have made more sense also, because his shouting at her meant no one had heard him that time, either. She had worried about it then, that someone might have followed him and seen him warning her, though she had not seen anyone behind him.

She glanced at the lad, hoping he would hurry as

she didn't want to delay seeing Odara any longer than she had to.

"But Da wasna alive," Connell said. "Like me. Our da wasna alive." He looked curiously at her then. "How many times has this happened? You said you played with children we couldna see when we were younger. Were they...like...I am now?"

# Chapter 2

Spying some kind of movement in the woods, Alana peered at the pines, trying to see what had caught eye. Branches dancing in the breeze cast dark shadows. But she thought… She shook her head at herself, yet the hair at her nape stood on end as a smattering of chill bumps coated her skin. Why did she keep feeling as though she was being watched?

"Alana?" Connell prompted her, wanting her to an answer his question about her seeing spirits.

Alana had seen several ghosts over the years after her mother had died giving birth and the child had not survived either. Had the children she'd played with been imaginary? Only to those who could not see them like she could.

"Aye," Alana said to her brother, sighing. "The children were like you and Da, Connell."

One child had been crushed by a falling stone as men tried to rebuild a wall. The lad looked just as he had before his death, all arms and legs and wide-eyed innocence. Although she had known better. He'd plagued her mercilessly when she was six, but he'd been wise enough to conduct his mischief beyond her father and brother's seeing. She had heard a maid tell another that when a lad was young, if he liked a lass, he would do such things.

Still, she had been sad to see him die and played with him until one day he just faded away.

"Our mother?" Connell asked, bringing her back to the present.

"Nay, no' our mother or the babe who died. Sometimes I wonder if the person needs me or feels he or she must be with me for some reason and that's why they stay with me for a time. Mother had to take care of the wee bairn and so she left with him to do so."

Connell snorted. "So why am I here then?"

She looked at him, wishing he could find peace. She missed him. Missed his laughter as he had teased the lasses. Missed his playful banter with her. "You have unfinished business here? I dinna know, Connell. I wish I knew the answer."

The boy stopped splashing in the water, and Alana looked in his direction. All smiles and sopping wet, the lad raced back to her.

"You are clean." She was surprised to see how much so.

Kerwin quickly mounted behind her and tried not to touch her as he gripped the saddle.

She continued on her way past the loch through the woods and beyond. He was quiet most of the time as they rode half a day's journey to the shepherdess's shieling where it sat near the stream that divided the MacNeill's border from the Cameron's. Most farmers lived within a short distance of the keep so that in times of strife they could herd their livestock into the outer bailey and take refuge. Odara's croft had been there for centuries, the roof of peat replaced several times, but the stone walls would be there forever.

She noted her brother rode along beside them as if he could protect her if she needed him to.

"Do ye speak with the fae?" the lad asked.

"Nay," she said, startled that he'd ask her that. Most were too afraid to do so. She hadn't lied. She spoke with the dead, not the fae.

"They say ye speak with the faery folk. If it isna them, who do ye speak to, my lady?"

"Do you never talk to yourself?" Alana asked.

Connell chuckled.

The lad said, "Oh, aye, my lady. When my brothers pick on me, then leave me quite alone, I talk a lot to myself, telling myself just what I will do to them when I am bigger. Is that what ye do?"

"Aye," she said.

"Have you no shame, lass?" Connell asked, raising a brow, yet she knew the way one corner of his lip twitched upward, he was again playing with her. "The lad asked you for your honesty. And you tell him lies."

She was about to respond that she did not lie. She did talk to herself, but she caught herself before she said a word.

"They say yer da brought ye home two days after he died. At least they say ye told them he had. 'Twas way before I was born. But they are still telling the stories. Do ye…see ghosts, my lady?"

She couldn't tell the lad yay or nay. If she did say she saw ghosts, he would return to his farm and tell his family, and the word would get back to the keep. If she said she didn't, then had she been lying about her father all along? She would not deny her father's help in getting her home safely.

"Do *you* see ghosts?" she asked instead.

"Nay," the lad said. "'Tis bad enough I see the living—my brothers, I am meaning, my lady."

"Ah." She expected the boy to ask again if she saw ghosts, but he grew quiet.

"You didna tell him you dinna see ghosts," her brother said, sounding surprised.

She opened her mouth to speak, then stopped herself and scowled at him. He was too easy to talk to, too real to her. She let out her breath in exasperation and rode the rest of the way in silence, though Connell seemed of a mind to vent about the man who had killed him and about the woman who'd been all too willing to sleep in Connell's bed.

She had been grief-stricken to learn of Connell's death. But how could she sufficiently deal with his death if he would not leave her in peace? She recalled how her uncle had received the news. He hadn't reacted outraged or angered. He had calmly looked at her as she stared back at him, shocked to the core of her being at hearing of her brother's murder. She thought her uncle was seeing her as his last sole heir to their legacy, his own wife having died barren three years earlier.

Had he been so disappointed in her brother that he hadn't cared one whit if he had become their clan chief or not? Or mayhap he suspected her brother would come to no good end, and he wasn't surprised when the inevitable had occurred.

Rumors had circulated ever since her father had been murdered that her uncle had hired men to kill him, so that he could become clan chief. He had raised her and her brother as his own with a heavy hand, but she'd always felt he cared for them as he would have if they had been his own children. She suspected the rumors were just that and that there was no good truth to them.

"You are no' listening to me," her brother said in mock disapproval.

You are a ghost, she wanted desperately to say.

"You cut me to the quick," he said as if he knew just what she had been thinking. Sometimes she felt her thoughts totally transparent.

She frowned at him. "I..." She caught herself, then shook her head.

He smiled at her and looked back at the boy. "He is asleep. Your secret is safe with me."

But she didn't speak to her brother as she saw the stone croft with its peat-covered roof in the distance, dark and quiet, the sheep in the enclosure, restless, hungry, bleating.

The lad stirred behind her, and Alana rode to the shieling, and when they reached it, she said to him, "We are here. 'Tis time you see to the sheep."

"Aye, my lady." Kerwin slipped off the horse, bowed his head awkwardly, and went off to do his task.

She slid off her mount and tied her to a tree branch where her horse could drink from the stream and feed on grass near the sheepfold.

The sheep all crowded around the gate of the dry stone wall enclosure, knowing Kerwin would allow them to graze in the hills now, and they were eager to be freed.

Alana opened the door to the shieling and saw at once that Odara was flushed and breathing hard as she rested on her straw bed, the air cool, no fire in the hearth. She feared the woman had taken a fever.

She stalked across the stone floor and reached down to feel Odara's forehead. No fever. She felt a little relief. Why was Odara so winded? So flushed? So sweaty?

She was dressed, not wearing just a shift to sleep in. Why, if she was so ill, had she left the bed to put on her *léine*?

Alana set her bag of herbs on a small wooden table near the fireplace where the fire had been banked for the day. "What ails you, Odara?"

"Oh, my lady, you shouldna be here." The woman wouldn't look directly at Alana.

With no one to see them together, why was she acting so… nervous?

Alana supposed someone, mayhap her da, or someone else, had told Odara years ago that Alana was the laird's niece and above her in rank and that she should not act so familiar with her. As children, no one had said a word, probably nobody noticing as the girls went down to the stream and played in the water, or picked berries in the woods. Now they were alone with no one to say anything and Odara was ill. It was Alana's duty to see to her. Why was Odara behaving so…oddly?

"But I am here to see you as it is only right that I do so," Alana said gently. "So what is wrong?"

"My stomach pains me," Odara said, her blue eyes closing, her hand on her belly. "I have no' been able to keep down the oatcakes I made to break my fast this morn. It has been the same on and off for three days."

"I am sorry that I didna arrive any sooner. I didna receive word until early this morn." Alana thought the woman might have eaten something that disagreed with her. Something that had spoiled, mayhap. She gave Odara a mug of herbs mixed with mead that would help settle her stomach as she rested, a thin wool blanket covering her.

"'Tis a brave thing you do, mistress. But your uncle will have me flogged if he learns you are here." Odara's voice was stronger, and she sounded more herself this time, but her eyes were shadowed with worry.

Glad to hear she sounded stronger, Alana took a deep breath. "I have asked a lad to tend to your sheep until you are feeling more able to manage, Odara. Another day and I believe the sickness will have passed if you are feeling no other symptoms and you have not grown more ill with the passage of time. 'Tis good you have no fever. 'Tis no doubt something you have eaten that has made you unwell. I imagine 'tis true my uncle wouldna have allowed me to see to you had he been home. I have heard he is still angry that you willna wed Gilleasbuig, though I had no idea my uncle had said you must marry him."

Odara sighed. "The laird canna understand that Gilleasbuig is a swine. He willna do a lick of work if he can avoid it, wenching in the village whenever he can. The man willna be my husband, God willing. But the laird fears that if I am alone out here so close to the border..." She didn't say anything further.

Alana didn't know what to say. Her uncle could be ruthless when he wanted something, but she didn't think that included ensuring one of his men took a wife who did not wish to be one. Alana had not known Gilleasbuig would shirk his responsibilities. She didn't think her uncle would allow any of his men to avoid doing his work. Mayhap that's why he wanted the man to wed Odara. Mayhap he believed he would accomplish some work if it was something different than he was doing now. Or…not doing.

Alana had seen the man leering at the maids and overheard him making a crass remark or two to them, so she wasn't surprised to learn he was rutting with women that he should not have been dallying with. She had even spoken to her uncle about his comments, but he had been annoyed with her, told her that men would be men, and she shouldn't be eavesdropping on men's conversations.

She hadn't been eavesdropping!

She wondered sometimes if Gilleasbuig spoke within earshot of her the way he did just to see her cheeks flush with embarrassment. She truly had never liked the man.

Odara was a hard worker, although a bit of a mouse when it came to men. Surely one of the other clansmen would take an interest in her.

"Is there no one else who intrigues you? Someone who might consider asking for your hand in marriage instead, who my uncle would approve of?" Alana asked.

Odara's face paled a bit. She shook her head too vigorously.

Alana raised a brow, folded her arms, and pursed her lips. "There *is* someone. Prithee tell me who."

Odara let out her breath. "'Tis best I no' say, my lady."

"Someone not of our clan? Someone who my uncle would not approve of?"

Odara looked down.

Alana had an uneasy feeling about this. "Who, Odara?"

"My lady, the laird would kill me if he learned of it."

Alana's skin prickled with unease. "Who?"

"'Tis one of our enemy. A MacNeill."

\*\*\*

Dougald MacNeill and his men searched for the Cameron brigands that had been spied attempting to cross their border and raid crofters' livestock, but they found no sign of them. From what the crofters had said in these parts, they had not seen any thieves. It wasn't the first time rumors had spread about a raid that did not truly exist. A flighty farmer's wife frightened by some noise that meant the Camerons were raiding again. A lad panicked when a flock of grouse scattered heavenward, sure that men had scared off the birds and were about to steal their sheep. A farmer thinking he'd seen men skulking around in the dark of night.

The farmers had faced the raiders before, so Dougald imagined they were jumpy when naught was truly amiss. Yet none of these people said they had sent word of trouble. Someone would have admitted they had sought help if they'd feared the worst even if it turned out there was naught that was wrong.

Dougald glanced across the stream that ran along the border between their lands and the Cameron's, unable to keep from looking for the lass riding the golden horse one more time before they headed back to Craigly Castle.

Gunnolf joined him. "Did you see the lass again?"

Dougald gave his friend an annoyed look. He knew what he'd seen. He couldn't help that no one else was as observant.

Gunnolf smiled. "When you begin seeing lassies that are no' there, they say 'tis time to find a wench who is."

"She was there." Dougald hadn't meant to sound so grumpy as he turned his horse away from the stream and led his men in the direction of Castle Craigly where his eldest brother James was clan chief, though they would keep an eye out in case they encountered any men who did not belong on MacNeill lands. Or a pretty lass that he knew he had witnessed despite no one else having seen her.

The trouble was, he couldn't deny he had wanted to see the lass again, not wanting to doubt himself. But now he wondered. Had he been mistaken?

His cousin Niall rode up beside him. "When you and Gunnolf leave to see your brother, Malcolm and his bride, will you take me with you this time?"

Dougald shook his head. "You know how much James needs you."

"Aye, but you and your brothers have always had all the adventures. I want to see the world, too."

"If Angus returns home, you can join us."

Niall scoffed. "Your brother is enjoying being away from James's rule too much to return anytime soon." He glanced at their Viking friend, Gunnolf. "Mayhap Gunnolf will stay behind this time."

Dougald smiled. "You would have to ask him."

Gunnolf laughed. "And leave you in charge of getting Dougald out of trouble with the lasses?"

"As if any of you are above reproach," Dougald said with a snort. He wasn't certain why he was always the one the rumor mongers accused of dallying with the lasses when his brothers, his cousin, and Gunnolf were all to blame as well.

They just smiled back at him, and he wondered if *they* hadn't helped to start the rumors to keep themselves out of trouble in the first place!

"So," Niall said, casting a look back over his shoulder at the land across the stream. "What exactly did she look like? This wee lassie that has had you looking on and off for her and not Cameron raiders for some time now?"

# Chapter 3

"A Macneill?" Alana asked Odara, so astonished, she couldn't believe it. They'd been raiding the Cameron's livestock for centuries and the Cameron likewise when it came to the MacNeill's livestock. "A sheepherder?"

"Aye. I met him selling some of his sheep to the butcher in the village. He and I talked about the raising of our herds." Odara shrugged as if it was of no consequence.

Alana saw the blush in her cheeks. The woman was smitten with the man!

"A MacNeill," Alana said, still considering the possibility, though she did not think Odara had much of a chance to make a union happen between a MacNeill and a Cameron. The two clan chiefs were both too stubborn, both too boar-headed about who was right and who was wrong.

No, her uncle would never agree to the arrangement.

Odara swallowed hard. "I…I think I may be carrying his child."

Alana stared at her in disbelief. "Odara, you should have told me this at once. The herbs I gave you will be all right for the bairn, but I could have given you something that would have done it harm."

Tears filled the woman's eyes.

Alana frowned. "I didna, but I could have. How can you be carrying a MacNeill's child?"

Odara's eyes widened as she looked at her as though she was surprised Alana wouldn't know about such things.

This time Alana flushed, her cheeks flaming with heat. Then she scowled. "I know the way of it. I have delivered a number of wee bairn. I know how they got there!"

Alana had overheard enough conversations between the women in the castle, bragging to each other about what their men did to pleasure them, that she thought she was quite enlightened. Though curious, too, as to what it would truly be like to have a man making love to her. "What I dinna understand is how *you* are breeding." She stared at Odara, still unable to see how it could have happened. The woman seemed so quiet when it came to men, Alana didn't think most men even knew she existed. "I dinna see how you could have a man's bairn growing in your belly when you are no' wed to him." A man who was from the enemy clan of all things!

"We share so many…interests," Odara said shyly.

Alana scoffed. "Och, the sheep are one thing, but…" She waved her hand at Odara. "This is quite another. What are we to do?"

"Naught can be done, my lady," Odara said meekly. "The laird will take my croft, my sheep, and send me away when he learns I am carrying a MacNeill babe."

"Does he know? The father of the bairn? Does he know you are carrying his child?"

"Nay. I didna think I was with child before today. I am still not fully certain."

"You canna wed Gilleasbuig. He would realize you were having a child no' his own if you are. No telling what he would do."

"The MacNeill has a sick niece staying with him also, and he came by last eve to see if you had come to bring me anything to settle my discomfort and wondered if you might check on her. He lives so close to the border, he couldna walk all the way to Craigly Castle to fetch their healer while leaving his niece alone."

"Nay, that wouldna do. What ails the lass?" Alana asked, worried even more now that some sickness was spreading.

"A fever, my lady."

Alana took a deep breath, knowing what she had to do now. "'Tis no' far across the border, you say?"

"Walking, aye, but riding shouldna take you too verra long."

"I will see to his niece and speak with the man you have been seeing about the babe."

If the sheepherder lived close to the border, Alana did not think she would have any difficulty. She was only a woman, not a man leading a group of raiders. Alana had delivered a wee bairn of a MacNeill crofter who lived near their border when the woman could not get help quickly enough from her own clan. Alana could meet Odara's man there, and she was certain no trouble would come of it.

"Where do you meet him?" Alana prayed his niece didn't have the same symptoms as her maid. What if Odara had the same sickness as her maid and the girl?

Though if Odara was breeding without a husband, that would not be good either. Especially when the da was a MacNeill.

Alana would get word to him. He had to know what kind of a predicament he had put the shepherdess in and that the bairn was his also. He had to have some say in the matter if he wished it.

"Where, Odara? And what is his name? I will go. I will say that I am looking for the man who is the da of the bairn growing in the shepherdess's belly by the name of Odara and that he must make this right by her. And I will see to the girl. I couldna forgive myself if she died when I might have saved her. Truly 'tis no' too far, is it?"

Odara looked pale again and was trembling so hard that Alana took pity on her, leaned down, and took her hand. Meeting her gaze, Alana said, "I will do this with or without your help. 'Tis the man's bairn also, and he has every right to know about it."

She hoped the sheepherder would come for Odara and take her to his own croft where they could raise his sheep, should they wish it. If he loved her as much as it appeared Odara loved him, Alana felt it could work.

Odara slowly nodded. "Rob MacNeill. He lives near the border. No' far from here."

"Near where I delivered the MacNeill bairn?"

"Nay, nay, north of there. No' south."

Letting out her breath, Alana nodded. She'd have preferred it was in the same area where she had visited before, where she had saved the MacNeill mother and her newborn infant. They would know her there. "I will go and seek out this man."

"What if he doesna want me? What if he only

wished to have a little fun and didna intend to wed me?" Odara asked.

Alana straightened. "I will learn what I can. 'Tis early. My uncle willna return for mayhap several more days. He never learned of the time that I had delivered a MacNeill babe. He willna learn of this."

Odara said, "He doesna intend to wed you to one of the McDonald's sons, does he?"

"I dinna know for certain. 'Tis none of my concern as my uncle would say." Though it bothered Alana to admit as much, it was the way of their world. "*Rest.* I will return when I can. I will pay the lad to take care of your sheep until the sickness passes. He will need to be fed…"

"I will feed the lad. You have your mother's ways, my lady, God rest her soul."

"Her temper also and her willfulness, I fear," Alana said smiling, then made for the doorway. "'Tis still early. I will return before dark falls."

The boy was already off with the sheep in the heather, letting them eat their fill, when Alana headed west toward the MacNeill border and the stream that divided their lands. This time it would be different from when she had crossed into the MacNeill land bordering her uncle's. She would not be as welcome as she sought to deliver a bairn and save the mother's life. She would be searching for the father of her clanswoman's babe who might not be willing to claim it as his own nor desire to wed the lass. What if he was already married?

Men like that would not be held accountable. She prayed this was not the case. That he would love Odara and return for her. That she would love him back. And she prayed his niece was not too ill, that she could aid her, and she would soon recover.

She thought her brother might accompany her for a bit. But he wasn't around now. She didn't know what triggered his appearances. Why he would leave her for days, then suddenly materialize into her life again.

She soon reached the stream that separated the Cameron and the MacNeill lands and crossed it, then traveled another hour north. She had seen nothing but emerald green hills, the lacy edge of a forest, a small blue loch, and several streams filled with mossy stones. The lands between the Cameron and the MacNeill were vast, but she thought the shepherd would live close to the border—as Odara had claimed—if he had been slipping over it to see Odara on a regular basis. After traveling a couple of more hours and finding no croft or a sheepherder grazing sheep, she worried that when she crossed the stream dividing their lands, she had headed farther north than the man lived or she was still too far south.

She sat upon her horse, surveying the lavender drifts of heather, purple thistles proudly swaying in the breeze, a hawk winging its way across the blue sky now covered in clouds so blended and flat that it was like looking at a soft pillow of thin white wool cloth.

The air was warm, a steady breeze blowing in her direction when she thought she saw movement on top of one of the green hills only broken up by a cairn and a smattering of trees. Was it him? The shepherd grazing his sheep?

Or was it a bird in the heather, flying off into the sky?

She wasn't certain. She rode toward the hill to see if she might find some sheep. When she finally reached the top, she saw no one. But she heard splashing down below the hill. Curiosity got the best of her.

She moved further to the edge of the sloping hill and stared down at the sight of a dozen or so men bathing in a loch. And froze. They were naked, their plaids, tunics, boots, and belts discarded on the grass, their horses grazing nearby.

A lad was running down the high hill toward them at a frantic pace, arms flying, fully clothed, and she wondered now if he was the one she had seen atop the hill, but he'd moved so quickly, he was like a red grouse flitting from the heather.

"There is a lady," the lad called out, pointing toward the hilltop, motioning toward Alana, not realizing she'd followed him here.

One of the naked men who had left the water was standing on the bank, plaid in hand, but not covering himself, his attention turning from the excited lad to the woman on the hill. The tall man was bronzed and muscled, his hair an earthy dark brown, a sturdy jaw, and dark eyes that stared at her as if he couldn't believe she really was there, staring back at him. Like a statue, she couldn't look away if she'd wanted to.

The other men stayed in the water where it licked at their chests. They were quietly observing her, not saying a word as if they thought she was a spirit or sprite or maybe the fae. Good, let them think that, and they'd stay put.

Breaking free from the shock that she'd felt at spying the naked Highlanders—and she was loathe to admit—fascination she experienced, she didn't wait to see what would happen next. Their grazing horses and swords lying next to their plaids and not a sheep around told her enough. A sheepherder was not among these men. A sliver of panic seized her at once. She tried to remind herself why she was here. That she needed to find the man named Rob MacNeill. To find the little girl who was ill who was his niece. But what if these men might wish her harm?

She whipped her horse around and headed back down the hill from whence she had come, careful to pick her way among the rocks lest she injure her horse.

She would have a good head start as it would take the men time to dress and mount their horses. Or so she thought. She had not taken in account how quickly her own clansmen would throw on their clothes and be ready to leave at a moment's notice when they were faced with trouble.

The men shouted to each, ribald comments of who would catch the Sidhe, the fae, and what they would do with her. "Your brother found a pearl in the sea. You are swimming in a loch and see the vision of the fae, Dougald. Mayhap this is your destiny to capture her and make her your own."

They truly couldn't believe she was one of the fae. Her heart pounding with fear, she attempted to keep her wits about her and tried to remain calm, resolute, determined to find the MacNeill and his niece.

As soon as she reached the base of the hill, she rode as if the devil was after her. The forest was too far away to reach it and hide before the men could dress, mount, and take after her.

She heard horses' hooves impact the earth as they headed toward the top of the hill.

She glanced back and could only see one man sitting tall on his horse's back. She could not see him well from this distance as much as she was running her horse, except for a silhouette against the bright sky. He was wrapped in plaid, a sword at his hip, the hilt poking out of its scabbard. She could not tell the color of his hair, or what he wore in his bonnet that would clue her in as to his clan's affiliation, though he had to be a MacNeill or a man from a clan that allied with them.

She believed he was the man who had been standing on the shore.

She could not tell the expression he wore as he sat quietly observing her. His head turned to survey the land behind her, searching, she assumed, for anyone else who might have come with her. From this, she gathered he was a cautious man, prudent, and for an instant she admired him for it.

Looking again toward the distant forest, she hoped he would think it a trap and would not follow her. Mayhap she should call out to her invisible soldiers and wave in the man's direction. Would he take heed then?

Or mayhap she should stop, wait for him to come to her, explain to him what she desired to know. The man would know she wished no one any ill will. Mayhap he could direct her the right way. Surely if he was riding in this area, he would know of the man called Rob MacNeill. She was getting nowhere all on her own. And the sky would begin to darken before long.

She stopped her horse and turned to see the man still waiting on top of the hill not moving in her direction.

As if she was facing down a wolf—though she did not want to think of herself as a sheep—she remained sitting very still upon her horse, the only movement, the mare's heavy breathing, and her tail swishing back and forth. Alana's own heart beat at just as frantic a pace. Alana couldn't tear her gaze away from the man's progress as he finally made his way down the rocky slope on horseback.

She couldn't decide. Should she continue to run for the forest? Or speak her business to the man? Since only one was coming to meet her, she could do this.

Cautiously, he maneuvered his horse over the rocky terrain. Again she admired the way he handled the situation, not tearing down the hill, risking his horse's neck and his own. No, he was a careful man, caring about his mount, just as much as she had been about hers.

That all changed when he reached the bottom of the hill. Without hesitation, he spurred his horse on and tore across the glen to reach her. Her heart nearly drummed out of her breast as the fear took hold again. She had to force herself to keep her horse in place and not move a hair from her position. To show him she was not afraid. That she had a mission, and she would not be dissuaded.

To her horror, a second man on horseback crested the hill, and then several others. No, this was not what she had intended. Just one man. A quick question. A direction to head in.

What if this was a raiding party that intended to breach the Cameron's territory, and she could be in the midst of it? What if they thought she would warn her people that men of the MacNeill clan were coming?

Her blood becoming ice and her only thought now being to flee, she turned her horse and headed for the forest. She was too deep into the MacNeill lands to easily make her escape. But she had a better chance if she was within the cover of the forest.

"Dougald!" Someone shouted from the hilltop as the men began making their way down to join the one who was trying to intercept her. "It could be a trap!"

Whoever had hollered after him sounded worried for his safety. As if the Highlander had to fear a lass such as herself. Not that she wasn't armed. She didn't believe in her wildest dreams she could fight off a man as big as the one chasing after her with nothing but her dirk though.

She glanced back to see him close the distance between them, his horse's legs longer, his determination to catch up to her evident in his expression, a grin splitting his face in two. So he wasn't as much worried about who she was as he was in taking pleasure in the hunt.

Her heart was racing as fast as her horse's now, and she knew her mare would never outrun the man's long-legged steed.

Dark-haired and his eyes just as dark a brown, he eyed her with a devilish smile and a body that screamed Highland warrior, which she had already seen way too much of. He was every lass's nightmare—a man who most likely bedded every wench he chanced to meet. Just like her brother had done. She was certain the lasses would be very willing.

She hadn't even reached the lacy fringe of pines edging the forest when the warrior rode up beside her, his leg brushing hers, shocking her with his familiarity.

Worse, he did not do what she expected. Instead of seizing the reins from her hands and yanking her horse to a halt, he seized *her*!

# Chapter 4

Shrieking in startled surprise, Alana fought the man who yanked her onto his lap. She tried to hit him and jump free. His arm was like a steel band gripping her tight against his body as he headed back toward the rest of his men still trying to catch up to him.

"Let me go, you barbarian!" she screamed.

He laughed, nuzzled his face in her hair, and laughed again. "'Tis a bonny lass I find this bright day seeking my pleasure, eh?" His voice was dark and filled with merriment.

"I seek naught of the sort from you, sir," she ground out. He was holding her so tight as she tried to wriggle free, she felt she was wearing a *léine* two sizes too small and could barely take in enough air to fill her lungs. "My horse," she rasped out, attempting to put some distance between her and the muscled Highlander, but he only tightened his grip on her, pressing her indecently against his hard chest and his groin.

"You will fall, lass. Sit still. My cousin, Niall, has reined in your horse. Although I must say I am certain he wished he would have been the one to rein *you* in instead."

"I am not a horse!"

"Of that I am *well* aware." He squirmed a little beneath her as if she was making him uncomfortable.

That's when she noticed just why he had the need to reposition himself beneath her. Though she'd attempted not to look at that part of him that had been growing in size when she had observed him naked at the loch, she imagined his staff was doing the very same thing now beneath his plaid. Beneath *her*!

She tried to move away from him, to not incite his desire for her any further, yet he let out his breath in a whoosh and said, "Lass, quit your wiggling. You are making me want you something powerful."

That made her sit stock still, her back as stiff as his staff pressing against her in such an indelicate way.

"If you were a gentleman, you wouldna be having such thoughts."

He gave a hearty laugh. "It has naught to do with being a gentleman, lassie, but the way your arse is seated against my…"

"Say no more," she quickly said. "I wish to hear no more."

He chuckled. Then he grew serious as his men joined him, and they began to ride back over the hill.

His cousin, Niall, looked similar to the man they'd called Dougald, the man she was riding with—so improperly. Tall, impressive, muscled, dark haired, though he had a reddish cast to his locks, and the same smiling dark eyes.

His dark hair curling about his shoulders, Niall was grinning his fool head off at her as he rode beside them, holding her mare's reins. "Your brother found his lass in the sea. Mayhap you have found yours in the heather?"

Dougald's brother? Dougald was the laird's third eldest brother. She had heard that James MacNeill, who ruled Craigly Castle, had recently wed a lass found half-drowned in the sea. Her kinsmen had joked that he could not find a suitable wife so he had to dredge up the sea, looking for one.

Dougald was one of four brothers. Malcolm, the second eldest, had married a Lady Anice, cousin to King Henry's wife, without the king's permission. Her uncle had said the man would not live once the king learned of the traitorous deed, but Henry had welcomed Malcolm into the fold. Alana had heard rumors that Anice had fae sight, and she'd thought she would like to meet her. Yet, would the lady appreciate that Alana could see the dead? Mayhap not. She probably attempted to hide her curse just like Alana did and would not wish others to know of it.

The youngest, Angus, she'd heard was wounded in a battle at Lady Anice's castle and did not know if he had survived or not.

Her uncle would kill the MacNeills, every last one of them, if he knew she had been taken against her will by the laird's brother himself.

"You are Dougald MacNeill? Brother of James? Laird of Craigly Castle?" she asked warily.

"Aye. One and the same."

He did not ask her name as if it was of no import. She would offer it and mayhap he would think better of ferreting her off to God knew where. Although she suspected he was taking her to see James.

"I am Alana, niece of Laird Cameron. You must let me go. Now!"

Dougald shook his head. "The niece of the Cameron wouldna be traipsing about our land, spying on naked warriors bathing in a loch."

She felt her whole body heat with mortification. A

couple of the men grinned at her. One said, "Ye should have joined us, lass, on such a warm day."

She held her chin higher, not about to respond to the rogue.

"Whose horse did you steal? 'Tis a fine specimen. She should bring a goodly sum," Dougald said.

"She is mine, you heathen!"

Dougald chuckled and the sound made her believe he enjoyed her calling him such an ungracious name.

"She wants you," Niall said sagely. "When the lasses begin calling men names, 'tis a good sign they want you. Dinna you agree, Gunnolf?"

That's when she noticed the man with blond hair and blue eyes who looked more like a Norseman than a Scot. He was just as rugged looking as Dougald and his cousin, just as carefree with his smile.

"'Tis a saga we tell at home—when a wench is beating on us and calling us names, she is indeed in love with us," Gunnolf said.

They had to be jesting with her. That last comment made Alana snap her mouth shut. For only a moment. She tried again, only this time declaring her mission here. "I came seeking Rob MacNeill."

"Which one?" Niall asked. "We have a dozen or more in the clan by that name."

"A sheepherder."

"That makes it more like...a handful." Niall sounded as though he was guessing.

"What do you want with him?" Dougald loosened his grip on her as if he suddenly believed she was in love with the man or some such thing.

She quickly had to make him understand the import of the matter. Then she reconsidered. What if their laird was angry that the man had left a Cameron clanswoman with child? He might not approve any more than her uncle would.

"'Tis only a matter that I must discuss with him. *Alone*."

Gunnolf scrubbed his hand over his blond beard as if contemplating the matter. "Sounds to me like a love match gone wrong." He glanced at her slim waist as if he was looking to see if she was indeed with child. "Are you certain the man would wish to see you? That he would acknowledge the bairn was his own?"

What? Did he think she was a wanton woman, spreading her legs for any willing man?

"'Tis no' for me!" she snapped. As if she longed for the touch of a MacNeill! Despite that one was holding her way too close for her own peace of mind. Which was probably the reason she could not keep her temper. "He has left one of my kinswomen with child!" She felt her face heat as hot as a rock warmed beneath the sun on a summer's day. Why had she blurted out what she did?

She had not wished these men to believe *she* was with child! That was why!

No one spoke a word, but Dougald's arm tightened around her again, as if thinking she might still be willing to have a romp with him, if he was interested. She'd heard of his reputation with the lasses, and she wasn't about to give in to a man such as he was. Not when her brother had been such a notorious rake and died at the hand of an angry husband.

Why would she want a man like that? Who could not find happiness in one woman? And then get himself killed over some other man's wife? She wondered then where her brother was.

"Who is the woman?" Dougald asked.

Cold fear spilled through her. What if the MacNeill wanted to kill Odara, to eliminate the child growing inside her, to end the connection between their clans?

She pursed her lips and wouldn't say.

"She is a stubborn lass and courageous as well," Niall said, winking at her. "Mayhap she *is* the Cameron's niece."

"'Tis trouble we will all be facing if 'tis so," Gunnolf said.

"Aye," Alana said, grasping at any reason to convince Dougald and his men to release her and allow her to go on her way. "So you best let me go before the trouble begins."

Dougald motioned to Gunnolf. "Have four of our men investigate the whereabouts of this Rob MacNeill the lass has spoken of."

"If they find him?"

"Send him to join us at Craigly Castle at once where James will determine the truth of the matter."

"He has a sick niece. I was to see to her," Alana said.

Dougald frowned. "If you find this Rob MacNeill and his sick niece, have her taken to Craigly Castle as well," he said to his men. "Our healer will see to her."

"Whatever possessed you to cross the border between our lands?" Connell asked, and she quickly looked to her left and saw her brother riding between her and Niall and scowling at her. If he hadn't been just a ghostly spirit, she imagined he would have fought the men to free her and gotten himself killed. "When you saw to Odara, she began to talk about breeding and that was *more* than I wished to hear."

She imagined so, being that the notion of bedding lassies and leaving his own offspring with them wouldn't have appealed. Not that he wasn't good with bairns, but he just hadn't seemed ready to settle down anytime soon to raise his own.

"I leave you be for a time and what happens? You fall into the hands of the MacNeill? And not just any MacNeill." Connell glowered at Dougald. Her brother's gaze shifted to Dougald's possessive arms around Alana, then again looked at her. "The most well-known rake of the whole lot of the MacNeill clan."

# Chapter 5

When Dougald had seen the lass sitting upon her horse on the hilltop frozen in place staring at him, and only once glancing in the direction of his other clansmen who had still been bathing in the loch, he had thought she was one of the fae.

Until she rode away. He thought that the fae would have just vanished. Poof! In a puff of mist. If that's what she'd been. Her horse's hooves pounding on the ground sounded too real for her to have been one of the fae. He knew then she was the same woman he'd seen briefly earlier on the Cameron's lands.

He couldn't decide what she was up to. First, watching them from the hilltop, and then running off. Then turning again as if in battle preparedness, waiting for him to draw closer, and then—mayhap—having a change of heart and running again.

He thought men might have been waiting to ambush them, and she was the siren's lure, the temptation that was supposed to lead Dougald and his men into the fray. Which was why he was bound and determined to get hold of her first and use her as a hostage, if her men valued her life enough. They might not have, which had been a genuine risk he'd been willing to take.

Part of him had been like the wolf on a hunt, and he couldn't let her get away. The chase was half of the fun. Catching her, holding her close, smelling her sweet fragrance of basil and thyme and lavender was enough to make him glad he'd caught her.

The lad who had first spied her as he had tried to avoid bathing, stating he had to be on guard duty, had been so flushed and excited when he had run down the hill that Dougald had left the water at that point to see what the matter was. The lad clearly was eager to tell him some tidings in a happy way and not that he was about to warn them of danger. Dougald could still envision the woman sitting on her horse, the blue sky covered in a haze of white clouds, the woman dressed in pale blue, the veils she wore, the same color, all matching the sky. Seeing the regal lass with the sunlight dancing off her features had given Dougald pause. But only for the briefest period of time.

Once he had shaken loose of the notion she was of the fae, he had believed she might have stolen one of his clansmen's horses from the castle. Then he reconsidered and thought mayhap she was one of his clanswomen in trouble. Though only the ladies of Craigly Castle had their own mounts. He feared one of them had left the castle alone. But for what purpose? Still, he knew all of them and this woman was unknown to him.

Mayhap, she was not of his clan at all and was clearly lost. Or worse, in trouble.

No matter what scenarios chased across his mind, he had only one plan, take her in hand, learn who she was, whose horse she had, and what she was doing here.

He'd left his men behind as they were hurrying to dress and join him, unwilling to wait for them. What if the woman just…vanished…before he had a chance to catch her? Like she'd vanished before and his men hadn't caught sight of her. This time he had every intention of proving she was real. Tavis, the lad who had brought him the news of the lady, was so excited, telling him in a whisper so his voice did not carry over the hillside how bonny the lass was while Dougald hurried to dress.

He had carefully picked his way down the hillside, not wanting to injure his horse, though he had been dying to reach her before she tore off. He had watched her, truly expecting her to dash away, so he was surprised when she observed him as if she was the commander of a contingent of invisible troops and did not flinch. Not until he galloped toward her, and she knew then his intent. Or mayhap she had been more concerned when his men tried to follow him. She couldn't believe he would approach her alone. Not when she could be part of a bigger threat to him and his men.

Then, she did what he'd thought she would have done first, ran for her life. He couldn't decide if this bothered him more, or if the fact she did not move at first did. He had expected her to run away, but when she didn't and waited until he grew closer, he considered this truly might have been a trap.

She should have known no woman could outride a man who was battle trained and as determined as he was to keep their lands safe for his clansmen. She'd stirred his impulse to hunt. When she had ridden off, instead of sitting still and facing him lassie to warrior, he'd felt his heart pounding with excitement. The chase gave him much more pleasure.

When no one appeared to attack him and his men, he wasn't sure what to think.

What he hadn't expected was the way his body had reacted so quickly to the settling of her arse against his cock already straining against his plaid. The way he'd wanted to hold her closer—though he told himself it was to keep her from squirming so much and causing him more pain, or to keep her from jumping from his horse and injuring herself. He luxuriated in the feel of her soft curves held tightly against him, the way her body heated his to the level of a blazing fire on a summer's day, the smell of her as if she'd been dipped in a bed of lavender with a hint of the spices of other herbs, sweet and feminine and sensuous.

She wasn't his type of woman though. She was too…stiff in his arms, not melting against him like he enjoyed his women, malleable and willing. He imagined she hated him and his men for being MacNeill clansmen, when the wenches he took to bed loved him for who he was.

He grunted. No, the woman wasn't his kind of lass in the least.

He didn't believe for an instant that she was the niece of Laird Cameron. She would not have crossed their border, offering herself up to the MacNeills like a prize mare to bargain with. She would not have been alone without a maid and an armed escort.

Did she think Dougald and his men would show her more respect if they thought her words the truth? They would have, not wishing a war between their clans. But they would not harm the lass, no matter who she was.

"Your name, lass?" he finally asked, his tone hard, willing her to give him her true name.

"Alana, daughter of Bhaltair, deceased older brother of Alroy, my uncle, the Cameron."

His men were watching Dougald's expression now, and he would not let them see what he thought of her claim. He was beginning to wonder if she was who she said, and what that would mean for their clan. She had entered their lands unescorted and without invitation, so what was he to do with her? He couldn't allow her to roam their lands and potentially get herself into real trouble with some who would not be so noble as he.

For one, he probably should set her back on her own horse. No matter that she was not the kind of woman he normally enjoyed spending time with, he could not give the order to have her horse brought around so he could deposit her on it as much as he told himself he should.

He had to admit he liked very much where she was seated right now. Cameron lass or no'.

"Your uncle," he said, humoring her if she truly was not the Cameron's niece, "has not seen fit to have you wed? You appear to be an eligible maid."

More than eligible. The lass was bonny indeed, her golden hair so light it was like seeing the sun misted in clouds. Her hair was veiled by a shimmering blue cloth, her eyes as bright as the grasses covering the glen, her skin as white and soft as a swan's wing. And her supple curves nestled against him in his hard embrace spoke of a lass who was *all* woman.

"He is in negotiations as we speak," she snapped, not sounding happy in the least.

63

Arranged marriages were often not marriages made in heaven but to seal bargains between clans so he understood some of her animosity. "With which clan?" he asked, curious.

"If you wish to know my uncle's plans, you will have to speak with *him*," she retorted.

"You dinna know?" he asked, surprised. Even if her uncle, if he truly was her uncle, was making arrangements for her marriage and didn't speak with her concerning the matter, which was often the case, Dougald would have thought she'd have heard some rumors.

Then again, mayhap she already knew all the details and just did not want Dougald to know. After all, if the Cameron ended up allying with a stronger clan, the two could fight the MacNeill clan on a larger scale.

Well, there was nothing to be done concerning the matter. His only sister had died years earlier, or James could have offered her to the clan chief who was attempting an alliance with the Cameron, although she'd had her heart set on another clansman, which had been her undoing.

"Where will we stay the night?" Niall asked. "If we escort her to a tavern this eve, the journey would take us out of our way."

"The night?" she said, perking up, her voice a bit shaken.

"We will not reach the keep until tomorrow eve, at earliest," Dougald said to her, then added for his men's benefit. "Nay, we will continue on our way the quickest route to escort the lass so that she may have an audience with James and he will decide her fate."

"My fate!" Alana sounded as though she would draw a sword on him if she but had one to unsheathe.

"Aye, lass. You are a Cameron and have violated our laws when you entered our territory without permission," Dougald said.

She slumped a little against him, and he liked the way she softened against his body, even if she did not do so willingly. He wondered if her people had told her what a fierce warrior James was, and she believed he would toss her in the dungeon. He would, too, if he learned she planned for harm to come to his people. He meted out justice as harsh as any clan chief when it came to protecting his own.

"He is a fair man," Dougald said quite seriously. "If you were not trying to lead an army across our borders, you have naught to fear."

"Oh, aye," she said haughtily, but she did not stiffen against him again, nor try to ease away from him. "They were hiding in the woods, waiting to see if I would be taken first. If I didna fight you off well enough on my own, they would run home, tails tucked between their legs."

The men all chuckled, unable to hide their mirth at the images her comment must have stirred in their minds. Yet when one of his men looked back in the direction of the woods, Dougald probably had the same thought as he did. What if taking her with them had been the Cameron's plan all along? What if it was a reason to go to war, or for James to grant some other concession? What if she had been offered like a virgin sacrifice, and Dougald had taken the bait?

God's wounds, when it came to women, Dougald was always getting himself into a bind.

Gunnolf was smiling at him in his smug, knowing way. He'd been with him on enough of his adventures to know just what he was thinking.

If the Viking warrior had had *his* way, he would have slung the woman over his shoulder and claimed her for his own, damn the consequences. Not that a Highlander wouldn't do such a thing if he wanted a lass badly enough also.

But Dougald did not want *any* woman that badly, particularly a Cameron lass who would not want him in return. No, when he wed a lass, she would smile up at him and melt in his arms as he asked her to be his wife.

Dougald said to Gunnolf, "Return to where the shepherdess lives in the croft across the border. You know the one. We passed by there on our way home earlier this year and remarked how close the place was to our border."

"Ja."

"Learn what you can from the wench, then return."

Gunnolf bowed his head, and then turned his horse and headed in a more southeasterly direction.

"You dinna believe me?" Alana asked, sounding almost hurt.

Dougald hadn't meant to refute her claim. "Nay, lass. 'Tis that you didna give any description of this Rob MacNeill. Gunnolf will learn further about him from the lass, mayhap discover where he lives, and we will more easily find him."

She took a deep breath, then as if she finally remembered her earlier concern, said, "I canna stay the night with you on your lands."

"You will be safe with me and my men." Dougald couldn't help being annoyed she'd think any of them would take advantage of her.

She cast him an irritated look over her shoulder, her green eyes sparking like the sun's rays reflected off emerald daggers. "When my people learn I have not returned to the keep, they will be frantic."

"What did you think would happen? Surely, you considered such contingencies."

"I planned only to speak with Rob MacNeill and let him know the woman who loves him is carrying his babe! And I would have taken care of his niece should she have needed something for her illness. I would have returned to the keep well before it grew dark."

"You didna know where the man lived, now did you, lass? Or how far away 'twas from your border?"

"From the way Odara spoke, I thought the man lived close to the border. I didna know your people have no' enough vision to call your lads by more than one name."

Dougald laughed. He knew for a fact many of her kin named their sons after fathers or grandfathers or favorite uncles also. It was their way and had been for centuries to honor a male clansman in such a manner.

Dougald waved to one of the lads who rode with him, who learned from the older men while on the hunts, but also served as messengers in a case like this. "Tavis, ride ahead and get the word to James we are bringing a guest home with us. If we have any trouble before we reach the curtain walls, he should be made aware of why."

"Aye," the lad said, and rode off in the wrong direction. Wrong, with respect to not being on a direct heading toward the castle. The lad knew he had to make a detour to the village to get a fresh mount if he was to ride through the night and reach James before they did.

"Your laird will be sorely disappointed in you when he learns you have taken me hostage." The fight was out of her words now.

He suspected she was tired, probably unused to riding for so long on horseback. Mayhap somewhat resigned.

"Aye, and it willna be the last time," Dougald said.

His men chuckled.

"Of that I have no doubt," she said, and he smiled.

Not long after that, Alana drifted off to sleep in Dougald's arms, and he couldn't help but notice the way her body fit against his, warm and soft, nestled against his chest as if she belonged there. He was torn between feeling protective and not wanting the responsibility.

Curious glances were cast his way, the speculation already on whether or not something more would come of this. But his men had to also wonder what a mess they could be in if James was angered at Dougald for bringing the lass to Craigly Castle.

When the sky turned various hues of lavender streaked with pink as the sun began to set, Niall drew his horse closer to Dougald's and said in a low voice, though he was careful to speak words that would not cause any trouble for them if the lass was only feigning sleep, "You know what James might do about this matter, do you no', cousin?"

Dougald didn't want to ponder what James might decide. James had to do whatever was best for the good of the clan. Options were too numerous to consider. Dougald didn't want to waste his time attempting to sort out and guess at what his brother might decide.

Dougald shook his head, not about to be drawn into

a conversation concerning the matter. Not when there was not much he could do about it anyway.

Before the sun disappeared behind the mountains, Dougald said, "'Tis time we make camp.      Here."

They had ridden out early in the morn three days ago, just looking for thieves or the like to apprehend, feeling their oats, unable to sit still at the keep while things had settled down since James had wed his wife, Lady Eilis.

Dougald had been thinking about returning to see how Malcolm and his Lady Anice were faring, seeing if they had more trouble there where they might need his sword arm. Now he couldn't leave. Not until this issue with the Cameron lass was resolved.

He handed the sleeping lass down to Niall, then dismounted. A lad led Dougald's horse away to join the others, tying them together in a group.

Niall waited while Dougald rolled out another plaid of his, then motioned to it. "She can sleep there."

Some of the men had gone off to hunt. Some were gathering kindling for the fire. Others were tending to the horses. A couple were standing watch. No one had to be told what to do. Everyone knew their duty.

"Watch her," Dougald said to one of his men, then joined Niall and strolled away from the camp with him so they could speak privately.

"I believe she is who she says she is," Niall said, "so why did you send Gunnolf back to look for the shepherdess?"

"To see for ourselves if what she said about the shepherdess and her involvement with one of our clansmen was true."

"What are you thinking, Cousin?" Niall asked.

"That Lady Alana didna tell the truth?"

"I am no' sure. What if the wench isna carrying a babe? What if this is all some elaborate scheme to cause difficulties between James and the Cameron? 'Twould not be the first time that a clan chief created such a ruse. Why was she alone? When she saw me coming down the hill, she didna run away, like any lass from another clan might have done."

"Aye, Dougald. But remember when Lady Alana came across the border to aid our kinsman? Delivering Kyle's babe when the mother and son would have perished? Kyle's wife had lost two bairns already, and our healer was too ill to travel far that day."

Deep in thought, Dougald rubbed his whiskery chin and thought he probably looked a bit like a barbarian to the lass, then folded his arms across his chest. "How did the lass know about Kyle's bairn?"

"Kyle told me he had ridden across the border in search of her as soon as he had learned that our healer was too ill and that Lady Alana was visiting the shepherdess. He begged the lass to help his wife. You have been away these past several months so you might no' have learned about it, but the word has reached our clan as to how the lady is a well-respected healer among her people. Even our own healer wishes to speak with her and share techniques someday."

"I see." That might have accounted for the other fragrant herbs he'd smelled on her, very pleasing.

"If you dinna trust the lass, think you we should have attempted to find Rob MacNeill first and let her go on her way?"

Now *that* Dougald couldn't have done. Not only because he would have feared for her safety if she'd been traveling alone at night, but because damn his hide, he'd caught her, and he really didn't wish to let her go. Not that he wanted to keep her, permanently, he kept reminding himself. She didn't even like him.

"Do you know how long it might have taken us to find the right Rob MacNeill? With us being near the border and remaining there for too long, a battle might have ensued. If she had spoken the truth about who she is and the Cameron had learned she was with us and come after us, she could have been injured or killed in the fighting."

"Aye."

Dougald looked back in the direction of the camp. "Mayhap, though, the Cameron knew that Rob MacNeill was a common enough name. What if the Cameron shepherdess isna carrying a child? Or if she is, 'tis no' one of ours? What if—"

"Lady Alana isna Lady Alana?" Niall asked, arching a brow.

"'Tis entirely possible. That is why I decided to place her squarely in James's lap. He's the laird. She crossed the border, and he can decide her fate."

"His lap," Niall said, his smile returned, the connotation that she had not been placed in the laird's lap but Dougald's own for the long ride here.

"'Tis too bad she is a Cameron wench," Dougald said, acknowledging that despite his feelings that he should not be interested in such a woman, he *was* a bit intrigued.

He motioned for them to return to camp.

They would eat, get a few hours of sleep, and ride again with all haste for the MacNeill stronghold, and James's quick resolution in the matter concerning the lass.

Then he and Gunnolf would be off on a new adventure. One that would have all to do with fighting battle-hardened men for a good cause, while leaving the lassies—and the trouble that always seemed to get him into—alone.

# Chapter 6

James MacNeill snuggled in bed with his bonny lass, Eilis, unable to believe she was now carrying his child, though as many times as he'd bedded her since they had wed, the news shouldn't have been all that surprising.

They'd made love and she was sound asleep, he only drifting off, when someone opened the door to his chamber. He was instantly out of bed, sword in hand, until he saw his advisor with a lad of six and ten, Tavis, who had ridden with Dougald to inspect their lands for trouble.

If the lad had returned this quickly and was the one wishing to speak with him near the crack of dawn, something was amiss.

James threw on his plaid and belted it, then joined the men in the corridor, shutting the door behind him. "What has happened?" He envisioned Dougald and Gunnolf in a dark dank dungeon again, needing his rescue.

The boy looked done in, having ridden long and hard to get to the castle that quickly. He swayed on his feet, his face dirty, his eyes bleary.

Eanruig's black hair hung about his shoulders, a shadow of a beard clinging to his hard jawline and his blue eyes narrowed with worry as he clasped his arm around the lad's shoulders to hold him upright.

James said, "Get him some ale and something to eat, would you?"

"Aye, that I will do." Eanruig hurried off to the stairs.

James sat the boy down on a bench and again asked, "Tavis, look at me. What has happened to Dougald and the others?"

"He bade me come as quickly as I could, my laird. I rode to the village to exchange horses, just as you taught me when word needed to be sent quickly."

"Aye, aye, but what of our men?"

"'Tis the lass they have with them that is the trouble." Tavis yawned, dark circles shaded the skin beneath his green eyes.

"A woman?" James would have laughed, knowing Dougald and the way he was always getting way over his head when it came to women. But the boy looked too worried to make light of it. "What woman?"

"The Cameron lass she said she was."

"Cameron lass?" James wasn't following the gist of the trouble.

"Aye. *The* Cameron lass. The niece of the Cameron himself."

James's mouth gaped for a moment. "Lady Alana?"

"Aye." The boy nodded vigorously, the mop of red curls covering his head shaking violently, shedding dirt from the long ride.

Eanruig rejoined them, mug in hand and a chunk of brown bread in the other and gave them to the lad.

"What is the trouble?" Eanruig asked James.

"Seems Dougald has captured the Cameron's niece."

Eanruig's eyes widened.

"Aye," James said on a heavy sigh. He looked at the boy as he greedily drank of the ale. "He took her hostage, I presume? She was trespassing on our lands?"

"Aye, my laird. She was indeed. Near Fairen's lands where he grazes his sheep. But he wasn't grazing his sheep, and instead she was spying on Dougald and the other men while they were bathing in a loch. *Naked.*"

As if there was some other way to bathe in a loch. James raised his brows. "Indeed. And you?" The lad looked like he hadn't bathed in months. Smelled like it, too.

"I was the guard. And I spied her first."

"Aye, good thing, too."

Tavis frowned up at James as if he had something really bad to tell. "Dougald took off after her without the rest of us to watch his back. The men said he shouldna have run off after her all alone like that. Gunnolf said Dougald wanted her for his own. Niall said he wanted the fae."

"The fae?" James asked, surprised.

"Aye. That was what they called her. She looked like the fae with the white clouds and blue sky behind her, while she was wearing blue like the sky."

*The fae.* James recalled rumors that some said Lady Alana was of the fae, that her father saw her home after he had been murdered. He'd heard Lady Anice, Malcolm's wife, had the fae ability to see into the future. Dougald had been worried about Malcolm's safety, should the woman turn out to be a witch.

James didn't believe in the superstitions of his people or of those of other clans'. As a young girl,

Alana had obviously been distraught to see her da and the others in her clan murdered in front of her. James could imagine Alana envisioning her father was with her, ensuring she made it home all right, when in reality she had been in shock, too scared to know what really had happened.

"What was she doing on our lands? Did she say?" James asked the lad.

Tavis put the half empty mug and partially eaten chunk of bread down on the bench, then rubbed his eyes. "Looking for Rob MacNeill."

"Rob MacNeill? There are at least a dozen or more men named such in our clan." Why would the Cameron lass be looking for one of James's distant kin? Or he may have been a man who had sworn allegiance to the clan and taken their name.

"Aye, that was what your brother said."

"Which one was she looking for and why?"

"She said Rob was the father of one of her kinswomen's bairns. She wanted him to know of it. She said he was a sheepherder."

James cursed under his breath, annoyed one of his men could be so foolhardy, risking his own neck for what? "Where is Dougald now?"

"He and the rest of our men and the lady are on their way here."

James closed his eyes for a brief moment, then opened them and said, "Tavis, get your rest, lad. You have done well."

Clutching the mug of ale and the chunk of bread again in his tight grip, Tavis nodded, then stumbled off toward the hall where he would take a pallet with others sleeping there.

"What will you do?" Eanruig asked, sounding like he wasn't even sure how to advise him in this matter, when he usually had no trouble speaking his mind.

"Return the lass home with great speed and take care of the matter of Rob MacNeill and the Cameron wench, who is carrying his bairn."

"Rumors are rampant that the Cameron is making arrangements with another clan to wed his niece off to their clan," Eanruig warned.

James frowned at him. *He* hadn't heard any of the rumors. "Which clan?"

Eanruig shook his head. "'Tis a guarded secret, which is why I have no' come to you with the news prior to this. Those who say he is in negotiations say he threatens death to any should we hear of it before he officially releases the word."

James let out his breath in a huff. "One of our enemies then, no doubt."

"Aye."

"'Tis fortunate she is on her way here then." James was coming up with a much different plan for the lass.

"How so? Will you blackmail the Cameron into giving up the negotiations for the safe return of his niece?"

"And once he had her back, he would wed her to whichever clan he decides on? Nay, if the lass is who she says she is, Dougald will wed her."

Eanruig offered a rueful smile. "He may no' like the idea."

James waved his advisor's concern away. "Dougald loves all the lassies. He has taken it upon himself to bring her to us. Seems only fair, he should have every right to claim her." James clapped his advisor on the back. "Ready a contingent of men to meet Dougald in the event the Cameron learns of this and attempts to pursue them across our lands."

"Aye, my laird. Will you be riding also?"

"Nay. I will await my brother's return. I will have enough to deal with on the morrow." Then James entered his chamber and closed his door, intent on snuggling with his own lassie, hoping that Dougald would find pleasure in the Cameron lass.

The last he recalled of seeing Lady Alana, she was bonny indeed. Whether they would love each other in time was another matter though. He hoped that his brother could have a woman to cherish as he treasured Eilis. But it was high time Dougald settled down. An alliance with the hot-headed Cameron clan would not be a bad arrangement either.

He yanked off his belt and plaid, tossed them aside, and climbed under the covers. Immediately, Eilis nestled against him, her hand sweeping across his bare chest. "What is wrong?" she whispered.

"Naught is wrong. Dougald is getting married is all."

"Dougald?" she said with such surprise, James smiled.

"He said naught about this to anyone, has he?" she asked.

"Nay. He doesna know it yet, lass. Sleep. We will see him and his bride-to-be tomorrow eve if all goes well."

***

Lady Alana could not sleep. The ground was too hard, the night air too chilly, the worry about how her uncle would react when he learned she was with the

78

MacNeill clan, and what Laird MacNeill would do with her continued to plague her. She breathed in the smell of Dougald's borrowed spare plaid, the scent of pine and heather and leather, of wood smoke and his musky smell. Or was it on her? Wrapping her in its essence from having ridden in his arms all day?

She'd never been so close to a man, not like that. To feel his heated body pressed hard against hers, his arm clamped tightly around her, possessively, protectively, to feel the way she'd aroused him, all wantonly intriguing. Yet, she reminded herself that any lass who sat on his lap would have stirred the same craving.

She opened her eyes and saw Dougald sitting on a tree stump beside one of the campfires speaking to one of the lads who had ridden with them. He was talking quietly so as not to disturb the others who were sleeping. She realized then that several of the men were wrapped in their plaids, stretched out near her in a semi-circle, probably to protect her and ensure she did not attempt escape. One was happily snoring, and she realized that was another reason her sleep had been disturbed.

"You see, Callum, when you find the right bonny lass, you must protect her and cherish her above all others," Dougald said quite seriously to the lad.

Alana nearly laughed at the notion. Dougald was known to have been with many lassies. He did not stay with one to cherish her above all others. She had thought he would be teaching the lad something about fighting or surviving if separated from his clansmen, or the tending of fires, or hunting, or something important. She should have known Dougald would be talking about the subject he knew best—lasses. Even if he did not know how to truly love one and forsake all others. In that regard, he was just like her brother.

Who had vanished after he'd scolded her and left her to her own devices, she just realized. Not that he could do anything for her anyway.

In response to Dougald's advice to the lad, she gave a soft snort of derision, not meaning for them to hear her. She couldn't believe he would speak to the boy of the matter of loving a woman. To her chagrin, both Dougald and the lad looked in her direction.

Dougald's mouth curved at one corner to see her awake. She should have closed her eyes, feigned sleep, ignored the man, but she glowered at him instead.

"Off to bed with you now, lad. Seems the lady has something to say to me," Dougald said, his gaze still on her, the sparkle in his eyes and the crinkles beneath them indicating how much she had amused him.

Callum's dirty face split into a grin as he observed her. "Do you no' think I should listen to what she has to say? Then what you have to say?" He glanced up at Dougald. "Seems to me that I could learn much."

Dougald chuckled. "Nay, no' this time. Off to bed with you."

Not seeming in the least bit disappointed, Callum rose to his feet, grabbed his blanket, then found a spot as close to Alana as he could without disturbing any of the other men. Which was why she realized he hadn't been upset about Dougald making him retire for the night. The lad unrolled his blanket and gave her a big smile before he lay down. Then he rolled himself up in his plaid and watched her.

She wanted to shake her head, but couldn't hide a

smile instead.

"Come with me, lass, if you canna sleep. Tell me what is on your mind," Dougald said, motioning her over to the fire.

She remained where she was. "You, sir, are a rake. How could you teach the lad the way of women when you clearly…" She paused when two of the men's heads lifted off their plaids to look at her.

At first she thought they were annoyed she had awakened them, but then she saw the sleepy looks of amusement in the crinkles beneath their eyes and the small uplifted turn of their mouths and knew they wished to hear what she would tell the laird's brother about the way of women.

She unfurled herself from Dougald's blanket, stood, then wrapped it around her, walked over to the fire, and looked down at Dougald. "I have naught to say to you regarding your interest in women."

"You had an opinion earlier, my lady." He raised his brows, daring her to speak her mind. "What were you going to say?"

She shouldn't say a word. She knew that whoever was now awake, including three guards who were watching over the camp, would be listening. Then again, she wasn't one to hold her tongue when she believed the words needed to be said.

"You have a reputation with the ladies, sir," she said. Just like her brother had had. She knew the appeal was there, the smooth charming way of them, their glib tongues.

The flames reflected off Dougald's dark eyes as he studied her, watching her every reaction. His mouth was cemented into a smug smile, but he didn't say anything to refute her claim. He was a handsome devil of a man, his dark hair windswept, making him look wild and untamable, and she could see where women could be intrigued by such.

"You are known to be a rake. You dinna cherish a lass above all others," she continued, as if he didn't get her meaning the first time.

"Ah, mayhap my exploits are more tale than true." The sparkle in his eyes said he very much liked the way this conversation was going.

She was not an unreasonable woman, and she did consider the notion for as much time as it required for her to take a seat where the lad had been sitting on the grass. "Some, mayhap." Because she knew how men told tales, sometimes over way too many tankards of ale, and the telling of these tales would grow bigger and bigger until the telling was so exaggerated from the original story, that no one would have recognized it. She also knew there was often truth to the tale, no matter how much it had been embellished.

"I wager you have enjoyed your fair share of lassies and have not cherished any above any other," she insisted.

"At the time." He said the words matter-of-factly.

"What?" She did not understanding his meaning.

Some of his men chuckled.

Dougald let out his breath as if he couldn't understand how his meaning wouldn't be perfectly clear. "When a man is with a lass, he willna think of anyone else at the...," Dougald clarified, but paused, then shook his head as if he realized his mistake in giving her this particular explanation. She swore his ears colored a little, but it was difficult to tell by firelight. "Never mind. When a man finds the woman of his heart, he will cherish her above all else, is my meaning," Dougald finished.

A couple of men who were supposed to be sleeping, chuckled again.

She was certain, as much as she meant to couch her look of disbelief, that her expression was one of astonishment at hearing his declaration. "So you mean to tell me you would set aside your interest in all other women if you married?"

"Are you asking for yourself?" Dougald sounded far too amused.

Her face felt like it was on fire, and the heat spread down her throat all the way to the tip of her toes. She needed to get away from the fire. And from him and this conversation.

"Nay, of course not. I would never consider marrying a man such as yourself," she said, too haughtily. Her mother had told her if a lady spoke too vehemently about some matter, she would give away her feelings, which wouldn't do. Always be subtle when speaking with others. Let them guess as to how she feels. Alana would never learn.

Again, a few soft chuckles escaped from some of the men who were *supposed* to be sleeping and from one of the guards on duty who was *supposed* to be guarding.

"If a lass was to be my wife, which I have no interest in at the moment, rest assured, I would be devoted to her," Dougald said, not sounding all that serious, though she thought he was attempting to.

"Och, you would never settle down, sir. 'Tis no' in your blood. Any lass is like any other by your way of thinking." She almost mentioned he was like her brother, but managed to bite her tongue in time. She would not speak ill of her deceased brother—who seemed far too real to her still—in front of a man who was an enemy to her clan.

Dougald laughed softly. "If you say so, my lady. I wonder how it is that you know so much about me. I wouldna think my reputation was such that it would have reached the Cameron clan. Or your ears in particular."

"We know of your laird and his brothers. That your youngest is living with your second eldest brother, Malcolm, at Lady Anice's castle. That Malcolm could have lost his head to King Henry for taking the king's wife's cousin for his own. My uncle was much impressed. That James wed a lady and was nearly at war with two clans over it. My uncle has oft remarked how interested he is in knowing how your youngest brother and you would fare when seeking a bride. He predicts the lady's da will have to force the marriage where you are concerned."

"Me?"

She raised her brows. "My uncle knows that you were in a dungeon and that a lass helped you to escape. 'Tis your charming ways, no doubt, that earned your release in such a manner. My uncle jested that he would have to lock up all our lasses if he ever took you prisoner. It wouldna be enough that he would put you under lock and key. So you see, sir, you do have a reputation among the people of my clan."

Connell laughed from a place across the fire and her gaze shot that way to see her brother—*speaking of the dead*—sitting upon a log as if he had been invited to camp with the MacNeill clan this eve. "See, I am no' the only one with such a reputation," Connell said, grinning at her with his rakish charm.

*And see where that got her brother! Dead!*

# Chapter 7

Startled by her brother's laugh, Alana wondered how long Connell had been sitting on the other side of the campfire listening in on her conversation with Dougald. She imagined her brother would have been in the same situation had he been locked up in a dungeon—a willing lass would attempt to free *him* also!

She took a calming breath and turned her attention back to Dougald. He smiled too wickedly at her, and Alana wondered just what he was thinking. She thought it might be something she did not wish to hear.

She was about to leave him to the fire to contemplate his roguish ways when, with a definite sparkle to his eyes and a small smile, he said, "And what about you, lass? Would you have to be locked up, too, so that you wouldna be tempted to free me?"

She should have told him she would not be tempted to release the devil who would seduce any of the lasses in her castle that he could get his hands on. But that was not her way. If her uncle had imprisoned Dougald for no good reason, she could see herself freeing him. Although she wasn't certain she would risk her uncle's wrath for just any man. So mayhap Dougald had won her over…just a bit.

She rose and very seriously said, "It depends on why you were manacled in our dungeon in the first place."

Then she turned and headed back to her bedding.

The sound of a horse approaching made some of the men sit up and take notice, their hands on their swords. She froze in place before she had a chance to lie down. The Norseman, Gunnolf, looked grim-faced as he rode into camp and cast a look in her direction.

Dougald rose and welcomed him. "Gunnolf, what did you find?"

"If the croft that I visited was the same one that Lady Alana had been to, and the woman within was the same one who is carrying one of our clansmen's bairns, she seemed no' to be ill or with child, as far as I could tell."

Alana frowned. "You spoke with Odara?"

"That was the lass's name, aye."

"You probably gave her a fright, riding to her place and questioning her so. Why would you think she lies? The sickness comes and goes, if you knew anything about it." Men. They had no clue about a woman's sickness when she was carrying a babe. "'Tis too early for her to show." At least she assumed as much if Odara had only just come to the conclusion she was breeding.

"She wasna alone." Gunnolf watched Alana expectantly.

She stared at the blond hulk of a man in disbelief. Then she considered that the lad she'd sent to take care of Odara's sheep until she felt better might have stayed inside her croft with her overnight. "I sent a lad to help with her sheep."

"'Twas no' a green lad I saw with her," Gunnolf said. "Beyond that, I had already discovered the lad sleeping in the shed."

That gave her pause. What was Gunnolf intimating? That the man who had been with Odara was her lover? "Mayhap he was one of my kinsmen seeing to her welfare, or mayhap trying to learn what had become of me."

"He was in bed with her," Gunnolf said bluntly.

Her cheeks flamed as if they were on fire again. "In bed?" She didn't want to know if they were doing anything more than just sleeping. Then she recalled how adamant Odara was about loving the man called Rob MacNeill. "Was it Rob MacNeill? The father of her bairn?"

"Nay, lass, and they were rather noisy while conducting their business, which was why they did not hear me enter the shieling. They were together as lovers, no' in any other way. Because of what you had told us, I thought I might have discovered our Rob MacNeill, and then the task of finding him would be finished. But 'twas no' him."

Her heart was beating erratically, and she felt her knees weaken. Dougald stalked forward and caught her arm before her legs gave out beneath her.

"No' Rob MacNeill," she said in a very small voice.

"She still may believe Rob is the father of the bairn, *if* there is a wee one," Gunnolf said.

"And then took another lover? She wanted Rob. She said so. My uncle is trying to wed her to a man named Gilleasbuig. She doesna love him."

"Gilleasbuig?" Gunnolf snorted. "'Tis the very same name the man gave me, after he tried to kill me."

"He...he had to have forced himself on her," Alana reasoned.

"Aye, when she was asking for more, begging him

to go faster," Gunnolf said, his ire raised.

Alana was certain she would combust into flames at hearing the crude remarks. Dougald was fully supporting her now, rubbing her arm in a soothing way. She couldn't quit thinking of how it would have looked had she returned to the croft and found Gilleasbuig rutting with Odara, and the woman wanting more of the same.

Alana would have been shocked to the core like she was now. And angry.

"Do you know her well?" Dougald asked. "Well, enough to determine what the shepherdess's reason was for having sent you on this errand?"

A fool's errand, Alana thought. "You must return me to the border at once," Alana said, her voice determined as she tried to mask her alarm.

"Do you know her well?" Dougald asked again.

"Aye," she said, then hesitated and shook her head. "Nay. No' really well. We played together when we were little and her da brought her to the castle when he sold sheep to my da. I tended to her another time when she had taken ill. She had to bring her sheep into the bailey when we had trouble with a neighboring clan once or twice after her da died." She paused, realizing the neighboring clan and the trouble was with the MacNeills. "She is a quiet woman, not one to chase after the men." Alana let her breath out. "She is too quiet. Mousy even. I canna see she would be behind this deceitfulness."

Although she could conceive that the shepherdess might have been forced to play her role. "She sent word that she was ill. My uncle refused to tell me the woman was sick. That since she refused to wed Gilleasbuig she

89

could just suffer her complaint."

"I can only report what I myself have witnessed," Gunnolf said, arms folded across his chest, standing by his observation, though he looked as though he wished the news had been otherwise.

"Was your uncle adamant about this? Did he suspect you would go against his word and see to the woman?" Dougald asked.

"He wasna at the keep. One of Cook's assistants gave me the word. She said the lad had spoken on Odara's behalf to my uncle. My uncle had already left before daybreak to meet with one of the bordering clans. I didna learn of this for three days."

"'Tis the kitchen help's claim your uncle knew about any of this," Dougald said darkly. "Are you certain any of it happened as she said?"

"That the lad spoke to my uncle? Nay."

Dougald furrowed his brow. "And that the woman was ill?"

"She was…flushed, hot, but not feverish when I arrived.

"What if she had run inside in a panic when she chanced to see you coming?"

Alana didn't say anything as she considered the notion and found it did indeed have merit as much as she hated to admit it.

"Was she dressed?" Dougald asked.

"Aye." Which hadn't made sense to Alana if the woman was so ill, she couldn't take care of her sheep. Then again, she wondered if she had been caring for them all along, had intended to take them out into the glen, when she'd heard a rider—Alana—and rushed to carry on the pretense that she was ill. Or mayhap, knowing she had to care for her sheep and not having any other choice, she was doing so, ill or not. Though if that was the case, why would she have sprinted into the croft and pretended to be resting? "Return me and I will speak with—"

"Nay. If someone put the shepherdess and the cook's assistant and whoever else might be involved up to this, you could be in harm's way. Who within your castle walls would benefit if the MacNeill took you hostage?"

"No one would benefit." Alana wiped the clamminess from her hands on her wool brat and was attempting to assess the dilemma. What was the shepherdess plotting and who would have solicited her involvement in such a scheme? And how had she sought Pelly to assist her in getting the word to Alana? When the two did not live close by. Pelly lived with the servants in the keep. And Odara had no horse to ride to the keep and give her the word that she was ill.

Someone else had to have asked or forced the women's compliance. But why had three days passed before the word was given to Alana? Why not earlier, if all of what she had said had been a ruse and they needed Alana to chase down a Rob MacNeill, lover of Odara's, who was not her lover?

Did Rob MacNeill exist? And what of his niece?

She couldn't imagine her uncle arranging such a ploy. What if she had *not* gone to see the woman? Then what? Besides, he would have been too concerned for her safety.

Anyone who knew her well enough would also know she would always go to someone's aid who was ill and needed her help.

After she had visited the shepherdess, what if she had not tried to find Rob MacNeill? Only treated the shepherdess with the herbs, then returned to the keep? But then there was Rob's sick niece, which would have ensured Alana would have sought the man out for that reason alone.

Again, anyone could have known she'd seek to aid the woman both to help her overcome her sickness and to search for the man who was the father of the babe and to see to his sick niece. Her uncle had accused her of being too tender-hearted as if she would suffer too greatly if she didn't harden her heart to the cruelty of others.

Now she wondered if Odara's child was a deception also.

Had Odara known that Alana wouldn't be returning this eve? If she had returned, Alana would have caught Odara with Gilleasbuig. She shuddered at thinking of how she would have seen them, him on top of Odara, naked, grunting, her clawing at him, urging him to go...*faster*.

She noted Dougald and the other men were all watching her, waiting for her to come up with some conclusion that would explain why she'd crossed their border alone.

"Are you absolutely certain, Gunnolf, that Gilleasbuig had not forced himself on Odara?" Alana asked one more time, not wishing it to be true, but wanting to believe Odara was innocent of claiming any untruth.

"She noticed me when I stole into the croft and watched them, to see if they were both agreeable to committing the act, and also to see if it might be Rob

MacNeill. She didna warn him that I was there, and I thought that odd. After the man finished with her and turned to see me standing there, he came at me with both fists."

Alana shuddered at the image of that—a naked sweaty Gilleasbuig, hairy and meaty and no doubt red-faced with rage.

"I broke the mon's nose, and he sat on the floor holding it, cursing me. I tried to learn who he was, certain it was no kin of the MacNeil," Gunnolf said. "He readily gave up his name. I wanted to ask the lass about carrying a babe, but thought better of it. She seemed to wish to speak with me alone, but couldna with the man in her shieling."

"Three days ago we were informed a Cameron raiding party had crossed into MacNeill lands, but we have seen no sign of anyone, except the lass this day. And she doesna appear to have done much raiding." Dougald said.

"My uncle has been away these past three days." Alana folded her arms. "His men wouldna raid when he is gone."

Appearing as though he was considering her sincerity, Dougald studied her for a moment, then asked of his men, "Who sent word that the Cameron had a raiding party on our lands?"

The lad, Callum, spoke up. "Tavis did. A man he didna know told him when he was hunting rabbits."

"When Tavis became separated from the other hunters?" Dougald asked.

"Aye. He told me that two of our men were chasing a deer. Unable to keep up with them, Tavis spied a rabbit and went after him instead. A man stopped him before he got very far and warned a raiding party had just crossed our border."

A frown furrowing his brow, Dougald rubbed his whiskery chin, then said, "Why did the man tell the lad? Why not seek me out?"

The lad shrugged. "Tavis was excited to learn of it and made haste to speak with you. He didna think to question him, but thanked him and hurried back to find and warn you. You were on the hunt with the other men and had just returned with another deer."

"Yet we discovered no raiding party near the border or anywhere else on our lands, nor have we had any word from our crofters that they had been plagued by raiding parties." Dougald cast a glance in Alana's direction.

Everyone else turned their attention on her. Her cheeks burned. "I told you there had been no raiding party. The men of my clan wouldna have left the keep to conduct one with the laird away."

"What if you were supposed to be told of the shepherdess's ailment three days ago?" Dougald asked.

"There is no need to speculate. I didna receive word, nor did I come earlier."

"But what if you were to be told? And somehow the plan didna going into effect like previously plotted?" Dougald insisted. "What if we had also been told to go to the border for that very reason and would have intercepted you then?"

She shook her head. She didn't know what was going on.

"Did the man who warned of the raiders know who was leading our men this time?" Dougald asked the lad, sounding suspicious.

"He said to get word to you. So aye, he mentioned you by name. That is why Tavis thought he knew us and was one of us."

"Aye." Again, Dougald looked in Alana's direction, and she couldn't tell what he was thinking. Probably was just as confused as she was. Or mayhap not. She wasn't used to men's scheming ways. Mayhap he knew just what this was about. Or worse, mayhap he thought she was part of the whole plan. Whatever it was.

"Even if we find every Rob MacNeill in your clan, I suspect none will come forth to say he has been with Odara. If anyone *had* been meeting her," Alana said glumly. "Now that she is seeing Gilleasbuig, you must return me to the border at once. This has all been a big mistake."

"Nay, lass," Dougald said. "I am certain there was some purpose in you crossing the border, and we shall learn what it was in time."

"You were warned a raiding party had crossed into your territory," she corrected. "It was a mistake and has naught to do with me."

His mouth curved up, but his eyes held no mirth. "Aye, led by and made up of only one wee lass three days late. We will let James decide what is to be done with you."

Alana scowled at Dougald. "I had a task to do and 'tis no more. You have no need to take me to your laird."

Stubbornly, he shook his head. "You remain with us for now."

"You wished to know if I would attempt to release you from our dungeon if my uncle ever put you there? Nay. I wouldna." She stalked over to the spot of earth

95

where she'd rested before, curled up on the soft grass in Dougald's blanket and jerked it over her head so she could not see the men watching her.

No one spoke a word, nor did anyone move from the ground they were rooted to.

Dougald finally broke the silence. "Go back to sleep. We leave before dawn."

And his was the word of God, Alana thought, figuring James would even be worse.

\*\*\*

Later that night, horses' hooves pounded the ground from a distance, and Dougald quickly rose from his plaid, grabbing his sword in the process, pulse racing as he readied himself to fight the enemy, and protect the lass.

No one would ever get any sleep at this rate, Dougald thought as the horses drew closer. All his men hurried to rise from sleeping on their plaids, wrapping the wool around their bodies, grabbing swords and readying for the assault, except for those already on guard duty.

With a slight moan, the lady stood shakily on her feet, looking tired and the worse for wear, particularly after the very long horse ride she'd had, and Dougald imagined she was feeling sore all over. Her golden hair was bared for all to see and in the full moon's light and the flames still flickering in the fire, he was momentarily entranced by the silky rumpled fall of it about her shoulders. Sometime during the night she must have removed her veil.

"You have to turn me over to my uncle," she said wearily, looking at Dougald, not in the direction of the horses.

Not when the lady had trespassed on their lands, he didn't. And not when his brother had a say in this as laird over these lands.

He directed three of his men to watch the lady and take her into the darkness away from the camp and the soft glow of the fires so that she was invisible to the encroaching party. Callum waited to learn where he would go, and Dougald motioned with his head for the lad to accompany the lady. The men watching her were there partly for her protection and partly to ensure she didn't try to slip away. They quickly pulled her out of sight.

Only minutes later, his sword readied, Dougald spied his youngest brother, Angus, riding with the party of twelve men, and he grinned. He hadn't seen his brother in a year.

Gunnolf resheathed his sword and chuckled. "I would not have expected him this eve."

Angus dismounted, as one of the men hurried to take his horse and led him away, and Dougald gave him a sound embrace, followed by a slap on the back by Gunnolf.

"We thought you were a raiding party," Dougald said, smiling at his youngest brother. His curly brown hair was longer now, his crooked smile as bright as always.

"I thought you were a raiding party as well, though it appeared you were not right in the head with having so many campfires about."

Dougald smiled at that.

Niall hurried over to embrace Angus. "You have arrived just in time. Now you can stay and protect James and our kin. I can go with Dougald and

Gunnolf."

Angus frowned. "I return home and you are both leaving?"

Dougald shook his head. "Appears we will be staying a wee bit longer. Where have you been all this time? Still residing with Malcolm and his wife?"

"I have returned from England where King Henry has taken up arms to hunt down a Welsh prince who stole away his former mistress, the Welsh Princess Nest."

Dougald shook his head. "Were you there?"

"In the vicinity, but the accounts varied as to what had occurred."

Dougald led his brother to the campfire and one of the men brought him a flask of ale. "To hear some speak of it, the man was welcomed into Gerald FitzWalter and his wife's castle with the pretense that he wished to visit with one of his kinswomen. Then he and his party planned to kill the lord, and she convinced her husband and his men to escape in the lavatory chute to protect themselves."

Dougald raised a brow.

Angus shrugged a shoulder. "That was one telling of the story. Some say she went willingly with him. She was the king's mistress, and he gave her to Gerald as his wife. She's very beautiful and the Welsh prince just as charming. Who knows what really happened? Gerald begged the king to help him recover his wife on his behalf and so the king and his men are off to do just that. Who knows how it will all play out?"

"So you have been in the south again? Looking for a bride?"

"Unsuccessfully." Angus glanced over to see

Dougald's men return Alana to the bed they'd made for her. His brows rose, and he smiled. "Well, what have we here? I should have never left the Highlands. Who is this, pray tell?"

"Lady Alana," Dougald said, "meet my youngest brother, Angus."

The lady gave him a curt nod of greeting.

"A lady, is she?" Angus asked.

"The Cameron's niece."

Angus's mouth gaped for a moment, then he looked back at Dougald.

"Your brother has taken me hostage." Alana sat down on the borrowed plaid, then lay down and covered herself up in it. "Mayhap you will convince him of his folly."

Angus grinned and slapped Dougald on the shoulder. "Well done, I say. Has James been informed?"

"Aye. Tavis took word to him already. We will hear what he has to say about this by tomorrow eve."

Alana directed her next comment to Angus, "You are as bad as your older brother and will be in just as much trouble if you dinna convince him to release me at once."

No one said a word for a moment, then Angus laughed. "No one can get into trouble over the lasses as much as *he* can. And I am sure this proves my point perfectly."

# Chapter 8

"Did they search for you?" Connell, her annoying spirit of a brother, asked Alana as she was not quite awake the next morn, though it was still dark out.

Startled, she opened her eyes and saw her brother curled up in his plaid a little ways away from her, watching her, the campfires casting a soft glow in the dark.

"What?" she whispered, annoyed. She wished he wouldn't surprise her so. Furthermore, he frustrated her with coming up with questions out of nowhere, making no sense at all, as if they had been having a conversation all along and she should know just what he was asking. Besides, she wished to sleep longer. But she knew her brother would not quit pestering her until she answered him.

"When Da and his men were murdered, did the men who killed them search for you?"

She closed her eyes, reliving the moment so long ago. Of hiding under the moldy, decomposing leaves. Of fighting the awful urge to sneeze. Of hearing the battle cries, the clanking of steel swords as they struck their enemies'. Of the grunts of the men, the cries of pain, and the silence accompanying the end of the fighting.

Her heart thundering, she had listened, waited,

praying her father would call out to her.

Movement. She had heard men's boots and horses' hooves tromping on the ground, drawing closer. Her blood rushed in her ears. Her breathing was too fast. She wanted to get up and run. No words were spoken. No orders given. Why wasn't anyone calling out? Searching for her?

Because her people were no more. And the ones in the area? They were quiet, not wanting her to realize she knew they were the enemy who had won this day. That they were looking for her. The sole survivor of the slaughter.

"Alana, did they search for you?"

Tears filled her eyes. "Aye. They did," she said, her voice a hush. She took a consoling breath and looked at her brother. "You think they knew I was with our da? That I would be a witness to the massacre? Or had they wanted me for some other reason?"

"Were you with the men as a group when they were attacked?" Connell asked, his questions focused while he didn't answer her own. He seemed both concerned and angry. Not angry with her, more…worried if anything.

She bit her lip.

"They were hunting," he persisted. "Da and the other men. Often when you went hunting with us, and they took chase after a stag, you couldna keep up. You were only nine at the time. Had you been separated from them so when they were attacked, the brigands had not spied you?"

"Why do you ask this of me now, Connell? Why not long ago?" She tried to keep her voice low, though she couldn't help the annoyance she felt. She'd been questioned mercilessly by her uncle, her father's advisor, her brother, by other clansmen. Only the women had let her be.

And she had emphatically told everyone the same thing over and over again. She had seen nothing and no one. The men had used no names between them. Which her kin had thought suspicious at the time. She remembered seeing glances shared between them every time she was asked if any names were exchanged and every time she said no. She would have shared their names with her kin. She would have told them if she'd known. Instead, she could identify no one.

"They moved in closer to you, nearly stepped on you," Connell persisted.

"It happened so fast," she said under her breath. "So very fast. Aye, Da and the other men had ridden after a stag. One of the younger men stayed with me when I fell behind. But when we heard the fighting, he told me to hide and he rode into battle. Landon, he was…he was only five and ten."

"Aye, I know. But you said Da told you to hide."

He had. That's what had confused her. He had ridden back and told her to send her horse away and then to run and hide. All she could think of doing was burying herself in the leaves. She left her bow and quiver of arrows with her horse. She had the dagger that Da had given her the year before, and then she'd hidden and prayed that he would come for her soon.

"Was Da already dead?" Connell asked.

She took a sharp breath. "I..I dinna know for certain," she whispered. Yet she wondered, had her father already died, and she'd only seen his ghost? He'd seemed so real. Just like when he'd come back for her and taken her home. Just like Connell appeared to her now.

"They had to have known a girl was with the hunting party," she finally said. then she frowned. "Dougald MacNeill found my horse and gave her to Odara's da, who returned her to the keep." Alana wiped tears away.

"But the MacNeills took no part in the killings, our uncle said. And the others who did, searched for you. You saw the men."

"Nay. I had my eyes closed."

"They drew close, Alana. They were so close, you felt a man's leather boot brush past your arm. He knocked leaves aside, and you said you feared he'd see you. You had to have looked up at him. You had to have seen him."

"I was buried. I...I lay very still. I didna move. I lay there as if I was a fallen tree buried by the leaves."

"Think harder. You saw him. What did he look like?"

"Why do you persist in this line of questioning? I saw naught that night. I saw naught."

"For weeks, you screamed out in terror when you tried to sleep at night. One of the maids said you saw one of the men who participated in killing our men."

Had she blocked the memory from her mind so that at night the terror revisited her, but upon waking, she could not remember what had happened no matter how hard she tried?

"Alana," Dougald said, crouching in front of her, his expression one of concern, his brows deeply furrowed. "Are you all right, lass?"

She felt her cheeks flame. "Aye."

"'Tis time to break our fast." He was looking at her curiously, and she realized most of the men had left to hunt and gather wood to rebuild the fire to cook a meal, but she had an audience of four—Dougald, Angus, Niall, and Gunnolf.

And her brother was…gone.

So just how much had the men heard?

\*\*\*

Not wanting to send any of his men with Alana to watch her as she left the camp for a bit of privacy, but wanting to speak privately with his brother and cousin and Gunnolf over what they'd overheard Alana speaking of, Dougald opted to stay with her instead.

He wanted to ask her what had occurred before dawn this morning, but it would have to wait. Storms were rolling in at a fast pace and though he had intended to continue onto the castle and to reach it by nightfall, he would not risk the lady's health and would stop by the nearby village and stay there until the brunt of the storm passed.

She had looked so startled when she had realized he was crouching in front of her and had been for some time that he wondered just who she could have been speaking to. At first, he'd meant to wake her, but when she opened her eyes and began talking—to him, he thought, he'd paused and listened. Her question—asked in a highly annoyed whisper and simply, "What?"—had taken him aback.

He had at first assumed he'd startled her awake, and she was attempting to cover up her fright by being annoyed with him. But then she began to talk about her da and the massacre, and he didn't know what to think. He certainly hadn't brought the subject up. He hadn't even realized she might have witnessed her da's murder. That they were on a hunt, he knew that much. That her brother...*Connell.* Damnation, that's what she'd called him. Well, not Dougald, but she'd been looking right at him when she called him Connell.

Had she been talking in her sleep? But tears had formed in her eyes, and she looked very much liked she'd been awake.

He'd heard rumors that she talked to the fae, or...if the stories could be true, ghosts. Had she been talking to her dead brother? He'd died...several weeks past, murdered for his transgression with a married lass. Alana asked why he was questioning her now...about her da's murder? So long ago?

God's wounds, he thought his brother Malcolm had married a lass with abilities no person should ever have. God save the man who married Alana if she spoke to ghosts whenever the need arose. He could just imagine being in bed with the lass and there was her brother...curled up beside her...or beside Dougald.

As much as he was dying to know the truth, so were his brother, cousin, and Gunnolf. They happened to be watching the whole situation once they saw him crouching before Alana, but not waking her to ready for the journey, and instead listening to her speaking to someone like she was having a normal conversation. Only her words were whispered. To an extent.

He heard them, and so did his kin and his friend.

He wanted to speak with her. But he'd already seen the tears in her eyes and the ones rolling down her cheeks that she'd brushed away, and he didn't want to start the waterfall again.

***

As they began their journey, the men were mostly quiet. A couple of them way in the lead talked about something Alana couldn't hear. She was riding her own horse, stiff, her arse killing her, and she would be glad to get out of the saddle for a couple of days.

Dougald rode at her left flank, Angus on her right, displacing Niall. He hadn't been happy about it, though he still looked hopeful that Angus would stay with James, and Niall would take off with Gunnolf and Dougald when they decided to journey somewhere else.

She felt the two brothers watching her from time to time. She'd barely been able to eat a bite of the bread and nothing more that they'd shared that morning. She couldn't believe she'd been talking to her brother, whispering, aye, but was startled to realize Dougald had been crouching before her. How much had he and the others heard?

The men had talked plenty before they got ready to ride again. All but the four who may have overheard her speaking with her ghost of a brother.

"Do you often talk in your sleep, Lady Alana?" Dougald finally asked her.

She turned her head sharply to look at him. "What?" She'd heard him, but she didn't know what else to say. Mayhap this would be the perfect way out for her. She was prone to talking in her sleep. Wouldn't that solve her problems? Except when she was perfectly awake and still talking to ghosts.

"My sister used to talk in her sleep when she was overly tired," Dougald said, watching her, his expression one of sympathy.

Alana considered the notion more carefully. If she talked in her sleep, she wouldn't know about it, would she? Only others who might have heard her would realize she did such a thing. Watching the men in front of them to avoid looking at Dougald and giving herself away, she shook her head. "Nay."

"That is true," Dougald said, agreeing cheerfully with her. "If you talked in your sleep you most likely wouldna remember."

"I dinna talk in my sleep," she said, as if saying so would confirm that that's what it had to have been.

"One time, I thought she was talking in her sleep, my sister that is, but she wasna," Dougald continued.

Alana looked at him. His sister couldn't have spoken to ghosts, too, could she?

Dougald's expression had darkened, but he didn't say anything further to explain what had happened.

"'Tis going to rain," Connell warned.

She glanced in Angus's direction but Connell was riding his borrowed ghostly horse next to her. He motioned to the sky. "They willna want to risk you getting sick. They will have to take you to the nearest village. It will be hours before you can travel again. Mayhap no' until the morrow. You could attempt to leave then. I could help you get home. Mayhap this is the verra reason I am here. To see you home like Da did."

She opened her mouth to say something to him when he vanished, and she realized Angus was studying her. She clamped her lips shut and focused on the sky. The wind had picked up and the temperature had dropped several degrees. The sky had progressively darkened from a pale gray to ominous blue-gray, the clouds shifting and reshaping into mountains.

"We willna make it," Angus said to Dougald.

"Aye, but we are close now."

"To Craigly Castle?" Alana asked. It was early morning. They weren't supposed to arrive there until nightfall.

Dougald shook his head. "To a village near here. They have a tavern. We will stay there until the storm passes."

So her brother had been right about Dougald taking them to the village.

"The rain doesna bother me. We can keep riding," she said, afraid her brother would convince her to try to steal away from the tavern, and she'd get herself in more of a mess than she was in now.

Dougald gave her a small smile. "It pleases me that you are so eager to reach Craigly Castle. But Angus, here, might catch his death. James would have my head for it. So we shall stop at the village."

"Are you no' going to defend your honor against such a remark?" Alana asked Angus.

He laughed. "Oh, aye, 'tis a bonny barmaid Dougald wishes to see. But I dinna mind that he uses me as his excuse."

She gave Dougald a smug knowing smile, thinking back to his comment about women and loving one to the exclusion of all others to the lad. "Just one?" she asked Angus.

He smiled back at her, and she realized he had the most wickedly charming smile just like Dougald. She imagined then all the brothers were the same.

Within the hour, they were drenched, the rain coming down is such thick sheets, the men stayed close together so they would not lose sight of one another as they made their way to the village.

Dougald had even taken hold of her reins to ensure he didn't lose her. She didn't believe he thought she'd run away, but that he might lose sight of her in the deluge.

By the time they reached the tavern, she felt as though she weighed a hundred more pounds as wet as her clothes were. The ground was slippery and muddy, and Dougald gave up his reins and hers to one of the men, then helped her down from her horse, only he wasn't letting her go.

She didn't mind. It was bad enough that she was soaking wet all the way to the skin, but she didn't want to add a layer of mud to that.

He hurried her inside with all haste, his brother and Gunnolf leading the way, his cousin and a couple of the other men following behind them, the rest taking the horses to be stabled.

As soon as they walked inside, the laughter and talking subsided and every eye was upon them. The place smelled of ale and mead and of something cooking, roasted boar, she thought.

Men sat at five of the long tables. Although some moved to another table when Dougald's men arrived, many greeting him, and she assumed he was a regular.

"I will get you a room so you can get out of your clothes and dry them by the fire," Dougald said. "The rest of you, have a seat."

"Did you want me to bring up something for the lady?" Angus asked.

Dougald waited for Alana to say. "Nay, thank you." She was shaking so hard, all she wanted to do was get out of her wet things and get warmed up by the fire. A woman brought him a key to a room.

"What about the rest of you?" Alana asked, concerned any of them could become ill.

"We will get another room. The men can strip down and dry off there."

She couldn't help the heat that crept across her neck and cheeks. All she could think of was the way she'd seen those same men naked in the loch.

He took her upstairs and into the room, then removed the brooch on her cloak and laid the brat out on a bench near the fire, setting the pin on top of it. "Did you need help with your *léine*?"

She held her hand to her breast, not wanting to look so surprised, or shocked, but she couldn't help herself. "Nay," she said, sounding so upset, he smiled.

"I was going to send up a maid. I would not make a good lady's maid, Lady Alana."

"Of…of course."

"You willna be going anywhere, will you?" he said, still not leaving her alone.

"Nay, of course no'."

"I have your word?"

"In this weather? I would catch my death."

"Aye, you would. I will fetch a maid at once." Then Dougald left her, locked her in—so he didn't trust her as much as she thought he might—although he might have done so to keep other men from intruding.

She sat down on the wooden bench and began to remove her stockings and boots. She was shaking so hard from the cold she could barely make her fingers work.

Someone unlocked the door and a bonny woman around Alana's age hurried into the room, her hair dark and her eyes a pale brown, and dark brows knit in a tight frown. She closed the door. "I am no lady's maid, but I will see what I can do for ye. Ye look like a drowned rat."

Alana should have been angered by the woman's condescending words, but she found her comment too funny and laughed.

The woman stared at her for moment, probably surprised to get that reaction, then roughly hurried to help Alana out of her *léine*. "Ye know Dougald well?" the woman asked.

"Oh, aye," Alana said, and realized the pretty woman was probably the maid Angus had mentioned Dougald had been seeing. "I had considered marrying him as he has said he loves me more than he has ever loved a lass. But alas, I have fallen in love with another."

"You would be foolish to believe he would love only one lass." The woman smiled at her, and Alana assumed this was indeed the wench Angus had referred to that Dougald wished to reacquaint himself with.

Which reminded Alana that Dougald was no better than her brother when it came to dallying with the lasses. She shouldn't have cared, but she did. Mayhap because she'd wish the way he'd held her so close on his horse had meant he felt she was someone special to him. Someone who appealed in the flesh and not just to be bargained with as in MacDonald's case if her uncle was arranging for her marriage to Hoel.

She helped Alana out of her sopping wet chemise, then handed her a drying cloth. "I have no' clothes to loan ye as Dougald asked. Climb under the covers, and ye can get warm that way."

"Thank you."

The woman nodded, then hurried out of the room and locked the door.

Alana had barely slipped under the covers when her brother appeared, and she shrieked.

And knew at once her mistake.

# Chapter 9

"Get out!" Alana screamed at her ghostly brother as he appeared in the tavern room, giving her a fright. She pulled her covers higher as her heart pounded and blood raced.

"Someone has to stay here and protect your virtue," her brother said, leaning against the wall, arms folded across his chest, obviously not about to do as she bid.

Heavy footsteps tromped up the stairs at a run.

Connell unsheathed his sword and watched the door. Alana stared at the door, waiting for a whole pack of men to come barging into the room to rescue her. Hoping to stop the inevitable and save her pride, she held the covers up to her chin and called out, "I am all right."

The key poked into the lock with such ferocity, she thought the bearer of the key could have slain a villain with the brass object alone. The door slammed against the wall and Dougald, sword in hand, rushed to the bed while Gunnolf and Angus followed, both with swords drawn. Niall stayed in the doorway, guarding it. Gunnolf checked the window and made sure it was locked. Angus was peering under the bed.

Dougald raised his brows at her when everyone confirmed no one was in the room besides her.

"It…was a *rat*," she managed to get out, giving her ghostly brother a glower. He cast her a small smile and resheathed his sword.

She let out her breath, holding her covers tightly under her chin as if they might somehow slip down and reveal any naked part of her. Even her bare arms were too much for these men to see, but she was afraid to release the wool coverlet.

"I am sorry. I told you I was all right. You had no need to check on me. I am fine. Go back to what you were doing," she said to Dougald, his gaze steady on hers, judging her sincerity, she felt.

Dougald nodded to the others, but as they left the room and shut the door, he didn't leave. She noted her brother hadn't either. He was waiting, observing Dougald as if he would fight him to the death if he so much as touched Alana. As if her brother could truly do anything about it. On top of that, it was *his* fault Dougald was here in the first place.

"You didna see a rat." Dougald sat down on the bed beside her.

She looked at her brother. He was *too* a rat. How could he invade her privacy and keep scaring her to death if he wasn't? He could knock…well, she guessed he couldn't. But still…

"Alana," Dougald said, drawing her attention. "Did you see who murdered your da?"

Her eyes widened. Oh God, he had heard her speaking the words to her brother. Had Dougald been crouching in front of her the whole time? Only she had seen her brother instead of Dougald?

"I…I dinna know what you mean."

"You said they were on the hunt. Your da and the others, and that you were with them. That you had hidden beneath the fallen leaves. It had been near

114

winter when your da and his men had been attacked. Did you see any of the men who murdered them?"

She shook her head. For all she knew, they could have been some of the MacNeill. That Dougald and the others had not taken part, but had arrived late to discover the carnage. Would the word spread through his clan that she'd witnessed the murders?

When she didn't answer, Dougald asked, "Who were you talking to?"

She opened her mouth, paused, then said, "I…I wasna talking to anyone." Then it sounded like she knew just when he meant and that wouldn't do. "You mean, before you reached the room?"

"At the camp. I came to wake you, but you were already awake and talking to someone."

He couldn't have heard everything she'd said then. "I was asleep."

"You were looking straight at me."

"I was asleep," she insisted, a lot more vehemently.

"You called me…or *him*, rather, Connell. Your brother? The one who died a while ago?"

She felt as though all the blood had drained from her face.

Connell clapped his hands. She heard him, though no one else could, but it earned a glower from her just the same.

Dougald glanced over his shoulder, then looked back at Alana. "Is he…here now? Standing over there? Protecting you?"

Alana stared at Dougald, her lips parted, her eyes misty with tears. Other than the times she'd mentioned about people she'd seen who she thought had still been alive, she had never told anyone she saw the dead and spoke with them as if they were still among the living. How could she ignore them when they were so real to her? And sought her attention?

"Alana, is your brother here with us now?"

She couldn't believe Dougald would ask her that. She couldn't help looking back at Connell as if confirming to herself he was still there. Which of course he was. He shrugged at her as if he couldn't help her out, and she was on her own when *he* was the cause of the trouble. Well, at least this time.

"Nay," she said to Dougald. She couldn't tell him the truth. How could she? But then she realized she didn't act indignant that he said such a thing to her. She couldn't rectify her mistake that quickly without him becoming even more suspicious.

"Did he tell you to say that?" Dougald asked.

Connell laughed.

She glowered at her brother.

"All right." Dougald let out his breath. "Your secret is safe with me, lass."

She wanted to ask him if his brother and cousin and Gunnolf had also overheard everything she had said to her brother at the camp. Would her secret be safe with them as well?

"A man will be posted outside your room at all times for safety sake. A meal will be brought up later. I dinna believe you got much sleep last night. Take a rest and I will be up to see you in a while."

"Thank you, Dougald."

He patted her bare arm, and she felt her cheeks warm.

Seeing her blush, he smiled, then he grew serious. "I just want to say one more thing. My sister by marriage to Malcolm, Lady Anice, sees…glimpses of the future. I canna say I wasna concerned about her visions when I first learned of them. But I have come to believe her special sight is a gift and no' a curse. Mayhap what you see is just as much of a gift."

Her brother smiled and nodded at her. She scowled at him.

"Just let whomsoever is guarding your door know if you require anything," Dougald finished.

"Thank you."

Then Dougald looked in Connell's direction and said with a brusque tone, "Protect her if you must, but in a way that doesna scare her half to death."

"I rather like him," Connell said to Alana.

"You should. He is a rake just like you…were," she amended, then saw Dougald studying her.

Her whole body heated all over again.

"I will be back in a little while," Dougald said.

She knew then he believed that she truly spoke to ghosts, that Connell was standing against the wall looking smugly satisfied, and that she should never have allowed her brother to get the best of her. She was usually so careful with keeping up her guard. With the other ghostly entities, they had found their way home after a short time. Not so with Connell, and she was getting too lax with seeing him come and go. She would have to be much more diligent in watching what she said to him when the living might be close by.

Would Dougald tell the others? Mayhap not. She hoped not.

Dougald leaned over and brushed her forehead with a whisper soft kiss that warmed every part of her all over again, and she quickly looked to see Connell's expression.

Connell shook his head, but smiled again at her.

So, he approved of Dougald because he wasn't concerned she could see ghosts?

"I will return." Dougald again looked in Connell's direction, nodded to him, then left the room, locking the door behind him.

"I like him," Connell said. "You could do worse."

"He is a rake like you!"

"Mayhap you will be the lassie he loves above all else."

"You were listening the whole time! At the campfire."

Connell smiled. "I love it when your feathers are ruffled. Not a soul who was there was sleeping, Alana. They may have had their eyes closed, but they were smiling."

She turned away from her brother and closed her eyes.

"And for your information, dear sister, I have no' been with a woman since...since...hmm, the predicament I found myself in."

"You are dead!"

"You need no' keep reminding me. I well know what has happened."

Tears filled her eyes as she studied her brother's expression and thought for the first time he truly looked repentant. "I am sorry, Connell. I miss you, you know."

"I know, lass. And I...hate myself for leaving you alone without protection. I should have been there for you until you were married and your husband could protect you."

Was that why her brother stayed with her? Because

he had to see her married off? She didn't know why the ghosts came to her, stayed with her for a time, and then finally departed her world. Or why he seemed to be taking so long to find his way to his final resting place.

"I will be all right, Connell. You need no' feel as though you have to stay with me to protect me."

He shook his head. "I dinna know why I canna leave you, lass. But I canna. Rest, as Dougald said for you to do. The rain willna let up, mayhap no' even until the morn. You still have a long day's ride to Craigly Castle."

She closed her eyes then, weary, worried about how she'd be received, what James would decide to do with her, and fearful Dougald would tell his clan how she could commune with the dead.

\*\*\*

Dougald returned to the table downstairs to join Gunnolf and Angus, and drank the tankard of ale that Angus had ordered for him, wondering if Alana truly had seen her father's murder. If so, would she be able to identify any of the men? If she could, it had been so long ago, most likely no one would believe her.

"What was that all about?" Angus asked, his voice low for Dougald's ears only. Although Gunnolf leaned in to hear also.

"She saw a rat."

"Nay, she didna," Angus said, looking annoyed with Dougald.

"A ghost of a rat rather," Dougald said.

Angus smiled. "Now that I believe. We had heard her dead father had seen her home safely after he was murdered. Think you she truly sees the dead?"

"Some, mayhap. Close family, if 'tis what I

suspect."

"Good, if 'tis only close family. Otherwise our sister might plague her also."

Dougald had not considered that. He shook his head.

"Who is the rat?" Angus asked.

"Her brother."

Angus leaned back on the bench and raised his brows. "*Connell*. He was murdered a while ago."

"Aye."

"He made her shriek?" Angus asked.

"Imagine being a naked lassie, who suddenly sees a dead brother appear in the room she is staying in. Would you no' shriek in fright?" Dougald asked, sounding annoyed.

Angus grinned. "I never imagined myself being a lassie." Then he grew thoughtful. "But I see your point. What do you think James will do about her?"

The maid came up to the table and smiled at Dougald as if Gunnolf and Angus were not even there. "I am free in a wee bit."

Dougald shook his head. "But I will take more ale."

She frowned at him. "She says she isna yours. That she loves another."

Dougald smiled up at her. "The lady? She was shy about declaring her love for me to a perfect stranger. We will wed as soon as we are able."

Angus choked on his ale. Niall joined them at the table and slapped Dougald on the back. "A wedding? When did this happen?"

It wasn't happening, he wanted to tell his companions. He just wanted Ragnall to know he was not interested in her today or any other.

Then Ragnall's scowl quickly changed into a calculating smile. "Aye, and when you tire of her bed, you know where I will be. I will bring more ale." She bounced off as if she was perfectly pleased with the idea.

Niall took a seat across from Dougald. "Think you James will go along with your plan?"

"There isna a plan," Dougald growled low under his breath.

They all laughed.

"You know," Angus said, still smiling, "the lasses will soon get word of this and some will shun you if you come to see them."

"And others," Niall said, having just as much fun with this, motioned with his tankard toward Ragnall, "will be just like the wench. The sport so much more intriguing when you are wed."

Wanting to get them off the subject, Dougald said, "The lass witnessed her da's murder."

Everyone's expression instantly turned somber.

"But there has never been any word as to who had done such a deed," Niall said. "If the lass knew—"

"She said she didna. But she was there. Hiding. Buried by leaves. What if she had seen one of the men, or more of them than that?"

"Would they have not killed the lass already?" Gunnolf asked, his face dark with concern. "Even if she had not seen them, they wouldna know that for certain. They could not risk her telling what she saw."

"What if that wasna the strategy?" Angus asked. "What if the plan was to kill the lass's father? No' the lass?"

"You mean because they wanted him out of the

way?" Dougald asked. "So that her uncle could take over?"

"Aye. But here is another thought, Dougald. Was Lady Alana betrothed already? Often a clan chief's daughter will be promised to another clan in marriage even at a youthful age. So was she? And if so, is that the same clan that her uncle has gone to see concerning a marriage agreement or no'? Did killing the lady's father change the marriage agreement?" Angus asked.

"Or what if the lass was no' betrothed, but her father had been approached concerning such an arrangement, and he had said no? What if the uncle was more agreeable?" Dougald offered.

"Suppose someone suspects as much. Someone who believes the new arrangement would benefit someone who had her father murdered. And that someone sends the lass away from the castle, from the safety of her people, only to keep her from falling into the wrong hands? The same ones who murdered her father?" Gunnolf said.

Angus slapped his hand on the table. "Then Dougald will have to marry the lass and that will be the end of that."

Dougald could just imagine attempting to bed the lass, and there her brother would be, watching over them, speaking to the lass and being more than a nightmare than he would know how to handle.

# Chapter 10

When Laird Alroy Cameron rode into the inner bailey surrounding his keep, he found utter chaos. He had successfully negotiated a betrothal arrangement with Laird McDonald's middle son, Hoel, and Alana, believing the match suitable for his niece. The man drank a little too much for Cameron's liking, but that was inevitable as he was celebrating the agreement. He didn't care for Hoel's slipping off with a serving wench later that eve, either. Though Cameron had to remind himself the man could avail himself of the wenches, until he was married to his niece.

If Hoel upset his niece, he would have words with the knave. That was one reason he planned to arrange a marriage where Alana's husband would live under the Cameron's roof and Cameron's watchful eye.

He stroked his beard as he surveyed his staff rushing out to greet him and his men. No one met his eyes in greeting, the whole lot of them cowering as if they were not pleased he had returned home so quickly. Business done, he had wished to give the word as to his niece's coming nuptials as soon as possible.

He noted his niece was disturbingly absent. She

was always there first, lady of the keep, all smiles for him, greeting him upon his return no matter if he'd been gone only a mere few hours or days. Was she upset with him for making the marriage arrangement without speaking with her about it first? He wouldn't have. It was his decision to make, not the lass's. She wouldn't have a head for deciding such a matter. She would go along with his decision no matter what because she knew how important such an arrangement was for their clan.

His advisor, Turi, stalked toward him, his continence grim, and Cameron knew before he even spoke that something untoward had happened to his niece.

"Where is Lady Alana? Is she ill?" Cameron snapped, dismounting, and not waiting for an answer as he stormed toward the keep.

"Gone, my laird."

Cameron whipped around and glared at his advisor. "Gone? Where? Spill it, mon. Where is my niece?" He didn't like the concern etched in his advisor's face. All at once Cameron felt the blood rush from his face. "Dead? She has died?"

Blue eyes widening, Turi quickly said, "Nay, my laird. She…she left the castle and hasna been found."

Cameron studied him, not believing that the man could have let this happen. Turi knew never to allow her beyond the curtain walls when he was gone for any length of time. A few hours, he would allow when he was in residence, but not when he was gone for days.

"How? How did she get beyond the curtain wall without my permission?" he snapped, heading again for the keep. He needed a meal and a good night's sleep. He didn't need this news. Not now. Not after having made arrangements for her marriage to Hoel. He motioned to one of his men. "Ready new mounts for us. Have food prepared that we will take with us on our journey. We will eat and leave again at once."

"Aye, my laird." The man quickly spoke to a servant and began issuing orders.

"The last we could discover was she crossed the border into the MacNeill's lands, but we have no clue as to why she would have done such a thing," Turi said.

Cameron stopped just inside the keep and glowered at his advisor. "What? When did she leave?"

Had she learned of her marriage arrangement to Hoel and thought to run away? Seeking James MacNeill's clan as refuge? Cameron would not put up with her disobedience.

"Two days ago, my laird."

"Two…" Cameron felt himself shaking with rage. "No man accompanied her?" He did not wait for an answer because he knew the truth of the matter already. "You sent men after her?"

"We scoured our own lands and the castle several times first, my laird. We didna learn until later that she had crossed the border. She left with several men and women headed to the fields early the morning before last."

Cameron sighed with a bit of relief. "So she wasna alone."

"When she headed to the forest, aye, my laird."

"How come you know she crossed the border between our lands then?"

"Odara, the shepherdess who lives near our border with the MacNeill, said she saw Lady Alana heading that way."

"Did she no' attempt to stop her?"

"She said Lady Alana was too far across the border for her to get her attention. She was riding fast."

"So Alana *is* on the MacNeill lands." Cameron had learned about her acting as a midwife to a MacNeill woman and her babe across the border and though he had not approved of her doing so, the deed had been done, and he let on he never knew about it. Had he been too lenient with her? Aye. Until she was Hoel's responsibility, he would not let her out of his sight again.

She was like the daughter he'd never had. Like his sweet wife who had died three winters past. Connell, Alana's brother, had been a hellion. He was a likeable lad, but because of his transgressions with the lasses, Cameron had suspected he would come to no good end. Alana was everything sweet and innocent, and God's wounds, how could he have let this happen?

"Has James MacNeill sent us a missive—" Cameron shook his head, trying to clear the fog from it. "Of course no' or you would know she was with them." He narrowed his eyes at his advisor. "Why did she leave? Did she know I intended to offer her hand in marriage to MacDonald's middle son?"

"No one has told her of any such news as I believe no one knew it might come to pass. Is the arrangement agreed upon then?"

"Aye, but it counts for naught if my niece canna be found." But he didn't care about that right now. All that mattered was he found his niece unharmed. "I must eat and we will be off." He paused again at the entryway to the great hall where servants were hastily setting out a meal for him and his men. "Did you already send men to speak with James?"

"Nay, my laird. We have searched everywhere for her and since you were arriving this eve and you have always said we are no' to cross the border and instigate a battle between our clans in your absence…we didna go there. I thought she would return before this."

"You should have sent men at all possible haste to learn if she is with James. If the MacNeill has my niece, no telling what he will do with her."

"He will keep her safe," Turi said.

Cameron glowered at him. He might not like the laird as the two clans had skirmishes over the borders for centuries, but he knew James was honorable enough that he would not harm his niece. But what if she was lost on his lands, or worse? What if men not under James's control had taken her hostage? "*If* James has her at Craigly and she hasna become the victim of some unscrupulous knave." And beyond that, what if James decided to marry her to one of his brothers? The man still had two of them who were unmarried and a cousin besides.

"Aye, my laird."

Cameron stalked into the great hall and took his seat at the head table where Turi joined him. "I have been way too lenient with her," Cameron said, then drank a goodly sum of a tankard of ale as servants rushed to feed him and his men. "I am afraid Hoel MacDonald will have to do a good job at keeping the lass in hand." *If* Cameron could find his niece before harm came to her. He looked at the haggard lines of his advisor's face, realizing Turi had to be just as concerned about his daughter, Brighid, who served as a maid to

Alana. "You must be worried about your own daughter's safety."

"Brighid wasna with her."

Cameron threw down the bread he had managed a bite of and rose from his chair so abruptly, the great hall turned silent. "Your daughter is *here*?"

"Aye, my laird. She had been feeling ill. Lady Alana had given her something to settle what ails her. She was sleeping when Lady Alana left the keep to cut herbs in the garden. She had gone to the moorland earlier than that. When Lady Alana went out again, no one believed she was doing anything more than gathering healing plants from the forest. She is gone for hours sometimes. No one thought she would fail to return. I told you she was alone when she went to the forest."

"Aye, but I believed you meant she was without men to guard her. She is always to have her maid or two of them with her at all times when she leaves the castle!"

Turi cleared his throat. "I am sorry, my laird."

"Aye, you are." Cameron stalked out of the great hall, his men scurrying to grab what foodstuffs they could before departing again. He knew they were weary. He was tired and could have slept a fortnight in his bed. Then again, with worrying about Alana's safety, he didna believe he could sleep one wee bit.

He'd never forget her appearance when she'd come home ten years ago, her brat gone, her *léine* torn and filthy, leaves and twigs sticking out of her pale blond hair. She looked half starved, as though she was an orphaned waif. She couldn't speak at all, just stared at him and his men, as he tried to learn where her da and his men were, why she was all alone and there at the gate, her horse nowhere in sight, like she had fought untold battles of her own.

She had peered over her shoulder as if looking for someone else to tell him what had happened to the rest of their men. Cameron had crouched before her, held her tiny shoulders, looked into those haunted green eyes and asked again and again what had happened to the hunting party, what had happened to her da, the laird, his brother.

Connell had broken through the circle of men crowding around her when he received word she had returned home alone and asked his sister where their da was, trying to look like the warrior he so longed to be. His sandy hair blowing across his still whiskerless jaw, he stood as tall as some of the men, though he was still lanky because he was only five and ten. Tears clouded his blue eyes, belying the truth that he was afraid of what he would learn—that the lass was there in such a bedraggled state because their father and the rest of his men had fought a battle and lost their lives.

Cameron remembered yelling at the boy, furious that he would be so angry with Alana for not telling them what had happened. Cameron had known in his heart, Connell was as frustrated as he had been that they knew not where the men were. What Alana's brother hadn't recognized was the lass was so shocked by what had occurred, she could not tell them what she had seen.

Days later when she began to eat and speak again and long after they had recovered her father's body and those of his men, she had told of how her father had brought her home. Fearing she would be ostracized for what she believed, Cameron had quickly made her promise she would speak no more of seeing her father when he knew his brother had been dead at the site of the battle in the woods and had never returned her home.

Rumors had abounded since she was little that she had imaginary friends, that she could speak with the dead, but he and her father had always warned her never to speak of such a thing for fear they'd believe her to be a witch. Now, had he lost the young woman he thought of as his daughter? The one he believed would carry the Cameron clan forth with her own bairn someday?

# Chapter 11

The rain was coming down as heavy as earlier when Alana and her MacNeill escort first arrived at the tavern. The wind was howling and blowing the rain against the small shuttered window near the bed. She was glad she was not out in this weather, though she felt keenly aware that she should not be here without a maid. Not that she should have been sleeping in a camp with her enemy without a maid either. Still, she was relieved as ill as Brighid had been yesterday morn, that she was not with her this trip, considering all that had befallen Alana.

Her clothes dry, she was famished and ready to eat as she sat before the fire in the tavern's upstairs room when footfalls headed toward her door. She was thinking it was the maid bringing up a tray for her. She never expected to see Dougald carrying a tray into the room, his mouth curved up a little, probably because of the shocked expression he saw on her face.

"'Tis still pouring out, as you can well see." Dougald's tunic and plaid were dry, and it looked as though he was well rested. He motioned to the small wooden table where he set the tray down, then to her surprise, once she had taken a seat, he sat down beside her.

His knees brushed hers, and she thought to put

some distance between them, but the table was too tiny and…she realized…she really didn't want to put any distance between them.

He was so huge, dwarfing the table with his height, sitting so close to her, it reminded her of when she sat in front of him on his horse. His arms wrapped around her, Dougald had felt as big and powerful as his steed. His body had made hers feel as though she was on fire.

She'd told herself it was because the day was so warm and sitting so close to him, their shared body heat had made her feel as though she sat too close to the hearth. Even now, she felt warmer in his presence.

"Alana?" he said.

She realized he must have asked her something. "Aye?"

"You wish a slice of bread?"

She nodded.

After he had told her some hours earlier that her secret about her ghostly visions was safe with him, she felt differently about him. Probably a mistake. Yet, she couldn't help but see him in a new light. No one had ever believed her, or if they had, they thought her bewitched, or one of the fae. Some had feared her. Others had brushed away her claims as just a bit of fanciful whimsy—something that most children were fond of. She appreciated him for not seeing her in that way.

Dougald's gaze met hers, his dark brown eyes observing her, studying her as if attempting to read her thoughts. "Is he *here*?" He didn't act as though it would bother him to hear that her brother was still in the room, but maybe that's why he thought she seemed so distracted.

She shook her head. She shouldn't have acknowledged that she could see her brother, but this was the first time anyone didn't act as though she was thoroughly possessed or that she should hide what she saw. A sense of relief washed over her that she could, well mayhap not speak with Dougald about it, but at least not worry if she had the notion to talk to someone else in the room that he couldn't see. That he wouldn't treat her as though he was in the presence of a mad woman.

She relaxed a little.

Dougald cut off a slice of brown bread for her, then buttered it with his knife. "Do you ever summon him, or does he just come and go as he pleases?" He handed her the piece of bread.

She took it from him, felt the warm connection between them as his fingers brushed against hers, and she wondered if he had solicited the touch on purpose or if he was all innocence. *Him,* a seducer of women?

She studied Dougald's face, saw the shadow of a beard covering his masculine jaw, making him look rough and rugged, the serious expression in his eyes, the slightly crinkled forehead.

Mayhap she was only hoping he was attempting a subtle seduction of her. What was wrong with her anyway? She should stay far away from such notions.

"I never talk about it...ever," she said, and speaking the truth, then took a bite of bread.

He nodded and cut off a slice for himself, buttering it with care. Concentrating on what he was doing, he said, "'Tis up to you. But I would be willing to hear what 'tis like for you, and I would make no judgment against you, my lady."

She hesitated. She couldn't believe anyone would not judge her. Was he being sincere? "I…I never summon him. Why would I? If I were in trouble, he couldna assist me. He comes and goes when he pleases, and sometimes he gives me a fright."

Dougald had turned to watch her again, just holding his bread aloft, but not taking a bite of it yet. "I see. Some have said they have seen my sister floating around Craigly Castle. Never me, nor my brothers. But even James's wife, Eilis, had a scare when she saw my sister studying her in the solar. Mayhap if you only see those close to you, you willna witness my sister's ghostly spirit. I wish to warn you, just in case you do."

She noted that he did not say that Eilis *said* she had seen the ghost, but that she *had* seen the ghost, which indicated to Alana that Dougald truly believed Eilis had seen his sister in spirit form. That gave Alana hope.

"Do…do your people talk about her? About the ghost, I mean?" She was optimistic that his people were more enlightened than her own.

"No' out loud. Whispered mutterings. A screech, and then…" Dougald smiled at Alana in a warm way. "…a claim that a maid has seen a rat."

She smiled at him then. "'Tis possible, you know."

"Aye. Do you ever help ghosts find peace?"

"I…dinna know if I do or if they find their own way."

"Aye." Dougald drew taller and asked, "Were you betrothed at an early age?"

She was surprised at the question and hesitated to speak. "To a MacIverson, aye."

"What happened? Why did you no' marry the man?"

She bit her lower lip, trying to recall what had happened so long ago. She was not exactly privy to the goings on back then, though she'd heard some rumors. "My uncle hadna wished it."

"But your da had?"

"Aye, but I was only nine at the time when he died."

Dougald pondered that. "Your uncle would have been obligated to still marry you off to the MacIverson, even if he hadna wished it. Do you know why he didna?"

She shook her head and took a piece of the quail he offered.

"Did you meet the lad?"

She raised her brows at that. "Aye, but he was no' a lad. MacIverson was old."

"Older than your da?"

"Mayhap younger than that. But he was old to me."

"As old as you are now?"

It was hard to tell about ages, but he was older than she was now. "Nay, older."

"Did MacIverson wed someone else then?"

"I dinna know. I was only nine. Think you my da or my uncle talked to me about such matters?"

Dougald nodded in agreement that they wouldn't. "Did MacIverson know about your gift? You said you met him. When did you meet him, how old were you, and how did he act toward you?"

A chill raced up her spine as Alana stared at Dougald. "What are you thinking? That my uncle believed MacIverson had something to do with my da's death?"

"I am only trying to learn what might have been a

reason that your uncle didna wish to marry you to the man when your da had already made an agreement with him."

Alana took a deep breath and let it out. "'Twas a chilly day, verra much like today, and I was nine summers. And aye, it was only a short while before my da and his men were murdered on the hunt. I dinna know if my da had arranged the marriage earlier. I had met the man already but I was too young to remember much except I did recall the castle. It was darker than ours, smaller. Mayhap my da had taken me there for the MacIverson to decide if he wanted me as a bride or no'."

"Oft times the bride is of no consequence," Dougald said, plainly. "Still, he may have wished to see your temperament even at an early age."

"Aye. I would have been just—a bargain between clans. I played with some kittens while I was there."

The corner of Dougald's mouth lifted a little.

"And…" She fingered her bread, "I did see a ghost girl, but I was verra careful not to let anyone see me speaking with her."

"Can you no' ignore them?" Dougald asked.

"If someone spoke to you and he or she was standing there as plain as day, could you ignore him or her?"

"Mayhap not. 'Tis hard for me to imagine. But they are very real to you then? Not just some misty version of themselves?"

"They are real." She reached out and rested her hand on Dougald's arm and felt the warmth there, the muscle, the strength. "As real as you are, though I couldna touch them." Dougald's eyes took on a decidedly hungry look, and she quickly released his arm. She cleared her throat. "MacIverson was a big man and though he pretended disinterest in me at times as he drank his ale and joked with his clansmen, he watched me like he was a falcon eying his prey whenever we shared meals. My maid kept telling me to sit up taller, to raise my chin, to lower my eyes when he looked my way. I wasna used to being stared at, so I just stared right back at him."

Dougald chuckled. She was glad he found humor in it. Her da had not. As evidenced by his dour looks, he agreed with her maid.

"I didna care anything about him. I had hoped to see kittens again when I returned, but there were none. The ghost girl was gone as well. I was more interested in the herbs and plants that grew on his lands than I was in him."

Dougald furrowed his brow at that.

"What are you thinking?"

"I have heard it rumored that your uncle wished you to reside at his castle."

"Aye. My brother still lived when my da made the arrangement for my betrothal. He wouldna have needed me to stay with our people. He would have wished to use me for an alliance with a clan. My brother would have taken over the Cameron clan, should the men have felt he was a strong enough leader when my da was ready to step down."

"Your uncle made no other arrangement for you to marry in the meantime? Between the time the one marriage was called off and this new one was being planned?"

"Nay. No' that I am aware."

"Did MacIverson act in any way that he was not satisfied with the marriage arrangement?"

She shrugged. "I was a young lass. I didna have any…"

She felt her whole body heat as she thought about how she'd only had the very beginning of a hint of breasts and her legs and arms had been scrawny. She recalled what one of his men had said to him—that she did not have wide enough hips either. Though at the time she didn't understand what he meant by that and only later learned that it had to do with child bearing.

Some loved her long pale golden hair. Some did not, so she didn't know which way he had viewed her tresses.

"I wasna a woman fully grown." She was thankful Dougald did not rake his gaze over her womanly assets that she very much now had and instead just gave her a wolfish smile.

He'd touched way too much of her womanly attributes on the long ride here. She shouldn't have mentioned it as she swore he blushed a little, and he had to be thinking about what she was thinking, and she was certain *she* was blushing a lot.

She cleared her throat again. "Mayhap my uncle did believe MacIverson had something to do with my da's death."

"Do you know why MacIverson might have wanted your da murdered, if that was the case?"

She shook her head.

"Did your uncle battle against any clan after that?"

She raised her brows. "Aye."

"The MacIverson?"

"Nay, the MacNeill."

Looking as though he was fighting a smile, Dougald shook his head. "Nay, no' us. Others?"

"Aye. We were always having trouble of one kind or another. Just like you have, I am certain. What do you think, Dougald? You probably know more about something like this than I would since I am no' privy to much that goes on with regard to a man's way of thinking."

He leaned back and studied her. "'Tis difficult to say without knowing more of the facts. Why did your da want an alliance with MacIverson? Clan ties? Aye, most likely. Why did your uncle no' want MacIverson's part in it? Did he feel differently before your da was murdered? If so, then mayhap he did feel that MacIverson had perpetrated the murder. But for what reason? To get out of a marriage arrangement? He wouldna have had to murder your da for that. Something more personal?"

"I dinna know."

"All right. If MacIverson wasna responsible for your da's murder, why would he have no' insisted that you still be his wife?"

"He found someone else who appealed more?"

Dougald shook his head. "Clan ties are all too important."

She felt the cold seep into her bones. She had not considered her father's death for many years as the clan continued to move forward. Now, Dougald was dredging up memories she wasn't sure she wished to relive. Had she truly seen her father's murderers?

If so, could she dig them up, and see the men receive their just rewards without getting herself and others killed in the process?

# Chapter 12

When Alana had put her hand on his sleeved arm, Dougald felt the heat sizzle between them. He had to keep reminding himself the lass was not wily in the ways of men, and that her touch was not tantamount to telling him she wanted his touch back. He was used to women pulling on him, wanting him in a carnal way, though he oft teased them and flirted just as much as they did with him, but it did not mean he followed through with even half of the suggestive flirtations.

Yet he was almost certain that the ladies who witnessed such frivolity between him and the lasses were intrigued or resigned that he would never settle down. He had no intentions in that regard anytime soon.

And the men? Well, they smiled wistfully, some shaking their heads, most, he assumed believed Dougald had had his way with every woman he chanced to speak to. Except mayhap Eilis, his brother's wife who was as devoted to his brother as he hoped a woman would be to him someday, when he chose a wife.

Alana was different. She was not a maid looking for a quick tumble. She was a lady who had an important position within her clan. She didn't know the ways of men in an intimate way. She was an innocent.

Yet the way she had touched him made him want her more than ever.

He wanted to pull her tight against his chest, to kiss her, to make her see the pleasure that could erupt between a man and woman. But he was not the one meant to awaken such needs, he kept reminding himself.

For a brief moment, while he glanced Alana's way as she supped on her boar soup, he considered what it would be like to share wedded bliss with a lady like her. To see her playing with kittens in the inner bailey. To see her bent over herbs in the gardens taking snippings.

That made his groin instantly tighten, and he quickly thought of something else. Of watching her on the hilltop as she took in every bit of his naked body and God's knees, his staff was rising to the occasion.

Bedding her in the heather, or on his plaid on a misty morn near a loch, in his bed, in hers...all of it instantly came to mind.

He groaned.

She glanced at him. "Are you all right? You are no' feeling ill, are you?"

She had that healer look about her—one of worry and concern and a readiness to make him well. He wanted to take her hand and press it against his groin, to show her what was making him groan.

She would be shocked. Any other lassie he was interested in who was equally interested in him would lift his plaid and her own and sit on his lap, joining with him, grinding against his body as he thrust into hers. Alana would be mortified at the notion.

He quickly shook his head with regard to his feeling ill and considered the situation with her further.

He should not worry about what would happen to her, but he did. Had he not spent time with her, not known anything about her, just another bonny lass, he would not have been as concerned. What he didn't like was that her father's murderers had never been identified. The mystery about MacIverson not marrying her, her uncle's changing the marriage arrangement but not making another one for years, even the circumstances concerning his rise to power and her brother's death all troubled him.

Yet it was not any of his business. He had no say in any of it. There was naught he could do about it. Unless he took the lass to be his wife.

"You look a wee bit pale, Dougald. Are you sure you are no' ill?" She furrowed her brow and lifted her hand to his forehead.

Her warm hand on his skin made him want her all over again. He couldn't even stand and attempt to leave the room without her noticing just how much she had aroused him.

She turned her head sharply to the door, and he looked, too, ready to stand and unsheathe his sword, to protect her from anyone who meant her harm, but no one was there.

Quizzically, he looked back at Alana, and she was staring at his lap, then her gaze shot up to his, and her face turned a lovely shade of crimson.

"I am done, thank you," she said quickly and nearly fell trying to move away from him as if he was so needy he'd ravish the lady without her wishing him to.

"Alana," he said, wanting her to know he was not going to attack her, "you have no' reason to fear me."

She glanced again at the door, and Dougald

couldn't help himself, though he assumed he would see nothing amiss, but he looked that way also. Sure enough, there was no one there. Turning back to Alana, he said, "Is your brother here?"

She nodded, eyes round. "You can leave now...if you are through eating."

He couldn't move unless he had to do battle, or...love a lassie. "If you dinna mind, I will finish my dinner. 'Tis foolish to let a good meal go to waste. No' to mention paying good money for good food that one doesna consume."

"You could take it with you," she said hopefully.

He looked over at her then as she stood near the bed, hands clenched at her sides, and he considered the mattress. He couldn't help himself! She was standing too close to the bed for him not to be thinking of her *in* the bed. And him in it with her. On top of her. Inside of her.

This was not helping.

He smiled, more at himself for his own folly, and at her brother, for being a rake like him and knowing just what Dougald had been thinking. The lass may not have ever considered his wayward thoughts if it hadn't been for her brother, Dougald believed.

"What has your brother said?" Dougald asked as he concentrated on his boar broth, hoping he could get his other thoughts under control and his staff to settle down before he had to leave.

When she didn't speak, he glanced back at her. She was now sitting on that bed as if she couldn't stand upright any long. She furrowed her brow and crossed her arms defensively beneath her breasts. "He says, being the rake that you are, I shouldna sit close to you or touch you in any manner. That you will have illicit thoughts about me like any other man who is just the same as you."

"'Tis true," Dougald said and watched as her lips parted as if she was surprised he'd admit to the condemnation. There was no sense in denying it. Her touch and sitting close to her *had* provoked illicit thoughts even if he hadn't wanted them. But he had to admit, he had wanted them, had craved sitting beside her, having her touch him freely when he had not solicited it.

And wanted much more.

"But 'tis also true I wouldna act on such desire." He watched her, waited for her to turn and hear what her brother had to say about the matter, and then direct her attention back to Dougald.

"You know, 'tis hard to defend myself when I have no idea what your brother is saying to you," Dougald said, never believing he would be having a three-way conversation where he could neither hear one of the parties speaking nor see him.

She took a deep breath. "He says he believes you are honorable, as long as I keep my distance. And that you continue eating with the intention of leaving soon. Keeping your mind occupied so that these other notions of yours will fade away should work."

He smiled then. These other notions of his were *not* fading away. Not when she was sitting on the bed, or when she stood next to him, or he held her in his arms.

He continued to eat. *Slowly.*

"He says he has never seen a man eat so slowly in his life," Alana said.

Dougald chuckled. "If the roles were reversed and

he was here instead of me, and you were a lovely lass that he..." What would he say next? That he lusted after? He quickly quit speaking before he got himself into a worse quagmire.

"What?" she prompted. Then she said, "Quit laughing, Connell! I dinna see what is so funny."

Dougald smiled into his broth. As much as her brother could be annoying, he rather liked the man.

He finished as much as he could eat and turned to speak with Alana. She was watching him as if she was afraid he had the notion of ravishing her. "I will leave the rest for you, my lady, should you decide that you are still hungry."

He rose from his chair and noted her gaze immediately descended to take a gander at his plaid, but the part of his anatomy that had not been behaving was now quite mannerly, *finally*. He smiled at her, then said, "I will check on you later."

And then he took his leave before he did anything he regretted. Like...kissed her.

As soon as he was out the door and had shut and locked it, he heard Alana say, "Go away. He is gone now. Leave me be."

Dougald thought the lass sounded as though she had some regret that he had left her alone and at that thought—though it should not have pleased him—he felt lighter hearted than he had when he had at first entered her chamber, still worried about her father's murder and her brother's as well.

\*\*\*

Early the next morn, they travelled again as the rains had subsided, though it was chilly today, the winds blowing cold and the gray clouds still hovering low in the sky. Alana was trying not to shiver overmuch, hoping the day would soon warm up the later the hour.

A short while after they had begun their journey, they saw many riders approach, and she stiffened.

The men in the lead of Dougald's party hollered, "They are our men!"

"James sent them," Dougald said, glancing her way. He looked as though he was judging her reaction, to see if it would upset her that her own people had not come to rescue her.

She sagged a little, though she was so cold, she was having a difficult time relaxing much. And then wondered why she should? Because she didn't want a fight between her uncle's men and Dougald's. That's why.

Dougald's men all gave the impression they were a bunch of owls, casting looks back her way, glancing at Dougald, grinning, then talking amongst themselves. A few rode past them to follow them, others flanking them.

"They act like a bunch of gossiping women," Alana said, more to herself than anyone.

Dougald smiled. "At first I was surprised to see James had sent such a large force of men. Either he worried your uncle was coming for you, or more of our men came to see the Cameron's niece."

She gave a little harrumph. "'Tis more likely he worried he might lose a brother if a battle had occurred."

Dougald laughed out loud at that.

She frowned at him. "You dinna think your brother would worry about you?"

"Oh, aye, lass, but he would never have sent *this* many men."

"Oh." What did she know about men and fighting battles?

Later that day after warming by a fire, eating and then going on their way again, they found the weather had not improved. The wind blew just as cold, the rain threatening again when a lone rider approached the front of the formation. He greeted some of the men, who motioned to the middle of the party, indicating that was where Dougald was. As the rider drew closer, she recognized him as one of the men Dougald had sent in search of Rob MacNeill. If he was looking for Dougald now, he had to have news. Since the rider was alone, she could only guess what that meant. The others were taking Rob MacNeill and his niece to see James. Or they hadn't found the man and were still looking for him.

Dougald rode out to meet the man, keeping her from hearing the truth. She scowled at the two of them as Angus and Gunnolf kept her moving in the direction of Craigly Castle and away from Dougald and the messenger.

She wanted to listen in on the conversation as if it pertained to her, which it most likely did. They stopped speaking and both looked at her, then Dougald nodded at the man, and he joined some others leading her escort.

When Dougald rejoined her, he didn't say a word. She could tell from the way he was looking straight ahead, brow furrowed, he was pondering the matter before he spoke, which again made her believe he was a cautious man, not one prone to saying whatever was on his mind before he had thought the matter through.

Well, she wasn't about to let him think about it any further without telling her what he'd learned. "Did they find Rob MacNill, or no'?" she asked, in a less than sweet and innocent way. But her sharp tone did get Dougald's attention.

A couple of the men in front glanced back to smile at her and to see Dougald's reaction.

She got practically everyone's attention, in fact, some looking a little surprised but then the smiles began to creep across their faces. All except for Dougald's. He probably wasn't used to a woman demanding that he tell her of some news, particularly when she was from the enemy clan.

"One Rob MacNeill they located was gray-bearded," Dougald finally said. "His wife said he would never think of straying. So they discounted him. Furthermore, he had no niece. He also had a lad of ten by the name of Rob."

"That was all? You said there were at least a handful. Or mayhap 'twas your cousin who had said so."

"None who live near the border, lass. There was another. He is three and thirty and has no kin. His wife and bairn died some years earlier. But my men couldna locate him. The other men are still searching for him."

That gave her hope that Odara had not lied to her. "He abandoned his sheep and his croft and went into hiding?"

"Nay, lass. 'Tis just that he wasna home. He may have been visiting a neighbor—"

"Like Odara?"

"'Tis possible." Dougald didn't say anything about

the fact that Odara had been with Gilleasbuig, and Alana was grateful for that.

She glanced at Gunnolf. "You said you knew the man who was with Odara wasna Rob MacNeill. Yet you went to speak to the shepherdess to learn what he looked like. How do you know he wasna Rob MacNeill if you didna know what he looked like?"

"He said he was Gilleasbuig. I took the man at his word," Gunnolf said.

Frustrated that the Norseman hadn't known what either man looked like and couldn't be completely sure he was Gilleasbuig, Alana let out her breath and rode in silence for some time. Then she thought even if he did not know what Gilleasbuig looked like, *she* did. She turned sharply to speak with Gunnolf again. "What did the man look like?"

"He was a burly man, nearly as tall as me."

That could describe Gilleasbuig or any number of men. The Highlanders were tall men, and well built. "The color of his hair?" she asked.

"Dark brown, nearly black."

"Aye. And the color of his eyes?" She was losing hope it was someone named Rob MacNeill.

"Brown, pale, not as dark as Dougald's."

Alana opened her mouth to speak to Gunnolf but Connell appeared between her and Gunnolf. "Gilleasbuig has blue eyes," her brother said to her. As if she didn't know!

She wanted to tell her brother to move out of her way so she could continue to question Gunnolf. She sighed. Though she still couldn't see Gunnolf because of her pesky brother being in the way, she said to Gunnolf, trying to pretend her brother was not staring at her, waiting for her to speak as if she was talking to him, "He has blue eyes, no' brown."

"Are you certain?" Dougald asked, drawing her attention.

"Aye. Gray-blue, if you must know." She again turned to Gunnolf—or her brother as he was still between her and the Norseman. "Does he have a scar on his face?"

"No, but he does have a broken nose." Gunnolf sounded pleased with himself for having given the man the break in his nose.

Alana clamped her mouth shut. What if the man in bed with Odara had truly been her lover, Rob MacNeill? But had been afraid to reveal such? She tried to remember anything else about Gilleasbuig. "Was the man hairy?"

That got a couple of hearty chuckles from the men riding ahead of them. Dougald was staring at her as if he couldn't believe she'd know such a thing.

Her whole body heated. Dougald was probably wondering *why* she would know that Gilleasbuig was hairy. She would never have spoken of the matter if she hadn't thought revealing such a thing might give them a clearer picture as to who the man was.

"How would you know that?" her bother asked, glowering at her. Or maybe he was worried the man had tried to molest her or some such thing, and he meant to glower at Gilleasbuig if he had been here.

Without thinking, she snapped at her brother, "He was injured, for heaven's sakes!"

# Chapter 13

Alana wondered what Gunnolf would think of her irritated reaction to her brother when it would appear she was reacting to Gunnolf. She couldn't see around her brother and had no idea what Gunnolf was doing right now. Looking straight ahead? Watching her? Smiling? Scowling?

Beyond her brother, she heard Gunnolf say, "He wasna...overly...hairy, to my way of thinking, my lady." His tone was decidedly amused, and she knew she should have let the matter rest.

A few chuckles erupted, and she was certain the men within hearing distance were highly entertained with the direction the inquisition had taken.

"So," Dougald said, proceeding with caution, "you know this Gilleasbuig well."

She looked at him then, wondering if he thought *she* had some romantic notions concerning the hairy beast! Mayhap that she was upset that Odara had been in bed with the man, and that the shepherdess had been trying to cover up the fact because Alana loved him and would be upset with the man?

God's teeth, what a horrid thought!

She frowned at Dougald. "I dinna know what you mean."

"You know him well enough that you would be

able to identify him."

"Of course. Aye." Wasn't that what she'd been saying all along?

"Did he have a hairy back as well as a chest?"

Not wanting to say aloud all that she was thinking of the matter, she felt her whole face heat. He had a very small staff and a hairy arse also. She had seen this as the men had hastily stripped him of his blood-soaked clothes so they could turn him on his side, and she could proceed with stitching him up.

"Not all men do, lass," Dougald prompted.

She had not seen Dougald's back and now she wondered was he hairy or not? His chest was only lightly furred, trailing down to his staff that had grown as she'd watched, before she swung away and had headed back down the hill, intrigued and mortified at the same time.

Her face had to be flaming red now.

"This man's back was as smooth as a bairn's…," Gunnolf said, pausing to finish what he was going to say.

She knew what he was thinking of and had she been one of the men, he would have said it. "Cheek?" she asked.

Several more laughed under their breaths.

Gunnolf said, "Ja."

Her lips parted. It could not be the same man. "'Twas not Gilleasbuig. Unless someone shaved his back."

More chuckles.

"So you treated him for an injury?" Dougald asked.

"Aye. A sword wound. It had gone through his side. I treated him while he lay on his uninjured side."

"Which side was injured?" Dougald asked.

"The left."

Gunnolf shook his head. "The man with Odara had no sword wound on either side of his body."

"So both his chest and back were hairy?" Dougald asked.

"Aye. The man with Odara canna be Gilleasbuig," Alana said, not wishing to discuss how hairy the beast was any further. If her uncle had heard her speaking thus, she'd be locked in her chamber for days!

"I hope Gilleasbuig was unconscious when you saw to his wound, Lady Alana."

She wondered why Dougald seemed concerned. When she didn't say, he looked again at her and raised a brow.

"He was awake. Three men held him down. He didna like that I sewed him up."

"But?"

"I saved his life. He thought I took pleasure in hurting him, which I wouldna have done. No' even with him."

"Does he ever show you disrespect?" Dougald's words were soft with threat.

"'Tis none of your concern, Dougald MacNeill. 'Tis only my uncle's."

Dougald seized her reins so suddenly, she gasped. He halted her horse. His eyes had grown nearly black. "Answer me, Alana."

She noticed everyone within hearing distance had stopped, waiting for her response and for Dougald and Alana to continue walking their horses.

"He is a brute. Mayhap he believes because I touched his skin and saw him naked, I wish more than that." She snapped her mouth shut. She had not meant to mention that she had seen him entirely naked, though Dougald may have very well assumed as much. She thought she would allow them to think Gilleasbuig was at least wearing his plaid, and only his tunic had been removed. Too late for amending her speech. "The man is a swine. But he would never be foolhardy enough to attempt to pursue anything with me or earn my uncle's full-fledged wrath. Truly, though, 'tis none of your concern."

Though she had to admit when she'd told her uncle of the things Gilleasbuig had said around her, her uncle had dismissed her concerns.

Still, she did feel better that Odara may have been seeing Rob MacNeill after all and not the odious Gilleasbuig. They just had to locate a Rob MacNeill who had a broken nose. Then again, if the man they were searching for now had no niece, that didn't bode well for Odara having told her the truth either.

Connell said, "You didna tell me about this. Did Gilleasbuig ever threaten you in any way?"

She closed her eyes, asking God why her brother was still here and had not gone on his way, when she felt herself lifted from her saddle. She gave a little scream, her eyes opening at once, her heart pounding as Dougald pulled her into his arms.

Dougald shook his head while Angus took her horse's reins. "You looked like you were ready to drop off to sleep."

"I wasna," she said indignantly. "I only closed my eyes for the span of a heartbeat. Let me ride my own horse."

He tightened his hold on her as she squirmed, then

he rode off at a canter. "The day is still chilly, and you are ice cold. It will only get colder this eve."

She relaxed against him, and he seemed to revel in the feel of her in his arms. The rake that he was, she had to remind herself.

"Tell me the truth, has he ever made you feel unsafe in his presence?" he asked her quietly.

"Gilleasbuig?" she asked, surprised Dougald was still concerned about the man.

"Aye. Tavia, our healer, has seen to men's wounds a time or two who thought she was interested in having more to do with them because she had been so…for want of a better word, intimate with them. She didna, but that was the way the men would sometimes view her."

"Aye. He says vulgar things when I am near enough that I can hear him, and I feel he wants to observe my reaction."

"To see if you are interested in dallying with him?" Dougald's face was so tight with anger, she thought if Gilleasbuig had been nearby, Dougald would have taken him to task in not so gentle a manner.

She let out her breath. "I hadna considered that. I thought he only wished to know if I would be embarrassed and watch me blush." Alana didn't want to believe it was more than that.

***

Dougald couldn't bed the lass, mayhap that was why he wanted her so badly. Every time he had any physical contact with her, he wanted more. Every time he saw her, he wanted to touch her. He hadn't been certain why she'd closed her eyes, but he'd seized the opportunity to put her where he wanted her…in his lap—again.

This time, except for her squirming a bit, she did not protest like she did at the first. She quickly settled into his arms this time. She was chilled, he'd noted right away. The rains had cooled the air considerably, and he didn't wish her to become ill. The air would only grow colder tonight.

He thought again about this Rob MacNeill and Gilleasbuig and realized Gunnolf might very well have broken one of Dougald's kinsmen's noses. If it was a MacNeill, why had he lied to Gunnolf?

To save his skin probably. He must have thought the Norseman would kill him for rutting with the woman who was their enemy, so he pretended to be a Cameron instead. Odara probably had told him how Gilleasbuig was to wed her and the name came easily to mind when Gunnolf questioned him.

This business with Gilleasbuig bothered Dougald even more.

"You have spoken to your uncle concerning Gilleasbuig's actions?"

"Aye. Drop the subject, Dougald. I willna speak further on the matter," Alana said.

He frowned at her. "I believe Gunnolf may have broken my kinsman's nose," he said, to appease her somewhat. He usually just kissed a lass to do the job. He knew she was concerned about this business with Odara, just as he was, and he wished to set her mind at ease as much as possible.

She took a deep breath. "I feel badly for him, but I think you may be right." She turned to Gunnolf. "Did the man with Odara have a sword?"

Gunnolf grinned and Dougald knew what he would

say before he said it. "He was naked, my lady."

Dougald smiled as he knew Alana would be blushing beautifully again. He still didn't like it that she had seen Gilleasbuig naked and if Dougald had been her husband she would never care for injured men like that again, who might take more of an interest in her than he would like.

She didn't say anything for a moment or two, then cleared her throat and managed to get out, "I mean, did he have a sword lying with his clothes on the floor of the croft?"

Gunnolf gave her a wry smile. "He had none. I made sure of it while they were so busy."

Dougald could envision Gunnolf leaning against a wall, arms crossed, enjoying the action in a wryly amused way.

"Gilleasbuig would have had a sword, and I imagine he would have come after you with it. I believe the man you hit was Rob MacNeill, a sheepherder."

\*\*\*

Late that night, the whole of Craigly Castle was astir as everyone waited expectantly for Dougald to bring the Cameron lass home with him, knowing this bad weather had to have held them up. James was glad to see they had arrived trouble free and hadn't encountered problems with the Cameron.

It was a shame his own wife was indisposed due to the babe, as James greeted Lady Alana in his private solar. He was surprised and pleased to see their youngest brother, Angus, arrive to join him also.

"Welcome to Craigly Castle, Lady Alana," James said.

Despite the late hour, the clan had waited on their

evening meal to welcome the lady. She looked as tired as the lad, Tavis, when he had arrived before daybreak the day before.

She curtseyed to James, but looked so unsteady on her feet that Dougald quickly took her arm. She glanced up at him, appearing grateful and when she seemed to have regained her balance, he inclined his head to her and stepped away.

"You have met my brothers, Dougald and Angus, and our cousin Niall. This is my senior advisor, Eanruig. My wife, Lady Eilis, my mother, Lady Akira, and my wife's cousin, Fia, will join us shortly. My wife has been unwell of late. But it comes and goes."

Alana's eyes widened, and she quickly said, "Can I aid her in some small way? I am a healer for my own people."

He gave her a half smile, believing his decision concerning the lass was a good one. "Our healer is with her, but I thank you for your kind offer. You will need food and rest. Cook is preparing the meal for everyone as we speak. A chamber has already been made ready for you."

"What do you intend to do with me?" she asked bluntly, and he noted then she'd clenched her hands together so tightly they were white.

He really had not wished to discuss the matter with her this eve. Best to allow her a hearty meal and a good night's rest.

Dougald was standing so close to her, he looked as though he would lunge for her again and rescue the lady if she needed his further assistance. James had never seen his brother take so much interest in a woman, the way he was protective of her and considerate of how she was feeling. James knew he had made the right decision.

He motioned to a maid standing near the door. "Mara, will you take the lady to her chamber to wash up? Then have her escorted to the great hall for the meal? We will be down shortly to sit with Lady Alana."

The Cameron lass glanced at Dougald. James swore something passed between the lady and his brother. Then she nodded, curtseyed quickly, and left the solar with the maid.

Angus said, "I will see you at the meal, then."

He and Eanruig left the room.

Once a servant shut the door to his solar, James and Dougald were alone. James asked, "What do you think of the lass?"

Instantly narrowing his eyes and looking wary, Dougald asked, "What do you plan to do with her? You are certain she is the Cameron's niece?"

"Aye." James handed Dougald a mug of ale. "I met her once a year ago and thought how winsome she was but knew there could be no alliance between our clans through marriage."

"Why no'? Seems to me you are an earl and the laird of our clan, a decent man, provider, warrior, and an alliance between our clans a good one. What could be better than that?"

James studied his brother, drank deeply of his own mug of ale, then said, "He wanted a man who was not a clan chief. He needs a man to take over when he grows too old to manage."

"The clan shall choose their own chief when the time comes."

"Aye, and he wants someone married to his niece

who will live among his people, show his strength, and what kind of man he truly is. If the clan feels that the laird has chosen right, his nephew by marriage will provide the leadership for the clan in the future."

"I understand. He is thinking of marrying her off to one of the MacDonald sons, aye?"

James shook his head. "If Cameron gains an alliance with the MacDonalds or one of the other clans through the marriage of his niece to one of their sons—"

Dougald frowned at him.

"Hear me out, brother. I hadna considered such an alliance before because for one, you were off with Malcolm searching for an English bride. Even when he found a Scottish lass to wed and you had found no one, I didna think you were ready to settle down with one woman." James straightened. "Bringing the Cameron lass here has changed everything. You will wed her. We will make arrangements with her uncle afterward."

Dougald frowned. "Her uncle would be furious."

"Her uncle would have no say in the matter. If he wants a nephew by marriage and an heir, he will have one. If he doesna want her back, she will remain with us."

"What about the lass? What about what *she* wants?"

"She would have no choice no matter how this plays out."

"And me?"

James waved his hand dismissively. "You love all the lasses. This one will be no different."

"James, you dinna understand." Dougald let out an exasperated breath. "The shepherdess lied when she convinced Lady Alana to seek out Rob MacNeill. What if Laird Cameron set her up to it? What if this is some grand scheme of his?" Dougald paced across the solar, then stopped and faced James. "What if Alana is truly no' the Cameron niece but an imposter? Then Laird Cameron would have a laugh, aye? Me wed to his supposed niece, and she still is very much at home in her keep safe from the likes of me?"

"She is Lady Alana, the same bonny lass I met last year, Dougald. I have no doubt about that. Whether this was a calculated ruse by either Laird Cameron or someone else in his employ, I canna say. The end result will be the same." James studied his brother and saw that he actually looked pleased with the notion. It was subtle, as if Dougald didn't want James to see how much he agreed with the plan, but it was there in his almost smile and his eyes, bright with intrigue.

"This past year, I have remarked 'tis time for you to settle down and now the time has come," James said.

"Her da was murdered," Dougald said, not remarking on James's comment. "I believe she has seen one or more of the men, but she canna remember."

James studied him for a moment. "Aye?"

"What if the reason she lived through that massacre has something to do with that marriage? She was to marry a MacIverson. The marriage was set aside when her father died. Now MacDonald wants her hand in marriage? Before, her brother would have been the next clan chief, but with his death, whoever she weds will stand a good chance to be the clan chief."

"Aye, you, Dougald."

Frowning, Dougald appeared exasperated that he wasn't getting his point across. "Why would her uncle no' wish the lass to wed MacIverson? Did her uncle have something to do with the lass's father's death? When he took over, he made the change in the arrangements for her marriage."

"And you are thinking that if he doesna have her wed to the MacDonald's son, her uncle will try to kill you?"

Dougald raised his brows. "I hadna considered that."

James stroked his chin, frowning, rethinking his plan.

"Everyone knows 'tis tough to kill me."

James had to smile at his brother. There it was. The admission, subtle as it was, that Dougald wanted the lass.

Dougald folded his arms. "What if her uncle thought MacIverson had her da killed?"

"Could be. And then he called off the marriage. Why would MacIverson have had her da murdered?"

"He knew the lass sees ghosts?" Dougald ventured.

James stared at Dougald for a moment, then frowned. "You know this for certain?"

"Aye. What if the MacIverson had learned the lass could observe ghosts and thought she was of the fae, or a witch? He had intended that her father and their party, including the girl, perish, and thereby negate the contract. Only she hid well enough that they didna find her."

"Hmm," James said. "But then MacDonald doesna know she can see…ghosts?"

"Nay. Or it doesna matter to him."

"But if it does?"

Dougald's jaw tightened. "The man could have her

drowned as a witch. He could wait until he was in charge of the clan, mayhap have a child by Alana, and conveniently dispose of her."

"Aye." James said, "What about her brother?"

"He is dead."

"Aye, but how so? We heard he had been seeing a man's wife and the man killed him for it," James said.

"Aye. Where are you going with this line of reasoning?"

"What if that wasna the cause?"

Dougald's eyes widened. "You mean he wasna cuckolding another man's wife?"

James waved his hand in annoyance. "Nay, nay, we know Connell Cameron was a rake. What if the woman set him up?"

Dougald stared at his brother. "She enticed him to her bed and her husband killed Connell for some more nefarious reason?"

"Aye. What if Connell had been an unwitting pawn in this?"

Dougald's jaw dropped for a moment. "Then whoever sent Lady Alana on a fool's errand was trying to get her to safety? Someone warned us of a raid and when we investigated, there was no one, no sign that anyone had bothered any of our crofters. What if we were warned so we found the lady and took her into custody? Brought her here in fact, only we were supposed to do it as soon as the laird was away, three days earlier?"

"Because whoever it was that set this into motion didna trust her uncle or MacDonald, or both?" James took a deep breath. "Then I say you may still be the lady's savior."

Dougald snorted. "She thinks I am a rake."

"Then you shall have to prove her wrong. Let us join the others for the meal." James took Dougald by the arm and led him out of the solar. He'd never seen his brother look so…intrigued. Though he could tell his brother was worried the lass might not like the idea. James was certain that Dougald's marrying the lass would be best for all concerned.

"But…," Dougald said, his ashen face reddening, "you dinna understand."

"What? That one lass is no' enough to keep you satisfied? If you need lessons in that regard, I would be happy to give you some tips."

Dougald scowled at him. "Nay, 'tis the lass's feelings I am worried about."

James patted his brother on the back. "For the good of the clan, an alliance with the Cameron when we can ill afford the MacDonalds to ally with them, and the lass's own safety, should the MacDonald not like that she can…see spirits, Dougald, you will do this." He knew from the way Dougald had acted around her and the way he hadn't denied wanting her for a wife, he was willing.

The manner in which he'd gone to her when she'd seemed unsteady, the way they looked at each other, they had a fondness for each other already.

But still, to give his brother an out, just in case, James paused in the corridor and looked squarely at Dougald and said, "Unless you would rather our younger brother have the opportunity to wed the lass. Angus looked as interested. Or even our cousin, Niall."

Dougald's lips thinned, his expression darkened. "Nay, she is mine."

James grinned. He knew the right of it. "Good, then on the morrow, you will marry the lady."

# Chapter 14

A maid brought Alana a chemise, *léine,* and brat to change into while two others brought her water to wash off the dirt from the long ride. She was so tired, she only wished to collapse on the bed and sleep.

But she wanted to know what James had decided to do with her, and she was irritated already with him that he had shooed her away as if she didn't have any say in this. Not that she had much say, but she liked to think she did.

The ladies helped her out of her mud-spattered clothes and set them aside. They helped her to bathe and dried her. They assisted her into a sheer soft chemise, and then the pale blue *léine*. "'Tis lovely," Alana said, running her hand over the soft linen.

"I always liked the color on me," a woman said.

Not believing anyone was standing behind her and thinking the woman was the owner of the borrowed *léine* and she should thank her, Alana turned, tugging her hair out of a maid's hands as she tried to plait it for her. A woman her height and approximate build stood beside the bed, admiring the embroidery work on the sleeves of the *léine* she had just donned.

She had beautiful dark brown hair and when she

looked up at Alana, she had eyes to match. Her coloration looked deceivingly like Dougald's and his brothers'. Was she Lady Eilis? James's wife? Or mayhap Eilis's cousin, Fia?

The woman's gaze shifted to Alana's, and she tilted her head quizzically. "You seem to see me but are no' afraid. No shrieking or fainting. How verra odd."

Alana's lips parted.

The maids had stopped fussing with Alana's hair and looked to see what she was observing. "Are you all right, my lady?" one of the maids asked.

"Aye, aye, I am fine." Alana's skin prickled, the hair on her arms standing on end. She hadn't expected to see a ghost this soon. It couldn't be Dougald's dead sister, could it? "Can I have a moment alone?"

"We have no' pinned up your hair yet, my lady," the maid said, looking concerned.

"'Tis fine. The queen herself doesna hide her hair behind veils and such."

"You are wanted in the great hall to dine," the maid said, as if she thought Alana didn't wish to join the MacNeill clan at the meal.

"Aye, I will be down in a moment. Please leave me."

"Aye, my lady," the three maids murmured, glancing in the direction that Alana was looking, then shut the door on their hasty retreat.

"Are you Dougald's sister?" Alana asked.

This time the ghost's mouth parted. "Can you hear me?"

"Oh, aye." Alana smiled brightly.

"Well, that is a laugh and what a surprise," the lass said, smiling, looking tremendously pleased. "Are you staying here?"

"Nay," Alana said, shaking her head.

"'Tis a shame. I would have enjoyed speaking to someone who could talk with me who did not shriek in alarm and when a manservant came to the woman's rescue say she only saw a..."

"...rat," Alana offered.

The woman raised her brows.

"'Tis the excuse I have used when seeing something that others canna see, and I have had no warning."

"You see *others* like me?" The lass's eyes widened and she seemed truly astonished.

Alana let her breath out. "Aye." It seemed a curse at times, but right now she couldn't imagine how difficult it had to be for a spirit who was lost in their world, just a fright to some, and nonexistent to others.

"Who *are* you?"

"Alana Cameron. Niece of Alroy Cameron, the laird."

"Ahh. Whatever are you doing here? I have heard the rumors spreading that Dougald captured a lass in the heather and brought her here to be his bride. My brothers believe anyone who sees ghosts is mad. So Dougald willna do for you. Besides, he is way too fond of the lasses. I am Lady Seana MacNeill, by the way. Pleased to make your acquaintance."

"And aye, you, Lady Seana."

"No need for pretense here. Call me Seana."

"Alana," she said, smiling brightly. "You say your brothers truly believe anyone who sees ghosts is mad?"

Why had Dougald professed to believe her, then? Mocking her. Pretending to talk to her brother, who as far as Dougald believed, wasn't truly there, even in Alana's estimation? She felt disheartened to the core and annoyed with herself for even trusting that he had told her the truth.

A firm knock on the door gave her a start.

"Lady Alana?"

"*Dougald*," Alana said under her breath, her skin warming. Why did he affect her so as if she was sneaking away with him for a lover's tryst? Mayhap it had more to do with her sending the maids away, her hair unbound and hanging about her shoulders, and she was speaking to Dougald's dead sister when he really thought Alana was mad and *not* gifted at all.

Seana hmpfed.

"Are you all right in there? The maids said you dismissed them, and they were worried you were…"

"Seeing rats?" Alana offered, opening the door, frowning at him. She couldn't help it. She'd trusted him! And *he* was the rat.

Seana chuckled.

Dougald looked at Alana in the new *léine* and brat and took a deep breath.

"Oh for heaven's sakes," his sister said. "He looks at you as though you were a new conquest. Leave the lass be, dear brother."

"Your sister was telling me I shouldna consider you for marriage, though I have no plans in that regard." Alana glanced back at Seana and whispered, "Later." Though she knew very well that Dougald could hear her, and if he thought her mad, so be it. What did she care what he believed?

Seana grinned at her, looking more than delighted to have found a friend in Alana. "Aye. Soon." And then she vanished.

Dougald took Alana's arm and hurried her into the hall and said under his breath, "If you see my sister, please dinna let others know this."

Which proved just what Seana had told her! Not about to let him think she was fooled by his rhetoric, Alana said, "She revealed to me you and your brothers believe anyone who witnesses ghosts is mad."

He narrowed his eyes as he looked down at Alana. "Before Lady Eilis saw my sister? Aye, 'tis true. After that? Nay. Dinna believe my sister. She is still angry with all of us for believing she shouldna have run away with the lad. And for what? She died. 'Twas a tragedy we all still feel."

Seeing Dougald clench his fists, his jaw tightening, then take a deep breath as if he was trying to ease the pain, she could tell his sister's death still affected him.

"What did your brother say concerning what he would do with me?" she asked, changing the subject, unable to quit worrying about the matter, which was more pressing at the moment. Though she was glad to hear that he had believed her about seeing ghosts after all.

Before Dougald could tell Alana, she was surrounded by women who hurried to introduce themselves as they rushed her to the great hall. First was Lady Akira, Dougald's mother, who was all smiles and looked positively thrilled to visit with her. Her brown eyes were bright with enthusiasm. She was dark-haired like her sons, but strands of her hair were streaked with silver.

Lady Eilis, Jame's wife, was just as dark haired, who looked rather peeked, her belly swollen with the babe she was carrying. She kept rubbing her belly and appeared uncomfortable.

Fiona, Eilis's cousin, was just as friendly, very similar in looks, but her attention was diverted. When Alana glanced around the hall to see what held the woman's attention, she noted Fiona was gawking at Gunnolf.

He was talking to some of the men and didn't seem to notice the lass's interest.

Dougald didn't look entirely happy with regard to whatever James had spoken to him about earlier, but he wasn't able to answer her as Alana was escorted so quickly away to the great hall.

Before long, she was seated between Lady Eilis, and Dougald's mother, Lady Akira. Since they had sat down, Lady Akira had been talking to her nearly nonstop about the castle and her sons, about Eilis and the baby, about their people and mostly how delighted she was to finally meet Alana.

Alana's attention was drawn to Dougald sitting on the other side of his mother. Alana tried not to look at him because every time she did he caught her glance. He appeared as though he wanted to say something to her, almost apologetic. Again she wondered what James had decided concerning her. At least she assumed he'd made some decision.

Trying to take her mind off her own troubles, she said to Lady Eilis, "I have some herbs that might settle your stomach."

Dismissing the notion, the lady waved her hand. "I am fine. I have been told this sickness will pass. And our healer, Tavia, has aided me greatly."

Alana nodded and again chanced a look at

Dougald. He gave Alana a thin smile, but it wasn't warm and endearing, nor did he look amused as if he believed she was giving him fervent looks because she was interested in him. Nor was it the kind of smile that said he wanted her, like he had given her earlier when he had pulled her from her horse and seated her upon his lap. *No*. This was more of a show for her as if he was trying to be civil and put her at ease, which it wasn't.

She said to James's wife, "Lady Eilis…"

"Eilis, if you please."

"Alana, if you would. Did your laird husband tell you what he intends to do with me?"

"Oh, dear." Eilis suddenly looked as pale as a puff of white cloud, then rose unsteadily, holding her expanded belly, and hurried away from the table.

Her healer and a couple of maids quickly joined her as she rushed out of the hall.

"'Tis the babe," Lady Akira assured Alana. She reached over and patted her hand. "James was easy on me and Malcolm, too. When I was carrying Dougald, och, he was a kicker and squirmer and unsettled my stomach something fierce. I fear Eilis is carrying such a babe."

"Dougald," Alana murmured, nearly feeling sick to her stomach herself. Not because of a babe, but with worry as to what James intended to tell her uncle. She said to Lady Akira, "Do you know what Laird MacNeill intends to do with me?"

"Oh, aye," his mother said cheerily. She squeezed her hand, and if Alana had not been so worried, she would have loved how the woman seemed to treat her as kin. "Why the perfect plan, really. On the morrow, you are to wed my Dougald, who needs a woman to tame his wild oats."

The lady's words had barely reached Alana before she felt herself drifting into a black void, and heard nothing more.

\*\*\*

Dougald carried Alana in his arms to her guest chamber, irritated with his mother for telling Alana he would wed her on the morrow and that the news had caused the lass such grief that she had fainted dead away. He had fully intended to tell the lass how much he wished to marry her.

James had the gall to laugh at him before Dougald carried her out of the great hall. Not hatefully, but just highly amused. He'd always scorned him for having such a reputation with the lasses, but a lot of it was exaggerated. Every time a lass was breeding and she was not married, Dougald was suspected as having been the father. Even when he was away on Crusade, or even when he was with Malcolm seeking an English bride south of the border. The timing could not have been proper for him to have spawned so many bastards, yet, there it was. He was the perfect man to lay blame to.

He hadn't even been with a woman in…over four months, he guessed. So it wasn't as though anytime a wench smiled wickedly at him, he lifted her skirt and had his way with her.

He placed Alana on the bed where two maids hurried to see to her as his mother walked into the room and gave him a brilliant smile.

"I believe she adores you already," she said.

Dougald frowned at her. "She fainted when you

told her we would wed. How does that show adoration?"

His mother clucked her tongue. "She couldna keep her eyes off you at the meal."

"She worried about what James would do concerning her and wanted to know if I knew."

"She wanted to sit beside you at the meal, to speak with you."

"Aye." Dougald folded his arms. "To learn what James told me he intended to do with her."

His mother tsked and took his arm and led him from the chamber. "I will tend to her, but tomorrow morn, you and the lass will wed, and you will show her just how good you will be for her." His mother gave him a look as if to remind him of his obligation to the clan and to the lady.

Dougald let out his breath, cast one last look at Alana who was coming to, and shook his head. He could just see them on their wedding night, he ready to bed the lass, and she swooning with distress in his arms before he could even get her to the bed.

***

Alana couldn't sleep. Again. Even though the bed was soft, unlike the hard ground when they were camping on the way here, or the lumpy bed in the tavern. But she worried too much about the coming marriage to Dougald on the morrow for her to sleep. She couldn't believe she'd fainted at the high table at the evening meal! What a sight that must have been!

She heard rustling in the bedchamber and pulled aside the bed curtain. Her brother was looking at the *léine* she'd worn that was now hanging on a peg on the wall, leaned against the door, turned to observe her, his arms folded, and his mouth curved down as he studied her.

She groaned. "What, Connell?" she whispered. "Why are you here? I am safe."

"I told you, lass. I canna help it. I was off feeding Spirit—"

"Spirit?"

"Aye. My horse. And the next thing I know, you needed me."

"I dinna need you!"

He raised a skeptical brow.

"Why do you believe I need you?"

"You dinna want to wed Dougald. He is a rake."

She shook her head. "I have no' choice it seems."

"Did you know there is a wench who is haunting the place?"

"Lady Seana?"

"I have no' been introduced. Have you met her? She is a terror. As soon as she saw me, she shrieked! Scared a maid witless. Then the ghost got angry at *me*! Just because I scared *her*. She threw a brass pot at me. The woman is mad."

Alana frowned. "A brass pot? Like your horse?"

"Since when is a brass pot like a horse?" He narrowed his eyes at her. "You didna drink overmuch this eve, did you?"

"I mean, Connell Cameron, that the pot was like you, a ghost."

"How can an object be ghostly?"

"I dinna know. How can a ghost throw a solid object?"

"*Here* you are, you *beast*." Seana glanced at Alana. "Dinna tell me you see *him*, too."

"Meet my brother, Lady Seana," Alana said with apology. "Connell Cameron. Connell, meet Lady Seana MacNeill, sister of Laird James MacNeill of Craigly Castle." She frowned at Seana. "Did you really throw a brass pot at my brother?" She was almost wishing the pot hadn't missed as many times as she had wanted to do the same when he was living!

The lady snorted. "Aye. But it did no good. Went right through him and all he did was laugh. No' that he didna jump a little." Her mouth curved up in an evil smile. Then her smile faded. "Then he grinned. The brigand. After he got over the shock that I could throw something at him."

"You were the one who made the poor serving girl faint dead away," Connell accused, waving his hand at her.

"Why are you still here?" Alana asked the lady. "It has been years since you…uhm, should have gone away, has it no'?"

Looking suddenly very sad, Lady Seana sat down on a bench. "I wished to wed Laird Dunbarton's nephew. His father and my brother, James, wouldna permit it. We ran off together and…" She gave a dejected little shrug. "We died. Caught a fever."

Alana felt terrible for her. She glanced at Connell to see his reaction. His brow was deeply furrowed as he watched the lass, his expression bothered as though he felt badly that she had run off with the man she had loved and died without finding the happiness she deserved; whereas, he was caught fooling around with another man's wife and had wasted his life without thought of finding the right woman to settle down with. He saw Alana looking at him and crossed his arms again and stood taller as if he was not affected by Seana's tale, but she knew her brother well enough to recognize he was.

"But you were together. In death. Aye?" Alana thought that the two should have been together for all eternity. But what did she know of such matters? "So why have you no' gone with him? Why have you returned here to Craigly Castle?" To her family, Alana thought. To be with those who loved her no matter what even if they hadn't approved.

Seana twisted her mouth as if considering what had occurred before she spoke. "Henwas said he loved me more than life itself. I believed him. At the first hint of trouble, he got scared and abandoned me. Every man for himself. He died, too, anyway. But he had left me to die to save himself, afraid he would become ill as I had done. I was so angry with him, I stomped all the way home, not realizing for a long time why some could see me and others couldna. Henwas never followed me home. Mayhap he passed over. I dinna care."

"The man was an idiot," Connell said, his tone angry.

Seana twisted a length of hair around her fingers and studied Connell, then furrowed her brows. "How would you know that? You, sir, were a notorious rake, by all accounts. Henwas may have feared dying and left me to die alone, but you would have never offered to settle down with a woman in the first place. That takes courage, you know."

"I wouldna have left you to your fate alone, lass," Connell said so sincerely, his comment brought tears to both Alana and Seana's eyes.

And the woman vanished.

"What did I say?" Connell asked, as if he couldn't believe his words would have or *should have* upset the lass. Before Alana could come up with a reasonable explanation, her brother vanished, too.

# Chapter 15

As tired as Alana was, she didn't believe she could stay awake through most of the night. All she could think of was her impending marriage to Dougald MacNeill, lover of lasses, and what being married to him would entail. The way he had looked at her in the hall over supper, he had not been happy about having to wed her.

She tried to tell herself he'd be a good lover as much experience as he had and that he had been protective and kind to her, not too bad a husband as men went. But she was certain he didn't wish a wife.

She didn't know the first thing about making love. Except for what she'd overheard other women speak of.

Still, hearing about what would happen and actually doing it… She shuddered. She would be a paltry example of womanhood. Trying to will herself to sleep, she closed her eyes, intending to make the best of the situation.

She was certain her uncle intended to marry her off to Hoel MacDonald, and he had a reputation with the lasses as well. She'd also heard he loved to drink with his men—a lot.

When she had watched Dougald, she hadn't seen him drink overmuch. Certainly not as if he was drowning the annoyance that he might feel with having to wed her in the morn against his will. So mayhap he would suit better than Hoel. Her own uncle was not a heavy drinker, and he did not allow his own men to imbibe too much, except for in celebration.

She sighed. She could refuse the marriage before she said her vows. Then she'd have to say them before Hoel instead. Especially after she had disappeared from the Cameron keep. Her uncle would have her wed just as quickly as James was trying to do. She did have to consider that Dougald's explanation about his sister made it seem as though he wasn't concerned that Alana saw ghosts and spoke to them. What would Hoel think should he ever catch her behaving so strangely? He might think her a witch or truly mad.

She closed her eyes. Tomorrow eve if she wed Dougald, she would be just as wide awake. Only for a much different reason than this eve. He would be bedding her as his wife, *if* she went through with it.

***

Dougald sat by the fire in the great hall, staring into the orange-red flames. His last night to be free to enjoy the loving of a willing lass, and three had offered themselves to him already, but he could only think of Alana. The fragrant way she smelled, of mint and nutmeg. The softness of her body pressed against his when they had ridden together. Her whispered breath against his cheek. Her expression so passionate—her cheeks full of color, her golden brows raised—even when she was calling him names, or looking for his support when she looked so weary.

Then her face turning ashen right before she fainted at the news she would have to wed him. He feared the lass would not hold up well during the ceremony, and he could just imagine what would happen on their wedding night.

\*\*\*

Before dawn, Alana heard someone thump at the guest chamber door, and she groggily tried to stir herself fully awake. She had slept hardly at all, waking at every unfamiliar sound, worried that someone would come for her before she was ready to face the day. *Like now.*

At first, she hadn't even been sure how she came to be in bed last eve, only woke to see concerned faces peering at her. Once they had told her what had happened, then were assured she'd be all right, the chamber had emptied of onlookers, and she had been left to sleep. Which she had been unable to do.

The heavy oak door opened, and four women hurried into the chamber, two carrying a lovely dark green *léine.*

"This should fit you, my lady," a maid chirped, smiling brightly, looking much more alert than Alana felt.

They hustled her into the *léine* trimmed with delicate silver embroidery. "'Tis lovely," she said, her eyes so scratchy from the lack of sleep, she had difficulty making out the intricate designs.

"Lady Akira said 'tis yours," the maid said.

A woman snorted.

Alana glanced up from looking down at the *léine* and saw Seana watching her, looking perturbed, face scowling, arms crossed. Alana wanted to ask if the *léine* was Seana's and if it was all right with her to wear it to the wedding, but she dared not dismiss the maids again.

Seana nodded. "'Tis fine that you wear it. 'Tis just

that my mother should have asked me first."

Alana didn't know whether to be saddened at the admission or amused. It was as if those who had died believed they truly had a say in the world of the living still.

"Thank you," Alana mouthed to Seana as the maids hurried to comb her hair.

"I told you that you shouldna wed that brother of mine. But I have a plan. If he intends to seek another bed for the night, I will make him wish he hadna."

Alana couldn't help herself. She asked the maids very sweetly, "Can you leave me alone for a moment?"

The maids all cast each other glances. The eldest said, "We are to have you to the kirk within the hour."

"Aye, just for a moment." They looked concerned, but nodded and quickly vacated the chamber.

Seana smiled at Alana. "Marry my brother with my blessings, and I will make sure he doesna stray. Although you will need to do your part as well."

Alana blushed.

Seana smiled again. "You will be fine."

Connell was suddenly standing by the narrow window, glaring at Seana. "Mayhap I shall have to protect Dougald from your scornful mischief."

Seana's brows arched and she shrieked, "Mischief?"

Alana glanced at the door and hoped the maids who waited beyond it could not hear Seana.

"I will give you mischief, you rogue, should you aid my brother in seeing another woman other than his bonnie bride, *your* sister."

Connell scowled at Seana. "When did this happen?"

"I told you I had no choice about this last night." Then Alana realized Seana was the one who'd stolen his attention last eve.

Seana rolled her eyes. "Where were you last eve when your sister fainted dead away, eh?"

Connells's eyes widened and he quickly looked at Alana to see her take on it.

"Hearing James wants me to marry Dougald came as a bit of a shock. I have to finish getting ready for the wedding," Alana warned. Wanting to straighten out a misconception Seana had about her brother, Alana said to her, "Dougald canna see you as I do, but he said he does believe that I can see and speak with you."

Seana let out her breath. "Good. 'Tis time he and the others quit dismissing that I exist."

"He canna marry you," Connell said to Alana.

"'Tis him or Hoel MacDonald, I fear. At least Dougald appears to believe 'tis all right that I speak with the two of you and others like you," Alana argued.

Connell looked at Seana as if he was getting her final view on the matter. She folded her arms and raised her brows at him.

Someone knocked on the door. "Lady Alana?" Lady Akira called out, sounding anxious.

"My mother," Seana whispered, just as worried.

"Aye." Alana hurried to get the door, her heart pounding. She hoped the maids had not told Dougald's mother she was having a ghostly session in the chamber, or that she was beset with a sudden case of nerves and didn't want to go through with this.

She barely had opened the door, when Lady Akira took Alana's arm in a firm, persuasive, but motherly way and guided her back into the chamber, motioning to the maids to hurry up and accompany them.

"We really must hurry, lass," Lady Akira said, stepping back to observe Alana and smiled. "You are beautiful. Dougald will be most impressed and his brother Angus and cousin Niall will wish they fought to have the right to wed you instead."

Alana didn't believe either of the men would fight over her, but she appreciated Lady Akira's words just the same. It made her miss her mother terribly though, and she fought back a shimmer of tears that threatened to spill.

The maids began plaiting Alana's hair again as Connell and Seana watched.

Thankfully, they did not attempt to engage her in conversation in front of Lady Akira and the maids.

"The men are betting on whether you say no to marrying Dougald at the ceremony," one lass said, looking very serious, then a smile curved her lips.

"Some are betting you will faint dead away," another maid said.

"Will you say no to marrying Dougald?" the first said. "I do believe 'tis the first time I have seen him so anxious."

Alana stifled a laugh. He was anxious because he would be tied down to a wife for the first time in his life.

"If I tell you what I will do, it will spoil the betting, will it no'?" Alana asked.

"Oh, aye, except we wouldna tell the others and we are no' betting."

Alana could just imagine the maids telling the men they might lose if they bet one way or another if they knew the outcome. The truth was that even Alana did not know what she would say when the time came.

"You look lovely, lass," his mother said. "I worried a wee bit about where Dougald was off to late last night, but one of my servants brought me news he had returned early this morn, so all is well."

So Dougald had left the castle to see a woman in the village or a neighboring farm, had he?

Seana cast Connell an evil glower. Connell looked as if to say *what did I do*?

Once they had attached a veil, they quickly moved her out into the corridor, and then down the narrow winding stairs where they hurried her through the great hall. They hustled her to the kirk as if they were afraid she'd bolt if she was not rushed through this. Or mayhap they worried Dougald would run away. She could not see him doing such, though.

As a duty to his brother and the clan, he would do what James asked of him, she was certain.

She would not faint this time, although she didn't remember fainting the other time, not until one of the ladies told her what had happened. She'd been in the great hall, attempting to eat, learned Dougald was taking her to wife, and then…

She collapsed. He must have really loved seeing her reaction to marrying him.

Now she was feeling lightheaded, her stomach jumping about, her heart beating wildly in her breast, and she barely remembered passing through the kirk to stand beside Dougald.

When it came to the vows, she actually spoke them without hesitation, as if she was repeating the words by memory and had no ability to control her own tongue. Dougald did likewise, his gaze barely leaving her, and he didn't look as though he was going into battle, but that he was actually content...mayhap even pleased with the way things had turned out.

She, on the other hand, having decided that the MacNeill clan had treated her with graciousness and even as family, believed the marriage to Dougald could not be all that bad. She had no idea what it would have been like in the MacDonald clan. Mayhap she would have been as well-received, but mayhap not. 'Twas her problem with seeing ghosts that could have given her difficulty with the MacDonalds.

The difficulty would be that her uncles wished her heir to eventually lead the Cameron clan. Would her uncle wish to kill James for having married her off to his brother instead?

Dougald's kiss brought her to full awareness that they were husband and wife, the way he took hold of her shoulders as if to keep her steady or ensure she didn't bolt away from him, the way he leaned down to press his lips to hers. In that instant, nothing else existed. The kirk. The MacNeill clan squeezed into the place, the rest of the clan members peering through the entryway, trying to catch sight of the wedding in progress. The silence. Not a murmur. Not a whisper.

Only Dougald's warm mouth pressing against hers, gently at first, then seeking a response. She'd never even kissed a man, well except for a knight who had kissed her, but when her uncle had caught them, he'd had him severely whipped. The kiss had been hastily done, not slowly, not like this where she could feel Dougald's thumbs sliding over her shoulders, building a fire low in her belly. Not like this where his mouth parted and she too parted her lips to take a breath because she felt so breathless and fully aware of him. Of the smell of him, of heather and the woods, of summer heat and all man. Of the heat radiating from him, his warm touch, yet she could see the raw passion in his eyes. If she had hauled him off to his bedchambers, she would have been in bed beneath him before she could stop him, she was certain.

His mouth curved up slightly, but then he did the unexpected, flicked his tongue over her lips, and she moaned, not believing how exciting and decadent that felt. She couldn't have moaned in the kirk, of all places. Her reaction seemed to please him, and he slipped his tongue quickly between her parted lips, stroking her tongue, shocking her. Thrilling her. She wasn't sure what to do, but touched his tongue back tentatively with hers, and this time he groaned, pulled her into a hard embrace and kissed her gently on the mouth, declaring she was his. That she was what he needed.

Murmurs began then, whispers growing until she could hear some of the bits of conversation. They were husband and wife. They had agreed to the union. They would make it work.

She barely remembered being escorted to the great hall where the feasting and drinking and dancing began. She only remembered Dougald's kissing her in the kirk, and she felt she would melt into the floor like heated candlewax. Now, his hand held hers beneath the table, his thumb gently caressing the top of her hand, soothing but also titillating. She'd never been touched in such a way by a man. The sensation was making her body tighten with a warm need she'd never known before.

"You have made me proud, my lady," Dougald said, smiling down at her.

She tried to summon a smile, but everything had happened so quickly, she couldn't adjust to the idea that she was married to Dougald MacNeill.

He fed her bites of his bannock cake, a spoonful of his cullen sink, the finnan haddie smoked and immersed in a thick soup filled with onions, and flavored with rosemary, fennel, mint, and parsley, chopped, and cooked kale, and shared his ale with her. Mayhap because she wouldn't have eaten had she been left alone, her stomach was unsettled from the reality of the situation as it was sinking in.

The hall was filled with conversation and laughing, of tankards clanking as they were set down roughly on the tables. The fragrance of mint in the soup and of the smoky peat burning at the great stone fireplace in the great hall filled the air. She tasted the rosemary and mint in the soup, trying to get her mind off what would come to pass.

All she could think of was Dougald bedding her this very eve, the way his warm touch made her feel connected to him, cared for. She was not a member of his clan, and she was far from home. Her uncle would not even know what had happened to her. She should have been worried about how her uncle would feel about what had occurred. None of that took her concentration as much as what the man, her husband, seated beside her was doing to her deep inside.

"You have naught to worry about, lass," Dougald reassured her, and she loved the way he seemed concerned about her silence, and inability to eat much.

Her body tingled, tensed with the fluttery feelings pooling in her belly. She wanted to draw closer to him, show she liked his attentions, wished he'd continue to want her after he'd bedded her. Just her, no other woman.

But what if she did not meet with his expectations? She was afraid to show him affection in front of all his kin.

Raucous laughter and shouts of ribald humor startled her to attention, but Dougald looked down at her, smiling sweetly, as if the man could look sweet in the least. He was the seducer of maids, and something decidedly wicked stirred beneath that smile that made her believe he knew she was thinking about their wedding night.

She was afraid he'd be sorely disappointed. She could barely stay awake because of not having slept last night. Now with the excitement and anticipation of what was to come, the early morning hour and the late one this eve, the food and drink that she'd managed to partake in, all of it was taking a toll on her ability to stay awake, focused.

Except for his touch.

# Chapter 16

Dougald thought Alana looked exhausted, dark circles beneath her eyes, her posture stiff when they had first taken seats at the high table, and then slumping slightly. He imagined she'd had barely any sleep last night, though she was holding up remarkably well. He could tell she was tired beyond what a body could normally endure. He admired the way she had come into the kirk, head held high, her gaze softening when she'd looked into his eyes, and he knew then the question in her gaze—would he be a good husband to her? Stay with her? Give up the other lasses?

He wanted to be that man for her and more. He'd given her a small smile to encourage her, attempting not to look at her like a man who was ready to bed the lass, when he couldn't help but think of such. Pleased at how beautiful she looked, how graceful, that she had not fought coming to the kirk, he knew he had won the bet. She would agree to be his wife as much as he would agree to be her husband.

The idea pleased him. He'd given it considerable thought all night long and had decided that wedding her for the good of the clan was the right thing to do. The notion that she would have to live with another man who did not make allowances for her gift and might even use this against her at some future date should he tire of her, had occurred to him. And concerned him.

He listened to the men talk of what they would do if they had such a bonny lass to take to the wedding bed, then much more laughter ensued.

He pulled a brooch out and leaned over to pin it on her brat. "My wedding gift to you, bonny lass."

Tears filled her eyes as she looked from the pearl brooch set in silver to him. "I have no gift for you."

"You are the greatest gift a man could have," he simply said.

She smiled up at him. "You, sir, are a poet." And he hoped she did not imagine him plying the lasses with such sentiments, but he felt moved that she would say such a thing. "Is it from your family?"

"Aye, lass. My grandmother's. She would have loved you."

***

It was already very late when the ladies came to take Alana away from Dougald to get her ready for the marriage bed, then much more laughter and the comments grew even more ribald.

He'd wanted to dispense with all the tradition and just slip away with her alone following the service in the kirk.

James smiled at Dougald. "Seems you won the bet."

"Did you place a bet against me?" Dougald asked.

"Aye. I wasna certain if one or both of you might back out at the last."

"Nay, no' me," Dougald said. "I did as you bade and I did this for the good of the clan."

"Then there was the wager that she would faint before you wed her. She did look a wee bit pale," James said.

"'Twas the lighting in the kirk." Dougald thought her cheeks were quite rosy, especially after he kissed her. He still couldn't believe how she'd nearly unmanned him when she'd played with his tongue in a tentative way.

"Ah. I wouldna wait too long to see your lass, Dougald. I imagine she didna sleep well last eve."

"If she is asleep, I will wake her," Dougald said grinning, then took his leave.

Several wanted to walk with him, but he waved them away.

And then he climbed the stairs to his chamber where the lass would be waiting for him.

When he reached the chamber, he smiled to hear the married ladies giving advice to Alana, and he was certain if any unmarried maids were in the room besides his bride, they would be soaking up all of the ladies' pearls of wisdom.

He knocked at the chamber door, and the women's voices within grew silent.

Light footfalls headed for the door and his mother opened it and frowned at him. "We would have sent for you when we were ready."

"I am ready," Dougald said simply, as if that was all that mattered. *His* being ready. Forget about the lass!

In truth, he wanted to see his bride before she collapsed from exhaustion. He moved out of the doorway, indicating the ladies were to make a fast exit.

"Really, Dougald, you have always been the most unruly of my sons."

He recalled a time or two when she'd said the same thing to his other brothers and his cousin Niall when they had done what she felt they shouldn't have, failing to measure up to her lofty expectations.

His mother kissed him on the cheek. "Be gentle with the lass." She and the other ladies left, all with smiles and backward glances before he entered the chamber and shut the door.

Alana was a goddess in her chemise, so sheer he could see the silhouette of her long legs, the blond curls nestled between them, her small waist and her very pleasing breasts, the nipples dusty rose in contrast.

"Alana," he said, his breath taken away. Her hair drifted over her shoulders like shafts of sunlight and her green eyes were wide with expectation. She licked her lips and swallowed hard.

He closed the distance between them and pulled her into his arms. Like he'd kissed her in the kirk, he would kiss her and have her melting to his touch once more.

"So beautiful," he whispered to her and ran his fingers down the soft slope of her throat until he held a delectable breast in his hand. His mouth was on hers, brushing a gentle kiss. As he stroked her breast, she parted her lips on a sigh, her nipple hardening between his fingers.

She arched her back slightly, appearing to revel in his touch, and he wanted to pull off her chemise and dispense with it, then take her to bed. It was her first time, he reminded himself. He had to make this initial time as pleasurable as he could or he feared she'd be afraid the sex would only satisfy his needs and not her own.

"Tell me what you want, lass," he whispered against her ear, both his hands feeling her bountiful breasts as he listened to her heartbeat quicken, heard her raspy breath, felt her tentative touch as she rested her fingers at his hips.

"I dinna know," she managed to say, looking enraptured in what he was doing to her.

"Help me remove my plaid," he said.

He guided her hands to his belt. She was trembling as she unbuckled it. He cupped her face and said, "We dinna have to remove our clothes if you dinna want to this time."

Her gaze shot up from his belt to his eyes. He couldn't tell if this pleased or displeased her. But in truth, he liked the notion. "I would be willing," he said, winking.

Then she visibly relaxed and backed toward the bed. He reminded himself he had to take this slow, but he believed making this the perfect night of wedded bliss might be the death of him.

\*\*\*

Exasperated with herself for being so anxious but unable to help herself because Dougald was so big, so feral looking, so ready for this and she was so new at what it meant to be a wife and a lover, Alana bumped her backside up against the high bed. Oh, aye, she'd seen Dougald naked already at the loch, but he'd been way down the hill. And she'd felt him prodding her with his rigid staff when she'd ridden with him, but they'd been fully clothed and nothing more would have come of it. This was entirely different.

He would be on top of her, inside of her, and would she be urging him to go faster? Mayhap the woman would say such a thing because she wished him to get it over more quickly. Yet Alana loved the way Dougald kissed her, and she didn't want *that* to end.

When he suggested they keep their clothes on, she had at first worried he was dissatisfied with the way she looked, or mayhap disappointed because she seemed so shy. The others he had been with probably had not behaved thusly.

She worried that she had displeased him, that she was not being the kind of wife he would wish in his bed.

Then she saw the wicked gleam in his eye and believed the idea fascinated him, and she liked the plan very much indeed. At least for the first time.

He lifted her onto the bed, then joined her.

The way he touched her made her feel as though she didn't have anything on, the chemise so soft as though it was transparent as his hands molded to her breasts, his body pressed against her leg, his mouth on hers.

She'd never felt anything so wickedly heavenly and wanted so much more.

His rough hands skated over her breasts, making her nipples sensitive beneath the light chemise, so needy. He stoked a blazing hot fire deep within, and she arched up against him, making him pause and smile oh so wickedly at her. But then his mouth was on hers again, possessive, commandeering, taking charge. She loved the way he made her feel—wanted, desirable, adored.

She wished to open up to him in every way possible, her lips parting to feel his wicked tongue between her teeth, to feel him stroking with the sensuous sweetened taste of it. She moved her thighs apart, wanting him to fill her with his rigid staff.

His eyes had darkened to midnight as he lifted his

head to look at her, his hand still on her breast, his thumb kneading the taut nipple. She was wet between her legs, aching, desiring him to enter her and show her why the lasses all wanted him to share their beds with him.

But this—the way he touched her, caressed her, watched her to see how she was feeling, this she loved and couldn't believe it could get any better. If this was what making love was all about, she was glad he took her for his wife as she didn't believe anyone could make her feel like he did now.

"I am ready," she whispered, unsure why he was waiting. Was he afraid she would faint? Or push him away?

He only smiled, his wicked grin so devilish, she frowned at him and began to push him away. Her whole body heated with a wash of embarrassment. She was too new at this, not knowing what she should say or not say, or do or not do.

But he was all solid Highland warrior, muscle, bone, and heated skin, and her efforts to push him aside only seemed to amuse him more. The skin beneath his eyes crinkled and his mouth curved just a hint, as she couldn't budge him in the least.

"Nay," he whispered against her ear, "'Tis only the beginning, lass." And then his sweet warm and insistent mouth kissed her mouth again, but he slowly moved downward, caressing her jaw with his lips, her throat, and before she knew what he was up to, he had pulled her chemise down to expose both breasts. With a hand on one, he kissed the other, licked her nipple, teased it with his tongue, then took her breast in his mouth and sucked.

She cried out, swallowed up in a world beyond. Inside her, the storm had built into a roaring frenzy, and she shattered with the strength of it.

He looked a little surprised, she thought. And at first she again felt mortified. She shouldn't have been so vocal, shouldn't have reacted the way she had to his touching her. It was too much, too soon.

He grinned and kissed her mouth again. "You were made for me," he said, his voice ragged with desire as his hand swept down, snagged her chemise and jerked it up. His large fingers brushed up her naked thigh, moving higher, making her tense with anticipation.

She thought she was ready for this. But she wasn't.

His hand was on her mound and she stifled a gasp, trying not to make any sound, afraid she'd displease him, barely breathing. She felt lightheaded, concentrating on the way his wicked fingers moved against her womanly folds, pressing into her, and she gave a gasp this time, unable to stop herself.

Deeper, he pushed, and then he withdrew his fingers and stroked a part of her that she hadn't known could give her such tantalizing pleasure. She couldn't take it. "Hurry," she said, her voice high and hushed and begging.

And he did. Stroked her, though that's not what she meant. She meant for him to plunge his staff inside her before she fainted from his powerful touch. But he didn't stop pleasuring her, ignoring his own needs until she'd felt the rush again of a firestorm spreading through her, taking her over the edge of the precipice.

"Oh," she cried out, unable to silence the word.

This time, he yanked up his plaid, pressed himself against her, and entered her woman's passage. She tensed and felt a pinch of pain as he breached her virginal barrier. He must have read her face, the way she winced, and he stopped. She loved him for it— loved how he was so aware of her feelings.

He watched her, then leaned down to kiss her and gently brushed his lips against hers. When she was ready for him, she nodded and he moved slowly, waiting for her to adjust to his size, his own body tense.

He was so big she wasn't sure she could accommodate him as she closed her eyes and reveled in the wonder of their joining.

Wanting to explore him, she touched his waist, her hands sliding over his hard muscles, felt the strength and tightness, but he stopped. She opened her eyes and saw him observing her, his jaw rigid, his gaze filled with lust. Had he not wanted her to touch him? Did it make him lose his concentration?

"I love it when you stroke me like that, lass."

Then she smiled and began to touch him again, sliding her hands over his warrior body. And then he moved into her all the way, or at least it seemed he had done so. She realized then, he had a long way to go before he filled her completely.

He slowly began to pull out of her, and she believed he was done, though she was surprised as she thought that a man pushed in more than once. And…went *faster*.

But still, she had loved the way he had made her feel, cherished and even now she felt lightheaded and in heaven.

How Dougald loved the woman who had sat upon her horse, so boldly eyeing his nakedness at first, then challenging him to race after her in the heather. He'd wanted this of her, to feel her beneath him, to burrow deep inside her soft willing flesh, to take her as a man takes a woman ever since he'd pulled her onto his horse and felt her arse pressed against him. And then again, when she'd been naked in the bed at the tavern when her ghostly brother had frightened her.

She couldn't imagine how much seeing her buried underneath the furs and covers had tortured Douglad's vivid imagination. When they'd touched over the meal, he couldn't help thinking what it would be like to join her in that bed, his staff tenting his plaid so much, he couldn't have moved quickly out of the room if he'd wanted to.

But this was different, more so than he'd ever experienced with any other woman. To see the way she came for him when he'd only suckled on her breast. To feel her come again just from his pressing his fingers into her soft woman's core. To watch the emotions playing across her face—worried that she was doing everything right—she had nothing to concern herself there. He'd witnessed the joy in her expression, and he'd felt it, too, at seeing her delight in the pleasure of lovemaking, so oft faked by the women he'd known. He hadn't known why they had wanted to see him again, if he couldn't make them feel the pleasure in the act like he could. Except mayhap those lasses wished to say that he had been their conquest because no matter how many thought he bedded every lass he chanced to meet, he had not.

He loved the way her fingers stroked his skin. Though her touch was tentative at first, he was certain as they grew to know each other better, she would trust her instincts more. He was having a devil of a time taking this slowly as much as he wanted to conquer and possess her, but he had to be careful so that she would enjoy the experience the first time and be all the more willing to want him again, because he knew one time would only lead to craving her more.

She looked startled when he began to pull out of her.

He pushed into her again, feeling her tense. He kissed her mouth and that made her relax as she was caught up in kissing him back, her tongue swiping over his, dueling, turning him on. As if she was so glad he was not done with pleasuring her, she wanted to show just how much so.

He began to pick up the pace, easing into her and out, and in again, until he was thrusting as if it would kill him if he didn't.

She wrapped her legs around his, her hands clasping his belt, and he swore the next time they made love, they'd both be naked. Although he couldn't deny seeing her breasts bared, the chemise clinging to her waist, while the rest of her was naked, had him burning hot with desire, too. Clothed or not, the woman had his devout attention.

She smelled of lavender, mint, and sweet woman, her body soft and willing, her skin sweetly decadent.

He thrust into her faster, so close to reaching the peak that when he came, he felt as though a bonfire had been lit inside him he was so hot. She moaned his name with such pleasure that he couldn't help but smile. He cherished his sweet wife.

When he finished, he rolled off her, got to his feet, and she looked alarmed that he was leaving her. But he quickly dispensed of his belt and plaid. Her gaze quickly shifted to that male part of him that even at her perusal had him beginning to harden again.

He pulled her chemise down her hips and tossed it on the floor. Then he climbed onto the mattress with her, yanked the fur covers over them and nestled with her.

"I thought you were leaving," she said, kissing his chest, still sounding concerned.

Had she thought he was such a rake that he'd leave his bride after lying with her and rut with some other wench? He sighed. He would have to prove he had no desire to do thus with some other woman.

"'Tis my chamber, lass," he said. "But I wouldna leave you for the world. Even if fighting broke out between my men and yours."

"The Cameron men are your people also, now," she said, snuggling against him.

"Aye." Though he did not feel the sentiment.

It might take years before he could earn their camaraderie. Dougald had to admit that his believing in the lass's ability to speak with those who had not quite departed this world and were in a state of limbo might relieve her uncle's mind somewhat, if he worried what a husband might do to her who believed she was possessed. The other matter of Dougald seeking another wench's bed? Staying in Alana's was the only way to prove to her uncle that Dougald wasn't about to stray.

# Chapter 17

Barely aware of snuggling with Dougald as she drifted off to sleep, Alana found herself in the woods again, her reoccurring nightmare that she never recalled upon waking, but remembered every detail upon falling asleep.

*She heard whispers. "Her horse is over there. She has to be nearby."*

*More hushed voices. "What if she didna ride with her da this time on the hunt?"*

*"He said she was coming. She always goes on the hunt with her da. 'Tis her horse. She is hiding."*

*"He willna like it if we return without her."*

*The voices faded into the distance. The tromping of boots walking through leaves and stepping on twigs moved away. Her heart thumped fast. Her blood pounded in her ears. Her nose twitched, tickled, the urgent compulsion to sneeze as she breathed in the moldy leaves, causing her to feel panic.*

*She dared not move. Dared not unsettle the blanket of leaves hiding her. What if one of the men was still standing nearby, watching, waiting while the others travelled farther away? Then as soon as she stirred, he'd pounce on her.*

*Forever, it seemed, she waited. Then horses ran through the woods, and the MacNeill men spoke with one another some distance from her hiding place.*

*That's when she heard the man standing near her*

*shift his position, moving closer. Felt his boot brush her arm. Thought she was going to die right then and there.*

*The MacNeill found something, Angus said.* Tears flooded her eyes. *They found...her men? Her da?*

Alana sobbed, waking herself.

"Alana." Dougald pulled her tighter into his arms. "Shh, lass, you are safe with me. Shh."

She snuggled with him, waking enough to remember she had a husband and he was Dougald and everything else fled from her thoughts.

***

As soon as Laird Alroy Cameron reached James MacNeill's stronghold, he studied the four towers rising up to the black night, torches lighting the massive entryway, the portcullis down, the gates shut, the massive gray stone walls thick and tall enough to keep out any rabid invader. He thought the structure impressive by even his own standards.

His military advisor, Bran, waited alongside him. "We have never been here to fight. Seems strange to be sitting outside the MacNeill stronghold with no intention of killing them. If she isna within, then what?"

"We will move on."

His men were restless behind him and were just as weary of traveling. He was certain the suggestion did not sit well with them.

He looked up at the two men watching them from the wall walk, the numbers increasing to five within minutes as the alarm was sounded as men hollered out, passing the word along.

"'Tis Laird Cameron seeking a word with MacNeill concerning my niece, Alana. I need to speak with him at once. We come in peace."

A guard on the wall walk called down in a gruff manner, "I will send word to Laird MacNeill, Laird Cameron." Then he disappeared from the curtain wall.

Five more men monitored Cameron and his men from the top of the wall walk as he waited for the word to reach James. Attempting not to appear annoyed with any delay, he was anxious about his niece, praying she was safely within.

"They will want to disarm us," Bran said, sounding like he did not care for the idea.

"We have been their rivals for years. It would be prudent for them to be cautious. They would expect the same if they came to our keep in the middle of the night with this many armed men."

He knew it would take considerable time for the guard to reach the keep and from there to wake James and for him to dress and then ready a force of men. Because in no way would he meet the Cameron unprepared. He half expected James to tell his men to speak on his behalf and not be bothered to see his enemy at this hour, that the gate would not be opened to a group of armed men in the middle of the night.

When the gates were unexpectedly opened, Cameron was more than a little startled. He was greeted by a number of armed men. That part he had expected. One of the men led the group, his hard jaw covered in black stubble, his black hair hanging loosely about his shoulders as if he'd just been awakened and hurried out of bed.

"My laird, I am Eanruig, Laird James MacNeill's advisor," the man said, his face tan, making it appear he spent a considerable time outdoors. He bowed his head in greeting. "He bade me welcome you inside. Your men must hand over their weapons, however. They can stay in the barracks for the rest of the eve. James will meet you in the great hall. I am to escort you there."

"My niece?" Cameron asked quickly. If she was not here, he had no reason to stay. Though if he did not find her here, he would welcome James's men to help search for her, if they would.

"She is sleeping in a chamber, my laird. Forgive me. I should have already said so," Eanruig said.

"She is well?"

"Aye, my laird."

"Take me to see James, then." Cameron motioned to his men to go with James's men.

Bran seemed a little reluctant, then dipped his head to Cameron in acquiesce and gathered their men as if he was in charge of the battle plan when James's men were instead.

"I am Fergus MacNeill," one of the men said. "We will take your weapons." As soon as the MacNeill men gathered up Cameron's men's swords and dirks, Fergus said, "Come, this way."

Seeing that his men were being taken care of, Cameron followed Eanruig. When they reached the keep, servants quickly opened the door. Inside, Eanruig led him to a table in the great hall near the fire in the stone hearth, the smoky, tarry fragrance of peat -- the compressed and partly fossilized loam of sphagnum moss and heather—burning blue, warming his tired body, and a servant quickly deposited a tankard of ale.

After sitting, but before he could take a swig of the ale, Cameron saw James stalk into the great hall, and he rose to greet the laird. Cameron couldn't help but admire the man for responding so quickly to his arrival.

But not only that, that he would actually see him and not send just Eanruig or someone else in his stead. Cameron felt more optimistic concerning the situation for the first time since he'd learned his niece had disappeared.

The man was impressive in stature, dark-haired and eyed, his shoulders straight, his bearing saying he was a man used to being in command. He did not smile, but was all business. Which was to be expected, considering the troubles they'd had with one another in the past.

"My niece, Lady Alana, I wish to see her," Cameron said, without further ado. He had to see her for himself, to know that she was indeed well. He'd been worried sick about her ever since he'd returned home and discovered she'd left the castle grounds.

"Aye. She was sleeping, but a maid is helping her to dress and will bring her down shortly. We must discuss another matter. Please, have a seat," James said, motioning to the chair.

He should have known the lass would take longer to prepare herself to meet him. Cameron sat then and drank deeply of the ale, his throat dry. But then he sat up taller, unable to hide his wary expression. "What other matter?"

"How the lady came to be on our lands. I believe she was to have left as soon as you journeyed on your way, except somehow she didna receive the word for three days."

"I dinna understand." MacNeill wasn't making any sense.

"She was told the shepherdess, Odara, who lives near the border between our lands, was ill."

Cameron narrowed his eyes at James, feeling his temper rise. That was *not* the story he had received from Turi. What in God's wounds was going on?

"My brother was warned at about the same time that a raiding party from your clan had crossed the border," James continued.

Cameron opened his mouth to refute the claim, but James held up a hand to stay him. "We believe it was a ruse. That someone wanted my brother to find the lass crossing the border and bring her safely here."

"Why did she navigate the stream? Seeing to the shepherdess's health would not have caused her to cross into your lands."

"Odara claimed she was with child, a Rob MacNeill's child, and that the man had a sick niece. Lady Anice went to find him and give him the news of the bairn and see to the niece's health. She said that you wished another man to wed the shepherdess instead."

Cameron would not deny that one of his men had wished to wed the shepherdess and Cameron had been agreeable because the man's reasoning was sound. Cameron didn't like that Odara lived all by herself near the MacNeill lands. Since no one had offered for her, Cameron thought the lass would be pleased that Gilleasbuig had wanted her.

But Cameron couldn't believe what he was hearing. The shepherdess had been with a MacNeill? And now she had been in on this plot to send his niece across the stream bordering the MacNeill and Cameron lands? "Who told my niece that the shepherdess had been ill?"

"A girl in Cook's employ by the name of Pelly."

Cameron opened his mouth to speak, then shook his head. How many more had been involved in this insidious plot?

"Dougald and his men made all haste to bring Lady Alana back here for her own safety," James said.

"Dougald MacNeill?" Unable to keep the scowl off his face, Cameron snorted. "He is as bad as my nephew was when it comes to lasses."

Ignoring his comment, James said, "Why would someone from your clan want the lady brought here? Was it because of the marriage arrangement you were seeking for her? Someone who felt she wouldna be safe if she were a MacDonald bride?"

"How did *you* know?" Cameron asked, furious with his people for letting the word reach the MacNeill's ears.

"'Tis of little import. Because of the circumstances that my brother found himself in, that is he could not leave the lass where she was, defenseless and far from home, nor could he have safely taken her across your lands without alarming your people, he had only one choice—bring her here. Since she had no maid, though he and my men had been completely honorable with her at all times, he wed the lass early this morn to ensure she would not be disparaged under any account."

Cameron just stared at James, his blood running cold. He couldn't believe it. All his plans upset in a single conversation with his enemy. He had considered that Hoel MacDonald might be angered that Alana had been with the MacNeill men without chaperone, that he might even wish delaying the marriage to ensure she was not breeding. But he never thought one of his MacNeill enemies would marry his niece.

He growled. He'd had no problem with her marrying Hoel. The man agreed to live with them, and if the clan approved of him, eventually he would be chief. But Dougald?

"Dougald MacNeill?" Cameron said. The man would *never* settle down with one woman, ever. He would break his niece's heart.

"Aye."

"You have forced this on them? I canna imagine Dougald settling down."

"They are both pleased. Neither the lass nor my brother were coerced into this."

Cameron rubbed his bearded chin, trying to concentrate on the real issue now at hand. "I dinna want my niece living here."

"She will live where her husband resides," James said.

Cameron pondered that further. He had no choice. He didn't know if his people would accept Dougald, but he wanted his niece home where he could still care for her and ensure her husband was good to her.

"I want her under my roof."

James didn't say anything.

"Dougald must agree to this. I wanted my niece to have an heir and her husband would be clan chief should the clan vote for him to take over when I am ready to step down."

"My brother will be agreeable."

"My people may no' be. We have fought for many years—your people and mine."

"Aye. Mayhap 'tis time to set aside our grievances and provide a unified front against our enemies. Someone, it appears to me, wanted the lass to come here. Why? To avoid an arranged marriage to Hoel MacDonald? Why did you no' want her to marry her first betrothed? MacIverson?"

Cameron glowered at James. "'Tis none of your concern."

"Was he involved in the killing of her da? Did she see any of the men who killed her father and his men? Mayhap someone knows 'tis MacDonald who had her father and his men murdered. And here is another thing to consider, why was her brother murdered?"

Cameron narrowed his eyes. "You canna believe this had anything to do with Alana."

"Mayhap no, but what if it did? What if whosoever sent her away from your castle did so to protect her? We have no quarrel with you in any of this—your nephew's death, Alana's father's death—but Dougald will do everything in his power to protect the lass should anyone wish her harm."

Cameron knew all of the MacNeill brothers had fought during the Crusades. Dougald had been a capable leader of men. But Cameron still didn't trust him as far as the lasses were concerned. "Aye, if Dougald takes his vows seriously with regard to my niece, then we will somehow live with this arrangement."

Cameron wasn't certain even if Dougald did live up to Cameron's expectations as a good husband, whether Cameron's people would want to kill the MacNeill over the past grievances between the two clans.

"And I will attempt to ensure my people dinna kill him," Cameron added for good measure.

James toasted Cameron with a small smile. "To the uniting of our clans."

# Chapter 18

A sharp rap on the door startled Dougald awake, but before he could unwrap himself from Alana's warm body to see to the matter, Angus opened the door a wee bit, and said, "Alana's uncle is here. James told me to send word for two maids to assist the lass with dressing. They will be here soon."

"Aye, thank you, Angus." Dougald hurried off the bed.

"James is speaking with Laird Cameron first. You can bring the lady down after that."

Dougald lit a candle, then threw on his tunic, glancing back at the bed. Alana was naked, but mostly buried under the covers, her cheeks red in the soft candlelight's glow as she tried to burrow further so his brother wouldn't see any part of her.

"Good luck, brother." Angus closed the door, his footfalls fading down the corridor.

The notion was just sinking in that marrying Alana and having the sweet lady for his wife meant taking on her uncle and moreover her clan as Dougald would have to live among her people, if the Cameron wished it. They might well not like it.

Dougald handed Alana her chemise.

He had been so tired when Alana had awakened him from a sound sleep earlier as she'd had a nightmare, he wondered if talking about it might help. "You had a nightmare," he said, gently, as he pulled on his boots.

Alana didn't say anything as she slipped her chemise over her head.

"Do you remember it?"

She shook her head.

"You were crying."

Appearing surprised, she looked up at him.

"You... dinna remember it?"

"Nay. If I dream, I never remember it upon waking."

He hadn't considered it before now, but if she had dreamed about her da's murder, mayhap she recalled some of what happened that day in the woods. Mayhap if he'd asked her at the time when she was just waking, she would recall it. Next time, he would give it a try.

The two maids tasked to help Alana to dress arrived and they quickly moved into the chamber, looking just as disheveled as Alana. They hurried to dress her in a *léine*, then covered her in the brat and pinned it with his grandmother's brooch.

The maids tried to plait Alana's hair but she could barely sit still. He watched her, her face flushed, her teeth worrying her lower lip, her eyes downcast as she looked at the floor again. She'd seemed so at ease among his people, but now the reality of the situation seemed to be setting in with the lass as well.

When the maids finished with her hair, they stepped aside to let Dougald comment. He smiled at her. "You are beautiful, Alana. Come, we shall see your uncle now."

She didn't make a move toward him and looked up at him, her eyes filled with tears.

It killed him to see her so distressed.

"Go," he said to the maids, then crossed the floor to

Alana as the maids left. He cupped Alana's face and looked into her eyes. "You are my wife. You have naught to fear."

"What if my uncle wants to kill you?"

"My brother willna allow him to."

She frowned at Dougald. "No' here. When we return to my home? What if you have an untimely accident?"

He pulled her into his embrace, loving the warm soft feel of her. "'Tis hard to kill me, lass. Many have tried and have proven unsuccessful. If he throws me in your dungeon, I have it on good authority you will slip down there and free me."

"Or half a dozen other lasses will do the deed before I even have a chance," she said, smiling up at him through her tears.

He chuckled. "I wouldna leave the dungeon until *you* came for me." He sighed. "As long as you dinna say I have harmed you in any manner...I would think the Cameron would be pleased to have me as his nephew."

"You are a rake," she said, "like my brother. My uncle willna be pleased if you..."

Dougald silenced her with a kiss, deepening it, wanting to pull the pins out of her hair so he could run his fingers through her silky tresses. He wanted to return her to bed and make love to her again.

When he looked down at her, he found her eyes closed, her lips swollen, her face flushed. He smiled and shook his head at himself. "Come, lass, 'tis time we speak to your uncle before I take you back to bed and forget he is wanting to see you. The maids willna like it if we have to call on them to plait your hair again. And you know how they would talk."

"You are a rogue," Alana said, but she was smiling when she said it.

"Only where you are concerned, my lady." Then he kissed her forehead and tucked her arm into his and hoped James had disarmed the Cameron, just in case. He could fight well, if he had his sword, but in an attempt to show that he only wished peace he was not carrying it.

He walked with her toward the stairs, found her step reluctant, and wished he had something he could say that would settle her worry. And hoped her uncle wouldn't be too incensed with her for leaving or Dougald would forget wanting peace with the Cameron.

\*\*\*

Alana was terrified. She had been so concerned about spending her first night with her husband, she had let that rule her thoughts completely and had forgotten about her uncle. She knew he would be furious with her. Her marriage had always been his decision to make. Would Hoel MacDonald, if that was who her uncle had made arrangements with to marry her, be furious she had wed another? Would the MacDonald clan want her still? Or would they be glad not to have her in the family?

And her uncle? How angry would he be with her? Especially after she had been with Dougald and his clan for so long without a maid to ensure propriety.

How would her people act toward Dougald? She hadn't really given it much thought since his people had only treated her with kindness. She could just imagine the rumors—Dougald had despoiled her, and she was no longer fit to wed Hoel MacDonald. Then James had forced Dougald, the man with a roving eye and hands, to wed her out of a sense of decency and honor.

She gritted her teeth. Would her uncle treat him ill?

Standing taller, she realized just what she had to do. Aye, his people had been her people's enemy for longer than she'd lived. She would protect him, show her kin he was a good man. Of course if he strayed to any of the lasses in her uncle's castle, she'd let her uncle clamp him in irons, and she'd keep the key herself. She smiled.

Dougald glanced down at her and smiled also. "Good. You appeared as though you believed you were about to be beheaded. I am pleased to see you are no' taking this so hard now."

*If only he knew where her thoughts had travelled.*

As soon as she saw her stern-faced uncle, although he was travel weary, he stiffened to see her, and she faltered.

When he rose from the chair to greet her, it was all she could do not to run across the hall like a little girl and into his arms to hug him. She had not wanted to worry him like this, and she still was afraid of what he'd think of Dougald.

"I am sorry, my laird," she said, rushing to bury herself against his chest, the gruff father he'd been since her own had died, hugging him as he wrapped his arms around her with a bear of an embrace.

Ever the indomitable Cameron laird, he said, "I canna pardon what you have done, running off to see Odara—"

"She lied," Alana said, looking up at her uncle with tears in her eyes. She could see her uncle was fighting tears of his own, so glad to know she was alive and well, yet how could he show that side of himself to his enemy? Even to his own people he might seem weak. So she knew why he acted the way he did, though she still didn't want him to believe she had left the keep for some other reason, such as to escape a marriage agreement he was in the middle of arranging.

"Aye, lass. But you shouldna have left the castle grounds while I was away for that long. You could have been killed." His voice choked a little on the words. He said to James, "I wish a word alone with my niece."

Dougald spoke before James had a chance. "Lady Alana is now my wife, Laird Cameron. Should you wish to speak to her, you may say what you will. We will have no secrets from each other."

She wanted to tell Dougald it was all right for him to leave her alone with her uncle. She knew he only wished to ensure she hadn't been bullied into the marriage or that she was able to speak her own mind *without* Dougald and his brother in the great hall listening in. Further, she was certain her uncle wanted to ask her questions she did not want Dougald or his brother to hear. At the same time, she needed to show allegiance to her new husband, and if she dismissed him—which she assumed wouldn't work anyway—her uncle would not respect him as much.

"Dougald will stay as he is my husband and it pleases me," Alana said.

"I will be in my solar should anyone need me." James raised his brows at Dougald and gave him a hint of a smile as if to say this was now his affair and bowed out.

Thankfully, her uncle did not seem perturbed with her for what she'd said, and motioned to the table.

Dougald and Alana sat across from him ready for the interrogation. Dougald took Alana's hand in his, warm, strong, reassuring as she realized her hands were freezing. She smiled up at him, although she was certain her smile was filled with apprehension still.

He held her hand in his lap, saying she was with him and he was with her every step of the way. Her uncle noticed. She realized—though she had not considered as much until now seeing her uncle and his witnessing her with Dougald—he would not be used to observing her in any kind of intimate way with a man. Her whole body heated as she thought about how she had so easily grown accustomed to Dougald's touching her and how her uncle must still view him as an enemy of their clan.

To Dougald, Cameron said, "Your brother assured me you were no' forced into this arrangement."

"Nay," both Dougald and Alana said, even though she knew her uncle was only asking Dougald. She wanted to make it perfectly clear that she had not been coerced to take Dougald as a husband either.

Her uncle studied them both, then appearing to have reconciled that they genuinely felt something for each other, he nodded.

"If you are to uphold this marriage agreement—though there has been no real agreement with me—I will have your word that you will live among the Cameron and our allies until which time I step down from my position. If my people vote to make you their clan chief at some date in the future, you will follow in my place, Dougald MacNeill."

"Aye, this is acceptable to me," Dougald said.

Alana let out the breath she was holding. Dougald

smiled down at her. His expression was a combination of warmth and acceptance and wicked interest. She believed he was still thinking of returning her to bed and what all that would entail.

"Good. I expect you to be a good and faithful husband," Cameron warned.

Dougald grinned. "All a man needs is a lass who he will love like no other. Alana will be that woman for me." He looked down at her, and she was reminded of the conversation they had had the first night they had camped together.

She swore she heard her uncle give a soft snort of disbelief, appearing not to take Dougald seriously.

Alana hoped this rake—unlike her brother—would truly settle down. Mayhap if her brother had also found a woman he had cared for, he would no longer have looked any further. Or mayhap Dougald appreciated her now, but when she was older or breeding, he may wish someone younger or prettier. She frowned at herself. She would not give into such negative feelings. He would treasure her always as he had said.

"That remains to be seen," Cameron said. "As to this other matter concerning Alana, James was afraid she was sent away from Cameron lands to ensure her safety. If so, who sent her into MacNeill lands? Aye, the kitchen maid, Pelly, and the shepherdess, but they had to have done so under someone's orders. I intend to learn who was behind this. James suggested it could have been to keep Alana from marrying Hoel MacDonald. If that was the reason, why the concern?

"He also mentioned Alana's father's unsolved murder. And her brother's murder as well. We found no evidence left behind in the forest where her father and the rest of our men were killed to give us a clue as to who the murderers were in her father's case. As to Connell, the man responsible was the husband of the woman Connell had been seeing. We know that for a fact. So no conspiracy there," Cameron said.

"Yet by eliminating Connell, you no longer had an heir to lead the clan," Dougald said. "And you were left with having to find a suitable husband for Alana who would be willing to stay with your clan. Could there be something more to his murder than an avenging husband ready to do battle?"

It was bad enough knowing Connell had been murdered for his own transgressions, but even worse if someone had set him up to be murdered because it would be so easy to do with his reputation, Alana thought.

"You are saying that the woman enticed Dougald into relations for the sole purpose of providing an excuse for her husband to murder him?" Cameron asked, his tone skeptical.

"'Tis possible. Because everyone knows how he was with the lassies, no one would suspect foul play," Dougald said.

Connell stalked across the great hall to join them, scowling, catching Alana's eye, and she twisted around to watch him.

"I will kill them both! To think I had any remorse for what had happened!" Connell roared.

Had he any inclination, thinking back on the circumstances prior to his death, to believe he might have been set up? Why had she not considered it before? Because like everyone else, she believed him guilty and the reason for his death justified at least from the enraged husband's viewpoint.

Dougald squeezed her hand. Her uncle was watching her with worried blue eyes.

"He knows I see them, Uncle," Alana said quietly to him. "Dougald is all right with it."

Cameron considered Dougald for a long moment. "Is this true?"

"Aye." Dougald's face brightened with a wry grin. "As long as Connell stays out of our bedchamber, I accept him as a brother." He said to Alana, "He realizes we are married now, does he no'?"

"Aye, he was at the wedding watching the proceeding as well as was your sister."

Dougald's eyes widened. "You have seen my sister?"

"Aye. She is well, but she and my brother have had a rocky start."

Cameron was observing her speaking to Dougald as if anyone might have such a conversation with her husband and it was perfectly acceptable.

"I may have misjudged you," Cameron said to Dougald. "I believe you might fit into my family after all."

Alana couldn't believe the huge concession her uncle was making. Then again, he had no idea how Hoel MacDonald would have treated her had he learned she could see and speak with the dead. Mayhap that had worried her uncle. Hoel might have wished to drown her in the loch as a witch if he'd learned the truth.

"Do you have any problem with my investigating Connell's death?" Dougald asked Cameron.

Connell spoke up as if Dougald had been talking with him. "No' at all. If you discover the two of them were in on it, I wish my murder avenged."

"Connell wishes it," Alana said to Dougald. "I wish it."

Dougald was waiting for her uncle to agree though. They were his people and Connell was no longer with them, as far as anyone else in the clan thought.

"If I said nay, I fathom you would investigate the matter anyway, would you no'?" Cameron asked.

"Aye," Dougald said. "I understand that some may no' wish me looking into the matter. Mayhap this is tied into Alana's marriage betrothal or her father's earlier murder. Or mayhap no'. Until I prove otherwise, I am concerned for Alana's safety."

"As am I," Cameron said. "Alana, can you ask your brother more about what happened that fateful night?"

She was so surprised that her uncle would ask this of her, given that he bade her never speak of being able to commune with the dead with anyone, including himself, she didn't respond right away. Then she overcame her shock and said, "I can. He may know naught more than what you and our men discovered, but because he believed the same as we all did concerning the situation, he had never considered other possible reasons for his murder."

Seana's expression alarmed, she hurried across the great hall to speak with Alana. "I just learned your uncle was here. If you are leaving, I wish to go with you, Alana."

Connell folded his arms and studied Dougald's ghostly sister. "I told you that you canna come with us when the Cameron arrived if you are going to throw pots around. You will have my uncle's staff in an uproar."

"I am no' going with *you*," Seana said indignantly. "I am going with *her*." She pointed to Alana. "She can talk to me. Everyone else just screams, runs off, faints, or calls me names. *You* are another matter."

"You would need Laird Cameron's permission to stay with us. I doubt he would give it if he knew how angry you become at the slightest provocation," Connell said, a devilish glint in his eye.

Alana realized he was teasing Seana. Even in death her brother was still a flirt and a tease with a lass!

"Our uncle would permit it, Seana," Alana said. "Just you quit provoking her, Connell."

She turned from the two of them to see Dougald and Cameron's mouths agape as they stared at her. "You were saying, Uncle?"

# Chapter 19

In the morning, Dougald and Alana would face Cameron's men, not to mention his own clansmen who would not be happy about the Camerons residing on the castle grounds. But for now, it was very late, and Dougald and Alana said good night to Cameron as he retired to a guest chamber after he'd discussed matters long enough with them.

Dougald took Alana back to bed, wanting to make love to her in the worst way, but knowing that she needed her sleep. He wished her well-rested for the feasting tomorrow and for the return trip to Braniff Castle. He also realized as new as she was to lovemaking, she would be tender.

Because of that, when he woke very early that morning and so that he wouldn't get ideas, he left the bed before she woke, dressed, and slipped down to the great hall. Sleeping with his wife had been overly enticing enough. He'd never stayed with a woman all night long, and he couldn't help but love how it felt snuggled up to her on the chilly eve and how much he looked forward to a lifetime of cuddling with her on such nights.

When he went down to the great hall, he found several servants were preparing for a feast, and his brother James and Angus were organizing things to an extent as they drank tankards of ale. Niall soon joined them and Gunnolf, too. Everyone looked expectantly at Dougald.

He raised his brows. "I believe Cameron has accepted me into the family—for now."

Everyone smiled and slapped him on the back as a servant hurried to give him a mug of ale.

Angus folded his arms. "We were laying bets on when you would come down to join us. None of us won."

Gunnolf shook his head. "We didna expect to see you until much later this morn."

"She is a sweet innocent," James said, coming to Dougald's defense, surprising him. "When you have such a lass to call your own, you will understand the need to take it a little slower. Even if it verra nearly kills you."

They all laughed.

Dougald loved his brothers, including Niall and Gunnolf, who were just as much brothers to him as the other two.

The servants were setting up the trestle tables and benches, a lot of movement and talking and noise, but Dougald saw Alana approaching, despite all the commotion. He turned, smiled, and headed for her. He was surprised to see her this early as late as they'd been up.

"The servants are preparing the feast for later, lass. You are looking lovely." He leaned down to kiss her mouth with good measure, and she blushed furiously, then glanced around him at his brothers, Niall, and Gunnolf.

They all wished her good morning with cheerful smiles.

She wished them the same, but she looked a wee bit anxious, her hands clenched together in a tight little fist.

"Is there something the matter?" he asked, frowning down at her.

She took his hand and tugged at him. "I…I need to speak with you in your chamber."

He tossed over his shoulder, "I will return shortly."

She said in a very determined wifely voice, "He willna." And then she pulled at him to come with her.

His brothers and the others laughed.

"Seems you were wrong, James," Angus said. "Can you find me such a lass?"

\*\*\*

When Alana discovered her husband missing from the bed so early this morn, the first thought she had was that there had been trouble. But then she worried that he was with another woman already. Why would a husband not be with his wife when they'd been up half the night what with lovemaking—that had been oh, so divine—nightmares, and then meeting with her uncle?

To her way of thinking, her husband should have been with her in bed still.

Then Seana was sitting on a bench, swinging her feet back and forth, waiting for Alana to wake, the wooden bench legs squeaking in an annoying manner.

When Alana had frowned at her, Seana had quickly informed her where her husband was and that he worried about how tender she might be and that he would have to be careful with her. So Alana was going to show him just how sturdy she could be. Though she was afraid she might be sore, she would not let that stop her. She didn't want her husband thinking he'd made a mistake with her and seek pleasure somewhere else.

"I thought you might need to sleep a little longer with as late as we were up last night," Dougald said, smiling down at Alana as they were crossing the floor of the great hall.

"You need no' worry about me, Dougald MacNeill. I would have slept longer if your arms had still been wrapped around me."

"I would have wanted *more* before long."

She smiled up at him, and she was certain her look was just as wickedly bad as one he would give her when he had been interested in making love with her.

"My mistake, lass," Dougald said, and swept her up in his arms, making her squeak from his sudden and impetuous action as he strode out of the great hall to the stairs that would take them back to the bedchamber.

When they were beyond his brothers' hearing, he said, "I truly do worry about how you would feel, Alana. You need no' concern yourself about me seeking pleasure elsewhere."

"I want this, husband."

"You do realize you are setting a precedent."

"Meaning?"

"I wake early."

She grinned up at him. "I will look forward to it."

He didn't give her much of a chance to change her mind. Which was fine with her! As soon as he reached the bedchamber and slammed the door shut with his backside, he set her on the floor. As she held onto his broad shoulders, he crouched and slipped one of her shoes off, then the other. After that, he was in a rush to remove the rest of her clothes. She realized he hadn't been fabricating how much he had wanted her, and it truly was the reason for his staying away! She loved him for it.

But when he removed her *léine*, he stared at her naked body, his lips parted, and he didn't say a word. Then he raised his brows as his dark, heated gaze met hers.

"What?" she said, thinking in the light of day he was not as pleased with the way she looked as he was when it was dark and she was half covered in blankets.

"Where is your chemise, my lady? And your stockings?"

She grinned. That was the only matter. She tugged at his plaid. "Hurry, husband. I didna want to fully dress when I would have to undress all over again."

He began tearing off his plaid and tunic, walking forward as he forced her to move backward. "You were half naked in front of my brothers and the others?"

"No' that they could see," she said, smiling up at him, loving how he teased her, while she yanked at his plaid to try to assist him in removing *his* clothes faster.

The chamber *was* chilly. Despite attempting to act as though being naked with him was perfectly normal, she still felt self-conscious. Particularly because the last time they had made love, they had both been fully dressed until he undressed her to sleep naked with her. But then furs and covers had buried them. And he had left the chamber this morn before she woke.

She wanted to get a peek at him when he'd removed all his clothes, but he kept his hot, hard body pressed close to hers as he continued to move her back toward the bed, his hands on her shoulders, guiding her. He was smiling wickedly down at her as if he thought she was just as sinfully intrigued as he was. And she *was.*

His hard as steel manhood was pressed against her. He was huge and she wondered how he'd managed to get such a big staff inside her. He had just a small amount of dark hair trailing down his broad chest, enough to appeal and make her want to run her fingers through it and to see just how low it went. She ran her hands over his hips and back and felt they were very smooth, no hair at all.

When her backside touched the mattress, he began to kiss her, his mouth warm and insistent, his hands cupping her face, his hard body pressed deliciously against hers.

She melted under his touch and forgot all about their nakedness as she felt the heat pool low in her belly, lower still into that place where he had been before. And the need returned, her breasts swelling, the area between her legs aching just as much. She craved the release she knew he could give her.

Somehow between his kissing her, and his hands molding to her breasts, caressing, lifting, his thumbs stroking her nipples, she ended up on the bed. She wasn't sure how it had happened, but all that mattered was that he was kissing her senseless, his body moving against hers, his staff rubbing her thigh and oh how she wanted him inside her.

She moaned as he moved his hand to stroke that part of her, and she felt the chilly room no longer too cool, but way too hot. Wonderfully hot.

His tongue licked down her stomach, tickling, heating her. Between that and the way his fingers were stroking the flame lower, when he pressed them into her womanly folds, she felt the pleasure wash over her in such a rush, she was heady with joy and cried out.

He smiled in a lusty way and moved slowly between her legs as if he couldn't wait any longer, but was careful not to rush in case she was sore. He pushed into her tight sheath, deeper, filling her with his staff all the way to the hilt.

Then he began kissing her again, rubbing against her, thrusting deeply, and she felt herself rising to that high place above the clouds, reaching, stretching until she shattered again.

"Alana," Dougald said, his voice raw with lust, as he came into her, having wanted to do this every time he woke last night with her sleeping in his arms.

The lass was so perfect for him, he couldn't believe how much she pleased him. He slid off her and pulled her into his arms, then shifted the covers over them.

He would never have left her this morning if he had known she could be ready for him again this soon. He loved her and smiled as she snuggled against him. His brothers and cousin and Gunnolf would have a fine time talking about Alana coming down to get him, and how she hadn't wanted just to speak with him of some matter. He was so surprised when she said she wanted him to make love to her. Even then, he still hadn't been sure she was ready for him, or just had felt the need to ensure he did not stray.

But she had no need to worry about such a thing. No' that the lasses who still might be interested could cause him difficulty, he thought grimly. He'd have to make sure Alana knew he wouldn't succumb to a woman's wiles, unless they were his wife's.

*\*\**

James had a maid carry a tray up to their chamber

with a word to Alana and Dougald that they were not to join the clans until they were good and ready. But Dougald knew it would be harder for Alana to face his people and hers the longer they were absent.

When they finally called on a maid to plait Alana's hair and make his bonny lass look presentable after their last bout of lovemaking, he escorted her to the great hall where the conversation soon died down.

Then smiles and welcomes greeted the recently wed couple and the feasting continued—to honor the Cameron clan, as far as the Cameron himself and his men were concerned, while they rested up for the return journey home. After eating boar stew and venison, Alana danced with Dougald, and he was pleased the way everything had turned out. Not that he was unconcerned about the prospect of living among those of the Cameron clan. He'd heard some of the laird's men grumbling about Dougald being just like Alana's brother, that he would come to no good end, either. Which made him wonder if someone had plans for him, if they had also plotted Connell's murder.

He'd released Alana so she could dance with his brother Angus with a look that told his brother the lass was a married lady and *his*. Dougald realized then that was the first time he'd ever felt possessive about a woman. He liked the feeling as he folded his arms and watched her dance. Angus had been highly amused.

Dougald was still watching them as his cousin Niall took a turn with the lady. She was in high spirits and seemed so at ease with his kin, he almost wished they could remain here. But he knew it was not in the Cameron's plans, and Dougald would do everything he could to make this work both for the unification of their clans and to make Alana happy.

"I told ye she would spread her legs for any, but I hadna expected it to be one of the men of our enemy clan," a man said bitterly somewhere behind Dougald.

His anger stoked, Dougald had his sgian dubh out at once. He whipped around and grabbed the man closest to him by the throat—who he believed had been speaking—so fast, the blond-haired man didn't have a chance to defend himself. Not that any of the Cameron's men were armed, per James's orders. Only the Cameron himself was allowed to wear his sword as a matter of honor.

The man's face was turning red, his green eyes bulging as he squeaked, "I didna say it. 'Twas him." He quickly motioned to the other man with a wave of his hand.

"Yet you said naught to defend the lady," Dougald growled. He shoved the blond aside and stalked toward the other man, turning his fury on him. This one was black-haired, his blue eyes narrowed in hatred. Dougald seized him by the throat and said in a manner that was low and threatening, "You will apologize at once."

"I am saying only what every man here is saying," the black-hearted knave croaked out.

"Mayhap," Dougald said, gripping the man's throat even tighter, "but I hear only you speaking such foul words. To speak thus so that I might hear means you dinna value your life overmuch or that you are verra brave or verra foolish. Which is it?"

"'Tis your right to deal with him as you see fit," Cameron said, laying his hand on Dougald's shoulder in a way that said he agreed with Dougald's being furious over the matter, yet he wished to have a say. "But 'tis your wedding celebration. I would have you enjoy it as I take care of him. If it pleases you."

Dougald wanted to deal with the vermin himself, but Cameron was right. It would not begin good relations with his newly acquired Cameron kin if Dougald killed one of their men so soon after he married his niece.

"Aye. Do what you see fit, but I will have no one speak ill of Lady Alana." Dougald looked fiercely from one Cameron man to the next. They glowered back at him, but not a one spoke his mind.

Cameron grabbed the man's arm and hauled him out of the great hall. Dougald looked for Alana and saw James had his hand on her arm, holding her in place across the hall, her face and his filled with concern as they furrowed their brows. The music had stopped and every eye was trained on him and the Cameron men behind him. He crossed the floor to Alana, took her shoulders in his hands and kissed her soundly. He motioned for the men to begin playing on their lyres again, and he began to dance with Alana once more.

"That was Gilleasbuig," Alana whispered. "He didna have a broken nose."

"I could have fixed that for him," Dougald said, his blood still cold with outrage, although he tried to rein in his temper as he danced with his wife.

"What did he say that riled you so?"

"Naught that would interest you."

She glanced back at her clansmen. "You wouldna have nearly strangled the man if he hadna said something that infuriated you so."

Dougald wasn't about to share the vulgar words the man spoke, afraid she'd hear them at some other time, but he wasn't going to repeat them here, not at their celebration.

"We were no' supposed to keep secrets from one another," she scolded.

"All right," he said, "the moment I saw you sitting on your horse on the hilltop, I wanted you for my own. I fought the notion, of course, the rake that I was. But I wanted you just the same."

She smiled up at him and he was glad he could get her mind off the subject of Gilleasbuig. "When I first saw you, I was shocked to say the least."

"Yet you didna ride away that instant," he teased.

Her cheeks blushed beautifully. "I was too shocked to move, at first."

"You were a vision. I had to see for myself if I could catch the vision. And then I didna want to let you go."

"I think my uncle likes you," Alana admitted. "I think he believes you are good for me."

"He is right."

"You are so conceited. I shouldna have said as much."

He smiled down at her, wishing he could steal her away to his chamber again.

***

Early the next morn, Dougald met with his brothers, Gunnolf, and Niall before Dougald left with the Cameron and Alana to reside at Braniff Castle, wondering just how well he was going to be accepted. "I will take Gunnolf with me as he has already vowed to go," Dougald said to James as the others looked on.

"I wish to go as well," Niall said in a hurry, as if he might be left behind this time.

James pondered the situation. Angus looked like he wished to go as well, but he admitted, "I just arrived. I will stay with you if Niall wishes so badly to leave with Dougald and Gunnolf this trip."

"Two of Eilis's maids said she'd accompany you and Lady Alana. And Tavis and Callum wish to go with you to serve you as you need," James said.

"Aye. The two lads will be welcome. I suspect they are more interested in serving Lady Alana. And I wish ten more men. Most, if not all of our men, can return with the maids later."

"Granted," James said. "When we get word of Rob MacNeill, we will send it to you."

Dougald hoped they'd learn sooner rather than later who was involved in the lass's leaving Braniff and the reason why.

***

Not too long after their journey began to Braniff Castle, Cameron said to Dougald, "Come, ride with me."

In the worst way, Dougald wanted to ride alongside Alana. He was a warrior, who in the past on a journey like this, would have been happy to be with the men. Before he'd wed Alana, he'd seen her as his responsibility when he had thought to turn her safely over to James. The manner in which she had objected to everything about him had made him smile and even want to prove she was wrong, when he wouldn't have cared what some other lass might have thought of him.

He would never forget the way she had faced him down when he rode out to capture her. Or took him to task about his way with women. She had accepted his sister's friendship, the ghost that she was, and had even asked Seana to ride with her to Braniff Castle. Even though he couldn't interact with his sister, he was pleased Alana could and was providing her with friendship that both the women seemed to need.

He didn't care if others saw him as not wanting to leave the lass's side as though he was tied to her by some invisible bond. He truly enjoyed her company, especially when she rode with him, tucked in his arms, settling in his lap, just where she belonged.

Dougald believed Alana to be in some danger and he worried if it had to do with the marriage arrangement between her and MacDonald or if whoever had sent her away had been concerned about someone harming her within the castle walls. Someone who was kin. Someone who could be riding with them now.

But Cameron insisted that he ride alongside him instead. "Come. I wish to speak with you."

Dougald gave Alana one last regretful look. She smiled at him as if she understood her uncle wouldn't be dissuaded, then Dougald dipped his head to her in a farewell and rode ahead while she stayed with the two maids. Niall and Gunnolf moved alongside the women, flanking them, protecting them if need be.

Dougald knew the lasses were in good hands, but he still preferred to ride with his wife. He joined Cameron and didn't say a word, just waited for the older man to say his peace. He looked out onto the moors covered with heather and moss, cotton grass, bracken and crowberry dotted with clusters of edible black berries, while the mountains in the distance were snow-capped already. A wisp of mist floating over a blue loch reflected on the water.

Finally, Cameron glanced at him. "My brother and

I didna always get along."

Dougald was surprised to hear Cameron speak of something so personal, although he and his own brothers fought a time or two so it wasn't something he was entirely surprised to hear.

"We didna see eye to eye concerning my niece's marriage."

"To MacIverson?" Dougald asked.

"Aye."

Cameron didn't say anything further and Dougald wanted to ask why, but held his tongue to allow the man to come out with it on his own if he was going to.

Cameron stared straight ahead, then said, "We were both stubborn."

"Aye." This time when Cameron didn't say anything further, Dougald said, "You are a leader of men, as was your brother, both strong in your own right. 'Twould be more than unusual had you no' disagreed on some things."

"Aye."

"My brothers and I have fought a few times."

Cameron still didn't say what was on his mind.

Dougald cleared his throat. "James, being the oldest, was in charge. We knew he would be laird when Da died, but that didna mean we agreed with everything he said."

"Aye, like with me and my brother."

"Aye." Dougald felt the urge to shake whatever the Cameron wished to say out of him! "One time, my brother wanted me to wed a lass who he believed would be good for the clan. The woman and I didna suit. She was too dour for me. James couldna see my side of it. I finally left to find a bride on my own. I was unsuccessful."

"I couldna say why I didna believe Alana should wed MacIverson. No' to my brother. I am no' sure he would have believed me. He was set on her marrying the chief."

"He is dead now, is he no'?"

"Aye."

The rumors had spread that MacIverson had been seeing a lass in the dead of winter, fell from a cliff, and died. He never took men with him, as he didn't wish his people to know who he was seeing. Had the man slipped off the cliff on his own? Or had someone given him a shove? Someone who believed MacIverson had murdered the Cameron chief?

"Why were you against the marriage?" Dougald finally asked, knowing James had already asked him as he said he had, but that Cameron wouldn't tell him the reason.

"You truly care for my niece?" Cameron asked, avoiding answering Dougald's question.

Thinking it obvious, Dougald was surprised to hear Cameron ask him. Then again, mayhap her uncle believed Dougald's mind was filled with lust for the lass, but that wasn't all that consumed his thoughts for now.

"Aye, I do," Dougald admitted without reservation.

"She is a bonny lass," Cameron agreed.

For some reason, the Cameron's words bothered Dougald. Aye, she was a beautiful woman, but she was much more than that. "She has quite a tongue," Dougald said, loving that about Alana as much as anything.

"Oh?" Cameron said, his eyes growing round.

"Aye," Dougald said. "She speaks her mind when she disagrees with others. And with...me."

"Oh," Cameron said. He seemed uncertain as to how to address the issue satisfactorily. Did her uncle think to give advice on how to handle the lady?

Dougald had no need of anyone's advice where Alana was concerned. They suited each other fine to his way of thinking. "I enjoy that she does. I love that she does. 'Tis refreshing and quite honestly, she reminds me of James's wife. I admire her greatly. I wouldna have wanted a wife who couldna speak her mind."

"I see." Cameron visibly relaxed in his saddle.

"She is beautiful, both inside and out," Dougald continued. "She concerns herself with healing the sick..."

"Even when someone feigns being sick when they are not," Cameron said, his face darkening.

"You mean Odara?" Dougald asked.

"Aye." Cameron rubbed his whiskered chin, then turned to Dougald, his brow deeply furrowed. "I shouldna ask such a thing of you or any other man who might have wed my niece, but I have to know—did the two of you suit?"

Dougald couldn't help grinning. He tried to wipe the smile off his face because he knew Cameron was concerned and quite serious about the matter or he wouldn't have asked. Still, he had a devil of a time controlling his smile. He couldn't be happier with his lady-wife.

"Aye, Laird Cameron. We have well consummated the marriage." He didn't intend to say any more than that, but he could see her uncle was still worried. Dougald finally said, "She is a delight and I will not stray from the marriage bed, if that is what you are concerned about. I vow this on my grandmother's grave."

He couldn't do such on his father's grave as he'd had many mistresses, to everyone's consternation. Mayhap Cameron thought Dougald would be like his da. But he had always vowed when he took a wife, he would never seek another woman's bed, not like his da who had distressed his good mother so.

"We will see."

Dougald nodded. He would prove to her uncle he would not dally with any other lass.

"You really dinna mind that she sees…what she ought not?" Cameron asked.

Dougald shook his head. "She's gifted. Mayhap 'tis because of her desire to heal those who are sick. Those who have not found their way still seek her comfort? I dinna know, but 'tis no' a problem for me. And I will take any man—or woman—to task who gives her a difficult time over the matter."

"Aye, that is good. Did you know her da showed her the way home, she said? Though she knew which berries and mushrooms and other plants she could eat, she didna know how to reach the castle. Some say she has a guardian angel who watches over her."

"Mayhap."

"But you trust her da took her home?"

"Do you no' believe so?" Dougald asked, surprised. Surely her uncle had not doubted the lass.

Cameron took a deep breath. "Over the years I have tried hard not to imagine what it must be like for her. She attempts to hide from me that she speaks to people who no longer live."

"At your behest."

"Aye. But we have all seen her talking to people who are no' there." Cameron paused, taking a deep, settling breath. "I didna know her brother was visiting her."

Dougald considered that for a moment. "Mayhap…if he should be able to recall anything that had happened before his death that might point to wrongdoing as far as the trouble he found himself in and shares this with Alana…"

"*That* we must keep secret. It would not be prudent for the word to get out that she might learn the truth of it."

"Aye," Dougald said. That only added to his concern over Alana's safety. "I rather like her brother. He's protective of Alana."

Cameron studied him for a moment.

Dougald realized her uncle must think he could see her brother as well. "I have no' seen him."

Cameron frowned. "He canna help her."

"Nay, but I think his presence is comforting to Alana to an extent." *When he wasn't scaring her out of her wits.* Dougald had to admit Connell had advised Alana not to touch Dougald when they supped together alone in the tavern room. So her brother had protected her then. It didn't make a whole lot of difference in the end as Dougald and the lass were now wed. Which had him thinking back to the bed and what he would be doing with her now if they could have stayed at the tavern tonight.

"Because you understand her strange ways and dinna seem to mind them, I have to admit I am relieved," Cameron said.

"You have no worry concerning me and how I feel about Alana's gift. She is safe with me."

"'Tis good to hear. I wasna certain how Hoel MacDonald would feel about her had he known."

Dougald had worried about that himself. On the other hand the thought that either his brother or cousin would marry the lass had him grinding his back teeth. The lady had been his the moment he saw her sitting so fae-like on top of the hill.

\*\*\*

Later that night, Dougald helped Alana down from her horse as camp was made.

Looking worried and stiff from the long day's ride, she asked him, "What do you think happened to Gilleasbuig?"

*That* was what she was concerned about. "He might have been whipped or just sent away from the clan. I have no' seen him unless he is staying clear of us and spreading his discontent among those at the fringes of the group. I didna ask your uncle. 'Tis his clan to guide and his decision to make." When she still appeared troubled, he said, "You are no' worried about him giving you difficulty, are you, lass? We will keep an eye on you always, my cousin and friend, the lads, and the men I brought with me."

"Aye, I know, Dougald. I just wish I knew what happened to him. I have looked, but have seen no sign of him. I dinna know how many traveled with my uncle, and everyone is so spread out, I canna tell how many are still with him."

"Twenty-one came with your uncle. James's advisor, Eanruig, counted them when they first arrived. But like you said, they are so spread out, 'tis hard to tell how many are still with us if no' all of them."

With help from his cousin and Gunnolf, Dougald and the others quickly set up a tent for the lasses. He wished he could be with Alana for the night. Of all the times Dougald had traveled with his men with nary a lass in sight, he had never been bothered by it. But this eve? He couldn't stand being away from Alana. The woman had thoroughly bewitched him.

Cameron motioned to Dougald to join him at the campfire after seeing where Dougald's attention was focused. They talked for a while about clan business, his military advisor, Bran, joining them and then when Dougald could beg off, he finally did.

Even though he could not sleep with Alana in the tent, Dougald curled up in his plaid nearby. He didn't care what anyone thought of his behavior either. He'd heard the taunts from the Cameron men and had seen the good-natured smiles from both Gunnolf and his cousin and his own men, knowing just what he wanted to do.

A couple of his men were posted on guard duty. The others settled down nearby. Gunnolf and Niall laid out their plaids close by. As did the two lads, Tavis and Callum, who had stayed near the ladies all day as if they were their personal guards.

Finally, Dougald closed his eyes, wondering just how receptive the Cameron's people would be to his living among them. Certainly, the Cameron's men he had dealt with already had not been all that welcoming.

Most of all, he wondered if someone would make an attempt on his life next if they didn't want him ruling the clan.

# Chapter 20

The night air damp and chilly, Alana wrapped herself in her husband's spare plaid, feeling comforted by the smell of Dougald—of the leather of his saddle and the fresh pine fragrance, even though she would have preferred his body wrapped around hers, warming her in the tent. Worn out from the long day's journey, Mary and Katerina, the maids accompanying her, had already fallen asleep.

Seana joined her in the tent and Alana whispered, "There are extra furs you may use." Even though it seemed odd that a spirit would need such a thing.

Seana laid down on a fur near Alana. Dougald's sister had ridden with Connell on Spirit all day, because he had said that Seana would give anyone a chill if she had ridden with anyone else. She had reluctantly agreed. Then they'd argued nearly nonstop the whole day, but Alana had been careful not to say a word to them with so many staying so close to her. She'd desperately wanted to scold her brother and tell him to hold his tongue a time or two. And Seana, too, but her brother should have been man enough to allow some of Seana's insults to slip by.

He was of a mind to keep the conflict going, however. Alana had just shaken her head at him, catching his eye. He'd only smiled back at her as if he was having the best time so not to worry.

"I dinna know why you are in here while he is out

there," Seana grumbled. "My brother, I am meaning. If it were me, I would be with my husband."

Alana suspected Seana was feeling badly that she had never had a husband before she grew ill and died. "He canna come in here with the other maids sleeping nearby. Can you imagine what the other men would think? What they would say?"

"That you were with your new husband where you ought to be."

"And he was with three women at one time," Alana whispered back.

Seana said, "Och, have you no legs to carry you into his arms?"

Alana pondered that. But she didn't want whoever was still awake to see her while she searched for her husband in a sea of sleeping bodies.

As if she read her mind, Seana said, "He is to the left of your tent, and I am certain he is thinking of you and no' sleeping either."

"What if the men give him a difficult time over it?"

Seana smiled. "'Twill be because they are envious and believe me, my brother willna be bothered by it. Instead, he will be proud his wife sought him out in the heather."

Alana sat up.

"If he doesna want you to join him, he is a fool," Seana added.

"What if he doesna want to sleep?"

Seana chuckled. "You think he would only wish to hold you close tonight? Nay. But he will because there are too many men about, and he wouldna want to embarrass you. Or make the others *too* envious."

Alana stood. "I will blame this on you if he doesna

like me bothering him."

Seana took Alana's place on the furs and snuggled in them, pulling them up to her chin. "He will be pleased. And you can tell him I sent you to him then. Now go before you change your mind and none of us get any sleep."

Alana studied Seana, wondering why the ghost would need to sleep. She left the tent and glanced around. The chilly fog settling over the area made her shiver. A guard sitting by the campfire watched her. He was one of her uncle's men. He probably wondered if she thought to join her husband or mayhap needed to take care of a more personal matter.

She glanced down at the bodies wrapped in their plaids around the tent—Callum, Tavis, Gunnolf, and Dougald. Niall must be off guarding. She walked over to speak with Dougald, but he suddenly jerked upright, sword in hand.

"Alana," he said, his voice gruff and hushed. "Is there something the matter, lass?"

He was getting ready to stand, but she quickly moved to him, crouched down, and said, "I wish to join you."

He grinned.

"Your sister put me up to it since I couldna sleep," she whispered.

He pulled Alana into his arms and snuggled with her. "It had naught to do with what you wanted, aye?"

"Oh, aye, it did. But she was the one who prodded me into coming out here."

"I am glad you did, lass." He wrapped her in his plaid, kissed the top of her head, and kept her snug against him.

The night was much like the time she was hunting with her da in the woods, the clouds filling the sky, the brush of the chilly breeze against plants making a wooshing sound. Only with a man wrapped around her in a comforting embrace and no moldy leaves to smell but leather and spicy male, she was warmer. With the heat of Dougald's body on the chilly night and the sound of his heartbeat against her ear, she soon fell asleep.

*The sounds of swords clanking against swords and her da yelling at her to hide filled Alana with dread.*

*Then they faded away and she heard the MacNeill say he had found her horse. 'Twas her horse and she wanted her back, but she was drawn to Dougald's voice, to his concern that he had not found her body. She headed for her horse—in Dougald's direction, a fleeting hope that he would rescue her from the others who were seeking her.*

*But then her da ordered her to go with him. She could not disobey him, as stern as he was and as angry. She glanced back in the direction of her horse where Dougald must be.*

*"Alana!" her da shouted.*

*She cringed, worried the others would hear him and come and fight him again. But mayhap the MacNeills would rescue her and her da also.*

*Her da made her walk until she could walk no more. "Sleep," her da finally said when she'd fallen so far behind.*

*She was cold and tired and afraid. She heard no more sounds of men. She only heard birds and saw a fleeting glimpse of a red fox.*

*"Sleep," her da said again.*

*Though she was cold, she found a place by another fallen tree and used it as a wall of sorts and again buried herself with leaves if only to provide a little bit of warmth.*

*When she woke, her da told her, "Eat, drink, lass."*

*She did as she was told, moving through her world as if in a fog, drinking from a stream, eating berries she knew were safe.*

*"We go now," he said.*

*She was so tired, her feet hurt something awful, and she didn't think she could move one foot in front of the other. She'd heard the men fighting in the woods most of the night—yet they hadn't been there. Just in her nightmares.*

*Her da was talking again, like he had the day before. But she couldn't focus on his words. His lips moved and he was speaking, yet she couldn't concentrate on them.*

*She closed her eyes, wanting desperately to sleep, stumbled, and fell.*

*"Landon," her da said.*

*She stared up at her da. He was looking into the woods, and she looked also, thinking that had Landon survived, he must be following them. Then she vaguely remembered her da mentioning his name before. She was certain he was angry that Landon had abandoned her to fight with the men. And then? Had he gotten himself killed? He must have or he would have joined them.*

*Her da shook his head and looked down at her. He began speaking again, but the words floated past her, and she could not make them out. She didn't wish to. She was tired and hungry and her feet and legs hurt.*

*And she was so cold.*

*"Alana!" her da said, breaking through her scattered thoughts. He sounded impatient, worried. "Come, lass. We must get you home. We canna let them find you."*

*Then she was again buried in the leaves, the leather of the boot brushing against her arm. She shuddered, heard the voices whispering.*

"Come with me," the man whispered.

"No," she moaned. He couldn't have found her. He couldn't have seen her.

Arms tightened around her and she gasped.

"Shh, Alana," Dougald said rubbing her arm, kissing the top of her head. "What do you see?" he whispered. "I am here. What is it that you see in your nightmares?"

She remembered them like she hadn't before, not until she was immersed in them again, only to forget them once she had fully awakened.

"He…he was standing next to me, his boot brushing up against my arm. I…I knew he saw me. Or…I thought he had. But then…but then I heard you talking to your brothers," she whispered. "You were close by."

She felt Dougald grow very still. "You were close to where we were?" he said, his voice hushed, upset.

"Aye, buried in the leaves. You found my horse. I didna want you to have her. She was mine."

She looked up at him and in the soft glow of the firelight, she saw him smiling down at her.

"What else, lass? What else do you remember?"

"My da was angry that Landon had left me alone."

"Landon?"

"Aye, a friend of Connell's. They were the same age at five and ten. When my brother was with me on a hunt, he was given the duty of watching over me if I got behind. But he had to stay at the castle that day, my da's punishment because Connell had stolen a loaf of bread from the kitchen that morn before we broke our fast. He was going to give it to a family in need. Landon had to stay with me instead. He was not happy about it. He wished to ride after the stag with the men. Connell never minded when he stayed with me. He said lasses were ever more important than chasing down stags."

"He had the right of it," Dougald said, kissing her again. "Landon left you to help the Cameron fight?"

"Aye. And then he never returned. My da rode back to me and told me to hide."

"Was he alive?"

"I thought he was. I dinna think so any longer. He was yelling at me, afraid for me, but wanting to get back to the fight. If he wasna alive, he must have still thought he was."

"He knew you could see and hear him if he was naught more than a spirit?"

"Aye. He didna wish to believe I could, but he knew it. When he took me home, my da talked to me for long periods of time, but I didna hear what he was saying."

"Why? If you can hear a ghost speaking, why did you no' hear his words?"

"I didna want to. He was talking about marriages and…" She shook her head. "I didna want to hear."

"Alana, he may have told you who murdered him and the rest of your kin."

Tears filled her eyes. She had blocked her da's

words out, so cold, so tired, hurting so badly, she didn't think she would ever find her way home.

She hadn't needed to hear her da's words. He would tell her uncle and the rest of their clan what had happened. She had just needed to reach the castle before she was too tired to care.

"Do you recall anything else?" Dougald asked. "If you wanted your horse, why didna you come for her?"

"My da wouldna let me. He shouted at me to come with him."

"I wish you had come for the horse, lass. My brothers and I would have taken care of you."

She wished it, too.

She shuddered from the cold and Dougald's arms tightened around her, and she settled into his warm embrace.

He might have spoken to her again, but she was tired, and drifted off to sleep until she heard her brother say, "I have been thinking."

She wanted to groan out loud, but she thought Dougald was sleeping, and she didn't want to disturb him.

She opened her eyes, and turned to see Connell wrapped up in his plaid next to her. She was glad Dougald couldn't see or hear her brother.

"After all that was said about my untimely demise, I was thinking back on the events that led up to my death." Connell rolled onto his back, arms folded beneath his head, and he stared up at the ghostly night. "She was verra insistent that I be with her that night. No' other."

"It was planned then?" she whispered.

Dougald stirred at Alana's back.

"Aye, I believe so. At first, I thought it was just that she was seeing me at such a time because her husband would be away."

"But he wasna."

"Nay. She was verra adamant that he would be gone though. Our uncle had sent him on an errand that would take two days."

"I didna know this. You didna tell me."

"I didna think it important because I wasna thinking my murder might have been planned."

"Aye. So I will verify with our uncle that he sent the man on an errand. What else?"

"She insisted on the time of night also. I was surprised because we were always more spontaneous in the time we would meet. Careful, aye, but we didna make plans to meet at such a specific hour, particularly when her husband was going to be gone for so long."

"That the situation was so different between the two of you makes it sound as though something was wrong. Did she behave differently toward you?" She couldn't believe she was about to ask this, but she thought it important to do so. "Was she as ardent?"

Her brother raised his brows at her as if saying she shouldn't be discussing such a thing since she was a lady and he was her brother.

"Or was she upset that you might be killed? Or shocked when her husband caught you two together?" Alana continued.

Connell frowned. "I never really thought of it in those terms. Now that I think back, she usually had her clothes off before I had removed mine. This time she made me take mine off first."

Alana was sure she was blushing furiously as hot

as her cheeks suddenly became. She hadn't expected this much information. Yet she had to know what was different this time between him and the woman if it meant learning that his murder was planned.

"Made you?"

"She helped me. She was always too busy removing her own clothes in the past—worried we would get caught. This time I just thought her slowness was due to her husband being away for so long, and she hadn't felt as rushed."

"But she didna want her husband to see her naked with you, in reality," Alana guessed.

"Mayhap."

"Did he know you had been with her before?"

"We were careful. We didna believe so."

"He must have found out. Mayhap had her set up the meeting. But had he another reason to kill you? And 'twas like taking care of two situations at once. Kill you because you were seeing his wife, but also eliminate you for someone else's benefit."

She chewed on her bottom lip, deep in thought. "Connell, after you died, what happened? How did she react? Distressed? Shocked that he would kill you? Happy?"

"Why would the lass have been happy? We were verra good together."

"All right, so she was distressed."

"Aye, weeping and going on."

"For anyone's benefit? Was there anyone there who would witness what had happened?"

"Turi. He had come to see to the matter."

Alana frowned. "If she was fully dressed, why would anyone believe she and you were...well, lovers that eve?"

"I hadna given it a thought. I was still so stunned to see her husband in the chamber, still trying to sort out what had happened, not even realizing I had died. Not at first."

"And then Turi arrived and reported it to our uncle?"

"Aye."

"But then Ward must have worried our uncle would have been infuriated with him for murdering you in a fit of passion, so he and his wife ran." She pondered that for a moment, then said, "Connell, when you were no' allowed to go on the hunt when da was murdered, was it Da who caught you stealing the loaf of bread? Or someone else?"

Connell didn't say anything, just stared up at the mist.

"Connell?"

"Landon. We had a fight. I was sweet on one of Duff's daughters and her family needed food. Da was punishing them because the two eldest lads, Firth and Alpin, had stolen sheep from the MacNeill without Da's approval. Landon had gotten into a fight with Alpin the day before, and he told me I shouldna be stealing for them. That the two boys would take the bread and never share it with the others. He said he would tell Da. And he did. I was so angry, I couldna think straight. Then when you came home alone and wouldna say what happened to Da and the rest of our men..."

"I wasna really...myself...for a time, Connell."

"I didna understand at first, but I did later."

"I was glad you were home when I returned." Alana sighed. "I didna know Duff's family needed food.

I might have sneaked it to them and gotten away with it. Landon wouldna have known for certain that Firth and Alpin would have taken the food and not shared it with their family."

"Are you speaking to your brother?" Dougald whispered to Alana.

She gave a little start. "Aye."

"Who told him the Duff family needed food?"

Again, Connell didn't say anything right away. Then he snorted and folded his arms across his chest. "Landon did. He thought it amusing that they were hungry after what Firth and Alpin had done. But all I could think about was the daughter that I liked and how she would go hungry because of her brothers' stealing."

Alana passed along the information her brother shared with her. She yawned, and vowed to ask her uncle first thing in the morn about whether he had sent the woman's husband on an errand or not, then snuggled again in Dougald's warm comforting embrace. And fell asleep.

Until later that night when one of the maids in the tent screamed.

# Chapter 21

When the maid screamed inside the tent, Dougald quickly pulled Alana to her feet and unsheathed his sword. Several men grabbed their weapons. Gunnolf and Niall charged forth to inspect the tent, the others standing guard, waiting to meet the attackers.

Dougald stayed steadfastly with Alana, not about to leave her side, his sword ready, Alana tucked under his free arm.

Gunnolf came out and shook his head. "Seems the man slipped away, whosoever he was."

"Who was he?" Alana asked, trembling in the cold.

Gunnolf said, "She didna know. 'Twas dark in the tent and when he pulled the plaid from her face and hair, she awakened and screamed. The other woman's head was already exposed to the man so he could see who she was without disturbing her sleep. When the woman screamed, he sprinted out of the tent."

"He was searching for Alana? It would have been too dark for him to see their faces. But he could see their hair, as light as Alana's is compared to the other women's," Dougald said, his voice harsh. "Who was guarding the tent at this early morning hour?"

No one spoke up.

"Who was *supposed* to be guarding?" Dougald tried again.

"Uisdean," one of the men said from the Cameron

255

clan.

"He is dead!" one of the men shouted beyond the camp. "Someone murdered him."

The Cameron strode forth and said to Dougald, "We need to continue on our journey." He looked at Alana with grave concern, and she felt a shiver go up her spine. Her eyes filled with tears. She hadn't known the man well, but was certain he'd had a wife.

Everyone looked stunned, several of the men's mouths were agape, Cameron was frowning, his fists clenched. Dougald put his arm around Alana and gave her a reassuring squeeze.

To his men, Cameron said, "You know your tasks. We will eat and be on our way."

He might have sounded harsh, but she knew him. Knew her uncle worried for the rest of the party's safety. He wanted her home within the protective curtain walls.

"Would it have been one of your men?" Dougald said in a hushed voice so only Cameron, Alana, Niall, Gunnolf, and the two lads could hear as they stood close to them.

"Mayhap and he was able to draw Uisdean away from the fire without him suspecting anything," Cameron said.

"Gilleasbuig?" Alana asked, since she had not seen him all day, and she wondered if he had no longer been with the Cameron's men.

"Mayhap 'twas him. Since the maids are MacNeill, they might no' have recognized him," Cameron said. "Although I would hope it was none of our men. But I am certain Uisdean wouldna have left his post if the man hadna drawn him from there and he knew him well. He would have otherwise called out an alarm. Which teaches others to be on the guard and no' to leave their posts without warning someone else."

Feeling chilled to the bone, Alana shuddered again, considering what the man had wanted with her. To carry her off? To murder her? She couldn't believe one of their men had been murdered.

She saw Seana watching her, eyes wide. *Seana.* Dougald's sister had unwittingly saved Alana from whatever the man's plans had been.

Dougald rubbed Alana's arm and said, "Let's get you over to the fire." He motioned to the other maids to join her.

"What would you have us do?" Tavis asked, the lad's expression anxious, but he kept glancing at Alana as if he wished to stay with her and protect her.

"Stay with the ladies. Both you and Callum. Niall and Gunnolf, you also. When you ladies wish a moment of privacy, let one of us know. You will have a guard escort at all times."

They murmured their ascent, but none looked comfortable with the idea. Worse, though, would be if the brigand attempted to grab Alana. As embarrassing as the notion was, she knew the other choice was more disagreeable.

"I could have stayed in the tent with the ladies," Tavis said, quite seriously, adding kindling to the fire. "Then the man wouldna be alive to threaten the lady any longer."

"Aye," Dougald said. "Mayhap you could pretend to be one of the ladies this eve."

Tavis frowned at that suggestion and Niall chuckled. "You have to be willing to do anything to protect the lasses, lad."

Callum was grinning at him. "I would like to see that. You, Tavis, dressed as a lady's maid."

Alana didn't like the notion at all. What if the man had intended to murder her, and he had mistaken one of the other women for her? True, the other women's hair were dark brown, nearly black and hers such a pale gold that he must have been able to tell the women were not her. She shuddered to think he might have killed the boy, just because he had been sleeping in the tent with a thought to protect the maids.

"Nay," Alana said. "'Tis too risky."

The men were too busy poking fun at the idea, trying to lighten the mood in their warrior way.

"Aye," Niall said, folding his arms across his chest, smiling. "'Tis too risky for the maids. The lad is too old to keep his mind on his duty if he was allowed to sleep with three lovely lasses."

Callum laughed. "Tavis, aye. But if *I* were to do so—"

Gunnolf ruffled the boy's hair. "You would be just the same."

Tavis grinned at that.

She noted that though the others were trying to make light of a bad situation in a good-natured way, Dougald looked concerned, his hard expression barely changing.

"Please, sit," he finally said to her again, with an almost smile as if he was trying to reassure her but wasn't quite able to manage it. "I wish a word with your uncle."

"Wait, Dougald." She thought he looked down at her with an expression that said he didn't want her joining him. She didn't want to, but she needed him ask her uncle about the man who killed her brother. "Ward murdered my brother for being with his wife. But Gwyn told Connell that my uncle had sent her husband on an errand and he would be away for two days. He obviously wasna. Can you ask my uncle if it was true that he had sent Ward on a mission?"

Dougald's hard look softened. He caressed Alana's cheek with his thumb, "Aye, lass. Anything else Connell remembered?"

"Turi was the first to find my brother." She told him about how things were different between her brother and the wench before the husband murdered Connell. When she was done, Dougald planted a soft kiss on her mouth.

With tears in her eyes, she sat down with the maids by the fire while Gunnolf bowed his head a little to Dougald, the silent acknowledgement that he would watch over the women. Niall and the lads would guard them, too.

Not that the rest of the men busy in the camp weren't also observing the ladies as they went about their chores. They knew her uncle was incensed at what had happened and all of them were ready to attack anyone who made any kind of threatening move toward her.

Between learning it looked more and more like her brother was set up to be murdered and the incident in the tent, Alana attempted to consider what was going on and not dwell on the upset.

Her uncle was speaking to one of his men, redheaded Bran, whose family had been from Ireland, and he had been born on Cameron lands. He was her uncle's right-hand man in everything to do with battle plans, and generally well-liked by everyone.

Dougald joined them and she was afraid that Bran would stiffen or react as though the MacNeill was an intrusion. She wasn't even sure how her uncle would react, but he slapped Dougald on the shoulder as if he was part of his fighting party and the three men spoke in earnest with each other.

She sighed, not relaxed after what had happened, but glad to see that her uncle seemed to have really taken a liking to the man she'd married, which meant everything in the world to her.

She noticed then that Niall and Gunnolf were also observing Dougald's acceptance into the clan. They were like brothers to him, just as protective of him as they were of her.

Niall glanced down at her and gave her a warm smile, then crouched next to her and said in a hushed voice for her hearing only, "You dinna have to worry about him with the other lassies, my lady. Now we will have to use Angus as the one we tell tales about. Truth be told, all of us were much affected by my uncle's, Dougald's father's philandering ways. He was our laird. Since my own da died when I was a wee lad, I was raised along with my cousins as their brother." He motioned to Gunnolf. "He was only a lad when he fought in a battle and lost his da. He has been a brother to us as well. We all swore when we found the right woman, she would be the only one for us, and we would never be like the MacNeill laird before James."

"Thank you for sharing that with me, Niall," she said quietly back. She couldn't tell him how much she appreciated his words. But she knew that some lasses might still try to gain Dougald's attention despite how he felt about his father's philandering ways when the newness wore off with her. What if she was breeding and another lass was too enticing to say no to?

She took a deep breath. She would not worry about what would be or would not be.

Niall rose, looking satisfied that he'd set her mind at ease and watched again to ensure everyone was doing what they ought to and no one made a move to join them that might be considered a danger to Alana.

Seana sat down next to Alana. "'Tis true, what Niall said about all the boys. They despised my da for keeping a mistress and dallying with others. Around us, my mother, Lady Akira, was good of heart and never spoke ill of our da, but I know she felt badly. She never knew I had witnessed her heartache. I believe what Niall said was true." Then she smiled impishly. "But if any lass attempts to steal Dougald from your marriage bed, you and I will have a wee bit of fun with the maid."

Alana grinned at her. She loved Dougald's sister. Which made the situation really difficult for Alana, too. She knew someday Seana would be gone with barely any warning, just like the others. She had to be glad for them, that they'd finally found peace. But she also had missed them.

The day was misty and damp and in the distance she could not see anyone. The sky was beginning to lighten by degrees, though the sun was not visible either.

After eating roasted grouse around the campfire, she and the other ladies took a time to perform their necessary personal duties while Dougald, Niall, and

Gunnolf kept their backs to them but stayed so close, Alana couldn't help being embarrassed. She had to remind herself she'd be much more mortified if someone tried to grab her when she was in the middle of washing or other chores and didn't have the men close at hand to protect her and the other ladies.

When she was done, she joined Dougald and asked, "What did my uncle say? Did he send Ward on an errand for two days and just came home sooner than expected? Or no'?"

# Chapter 22

Dougald hated having to tell Alana the news concerning the man who had murdered her brother. He cleared his throat and helped her to mount, then climbed onto his horse. "Cameron had not sent Ward on an errand. But had the lie been perpetrated by the two of them, just the wife, or mayhap just the husband? Cameron, Bran, and I suspect they both knew about it or her behavior would not have been so altered when she met with Connell. But was the wife coerced into saying her husband would be gone? We all believe so. If she liked being with Connell, we think her husband must have discovered their relationship and had her arrange to meet with him so that Ward would have more of a legitimate reason for murdering him."

"My uncle didna seem verra upset when he heard the news." Tears formed in Alana's eyes.

"He was...I am certain." Dougald heard the sorrow in Alana voice, not wishing her to be sad about this all over again and wanting to comfort her. "Lass, ride with me."

She sighed and looked at him with such tenderness, he stopped his horse and reached over to pull her onto his. "You realize," she said, "my people and yours will think I no longer know how to ride a horse by myself."

"They will know I dinna wish to be far from you, sweet lass." He tightened his arm around her waist and kissed her cheek, loving to hold her when they rode.

Niall rode up beside her to gather her horse's reins, winked at her, then moved away.

"Cameron must have been in shock," Dougald said to Alana. "When you came home without the hunting party, did he rant and rave and throw a fit that you were alone?"

"Nay. He was verra calm while he was trying to learn what had happened." She snuggled closer to Dougald. "He could have had someone else take me to my chamber, but he didna. He carried me there while Turi waited to hear what my uncle wanted him to do. My uncle had said to my maids, 'bathe her, feed her, and put her to bed,' and then to me, 'I will return soon, Alana. Is there anything…' He choked on the words. I dinna recall my uncle ever being that upset. 'I will be back,' he said, and then he left with Turi. After that, I had nightmares, and I didna want to speak to anyone. No' even to the ghosts I saw. They were sad for me. One girl went everywhere I did until she finally got me to laugh at a silly face she made. My maid was so distraught to see me laughing at naught that she called for a servant to fetch my uncle at once."

"But he didna wish to hear that you were laughing at something a ghost had done, I take it," Dougald said, wishing he could have been there for her. Had they only known she was hiding in the leaves so very close by, he would have seen to her safety.

She gave a little chuckle. "He was glad. First time ever. He took me away to his solar and spoke with me in private. He wanted me to tell him what I had thought was so funny. I was reluctant to say since he had always told me not to speak about ghosts. But he forced a smile and said, 'Tis all right, lass. Tell me what made you laugh.' I told him. The little ghost girl had followed us into his solar and was making faces the whole time. Then she smiled at me and left, and I never saw her again. My uncle warned me about speaking of what I saw, but he also said he was glad I was back. I hadna gone anywhere, so I wasna sure what he meant. But he also had a great feast in my honor.

"Connell plagued me mercilessly, trying to make me laugh, which he succeeded in doing. I think that losing our da like that made us even closer than before. Many asked me over and over again what I could recall. I think I...I didna want to remember."

For a while, they rode in silence.

Dougald envisioned that day so long ago. He had been Connell's age, five and ten, wanting to find the lass, but unable to. James had been concerned that whoever had killed the men were still in the area, and he worried for his brothers and their cousin and Gunnolf. They would be no match for a bunch of armed men since they were vicious enough to slaughter Cameron and his men. Yet, Dougald feared that the girl was somewhere about, and they needed to protect her. James was in charge though, being the eldest of the brothers and chief of the MacNeill clan at just nine and ten. He believed if the girl lived, the brigands, who had done this, had stolen her away.

Dougald and the others had taken her horse, the only one that had survived, to the sheepherder in the shieling near their stream between their borders, and told him what they had found. And then they returned home. He thought it odd that the man hadn't suspected the MacNeill of causing the slaughter. James had still been of a mind that they needed to return home before they had difficulties with the men who killed Cameron and his kin, and with the Cameron themselves should they believe the MacNeills had done the killing.

Dougald thought about how Alana had been buried in leaves nearby, of the man who had been standing there, his boot brushing her arm. Had she recognized him? His voice?

"Who was the man who was standing beside you when you were hiding, Alana? Who was he?"

She didn't say anything for a long time. He thought he might have upset her with asking when so many had questioned her before and she hadn't known, or couldn't remember.

"His voice was familiar," she finally said.

Dougald stopped breathing. Had she told anybody that he sounded familiar?

"But he whispered." She also whispered and said, "A mon's voice is different when he whispers, do you no' think?" Then she spoke in her normal voice again, a shudder wracking her body. "A woman's is the same way. I dinna sound like I normally do when I am whispering. I may have been mistaken. He may have no' been anyone I knew."

"Who did you think it was?" When she didn't say anything, he rubbed her back. "Alana, I willna tell anybody, if you wish. But I will make inquiries. Subtly."

"You promise?"

"Aye."

"I may be mistaken."

"Aye, lass, I understand." It was killing him for her not to just come out and say what was on her mind.

She let out her breath. "Alpin."

"Tell me about him."

"He has always caused trouble since he was a lad. He is older than you and Connell by two summers.

"Wait, this is not the same lad who was in trouble for stealing and his family was going hungry for it? And Landon had told Connell, who then tried to take a loaf of bread from the kitchen to feed the family?"

"Aye, the same."

Dougald contemplated that for a good long while. "If he was always in trouble, he was always getting punished. Alpin, I am meaning. He wasna on the hunt, I take it?"

"Nay, never. His father worked for my da as one of the guards. Duff is a pleasant enough man, though he thinks his sons can do no wrong. And he never disciplined them. Now, they are too old and still causing trouble."

"Where are they now?"

"I dinna know. They may be home still. They never work. Just steal when they can."

"Does your uncle do naught about it?"

"Have you ever known anyone who does bad things, not terrible, but mischief that he gets in trouble for, and you still like the person? The boys are just affable. Well, men, now. 'Tis hard to find fault with them."

"What is it that they do wrong?" he asked. She didn't say anything, her back leaning against Dougald's chest as they rode, relaxing a little, and he thought she might have fallen asleep. "Alana?"

"They…stole…sheep."

"From?" he asked, his voice darkening.

"The MacNeills."

"No longer."

"They shared the feast with others, which is why so many stick up for them when they should be in trouble more often," Alana said.

Dougald mulled that over. "Why would Alpin have been involved with the men who murdered your da and then was attempting to turn you over to someone else?"

"If 'twas him. We dinna know that for certain. I could only think of one reason. My da intended to banish him and his brother from the clan and my uncle didna wish to, or he didna know of it and after my da died, he threw the two boys in the dungeon every time they misbehaved."

"Banishment. Life is hard enough, but being banished from the clan would be hard to live with if they have no skills but stealing sheep. There is no other reason you can think of?"

"Nay."

"Did you see them that day? Before you left on the hunt?"

"I dinna remember."

"And when you returned, did you happen to see them? They were not in the dungeon at the time, were they?"

"I wouldna have known."

"Did you ever hear your da speak of banishing the men?"

She shook her head.

"Would Connell?"

"He might have overheard Da talking, mayhap. Turi would know. He was my da's advisor. They would have discussed it."

"But no' with your uncle?"

"He…was seeking a bride. He wasna always at the castle." Alana stiffened a little as she watched a couple of men ride off ahead of their escort, and Dougald saw the matter at once.

Alana's uncle told some of his men to ride ahead. Had they been given orders to take Odara into custody?

Alana was afraid her uncle's men might treat Odara poorly, believing her to be a traitor to her uncle. But what if Odara had done what she had out of concern for Alana's safety?

She cast Gunnolf an annoyed look. "Why do you and Niall no' ride with the Cameron men and ensure they dinna hurt Odara?"

"I will stay with you at all times, Lady Alana, should Dougald wish it." Gunnolf bowed his head to her. "And I wouldna leave your side for anything except to protect you on our journey."

"The same is true for me," Niall said, offering her a small smile.

"Someone needs to look out for Odara's welfare. If 'tis true that she sent me away for my protection, it seems to me she should be honored, not badgered about it."

"Your life could have been endangered when you left without escort," Gunnolf said.

She frowned at Dougald. "They better no' harm her."

"Laird Cameron will wish the truth. We all do. The sooner, the better. If she knows of some matter concerning you being in danger, then we all need to be aware of it," Dougald said.

"I want to ride ahead to make certain no one harms her," Alana said. "I will ride my own horse now."

"Nay. 'Tis safer for you here."

They all rode in silence. Gritting her teeth, Alana wanted to question Odara herself about why she'd said the things she had, to learn if any of it was true. She did not want her uncle's men mistreating Odara if she thought to protect whoever was behind Alana's leaving the Cameron lands.

Before they even reached the shepherdess's shieling, one of Cameron's men returned to speak to her uncle. The man shook his head at something that her uncle said.

Dougald moved Alana to her own horse. "Wait here."

But she wasn't waiting. She rode after him and Dougald glanced at her and shook his head, resigned.

"Odara was gone," Cameron said before Alana had a chance to ask him as soon as they reached him. He sounded disgruntled. "As were her sheep."

"What about Kerwin?" Alana asked, feeling a mix of relief and concern for Odara and the boy. "The lad was helping her take care of her sheep."

"We will check with his family on the way home," her uncle assured her.

Again, the men who had searched Odara's shieling led the way to the croft where the boy lived. Only this time, Alana rode off to hear the news herself as she did not want the men treating the boy ill just so they could learn what had become of Odara.

When they reached the croft, a haggard-looking middle-aged woman walked outside, streaks of dirt on her clothes, her hands dirty, sweat on her brow as she frowned at the men and Alana. "What do you want with me? If 'tis about any of my lads—"

"Kerwin," Alana said.

"He run off and good riddance to him. Naught more than another mouth to feed." She waved her hand in dismissal and went back inside her croft.

"Mayhap he and the shepherdess were grazing the sheep?" Alana asked hopefully, but she knew they would have seen her as they rode to her shieling. She prayed she and the lad along with her sheep were living with Rob MacNeill at his farm. It had to be better than living here with a mother who didn't care anything about his welfare.

Dougald said, "Our men are still searching for this Rob MacNeill. If they locate him, they will take him to see James and send word to us. The shepherdess and the lad, as well, if they are with him, to learn the truth of the matter as it pertains to you, lass."

She nodded, trying not to show just how relieved she was that Odara and Kerwin had escaped her uncle's wrath.

When they reached the castle, Turi, her uncle's advisor, hurried out to meet them. But the warning look on his face didn't bode well. His blue eyes were narrowed, and his dark brown brows knit together in a frown.

"My lady," Turi said quickly. "'Tis good to see you return." He gave a quick nod in greeting to Dougald, but then in a rush said to the Cameron, "My laird, Hoel MacDonald and his father and his brother are here, along with a force of eight men. They are in the great hall awaiting your return and were most concerned that Lady Alana was missing and in some danger."

Cameron said gruffly, "She is already married to Dougald MacNeill."

Alana swore a ghost of a smile appeared on Turi's face, but the expression vanished so quickly if it had been there at all, she thought she might have imagined it.

"MacDonald and his men willna be pleased," Turi warned.

"We shouldna have returned so soon," Alana said, but she knew as soon as she spoke, she should not have said such a thing. Not to a bunch of Highland warriors.

Both her uncle and Dougald cast her an annoyed look.

She stiffened, irritated with them. What if fighting broke out between the men? What if Dougald was injured or worse? She just married him, for heaven's sake!

"'Tis best we get this over with as soon as we can," Cameron said. He steeled his expression and rode into the inner bailey.

There, stable hands quickly took the horses in hand as the men and the maids dismounted. Dougald strode beside Alana, flanked by his cousin and Gunnolf. The lads trailed behind.

"I would have you retire to your chamber, Alana," her uncle said. "Wash up and rest. I will arrange for you and the maids to have your meals sent up to you. When we are assured you will be safe, I will have someone fetch you, but no' before then."

She glanced at Dougald to see how he felt about it. In the past, had her uncle told her what he expected of her—except with regard to Odara and her being ill—she normally trusted her uncle's decisions.

Dougald nodded his agreement, a hint of pleasure in his concerned expression making her believe he appreciated she would seek his approval. She didn't do it because she felt she owed it to him now that he was her husband, but because she trusted his judgment also. Her uncle seemed to approve of her actions, which she was grateful for. She wanted him to like Dougald as much as she cared for her husband.

Niall said, "I will go with the lass and her maids."

"I will stay with you, Dougald," Gunnolf said, and Alana was pleased that he would do so and safeguard her husband should he need protecting.

"All right." Dougald smiled at Tavis and Callum who stuck close to Niall, making their preferences known. "Go with Niall and the lasses, both of you."

As they entered the keep, Cameron directed four of his men to accompany Alana and the maids as well, and the remainder of his men and Dougald's accompanied them into the great hall as a united force, while the ladies and their escort headed up the stairs to her chamber. Her skin tingled with dread as she thought about that day so long ago when her da fought in the woods. She prayed she would not hear swords clanging against each other in a real battle before long.

\*\*\*

"Hoel MacDonald is the man on the far right," Cameron said to Dougald as they entered the great hall, "the one with the sandy red hair. The one next to him is Evnissyen, his brother, and believe me his red hair only gets brighter red when he is angry. Their father, Laird Uisnech MacDonald, is the dark-haired man with the red beard. All are fierce fighters. Watch yourself, Dougald." He glanced at him. "I wouldna want to lose my nephew by marriage so soon."

Dougald gave him a half smile. "I intend to watch

my back and yours as well if the MacDonalds dinna like the way of things." He dipped his head with respect.

Cameron gave him a hint of a smile.

Dougald believed he might have won Alana's uncle over after all.

When they drew close to the head table, Cameron motioned for them to take seats.

"Did you find the lass?" MacDonald asked, sounding concerned.

"Aye, that we did," Cameron said. "Lady Alana left Cameron lands to aid someone who was supposed to have been ill."

The MacDonalds did not even look in Dougald's direction, most likely assuming he was one of the Cameron's men and of no importance.

"Sit." We have ridden a long way today, and we need food and rest. And then I will tell you what I know." Cameron took his seat and motioned for Dougald to sit on the other side of him in a place of honor, which made MacDonald finally take notice.

Ducks and grouse were soon served and Cameron began to relate what had happened concerning Alana, the shepherdess, the shepherd, and the ill niece.

The whole while, as Cameron spoke, none of the MacDonalds sitting at the head table ate any of their food. Dougald was happily enjoying his meal, while Cameron ate bites in between relating the story.

"But you found her safe, I take it, though she isna at the meal," the MacDonald chief said, his brows knit together in a tight frown. "Which I hope means 'tis only because she is so weary."

"Aye. She is tired and is taking her meal in her

chamber with the maids. My niece was riding her mare on the MacNeill lands without an escort, I must confess," Cameron continued, stopping to eat a few more bites of his fowl.

MacDonald stiffened. "She had no *escort*? No *maid*? No one with her at *all*?" He glanced at Hoel, who was frowning just as deeply, then turned again to speak with Cameron. "If she has been compromised, the bride price will have to be much more than we agreed upon if my son is to take her off your hands. We will also have to delay the marriage to ensure she is not breeding."

Dougald fought smiling. MacDonald would *not* take Alana off anyone's hands and he was dying to say so. And if she was breeding, all the better. But this was the Cameron's business to deal with at the moment. He waved his empty tankard to a servant who quickly refilled it.

"Dougald MacNeill discovered her on their lands and took her to see his brother Laird James MacNeill of Craigly Castle," Cameron said, as he held his tankard out for more ale and the servant quickly obliged.

"Dougald MacNeill…," MacDonald said, his voice turning dark.

"She wed Dougald MacNeill, owing to the circumstances and because—"

MacDonald rose from his chair so suddenly, he knocked it on its back.

His men abruptly stood, Hoel finally coming to his feet as if he was so in shock to hear the news that he no longer had a bride-to-be, he couldn't fathom it and was struck dumb.

"You have married her off to one of the MacNeill's kin?" MacDonald roared, his face red with rage.

Cameron and Dougald remained seated, but the rest of the men—Cameron, MacNeill, and MacDonald men were standing, ready to do battle.

"You have gone back on your word," MacDonald said, his voice hard with condemnation.

"Lady Alana was with the MacNeill men for two days without a chaperone. Though Dougald was a gentleman when it came to the lady, he and his brother felt they must do right by her. They couldna have returned her home without the same difficulty. 'Tis best for all concerned. I will still concede paying what I promised as a bride price, but without the bride. Dougald has said he only wishes the bride."

"He does, does he?" MacDonald eyed Dougald, who was eating a chunk of cheese. "Is this the man?"

"Aye," Dougald said. "'Twas the only decent thing to be done under the circumstances."

"He canna have her," Hoel said. "You said she would be mine! He canna have her."

MacDonald ground his teeth. "Have you lain with her?" he asked Dougald.

"The marriage has been consummated, though as you well know 'twas no' necessary to make the marriage official in the Highlands," Dougald offered.

"We will give up the bride price in order to have the bride," MacDonald said, looking as though it killed him to concede the payment. Particularly when he thought he could coerce Cameron into paying him even more.

Why did he want Alana so badly? So his son, Hoel, could someday rule the Cameron clan if they should vote him in as their laird? But how could he even consider such when Dougald had wed the lass?

276

Cameron cocked a brow at MacDonald. "From the way you spoke before, you were conceding overmuch by allowing your middle son to wed Lady Alana in the first place. Then you stated you wished even more in payment for her having been without chaperone."

"'Tis a prudent man who bargains well. Hoel had his heart set on wedding the lass." MacDonald's jaw tightened. "Who perpetrated this charade to draw the lady away from your lands and onto the MacNeills? Are you led to believe that the MacNeills had not planned this all along? Had they word of the lady's marriage to my son and sought to stop it at all costs? Even going as far as having one of James's brothers wed her?"

"'Tis done," Cameron said wearily. "It canna be undone. You will keep your bride price. Sit and enjoy the meal with us if you wish."

Dougald expected MacDonald and his men to stalk out of the place in anger. They were vastly outnumbered if they thought to fight the combined forces of the Cameron and Dougald's men so Dougald did not believe MacDonald would start a fight.

To Dougald's surprise, MacDonald resumed his seat, and then he motioned to the rest of his men to take theirs again. Cameron did likewise with his own men as Dougald bowed his head to his kinsmen.

Gunnolf stayed near Dougald, eating, but ever watchful in the event MacDonald or his men decided to do away with the troublesome MacNeill.

*** 

Alana tried to concentrate on eating after she had bathed and hoped that she would not hear fighting break out down below. Twice she'd peeked out her chamber door and saw Niall and the two lads and her uncle's men all looking at her to see what she wanted. She wanted nothing but peace of mind where Dougald was concerned.

Niall smiled at her. "Tavis checked a while ago, Lady Alana. Everyone is eating the meal, though he said when Cameron told MacDonald that you were wed to Dougald, MacDonald was angry. Then he settled back down to eat."

She took a breath, glad to hear they were not fighting.

"Think you he has accepted my marriage to Dougald?" Alana asked, hopeful, though she could not imagine that they would like that this had changed their plans.

"He has no choice. For now, he seems to have accepted it. Your uncle said he would still pay the bride price to MacDonald as Dougald said he doesna need it."

"Dougald said that?" She shouldn't have been so surprised since her uncle had not made arrangements for her to marry Dougald. But still, it did sweeten the pot, and she couldn't believe he'd want her just for herself especially since he hadn't planned any of this.

"Aye. Dougald said he wanted only you." Niall smiled. "I would say you have bewitched the poor mon. So then MacDonald said he would forgo the bride price to have you wed to his son anyway."

She snapped her gaping mouth shut and glanced at the others in the corridor guarding her. They all smiled at her as if she was a treasure anyone would want who had his wits about him.

She again looked at Niall. "But I am already wed to Dougald."

"Aye. But MacDonald still wants you for his son."

Tavis spoke up, "He asked if you had…" His ears turned red as if he realized his mistake in bringing the matter up to the lady. "Uhm, you know. And Dougald said aye, and MacDonald said he still wanted you for Hoel."

Alana felt her face heat with mortification. She knew in noble English manors the whole household would be made aware of when the husband and wife consummated their marriage. But in a Highland marriage, they didn't even have to have anyone perform a ceremony. Just declaring they wished to wed each other was enough. Even if the marriage wasn't consummated, they were still married to one another. They didn't even require witnesses.

But she and Dougald were married and *had* consummated the marriage. Still, she hadn't wanted all of her kin and neighboring clans to know about it at a meal. She knew they'd realize it when Dougald joined her tonight. It was just something she hadn't expected anyone to speak about out loud to her assembled clansmen. At least she had not been at the meal when the discussion was going on.

Niall cleared his throat and tilted his chin down as he gave Tavis a vexed kind of look, saying to mind what he said in front of the lady.

Tavis's ears turned a bit red.

"It seems odd to me that he would still want me," Alana finally managed to say, pondering the matter. "Even though Dougald and the rest of you were perfectly honorable, and I had enough witnesses to say so while we journeyed to Craigly Castle, I doubt MacDonald would have been so enlightened to feel that everything would have been fine in his estimation had I not married Dougald and still been betrothed to Hoel."

To her consternation, she saw Seana and Connell coming toward her, both highly agitated with each other. Connell was looking down at Seana and saying, "You didna have to practically sit in his lap."

"I had to get close enough to hear what he had to say," she snapped back.

"You were practically falling out of your *léine*, you were leaning in so close to him."

She stopped in her footsteps, placed her fisted hands on her hips and scowled up at Connell. "Who was to see? Huh? Any of the men?"

Alana couldn't believe it when her brother's face actually flushed crimson. He folded his arms across his broad chest. "Me."

Seana's mouth gaped, then she copied his stance and defensively crossed her arms beneath her breasts. "Well, then you are no' a gentleman if you were looking, though I should have known this already."

"And you are no' a lady if you show off your womanly endowments the way you do," he said, motioning to her breasts.

This time Seana's face was filled with color. She stomped off and walked straight through the wall into Alana's chamber although the door was still open. Connell followed right after her.

Alana closed her eyes for a moment, then opened them and said to Niall and the others, "Excuse me."

"I bid you good eve, my lady," Niall said.

"And you," she said as the others wished her good night. She retired to her chamber, and Niall closed her door for her.

It was getting late and Alana was tired. The maids had already retired to pallets in the adjoining chamber, and she shut the door to their room. She couldn't sleep though, what with worrying about what was being said in the great hall. And now with her brother and Dougald's sister standing in the middle of her chamber scowling at each other, that didn't help matters. Either they didn't realize they had an audience, or didn't care as she entered the chamber.

"Go away, Connell," Seana said, "or I will be forced to throw another pot at you."

"And miss like you did the last time?" Connell turned to look at Alana. "See what I have to put up with?"

"You dinna need to follow her around, Connell." Alana sat down on a bench where she began to unplait her hair, feeling as though she was the mother of two unruly bairns, ghostly kind.

"I dinna always follow her around. She trails behind me!" Connell said.

Alana raised her brows at her brother. He was older than she was by several summers and yet he sounded like a petulant child.

He gave her the same raised brow look. "She *does*. I was coming to tell you what I heard at the trestle tables in the great hall, and she had to leave at the same time as me."

"*Everyone* was leaving!" Seana gave Connell a look of annoyance, her mouth pursed, brows knit tight in an annoyed frown. "Besides, how can it be that I trailed you, down to the great hall when *I* arrived first?" She sighed. "'Tis time for bed. And *you* dinna belong in here. This is the ladies' chambers. So be off with you!"

It wasn't the ladies' chamber either, Alana wanted to say. It was hers and she would be sharing it with her husband for the first time. That gave her a little thrill of expectation, but at the same time she felt odd that she would be sleeping with her husband in this room when she'd really never envisioned it. The adjoining room was the ladies' chamber, and she hoped the walls and doors solid enough that what went on in here between husband and wife remained a secret.

"You canna stay here either as my sister will have her husband in bed with her before long." Connell didn't budge.

Alana felt her own cheeks warm with embarrassment. Did her own brother have to speak of this?

"Besides, you didna have to listen to the men at the same tables where I was trying to listen," Seana continued, in a fine snit, ignoring the part about having to leave because Dougald would be joining Alana in bed.

"I had to go where only the MacDonald men were seated, same as you. Wherever your kin or mine sat with the MacDonalds, the MacDonalds said nary a word. Only scowled furiously," Connell argued.

Like Seana and Alana's brother were doing with each other right now.

"You could have gone to any number of other tables where only the MacDonalds huddled together in conspiratorial talks," Seana insisted.

Alana finished unplaiting her hair, suspecting they would bicker all night in her chamber if she didn't put a stop to it. "Enough! If I didna know better, I would think the two of you were an old married couple."

That shut them up. Seana's skin blushed beautifully. Connell glanced at Seana to see her reaction and smiled.

Alana fluffed out her hair. "So what was being said at the tables where only the MacDonald men sat?"

Seana seemed so flustered by Alana's marriage comment, she remained silent—first time ever. Connell watched Seana as if he was waiting for her to speak first. Alana looked from one to the other. She couldn't help the smile that crept across her face. Connell must have been too busy watching Seana and the way she had leaned over—exposing her "endowments" to the men when no one could have seen them but Connor—to have heard what the men said!

"Seana?" Alana prompted.

Seana cleared her throat. "They didna like it that Dougald married you."

"But will they try to do anything about it?" That's what had worried Alana.

"I dinna know for certain. There was speculation, to be sure. None of the men seated at the lower tables would know what their laird would do. And no one at the high table would speak of it for fear the Cameron or my brother might overhear."

"And the speculation?" Alana asked.

"That the MacDonald wouldna let the insult go."

That's what Alana was afraid of.

"There is one another thing," Connell said, straightening, his eyes narrowed at Seana as if he was expecting her to object.

Which she did. "You are wrong, Connell. Dinna mention it."

He turned his attention to Alana. "Hoel MacDonald

was watching Seana's endowments as well."

# Chapter 23

Cameron had suggested the men stay for a hunt the next day, which had surprised Dougald. He thought it best if the MacDonald men left Braniff as soon as possible. He couldn't help worrying that the men might decide to steal Alana away if they had a chance.

If they got her to their castle, it could take weeks or longer to lay siege to get her back. He still couldn't understand why they would want her after he had married her and consummated the marriage. Wouldn't they be concerned that a child of hers would be a MacNeill and not a MacDonald?

Other than that, Dougald had suspected that MacDonald wanted his son to take over Braniff Castle and lead the Cameron clan someday. And that was why he wanted the marriage to go through, not to mention they would be allied with the Cameron rather than the MacNeill having ties to the Cameron. Then again, if they thought to steal her away, how could they and still be on good terms with the Cameron? Dougald didn't believe Cameron would forgive them that easily.

Unless Cameron's people were more interested in an alliance with the MacDonald clan than the MacNeill.

After the MacDonald men and the laird and his sons retired in the barracks for the night, Cameron invited Dougald into his solar. With full tankards of ale in hand as they sat on cushioned benches next to the fire, Cameron said, "I know your concern, Dougald."

Dougald bowed his head slightly to the laird. He was anxious to see Alana, but it was important to learn what Cameron had in mind when he decided to invite the MacDonalds to hunt.

"Here is my thinking on the matter. What if some of my people were in collusion to send Alana away? If 'tis true that they attempted to get word to you to come to our border to investigate the claim that my men had crossed to raid your farms just so you would find Alana and keep her safe, then had it to do with not wanting her married to Hoel MacDonald? If so, mayhap if the MacDonalds stayed here a wee bit longer, we could determine who had tried to protect her and why."

"I worry that she will be at risk while the MacDonalds are within your castle walls."

"Aye, I understand and your men and mine will safeguard her at all times."

"Who do you suspect might have had the lass sent from here? And why the delay of three days?"

Cameron took a swig of his ale and wiped his mouth off with his tunic sleeve. "I have been giving the matter great thought. What if whoever set the plan in motion left Braniff before the word was given so that he wouldna be implicated? When he returned three days later, expecting his word to have been carried out three days earlier, he discovers it hasna. Which means he must attempt the ruse again."

"Yet this time he didna send anyone to warn us that your men were crossing the border. What if we hadna found the lass before she got herself into trouble?" Dougald asked, frowning.

"I have wondered that as well. If the person was concerned for her safety, it would seem that would be a risky thing to do. But what if whoever planned this whole thing had her watched? Made sure no harm came to her?"

Dougald stared into the fire, thinking back to when he spied the lass sitting atop the hill. "Mayhap. Though I never saw anyone watching us. And why someone of your clan thought the lass would be safe with me and mine…"

Cameron nodded. "I have pondered that as well. Think you that it was someone who knew *you*?"

"I didna know this Pelly woman who works in your kitchen, nor Odara, the shepherdess."

"Nor Rob MacNeill?" Cameron raised a brow.

Getting the distinct impression that Cameron might be thinking Dougald had everything to do with the lass's leaving her lands and crossing the stream, Dougald frowned at him. Or mayhap Cameron thought that James might have planned it, considering that if they didn't grab the lass, she'd be wed to an enemy clan.

"Nay. We have a handful of Rob MacNeills who raise sheep. I dinna know each one personally. He may be a distant cousin or someone who had sworn loyalty to James and has taken the MacNeill name. Have you had someone speak with this Pelly who works in the kitchen?"

"She has disappeared just like the shepherdess."

Dougald should have figured that would be the case. "Do you know who left the castle for three days, then returned and could have learned that his plan to have Alana leave had not been carried out?"

"I am having my advisor make enquiries. You

know how it is. So many come and go on a daily basis with tasks to perform outside the curtain walls. Beyond that, the time that has passed has been near nine days, learning the truth may be difficult. But I am thinking, what if you, or mayhap James, had this Rob MacNeill seduce the shepherdess. He had Odara bribe Cook's assistant, Pelly, and the word was given to Alana that Odara was sick."

Not about to become angry that Cameron was still thinking this whole situation might have been because James or any of their kin had planned it as Dougald wished to treat his uncle by marriage with all due respect, Dougald looked back at the fire and tried not to frown too deeply. "Alana said that the shepherdess lives so far out that she wouldna have had the opportunity to meet with Cook's assistant."

"Guards!" Cameron bellowed.

Dougald sliced Cameron a look, wondering what was going on, thinking that someone had slipped into the solar, someone like a MacDonald and intended to harm either Cameron or himself. Five of Cameron's men with swords drawn rushed into the solar. Thinking now he had the whole scenario wrong when the men came for *him,* Dougald jumped up from the bench. One of the men grabbed for him and Dougald tossed the remainder of his ale in the man's face. He had halfway drawn his sword to fight off another, but two of the men grabbed his sword arm and he was quickly disarmed. Sorely outnumbered, he couldn't do anything as they wrenched his arms behind his back and held him tight.

"Be easy with him," Cameron said, scowling at Dougald. "He is my niece's husband, after all."

His blood pounding, Dougald was so angry, he

couldn't tell if the Cameron was jesting, or being serious. "You canna believe I had anything to do with Alana's crossing into the MacNeill lands," Dougald shouted. "I hadna anything to do with any of it. And if someone among your own kin fears for her safety, you could be putting her in grave danger!" He jerked his arms hard, trying to pull himself free of the men, but it was of no use. He had thought to be with her tonight, sleeping, loving her, keeping her safe. He suspected he *wasn't* going to be anywhere near her tonight and that made his blood sizzle with outrage.

"Cameron, have your men release me at once," Dougald ordered. He didn't want to leave her alone. Cameron would still keep his men as guards for her chambers, or at least he thought her uncle would, but what about Dougald's men? Had they been arrested as well?

Cameron didn't speak another word, but inclined his head to his men, giving them the silent order. They hauled Dougald out of Cameron's solar, roughly, because he wasn't making it easy for them.

The laird had to have planned this all along. When? When they could not speak with Odara? Pelly? When he could not confirm that Dougald and his kin had nothing to do with Alana's leaving the castle? Had he planned this on the journey here? He'd had ample time to make arrangements while Dougald spoke to his cousin or with Alana. After they had arrived at the castle? He didn't think so. He'd been with Cameron since they arrived here.

"Cameron!" Dougald shouted again, trying to wrench himself free.

"MacNeill willna have the lass to bed this eve," one

of the men said.

"Never fear, we will keep Lady Alana safe, MacNeill," another said.

But he couldn't help worrying about Alana and fought for his freedom. What if Cameron had decided the only way he could get Alana away from the MacNeill was to pretend to agree to accepting Dougald's marriage to Alana, and in truth, he had fully intended to turn her over to Hoel after all?

Everyone had begun setting up pallets in the great hall to sleep and so the corridor the men took Dougald down was deserted except for a servant or two who witnessed his predicament. Once he got free—and he would get himself out of this, somehow—he had half a mind to take Alana back with him to Craigly Castle or even with him to Malcolm's castle and her uncle would never see her again.

The only thing that did not make any sense was the men were careful not to injure him, despite the way he fought them, which made him think Cameron truly did not believe Dougald was guilty of any crime. Mayhap only his brother, James's pawn. That did not lessen Dougald's worry concerning the lass and what Cameron intended to do with her. Or that she might not be protected well enough without him there.

When they reached the dark, dank dungeon, he was shoved into a cell, minus his sword, but they left him with his dirk. He wondered what was going on. Anyone with half a thought in his head would know not to leave a prisoner armed.

The men quickly locked him in, and then left him alone without another word. His eyes adjusting to the dark, he saw two more men each sitting on pallets in another cell. One—a blond, and the other, as dark-haired as Dougald. "God's knees, Gunnolf? Is that you? Niall, you, too?"

Niall snorted and folded his arms. "This wasna what I had in mind when I wished to have an adventure."

Gunnolf shook his head. "You should have known Dougald would get us thrown into a cell like this. This *is* part of the adventure when you go places with him."

"I am no' the *only* one who manages such a feat," Dougald said darkly.

"'Twas no' over a lass was it?" Gunnolf asked, cheerfully, a teasing lightness to his words.

"I am no' certain what Cameron has in mind. His men left me with my sgian dubh," Dougald said, not answering his question. Gunnolf had to know better.

"Same with us," Niall said. "I thought they were careless."

"I dinna believe so," Dougald said. "No man in his right mind would leave prisoners well-armed with their daggers."

"They attempted no' to injure us," Gunnolf said, "though I split one mon's lip."

Dougald smiled at that. "He is lucky you didna get his nose. What of our other men? The lads?"

"They were relieved before Cameron's men came for us. They were to sleep in the barracks with Cameron's men. The lads were taken to a special chamber to sleep, with honeyed milk and slices of bread and cheese. The lads thought they were in heaven," Niall said. "After they were led away and our other men exchanged with relief guards who were all Cameron men, they came for us."

Frustrated, but unable to do anything at the moment, Dougald sat on the pallet.

Gunnolf lay back down on his. "They didna take our clothes away, either."

"Aye." Dougald looked over at Niall. "You may have to remove yours."

Niall frowned at him. "Why?"

"The dungeon is too cold for *me* to do it. Besides, 'tis part of the adventure, and Gunnolf and I have already done so before. Someone has to entice the lassies to come and rescue us," Dougald said with a slight shrug of one shoulder.

Gunnolf chuckled.

"You didna do such a thing before," Niall said.

"Nay, we had no choice in the matter. We were stripped naked in the bailey in front of the men and women. 'Tis supposed to degrade us, but in fact by doing so, it enticed a lass to free us." Then being angered again, Dougald rose from the pallet and paced across the cold stone floor. "I canna believe the Cameron did this to us."

"Canna the likes of you shut up and go to sleep?" someone groused at a cell in the darkest part of the dungeon.

Dougald looked at Gunnolf, who smiled back at him. It was tempting to talk all night long just to make it inconvenient for whoever was locked away, who had no doubt done something that had warranted it.

"Who are you?" Dougald asked.

"Firth and Alpin. Who are you?" the man asked, sounding surly.

"Dougald MacNeill."

"A MacNeill," he said in a huff.

"What are you in here for?"

"Stealing from you."

"Really. Well since I have married the Cameron's niece, mayhap I can find a place where you could hang, rather than languish in the dungeon."

"Hey, Firth, ask him why he is in the dungeon with us if he just married Lady Alana."

"Yeah, why?" Firth asked.

"To hear your confession. Now that I have heard it, I will advise Cameron on what to do with you."

The men said naught after that. Niall grinned at Dougald. "So what do you think Cameron is up to?"

"Mayhap he has a plan," Gunnolf said.

Dougald glanced at his friend. "I suspect so. But what would that be?"

Gunnolf shrugged and closed his eyes. "It doesna matter as long as *you* are coming up with a plan for us."

"I am," Dougald said, and resumed pacing.

\*\*\*

"What do you mean that Hoel MacDonald was admiring Seana's..." Alana paused, seeing Seana blushing furiously. "You mean he sees ghosts? That he saw you even, Connell?"

"How would I know *that*?" Connell growled, his eyes narrowed. "He was only looking at Seana's...attributes."

"Mayhap he was watching his men seated at a lower table across the great hall," Alana reasoned.

"Nay," Connell said.

"Aye," Seana said. "That was just what he was doing."

"Did you walk around the head table?" Alana asked, still concerned her brother was correct in his assumption. She wasn't sure how it would change things, but she was certain it would. "You said you didna overhear anything spoken there that was important to us."

"Nay, and if Hoel MacDonald could have seen me, he would have been watching me, but he never once looked in my direction. Nor at Connell either," Seana said.

"That's because he was busy shoving food into his mouth." Connell turned and headed for the door. "Fine. Believe her, but I know I am right." He vanished through the door.

Seana made a scowly face at the door. "Connell is wrong. I even leaned around Hoel when Connell told me the man had been watching me, just to see if he reacted. And he didn't. He took another drink of his ale and went back to eating."

"Did Connell tell you that Hoel had seen you before you moved near MacDonald? Or after you were near enough he could hear you speak? Though, I suppose some might be able to see you and not hear your spoken words. I wouldna know for certain."

"Connell told me before we crossed the great hall to the high table. He practically dragged me to get close to Hoel, and then he said, 'See now if he reacts in any way.'"

"Then if Hoel could see you and could hear you, he might have pretended no' to see or hear you."

Seana pondered that, then ignored the comment as she might have to admit Connell could be correct in his assumption. "I am tired. May I sleep with your maids? Well, your borrowed maids?"

"Aye."

"Good eve then." Seana disappeared through the door to the ladies' chamber.

Alana glanced at the door and took a deep breath. She imagined her uncle was still speaking with Dougald, but she was too tired to stay awake another moment. And she wondered what had become of Turi's daughter, Brighid. She should have been there in the inner bailey to greet her first. She wasna sleeping in the maid's chamber. Where was she? That had Alana worrying that her illness had… She couldn't think of it.

She headed for the door and opened it. Only her uncle's men guarded it now. Gunnolf and Niall and the lads must have retired for the night. None of the MacNeill men had remained either. But she thought the show of force too much anyway. Three men remained and all waited for her to speak.

"Brighid, where is she?"

"She has gone to see her sister." Her uncle's advisor, Turi, hurried down the corridor, speaking as he moved toward her. "She hasna seen her in a fortnight, forgive me, my lady. She didna think you would mind."

"Of course not." Brighid had always been loyal to Alana, and the woman loved her married sister dearly. She had two nieces and a nephew she adored as well. "Is she feeling better?"

"Aye. The herbs you gave her settled whatever ailed her. She is fine."

Alana frowned at him. "Are my uncle and husband still talking?" She was afraid mayhap they were doing a bit of drinking.

"They are still talking. It might be quite a while before he retires. You might as well get your rest until then."

Alana let out her breath. It was only her second night of married bliss, and she hoped the night before had not been her first and last. "'Til the morrow then," she said and returned to her chamber as Turi closed her door.

Alana crossed the room, removed the brooch from her brat and laid the wool cloak over the bench. She pulled off her *léine*, then climbed onto the mattress. She yanked the furs over her and closed her eyes, willing Dougald to hurry up and come to bed with her.

But she wondered—did Hoel also see the dead? If so, was that the reason his da wanted him to wed Alana? Because they knew she could also? Then he wouldn't think she was mad and she wouldn't think that of him?

Or was Connell mistaken and it just seemed as though Hoel was looking at Seana and then not looking at her—in an avoidance kind of way?

Alana must have drifted off finally because a hand on her bare shoulder brought her instantly awake. Or at least she thought it was as she opened her eyes and couldn't see anything in the dark. She swallowed a scream, remembering that Dougald was her husband and that he must have come to bed with her sometime after she'd fallen asleep.

Until Connell dispelled that notion and whispered, "Shh, Alana, 'tis only me."

She must not have been fully awake after all, as she couldn't seem to clear her mind and figure out what was going on. She glanced in the direction Dougald would have to be sleeping, but still, it was too dark for her to see anything.

"What are you doing here?" she asked, her voice

low and irritated. She was not only alarmed that her brother was in the chamber when her husband had to be sleeping beside her, though he must not have wanted to wake her so he wasn't touching her, but she was naked.

"Dougald has no' come to your bed," her brother said.

She glanced in the direction Dougald should be and frowned. If her brother was going to tell her that her husband was dallying with another maid, she would kill Connell. Well, if he wasn't already dead. Then she'd kill Dougald. And *he* wasn't already dead, but he'd wish he was as soon as she got hold of him.

Then again what if something untoward had happened to her husband what with the MacDonalds still being here? But what if it was just that Dougald had drunk too much and was sleeping it off somewhere else? Too many scenarios were flitting through her mind all at once.

"Where is he?" she asked, her voice hushed, certain guards were still posted outside the room, though because of the thick walls and heavy doors, they probably couldn't hear her speaking anyway.

"Nowhere."

She frowned at her brother. Could a ghost see in the dark?

"Our uncle has gone to sleep, but went to bed some hours earlier. I have looked for Dougald everywhere, and I canna find him."

"Why were you looking for him?" She started to pull her covers aside, then paused. "Can you see in the dark?"

"Aye."

"Oh. Leave and allow me to dress then."

"I was looking for him because I thought some of his men were to watch you at all times."

She stared in her brother's direction. "I...I noticed. I thought mayhap he believed it safe enough not to have any of his men posted."

"Nay. He wouldna. He believes that someone from our own clan was possibly in collusion with someone that might wish you harmed...or...something. Not sure what. But Dougald doesna fully trust our people. He believes that someone from here also knew this and was the one who planned to have you leave—using Odara as the reason."

"You...you dinna think that whoever had our da murdered was one of our own people, do you?"

"I think it was too long ago to make a connection."

"What about with you? Your death?"

Connell didn't say anything.

"All right, well, leave, Connell, and I will dress."

"I will turn my back. I am no' leaving you." Connell was so sincere, she felt he truly believed he could protect her.

"Oh, all right." Since fumbled around for chemise and *léine*. Finding them, she began to dress. "Where do you think Dougald is?"

"The dungeon."

Alana paused. "You are jesting, aye?"

# Chapter 24

Cameron thought someone would make a move soon. Someone who thought to protect Alana and sent her away from Braniff Castle would come to free Dougald so he could shelter her. Or someone would attempt to get to Alana.

One or the other. He knew he couldn't convince Dougald or his men to agree to his scheme. Not willingly. So he'd done the only thing he could think of to protect his niece. Locked Dougald and his cousin and boyhood companion, Gunnolf, away and continued to provide a safeguard for Alana. Then see who made a move after that.

Turi was pacing across Cameron's solar, wringing his hands, acting like an old hen worried about her chicks.

"Sit, Turi. You are wearing me out, and I am weary enough." Cameron wanted to get this over with quickly. He was tired and wanted to sleep. But he had to learn who was behind what had happened to Alana.

He thought whoever was responsible would make a move, and he hoped he would because he didn't know what he would do in the morning. Alana would be upset her husband never came to see her that night. She might even suspect he'd been with another woman. And Cameron didn't want her to think that. Dougald's men would become restless if they should learn Dougald, Niall, and Gunnolf were not about to greet them when they broke their fast. Hell, his own advisor, Turi, was about ready to have a stroke over locking Dougald away.

"The MacNeill willna be pleased with what you have done. They might even take Lady Alana back to Craigly Castle once they have a chance," Turi warned.

Cameron shook his head. "We have a deal. He married my niece and he will stay with us and earn his place among our people. Mayhap take over someday when I am too feeble to lead our clan."

"The plan was not to place the man in the dungeon. Per your order, I have no' told our men why you have done this, but some are thinking 'tis where the MacNeills belong. 'Tis no' a good way to mend walls between our clans. 'Tis no' a good way to begin your niece's marriage."

"You didna come up with a better plan, Turi. Do you have another idea?"

Turi shook his head.

"All right, then. We wait."

But no one had made a move yet. And Cameron feared no one would as if everyone knew this was just a ruse to catch the culprit or culprits at their game.

\*\*\*

"How am I going to get past the guards at my chamber door?" Alana asked her brother, motioning at her guarded doorway. "They willna allow me to leave my chamber to go traipsing about the keep."

"I know of another way out."

She arched a brow.

"Through the ladies' chamber."

"A secret passageway? Oh, Connell, dinna tell me you would sneak into Brighid's and the other ladies' chamber to see my maids." Before he could answer, she waved her hand in the direction she'd heard his voice. "Forget it. I dinna want to know." She let out her breath in exasperation. "I canna see. How will you show me the way?"

"Light a candle. I will guide you."

"The maids might wake."

"It canna be helped if you canna see in the dark like I can."

She fumbled to light a candle, muttering to herself about Connell and her maids and his rakish ways. Two of her maids had left shortly before he died. She was told it was because they wished to marry someone in another clan. Had they? Or had there been another reason? One to do with her brother's dallying with them? Had Brighid fallen under her brother's charismatic spell as well? Brighid had assured her she hadn't. But it was hard to tell what the maid was thinking from time to time.

As quietly as she could, Alana opened the door to the ladies' chamber and waited to ensure no one stirred. When she stepped into the room, she noted her brother was looking at the sleeping ladies, and she wanted to poke him and remind him of his business in here. Then he spied Seana sleeping next to another lady and smiled.

The rogue appeared truly smitten!

Alana moved around the pallets, and that got her brother's attention. He quickly stood before a tapestry hanging against one wall and motioned with his hand.

She hurried to the wall, lifted the edge of the tapestry, and saw a small door only about three feet tall. She'd have to crawl through it. In long skirts and holding a candle, not to mention trying to hold the heavy tapestry aside while she attempted everything else, would be a trial. At least she could stand up in the stairwell.

Somehow, she managed to use her back to hold the tapestry away from the door, bunched her skirts on top of her lap, and hoped her brother wasn't watching her. Once she was in the corridor, she was actually able to crouch through in a really strange walk, which she could feel straining her legs right away.

She only took a few more steps before she found herself at the stone stairs leading downward into the blackness, winding around in a circular fashion like all stairs did as if even hidden inside the walls it was used for defense, the person at the top of the stairs being able to yield his sword much more easily at the one coming up the stairs.

"Connell," she whispered, not liking that she didn't know where she was going.

"I am right ahead of you, lass. Keep going."

"Where will we come out?"

"My chamber."

"You had a secret passage straight to my ladies' chamber?" She couldn't help the annoyance in her tone of voice.

"Nay, lass. What do you think of me?"

"That you are a rake, Connell. As you always were."

He snorted. "This leads to a hall that connects with

several chambers. But we will come out through my chamber was my meaning."

"Oh." She didn't regret what she had said. How else did he know about the secret passageway that led to the ladies' chamber?

"I was exploring the castle when I was a wee lad," he said, as if he surmised what she was thinking

"Och, Connell. You dinna expect me to believe that, do you?"

"The truth?"

"Aye, if you can manage it." Mayhap she shouldn't have asked.

"Do you remember Lizzy?"

She furrowed her brows. The lass was the first maid who served her when she was ten summers. The girl was about Connell's age, she believed. "Aye."

"She knew about the secret passages."

"Truly?"

"Aye. She was my first, you know."

Alana snapped her gaping mouth shut. She didn't want to know this.

"'Twas no' my idea, but hers. She was a wild one."

"Why did she leave my service?" Alana shouldn't ask, but now she had to know.

"Our uncle was afraid I would have to wed the lass before long. Yet I wasna the first to be with her. Which was another reason our uncle wished her to be gone. He was concerned she might influence you to begin to take lovers as well."

She frowned at her brother.

"'Tis no' always me who is pushing to go to bed with a lass. Some of the lasses are more than insistent."

She gave a quiet laugh of disbelief. "As if you had

ever needed any encouragement."

"Ask Dougald. He knows the way of it. Half his conquests were no doubt *no'* his own, but some lass's as she forced herself upon him."

She couldn't help it. She laughed under her breath. "Oh, aye, I can just imagine."

"'Tis true. Here is the door to my chamber."

"Is anyone in there?" she whispered.

"The two lads who are with the MacNeill clan. They were sleeping when last I checked."

She pushed open the door, thankful that it didn't make any noise.

Tavis and Callum were sound asleep on pallets, and she quickly moved past them to reach the door.

"My lady?" Tavis whispered, nearly giving her a heart attack. She turned slowly to see the lad wiping the sleep from his eyes. "What are you doing in here?"

"I…I worried about my husband. He hasna come to bed."

Tavis frowned and looked at Callum sleeping on the other pallet. "And you thought he was here? He was still with your uncle last I know."

"My uncle went to bed long ago."

"Let me see if anyone is in the hall." Her brother walked through the door.

"You canna be wandering around the castle all by yourself, my lady. I will go with you," Tavis said.

Callum stirred, sat up, and rubbed his eyes. His eyes widened as he saw Alana in the chamber. "My lady," he whispered, frowning.

She held her finger to her lips to silence any further discussion.

Connell walked back through the door. "Something

is the matter. My chamber is being guarded. Only one mon, but that is enough. You canna pass this way."

Now what? She didn't want the lads to know she'd slipped into the chamber through a secret passage, but she had to find a way to see if Dougald was truly in the dungeon. She couldn't believe it. Unless he had been caught dallying with a maid and her uncle threw him down there. Then afraid the lads or Dougald's men would attempt to free him if they learned of it, her uncle had placed the lads under guard, without their knowledge, and sent Dougald's men to the barracks to sleep, without them knowing what had happened to him.

If Dougald had been with a maid, she'd give him a piece of her mind and leave him down there. Then she'd have a few choice words with the maid. She'd be sure to let any woman know that if they had any notion of securing her husband's affection, they'd find themselves without a job and home. As for Dougald? He could stay down in the dungeon until he begged her to have him freed and promised to mend his ways.

"I am looking for Dougald. My..." Och, she couldn't tell the lads that her brother had told her that Dougald was missing. "I heard rumors he might be in the dungeon." Then how could she tell the lads she knew a guard was at the door? Her brother was a big help, yet trying to explain how she knew things when she should not...

The lads' eyes grew round, and they looked at each other. Tavis said, "I will dress and come with you. You will need protection and help with the guards to free him."

"I am coming also," Callum whispered.

Connell folded his arms and grinned. "You would make a great leader of men, Alana. The lads are falling all over themselves to aid you."

She wanted to say that he'd better be correct about Dougald. It was one thing to go looking for her husband on her own without anyone to witness it and then discover Connell wasn't right in his assumption. Quite another if she had an audience. Although she wished her husband was not down there, either.

"A guard is posted beyond the door. I will step inside the secret passage and wait for you." She pulled the tapestry aside.

The lads' mouths hung agape.

Tavis managed to say, "I wondered how you got in here if you were able to get by a guard. I guessed mayhap he was away from his post for a moment." He frowned. "But then why did we have a guard in the first place? And how would you know he had returned to his post?"

Both of the lads watched her, waiting for an answer.

She sighed. She did not like making untruths, although telling the truth could be troublesome. "My brother told me a guard is posted at your door. Why, I dinna know. Be quick," she said, then pushed the small door open, and hid in the secret passageway.

She didn't bother closing the door again hidden by the tapestry and heard Callum whisper to Tavis, "She is of the fae. I told you so. She will bring us good luck."

The rustling of the wool and straw on the pallets and the pulling on of tunics and their plaids followed. "Aye," Tavis said, sounding wise for his years. "But I was the one who first saw her. Think you we can convince Dougald to allow us to guard her always? Between the two of them, we shall always have an adventure on our hands."

"Aye," Callum said. "If we do good with breaking him out of a cell, I think he would agree, dinna you?"

"Aye."

She shook her head. She would prefer sleeping soundly in her husband's arms at night and not having "adventures" such as these to break him out of a cell in the dungeon.

Boots tromped toward the hidden doorway, and Tavis lifted the tapestry and peeked into the passageway where Alana was standing a little ways away holding the candle. "This way," she said.

As she followed Connell, she wondered which chamber he would try next. He said to her, "Stay. I will be right back."

She couldn't tell from the passageway which rooms would be connected. The lads were right behind her, taller than her, breathing down her neck, the heat of their bodies warming her in the chilly passageway.

"What are we waiting for?" Tavis whispered to her.

"To see if anyone is in the chamber first."

"Oh."

She forgot how odd it must be for others to wait for a figure they could not see who was helping them on a quest. Connell returned and shook his head. "Our uncle has moved MacDonald and his two sons in there."

"One of the maids told me they were staying in the barracks," she said.

"They were moved there initially, but told later they could retire in the castle. I wonder what our uncle is up to." Connell rubbed his chin that was still shaved, and she supposed it would always be that way until he found his way to his new home.

"You dinna think our uncle wishes to turn me over to the MacDonalds, do you?" she asked her brother.

Tavis said behind her in a hushed voice, "He canna. You belong to us!"

She smiled at the lad's words, but she said to Connell, "Too risky to go through that room. Let us find another."

"I dinna know what our uncle is planning. I hate to tell you, but they didna have a guard posted at their door."

"No guard? Why would *they* have no guard?" She waved at him to not speak. "I dinna need to know. We free Dougald, gather his men, and leave at once for Craigly Castle."

"How will we get the MacNeill men out of the barracks without the Cameron and MacDonald men knowing?" Tavis asked. "I assumed we would only be facing one guard in the dungeon and Callum and I can take care of him. But taking on all of the other men would be hard to do."

"Dougald will come up with a plan," Alana said. She was not the military commander of troops. She'd leave battle plans like that to the men who knew how to manage them.

Connell went through the hidden door at another room, and she paused, expecting this time they would find an unguarded chamber. She had hoped they'd be out of here by now, yet she felt some comfort in being hidden in the passageway, and some apprehension at being discovered and still being stopped.

Connell quickly returned. "This chamber belongs

to Turi, but he is not within."

She thought it odd. Why would he not be in bed at this late hour? "No guard?"

"Nay."

Not that she thought he would have anyone guarding his room. "All right. We will use his chamber." Though she hated to. She'd always cared for the man, who had been like a father just as her uncle had been with her. Everyone was fond of him, which was why when her da died, his advisor became her uncle's advisor and no one questioned it. So she didn't feel comfortable sneaking through his chamber like a thief.

When she and the boys were in the room, she hurried to the door, but Tavis quickly moved in front of her. "Allow me." He was armed with his sword and dagger, as was Callum, though she didn't want either of the boys fighting her battles.

He opened the door and seeing no one, motioned for her and Callum to go with him.

After they entered the corridor, Callum shut the door, and they hurried off to the stairs that would lead them down to the kitchens and then to the dungeon.

In all the years she'd lived here, she had not once left her chamber in the middle of the night to roam through the keep, and it felt eerily spooky. Particularly when she saw two maids who had died from a fever this past spring near the kitchen, and they both watched her curiously.

*Please don't speak to me*, she pleaded silently to them, tearing her gaze away from them as if she didn't see them. Connell glanced at them and smiled and winked. *Och, Connell.*

Even now her brother couldn't quit flirting with the lasses.

"Where are you going?" Seana asked behind them, giving Alana a start.

# Chapter 25

"Seana," Alana said in a hushed voice as they neared the dark kitchen, surprised to see Dougald's ghostly sister following them. Had she come to check on Alana in bed and found her gone? Or had she been searching for Connell to see what he was up to? "Connell thinks Dougald is in the dungeon."

Seana's brown eyes grew round. "Where is it?"

"We are going there now."

The two ghostly maids were still watching them, and Seana cast them a narrow-eyed look like they'd better leave or else. They quickly curtseyed to her—the word must have gotten out she was a lady and even in the spirit world rank must have counted, or they were used to such courtesy—then they vanished.

Now if they could have used all the ghosts roaming around tonight to help free Dougald from the dungeon—if that's where he was—they'd have no trouble.

Callum whispered, "Who are you speaking to now, my lady?"

"These are your guards?" Seana asked. She glowered at Connell. "Dinna think I didna see you making eyes at the maids." She shook her head.

"Lady Seana has joined our party," Alana said to Callum.

Connell said, "I only smiled at the lasses. Did you want me to scowl at them? Why should I?"

Seana frowned at Connell. "There is smiling and then there is smiling. The kind you do is the kind that gets you into trouble, Connell Cameron."

Alana rolled her eyes. How was she to rescue Dougald if she had to quell the bickering between her brother and *his* sister?

They'd barely passed the darkened kitchen and had quite a ways to go before they reached the stairs leading down to the dungeon, when a force of several men dashed out of the room, startling Alana. She cried out. Men rushed up the dungeon stairs, as evidenced from their heavy tromping boots on the stone steps as they moved in their direction and quickly surrounded Alana, Callum, and Tavis.

Her uncle was among them and stared down at Alana, then looked at the lads and scowled deeply. He folded his arms. "How did the three of you get past the guards?"

"Where is Dougald?" she demanded. She had never acted in that manner toward her uncle. She was always very considerate when she was with him in front of his men. She couldn't help herself. If her uncle was in the wrong, or even if he was in the right, she wanted to know what was going on.

Then she spied Turi standing among the men, looking more than concerned. But she was not about to be sent to bed without an explanation, and if Dougald had done no wrong he was retiring to bed with her.

"Come with me, Alana," her uncle said, then motioned for his men to take the boys back to their chamber.

She saw then that they'd quickly been disarmed. She hadn't wanted any harm to come to them, so she was glad they hadn't been given the chance to fight.

"No," Tavis said, bullheadedly. "We stay with Lady Alana. She is one of us now. You canna hand her over to the MacDonalds."

Cameron chuckled. "I didna intend to, lad. Return to your chamber and stay there or I will lock you in a cell down below."

"Go," Alana implored. She didn't want the boys locked in the dungeon, and she was heartened to hear that her uncle did not intend to give her up to the MacDonalds. "Why is Dougald in the dungeon?"

She shouldn't have asked her uncle in front of her clansmen when she was so angry.

"Alana," he said, reaching for her arm.

She stepped back out of his reach.

He frowned and turned to his advisor on battle matters, Bran. "Take her to my chamber and keep her there."

She could have fought her uncle, the men, every one of them. But she knew in the end, it would be of no use.

She opened her mouth to speak, but her uncle cut her off and said to Bran, "Now."

"Aye, my laird." Bran grasped her arm and took her away with two men leading the escort and two following behind.

When she was beyond her uncle's hearing, she scowled up at Bran. "You can release me now. I willna be running away."

He smiled down at her. "I agree." But he didn't release her, either.

"What is this all about?"

"When the laird is ready to tell you, Lady Alana, he will." Bran took her to her uncle's chamber, once her da's.

"I wish to be returned to my own chamber so I may sleep."

"It isna your uncle's wish."

"I canna sleep in his bed. I am tired."

He chuckled. "If you hadna *left* your bed, you could be asleep in it."

Two of the men inspected her uncle's chamber before they allowed her to enter. She thought it odd. Why would anyone be hiding in her uncle's chamber?

"Tell me this then," she said, taking a seat on a cushioned bench, when two of the men were posted outside the room and the other two inside along with Bran, "what has Dougald done to earn him a stay in a cell?"

"He hasna done anything wrong, my lady, but continued to be the heroic individual he has been all along with regard to you."

She folded her arms and scowled up at him. "Then why is he in a cell!"

"I canna say for certain, only that your uncle had a plan, and he knew MacNeill would no' go along with it."

She noted then that neither Connell nor Seana had joined her. Where were they now? If only *they* could let Dougald out of his cell.

Still, she was furious with her uncle, and she would let him know it as soon as he came to see her.

\*\*\*

"Alana! Cameron, God's wounds let me out of

here!" Dougald shouted, after hearing Alana scream. He knew she'd been startled, not hurt after he'd heard the words spoken near the kitchen. He'd listened quietly, trying to hear what was being said.

Bran was escorting her to her uncle's chamber, the lads to the one they shared, and guards would be posted. But he'd heard her uncle say he didn't intend to give her up to MacDonald. Which was a relief.

Gunnolf yanked at the bars and said, "I believe we are down here so he could see who would come to rescue us. Seems your lass and the lads were the only ones brave enough to do so."

Dougald should have known Alana would try to free him. He smiled to himself, then he was irate with Cameron all over again.

"Cameron! Release us at once!" Dougald shouted. To Niall and Gunnolf he said, "I believe this is the only time I have ever been used as bait. I dinna like it. Especially when I meant to protect my wife." Dougald stood at his cell door, then called out, "I am ill and in need of a healer!" He swore he heard Cameron chuckle along with a couple of his men.

Even Gunnolf and Niall were grinning at him.

Dougald stalked over to his pallet and sat down. "Who does he believe intended to come down here and rescue us?"

Niall snorted and crossed his arms over his chest. "According to you, if I got naked, a lassie would have appeared."

Remembering when Alana had seen all the men naked at the loch, Dougald studied him for a moment, then shook his head. "'Twas good that you didna if Alana had happened to join us."

"You asked if the lass would come to rescue you if you were locked in the dungeon," Niall said, taking a seat again. "Now you have your answer."

Aye, he did. He loved her.

Dougald stood and walked over to the bars again. "Cameron! It willna work. Whatever your plan was, it didna work! Release us! Now!"

They heard the stomping of boots on the stairs, then several armed men strode toward Dougald's cell and at once he felt relief, anger, and apprehension.

"Dinna cause any trouble," one of the men said, poised to unlock the cell. "Laird Cameron asked that we free you so you can take Lady Alana back to her chamber and stay with her the rest of the eve."

"Because whosoever was supposed to free us didna show?" Dougald asked.

"Aye. His lairdship didna believe his niece would be the one to try and do so." The man chuckled softly and unlocked the cell door.

Dougald was sorely tempted to slam a fist into every Cameron's face there, but he reined in his temper. He had to make peace with these men if he was ever to someday lead them. And he knew his actions and his reactions would always be judged by the rest of the clan.

"Why didna he speak to me first of the matter?"

"He knew you wouldna go along with it." The man turned to unlock Gunnolf and Niall's cell, while another handed Dougald his sword. Then they waited for Niall and Gunnolf to leave their cell. Another man returned their swords.

In a rush to gather Alana up in his arms and sequester her away to her chamber—to his also now—

Dougald led the group out.

Cameron had that right. Dougald would never have agreed to be locked up while his wife was without his protection. "Where is Laird Cameron?" Dougald asked.

"He has gone to speak with his niece to explain to her his reasoning. He didna want her to believe you had done anything wrong."

"Too late for that," Dougald scoffed.

"Everyone wishes to know how you do it," the man said.

Dougald glanced back at him. The man was smiling, blue eyes sparkling as he scratched his red beard. "You know. Always have a bonny lass come to your rescue when you are locked in a dungeon. We all were wagering which maid might come to free you, hoping they wouldna spoil the plan. But none of us believed the rumors were true, that a lassie would make the effort."

"Which of you won the bet?"

"None of us. No one thought to bet on Lady Alana. She had guards keeping her in her room. That was another reason Laird Cameron went to speak to her, to learn how she managed to break out of her room without alerting the guard."

"And break out the lads as well?" Dougald asked. He'd heard Tavis defend Alana by proclaiming her to be one of the MacNeills. He was proud of the boy. He assumed Callum, usually the quieter of the two, was ready to do battle as well.

"Aye, and them, too. They also had a guard. If the guards left their posts, they will regret it when Cameron gets through with them. Did you need anything?" the man asked.

"Your name?"

"Duff."

"Well, Duff, ensure Gunnolf and Niall have a chamber to sleep in, and ask two of our men to keep watch outside Alana's chamber door."

"Aye." The man said to one of the others, "Do as he says." To another man, he said, "Take Niall and Gunnolf to their chamber. I will escort MacNeill to the laird's chamber."

When they reached the laird's chamber, they found Bran outside of it, guarding it. He smiled at Dougald and bowed his head a little in acknowledgement, then he knocked on the door. "Dougald MacNeill is here, my laird."

Before Cameron could call out, Alana threw open the door and rushed into Dougald's arms. "Take me to bed."

Dougald smiled down at her, all his worries washed away in that moment. He looked up to see Cameron shake his head. "I will speak with you about this in the morn. Do as the lass wishes," Cameron said.

No apology, not that Dougald expected it. Bran was grinning.

Dougald swept Alana up in his arms and stalked off for her chamber. They were not rising early for mass or to break their fast. "I want to know how you escaped your chamber as well as the lads escaping theirs without alerting the guards."

In her chamber, he set her on her feet and went to shut the door and bolt it.

She said, "It was a secret chamber in the maids' room. Connell showed it to me."

Dougald shook his head. "I should have known he

would get you in trouble."

"Only to come rescue you," she said, in defense of her brother.

He was already removing her brat as she spoke. She was so bonny and all his.

"How did you think to rescue me with just two lads to aid you?"

"We thought there would be only one guard and three of us."

He dropped her plaid and began to pull off her *léine*. "You?"

"I have my dagger. And he wouldna have wished to harm me or fear my uncle's wrath."

"As well as he would have feared your uncle's wrath should he have allowed one woman and two lads to free us." He slipped off her chemise, then dropped it onto the floor and hurried to strip out of his own clothes. "But I will speak with him further of this matter of using me to get at those who had you leave the keep." He paused, looked at her, loving the sight of her, thinking of the difference from being in the dungeon to being in the lass's chamber ready to make love to her.

He gave her a wolfish smile as she smiled up at him, her brows raised slightly. Then he scooped her up in his arms and deposited her on the bed.

"This is where I belonged hours ago to keep you safe and from roaming freely about the castle on your own, lass." When she opened her mouth to speak, most likely to remind him that the two lads had accompanied her, he said, "With Callum and Tavis, aye, which wouldna have been enough."

Then he kissed her long and thoroughly, his tongue stroking hers. Her mouth curved upward, and her eyes were dark with intrigue. "You are so bonny."

He smiled and stroked her silky hair. Then he was kissing her again. She responded with the same kind of rabid enthusiasm, her tongue exploring his mouth, her tongue caressing his, encouraging his already heightened need to investigate every bit of her and give her pleasure. He loved how quickly she was beginning to be accustomed to him and was just as eager to make love back.

He cherished her and he couldn't imagine being anywhere else in the world but here, pleasuring her.

He settled between her legs. He was so ready to enter her, to fill her completely. Her body relaxed beneath his, her nipples hard against his chest.

He wanted to feel every luscious inch of her writhing beneath him as his mouth left hers and his tongue swept over her warm, soft skin, down her throat to a swollen breast, the nipple puckered. He licked and tasted and smiled as she moaned, her fingers grappling with his hair. She arched her body against him.

He prized her responsiveness, the way she wanted more. Her eyes were closed now. She sighed with pleasure. She was a dream. *His dream.* He stroked her woman's need, rubbing the knotted area that made her moan and writhe.

When he slipped his fingers into her wet heat, she cried out, shuddering. He continued to stroke her, to enjoy the way her body responded so quickly to his touch.

Unable to wait any further, he pressed his staff between her legs, parting her folds, entering her until he'd buried himself to the hilt. He loved joining with her, thrilled that she enjoyed their lovemaking just as much. He began to thrust into her and pressed his lips against hers again, her breathing fast, her heart beating hard. Her mouth kissed him back with just as much enthusiasm. She wrapped her legs around his waist, making the connection between them even more pleasurable.

"Dougald," she said on a half sigh, half whisper.

How could he ever have gotten so lucky to catch her in the heather?

She dug her heels in, her hands gripping his back as he dove in again and again. He never wanted the night to end as he drew close to completion. So close, wanting to hold on, to enjoy every minute. He thought of the bairn they would have. The bairns. Loving and laughing, and just as lovely as their mother.

Then he released, joining her, filling her, loving her.

He collapsed, kissed her cheek, combed his fingers through her silky hair and wondered why he hadn't stolen her away from her uncle years earlier.

"You, lass, *mo chridhe*, my heart," he said, then kissed her mouth, "you are the reason a man wouldna look any further."

"Just remember that, husband," Alana said, smiling, as he moved off her, pulled her into his embrace, and tugged the furs over them.

She felt as though she was in heaven, her body thrumming with the pleasure of his lovemaking, and the general overall happiness that being held in his arms, snuggling as man and wife, brought her.

She and Dougald were feeling naught but delight and pure satisfaction, so she knew she shouldn't bring this issue up now—though she had discussed it thoroughly with her uncle and he was agreeable. Yet she was afraid Dougald would leave on the hunt without her, and she wanted to go also. She didn't want to wait until tomorrow to tell him what she intended to do, either.

"About the hunt on the morrow—"

"Aye, lass," Dougald said, his voice already taking on a negative tone as if he thought she was going to tell him she didn't want him to go.

She tried very hard not to stiffen in his arms. "When we go on it tomorrow—"

*"We?"*

She knew he wouldn't like the plan.

# Chapter 26

It was one thing for Alana to come to rescue him from the dungeon while only the two lads guarded her—though Dougald hadn't liked that she had been running around the castle without a dozen of his men as escort to protect her should MacDonald have learned she was practically roaming about the keep alone—but the lass was *not* going on the hunt with them.

He could already feel her tensing in his embrace and wanted to head this argument off right away. He opened his mouth to speak, but she said, "My uncle agreed I would go on the hunt."

He snapped his mouth shut. Her uncle was no longer her guardian. She was Dougald's wife, and *he* was the one responsible for her protection.

Dougald wouldn't allow her to go with them when the MacDonalds would also be on the hunt. "Lass…," he said in a consoling manner.

"We will go to the place where my father was killed. My uncle has agreed."

Stiffening at the idea, Dougald knew he shouldn't have tried to placate her and instead told her the way of things. The forest she was talking about was near the stream that bordered their lands. He didn't want her that far from the safety of the keep—not with MacDonald and his men with them. Truth be told, he didn't want her that far away even if MacDonald and his men *weren't* riding with them on the hunt.

"Alana…"

"I have no' been back since my da was murdered," she said, her voice soft. She was stroking his chest in a tender way.

He wondered if she did so because it gave her solace or if it was a means of appeasing him. "Lass, I dinna—"

"I have been afraid to return," Alana admitted.

He couldn't see her face, but he thought she was fighting tears the way her voice choked a little with emotion. He hated for her to be distressed. He pulled her tighter and kissed her head. "You dinna—"

"I must return." She didn't sound like she was willing to concede.

"I canna—"

"MacDonald's men will stay at the castle tomorrow. Only he and his sons will be permitted to ride with us. All of your men can come on the hunt. My uncle will bring some of his men while the remainder will ensure MacDonald's men dinna cause mischief."

"Alana—" Dougald couldn't keep the censor out of his voice. He didn't want her to go. What was wrong with her uncle?

"Do you want to know why I am going?"

To give Dougald gray hairs!

"My uncle and I discussed it, and you know how he hasna wished me to talk about my ability to see and speak with spirits."

He scowled at the thought that his wife was discussing such matters with her uncle while Dougald was left out of the conversation! He would put a stop to it at once.

"It was many years ago, but what if some of the men are still there? The ghosts, I mean? What if they could tell me what they know? Mayhap even who had fought them?"

Dougald ground his teeth. He still didn't like the idea that she would return there with the MacDonald men. It was too far from the safety of the keep. Yet he was glad that her reasoning wasn't just that she always went on the hunt. If they could learn who the murderers were, he had to admit that was a sound motivation for taking her. As much as he *hated* to confess it.

"Of course," she said, still stroking his skin. If he wasn't so uptight about her going on the hunt, he would have had other thoughts in mind as she caressed him. "The ghosts may no longer be there."

True, which was a very good reason *not* to go.

"But if any of the men are still there and could help us clear up the matter concerning the murder of my da, wouldna it be a good idea?"

"Alana, lass…"

"I knew you would agree. That is what I love about you. You are strong and every bit a warrior, yet you are also verra clever."

He shook his head, but then kissed her forehead and held her tightly in his arms. "If it could help us to learn the truth about your da and the other men's death, 'tis worth a try. No' that I am saying I am keen on the notion of you going along. If someone else had your talents, I would take him or her with us instead and keep you safely guarded at the castle."

"Aye, but no one has my talent. And I thank you, husband, for calling it that."

"Ah, lass, your safety is all that matters to me."

"And in keeping me safe, we need to learn who was behind the murders."

"Do you really believe anyone will still be haunting the forest?"

She shook her head. "I dinna think so because the only ghosts I have ever met are ones that have no' been dead for verra long. But we shall see."

*\*\**

The next morning, they broke their fast quickly so they could be on their way to hunt, but Alana could barely eat because of the way the MacDonalds watched her. She was certain they were annoyed with her because she had left her uncle's lands. Then the MacNeills found her in their own territory, and Dougald had felt compelled to marry her.

The MacDonald men didn't scowl though, as if they were trying to be civil with her in the event that if someone dispatched her current husband, she'd suddenly have need of a new one. They didn't smile exactly, either, as if they were still so irritated with her, it was impossible to act pleased to be dining with her that morn.

She didn't care. All that mattered was that she was married to Dougald. She loved him for his protectiveness and—despite his misgivings about her going on the hunt and his desire to make her stay home to keep her safe—he had agreed to allow her to come. He fully accepted that she might be able to speak to someone at the site where her da and the others had died and no one—*but the dead*—had ever truly tolerated that she could do so. His believing in her meant the world to her.

With that thought in mind, she drew her chair a

little closer to Dougald's and smiled up at him. He returned the smile, though his brows were raised a little in question.

She mouthed, "I love you."

He chuckled and shook his head. "'Tis no' because you had your way with me, eh, lass?"

She laughed. "For that and so much more."

"I am speaking about the so much more."

That made her face flush. He was such a rogue, and she loved him for it. It was true that after he had conceded she could go on the hunt, they'd made love again. And that was another thing she treasured about him. He made her soar to the sun and to the moon and every bit of sky in between.

"Do you think 'tis a good idea to bring the lass with us?" MacDonald said to her uncle, garnering her attention.

Dougald immediately said, "Aye." He didn't give any reason to MacDonald, but instead winked at Alana and squeezed her hand. She appreciated him all the more.

She knew, despite what Dougald said, he was reluctant for her to go with them still. Yet, she assumed he had quickly responded to show MacDonald that *he* would answer for Alana, not her uncle. And that he was agreeable with Alana's participating on the hunt, particularly if MacDonald wasn't.

Cameron nodded, but continued to eat with haste.

"I didna believe she liked to hunt," MacDonald said, casting a concerned look her way.

She didn't think he appeared sincere.

"She has hunted with me and my men for years," Cameron said, then finished off his ale and rose from his seat. "'Tis time to ride."

Not only had he signaled the end of the meal, but the end of the conversation. Did her uncle think anyone might let it slip that she was going to try and commune with ghosts at the hunting site? Neither her uncle, nor her husband would speak of it to anyone. Certainly, she wouldn't.

Her uncle had not told MacDonald or his own men where they were going, either. Only Dougald's men were well aware of the location and knew to say nothing to the MacDonald or Cameron men about it.

She liked the MacNeill men. They all seemed to view her as one of *their* clan, rather than of the Cameron's. Just as Tavis had said last eve.

The lads were eager to hunt, but they knew that taking down a stag or wild boar was only incidental to why they were going. Every MacNeill man there, and the Cameron also, knew to safeguard Alana. If she hadn't planned to attempt to communicate with any spirits lingering about the woods, she wouldn't have gone because she knew she would be too much of a distraction.

Since they left the castle grounds before it was light, they would reach the killing grounds when it was late morn. She tried not to observe MacDonald and his sons too overly much, but she was curious to see how they reacted when her uncle led them so far away from the castle to hunt.

She and Dougald were riding behind MacDonald and his sons and her uncle, while Gunnolf and Niall flanked her and her husband. The lads and the rest of the men rode around them in a protective stance.

Not to her surprise, MacDonald finally said, "We

are going quite a distance, Laird Cameron. Seems the forest nearer your fortifications would have the same prey as the woods this far out. If we keep going in this direction, we will soon come to the MacNeill lands, will we no'?"

"We will hunt before we reach the MacNeill lands," Cameron assured him.

Hoel kept giving Alana backward glances the nearer they got to their destination. Which again made her think of her brother's words. Had Hoel actually seen Seana? And her brother?

If he could see ghosts like she could, and she was able to see some who remained behind where her da and his men had been murdered, would Hoel also be able to see these men? And hear what they had to say?

What if MacDonald had sent his own men to kill her da because he hadn't wanted her to marry MacIverson? And he thought he'd have a better chance convincing her uncle to agree to have her wed to Hoel instead?

She wondered where her brother and Seana were now. If they showed up, she might be able to observe Hoel's reaction to their arrival. Unless he saw them, but pretended not to.

They were getting close to where they needed to enter the woods when a man on horseback raced toward them. It was Angus, Dougald's youngest brother. She tensed. Something must be wrong.

Dougald went off to meet him and talked for a moment in private. She knew he did so, not wanting MacDonald and his sons to hear what was being said. She wanted to join them also, but Gunnolf and Niall kept her from going anywhere. She should be irritated, but she knew they only had her welfare in mind.

Dougald listened to his brother, nodded, then rode back with Angus to the group. He gave Cameron a slight tilt of his head, indicating they should move on.

"What happened?" Alana asked Dougald in a hushed voice as he rejoined her.

"Rob MacNeill was found." Dougald glanced at Gunnolf. "He has no hard feelings that you broke his nose and stated he was afraid if he told you who he was, you might have done worse."

Gunnolf shook his head. "Teaches the mon to lie to me."

"And the sick niece?" Alana asked.

"She is well now. By the time our healer saw to her, the cough she had was subsiding."

Alana's mouth gaped. She hadn't thought Odara had told her the truth. "But I thought you said the sheepherder had no niece."

"He hadna. At least that we knew of. And certainly before that, he wasna caring for her, until this last summer. His sister died and he took in the young lass. The girl and Kerwin fight all the time, but in a good way, Rob said."

She frowned. "Where was the niece when you gave the man a broken nose? Surely he didna leave her alone."

"She was sleeping in his shieling," Angus said.

"But where was the man's shieling? He wasna close to the border between our lands."

Angus shook his head. "You must have crossed the creek too far north."

"Och." She was annoyed with herself until she remembered what had happened because of not finding

Rob MacNeill—she was now married to Dougald MacNeill. "And the bairn?" She hoped that if the sheepherder had taken Odara in, he was marrying her and providing for the bairn she was carrying.

"Aye. Tavia, our healer, said the lass is breeding. Odara is living with the sheepherder. After one of our men took her, Rob MacNeill, and the lad, Kerwin, with them to see James, he had Rob and Odara wed."

Alana chewed on her lower lip. "They are keeping the lad?"

"Aye." Angus smiled at Alana. "The boy seemed verra happy to be living with the couple. He loves the sheep and said he has no brothers to throw him into smelly places now. And he said the girl, Tristina, has been a pest, but he smiled when he said it."

Relieved beyond measure that Odara had not lied to her and that she and the others were well, Alana smiled. "I am pleased they are all content, though I am certain my uncle willna like that Odara's shieling has been abandoned."

"Rob told James if the Cameron doesna mind, he can move his sheep and Odara's back to her shieling. She has an attachment to it as she was born there and her mother and da died there. Her shieling is bigger so will accommodate the burgeoning family. He wanted Cameron's permission first though," Angus said.

"What about Rob's own place?"

"He has a cousin interested in it."

Alana took a deep breath. "How did she get word to Pelly, Cook's assistant, that she was ill?"

"A man said that she would be paid well if she said she was ill when you arrived. She was already feeling unwell, so she didna believe she had done anyone any disservice. He said that you were in grave danger if you should wed the MacDonald's son, and if she cared for your well-being, she must do this. Concerned for you, she wished to aid the man—and you."

"So she hadna asked for me to see to her. But she was ill."

"Because of the bairn, aye. She had not sent anyone for there was no one to send. She thought she would get better. She had been fetching water when she heard a rider approaching, and though she thought you would come days earlier, she ran into the shieling and hurried to the bed just in case it was you."

"Which was why she was so flushed. I suspected since she was dressed, she might have been doing chores. Who was the man?"

"She didna know. Since she lives so far from Braniff Castle, she doesna know everyone."

Alana frowned. "Then she needs to be returned so she can identify the man for me, and I will thank him most profusely." She looked up at Dougald.

"I will reward the lass myself for sending you to me," Dougald said.

Angus looked at the three men riding ahead with Cameron. "Is that MacDonald and his sons?"

"Aye," Dougald said.

"What are *they* doing here?"

"They were concerned that Alana was missing. They didna like that I had married her."

Angus gave Alana a worried look. "Are you certain you want to return to the place your da died?"

"Aye, I am. 'Tis time to bury the past and learn the truth if 'tis possible."

They rode into the ancient pinewood forest mixed

with deciduous trees now, having to go single or double file in some places where the trees clustered together. The ground and tree trunks were covered in green moss. Leaves littered the forest floor and creeping woody undergrowth. Catching her attention, a red squirrel scampered up a tree while a bird pecked at a fallen pinecone nearby.

Before they rode much further, Dougald took hold of Alana's reins. "Sit with me, lass."

"You worry overmuch," she said, but didn't argue as he pulled her onto his saddle and Angus took her reins.

"Do you see anything?" Dougald asked, leaning forward, whispering in her ear.

"Trees."

He chuckled.

Cameron cast a look over his shoulder to see if Alana was all right. She smiled at him, but it was more of an anxious smile than anything. She knew he was leading them to where the actual battle had taken place. She had not seen where the men had killed her clansmen that day.

A shiver trailed up her spine, and she suddenly felt chilled. Dougald wrapped his arm around her tighter, pulling her closer to his body.

Then to her surprise, she heard Connell arguing with someone else in the woods up ahead. Seana? She couldn't see them.

No, not Seana. It was another man's voice. But she couldn't hear the words yet.

What was Connell doing here? He must have followed them, staying out of sight. Because of Hoel, mayhap?

She strained to recognize the sound of the other man's voice. If Connell and he were having words, the man had to be dead.

*Landon?*

A chill sliced through her.

"That way," she said, pointing in the direction of Landon and Connell's voices.

She glanced toward Hoel to see if he'd heard the voices, too. He was looking in the same direction. Another shiver stole through her. Dougald rode off toward the voices she heard and several of the men stayed with them.

Cameron said to the MacDonalds, "They must have spied something to hunt."

"Here, stop." She almost neglected to tell Dougald, forgetting he couldn't see them and would have run his horse right through her brother and Landon if she hadn't told him to stop. Because the men appeared so real, she kept thinking everyone witnessed what she did.

She wondered if this was in the vicinity where the killing had taken place. Whatever blood had been shed on the ground during the massacre had washed away over the years. Now ten years later, Landon and Connell fought each other with their ghostly swords, slashing at each other, attacking, parrying, falling back, and lunging forward. How could they fight? Why would they fight? They had been the best of friends.

She hated seeing them battling one another, flinching every time they sliced through each other, fearing they'd be injured, despite being dead.

Was Connell angry Landon had abandoned her to join their men in the fight? Or angry that Landon had told on him when Connell stole the bread and couldn't go on the hunt and hadn't been able to be there for his da or Alana?

Connell was ten years older than Landon now, but it didn't seem to matter. Neither could have the advantage fighting in their ghost forms.

Seana was nearby, her face ashen. How a ghost could look so real and lose all its color like a living being, Alana didn't know. Seana glanced at Alana, finally realizing she had arrived and shouted, "Make them stop!"

MacDonald said, "I see naught. Did someone see a stag and lose sight of it?"

That's when an arrow went whizzing through the air headed straight for Alana. The next thing she knew, she was falling or rather she and Dougald were falling from his horse.

# Chapter 27

The arrow came at her so quickly, Alana didn't even have time to scream. Thinking Dougald had been hit, panic and dread welled up inside her. She could barely breathe as he pinned her to the earth with the length of his body.

"Dougald," Alana said, trying to determine if he was all right as he took a heavy breath and didn't move off her right away. "Were you hit?"

"I am fine, lass," Dougald finally said, kissing her cheeks, her lips, her chin, his eyes dark with concern. "Are you?"

Seana was looking down at them, tears staining her cheeks as she wrung her hands.

"Aye, I am." She placed her hands on his face and saw the worry in his expression. "I am fine."

Several men galloped off in the direction the arrow had come, the MacDonald men with them. Others quickly surrounded Alana and Dougald, some to help, some to protect them. Angus and Niall quickly dismounted and drew close.

"I pulled you from the horse quickly enough that the arrow missed. I couldna have moved the horse out of the arrow's path that fast." Dougald moved off Alana and helped her to sit.

She let out her breath. "Thank the heavens he missed."

Connell appeared beside Seana, and she gave him a shove. As if she had given him an actual *physical* shove. When he fell back a step, he appeared as surprised as Alana was, his blue eyes wide, his mouth agape.

Seana furrowed her brows at him. "Why were you no' watching out for your sister? This Landon friend of yours is dead. You should have been looking out for Alana."

"He *isna* a friend of mine." Connell glanced over his shoulder.

Alana couldn't see if Landon was there or not. "What did you fight about, Connell? Did he know who killed our da and the others?"

"I was angry that he had left you behind. He wasna supposed to do so! Da would have had his head for it. But I wanted to know why he told Da that I had stolen the bread. *He* was the one who told me the family needed it. Then he waited for me to steal it before he reported that I was sneaking out to take it to the family before we broke our fast that morn."

She frowned. "And?"

"He...he said he knew the men were going to have a confrontation during the hunt. But he only thought the men would talk to Da. He didna want me there. He was afraid I would be killed if a fight ensued."

Alana stared at her brother, her lips parted, speechless.

Dougald rubbed her arm, looking anxious as he watched her closely. "What is he saying, lass? What does Connell know?"

She couldn't answer Dougald. She had to know more about what had gone on that day.

"If he…knew Da and the others were going to be attacked, he was in on it. How…why…?" She couldn't even form the rest of the words as she tried to think back to that day. Landon had acted hesitant to leave her, yet he also seemed to want to help the others. Had he had a change of heart when he heard the cries from their men as they were being butchered?

"He said he thought the men would talk, but Da wouldna hear of it," her brother said.

"Landon lies!" she said, as the grief at having lost her da and all the rest of the men washed over her.

"Aye, that was what I told him," Connell said.

Alana folded her arms, her brow furrowed. "I want to speak with him."

Dougald helped her up from her seated position on the ground. As she looked for Landon, she didn't see him at first. "Landon! Show yourself."

Then he was there, as real as life. His mouth curved down, his blue eyes looking at her, he lowered his gaze to the forest floor as if he couldn't stand to see the recrimination in hers.

"Who killed our people?" More than anything, she had to know who had done the horrible deed.

"MacIverson's men," Landon said. "He said you were a witch. That you could…" Landon motioned with his sword at her. "…speak with the dead. Like this."

"I dinna understand." Tears streaked down her cheeks, and she brushed them angrily away. She didn't want Landon to see her in distress, to show weakness, when she wished only to show strength. "Why did he no' just say he didna want to go through with the marriage contract?"

"Your da wouldna agree. He wanted an alliance

with their clan. He didna know MacIverson believed you to be a witch."

"Why did he want to marry me in the first place?"

Landon licked his lips and wouldn't look at her.

"Landon, why?"

"He was seeing someone else. He wanted to continue to see her. She said if he married you, she could."

"Who?"

Landon shook his head.

"You dinna know?"

Landon wouldn't say. Either he didn't know, or he didn't want to reveal the truth.

"But...but the man in the woods said that MacIverson wanted me. That they were to take me to him."

"Nay, someone else. But I dinna know who."

She did not believe MacIverson and his men had any intention of talking with her da to change his mind. They had decided the sword was the only way to settle matters.

"I dinna understand. If he wanted to see this other woman, than why did he decide he no longer wanted me?"

"The woman's husband learned of her indiscretion and said he would kill her and him if he discovered she went to MacIverson again."

Alana's mouth hung agape, and then she swallowed hard. She thought frantically about what she needed to ask. Landon was already fading, as if his mission was to tell her the truth about what had happened, and then he'd be free from this world where he no longer belonged.

"Who is she?"

He shook his head, his gaze on hers now.

As much as she hated that he had not warned her da, she had to remember Landon had protected her brother. "You saved my brother's life."

"Aye," Landon said. "But when our men were set upon, I was torn. Protect you, or help them."

"And you got yourself killed."

"I didna deserve to live. Your da was furious with me for leaving you behind. But then one of the men trying to kill him was angry with me for leaving you. He shouted at me that I was supposed to stay with you and keep you from running. I thought your da would kill me instead for the traitor I was. He didna. I will never forget the look on his face—of condemnation and disbelief. He turned his back on me, but couldna know if I would shove my sword into him or no'.

"Still, he continued to fight the man in front of him as if he had no choice as the other man was older and more battle-trained, or your da didna think I would kill him. Our men were outnumbered. I knew if I fought the MacIverson men, I would die, too. But I also believed that my leaving you alone, and mayhap their worry I might turn on them in the future, meant I wasna going to live long either. I fought the man alongside your da. We killed him, but then I was attacked and the much bigger man struck me such a blow, I didna live."

Alana couldn't help the shudder that wracked her body. He had done wrong, but how many times over the years had she made wrong choices? Reckless decisions, thinking she knew best? Only his wrong decision caused men to lose their lives.

Landon took a deep breath, then frowned at

Connell. "I save your life and this is how you end up anyway?" He waved his sword at Connell.

Connell glowered back at him. "You were a traitor to our people, to Da. If I could kill you to avenge him and the others now, I would."

Dougald had wrapped his arm around Alana's shoulders, though she could barely feel his warmth she was so cold and concentrating—trying to concentrate—on what to ask next.

But Landon spoke again. "Your da rode back for you, only he and his horse were already dead. I heard him shout for you to hide. I felt badly for you. You were so young. I was afraid of what they might do to you should they find you. But there was naught I could do about it then. Your da led you home. I couldna follow. I was stuck here. Everyone else left me. How long has it been? I canna believe you are a woman now full grown."

"Ten years," Alana said. "Who was the other man who wanted me, Landon?"

"I dinna know. I never knew. Just that the one didna want you, and he thought to turn you over to the other who did."

"MacDonald?" she asked. She was glad MacDonald and his sons were not hearing this.

Landon shook his head. "I dinna know." His voice was merely a whisper as his body was fading fast.

"Why did you turn on our people?"

"They said you were a witch. MacIverson would have drowned you. I couldna let that happen. The other man who wanted you knew, yet he would have kept you safe."

She thought again of how her da had come for her

to help her find the way home. Tears welled up in her eyes again, and she swiped away more trailing down her cheeks.

"I couldna tell Connell." Landon looked in her brother's direction. "He believed, as everyone else did, that MacIverson wanted you. Only your uncle—he didna like the man and tried to convince your da to choose another."

"I chose another," Alana said, holding Dougald's arms around her.

Landon looked at Dougald. "A MacNeill?" He snorted. "What are our Highlands coming to?" He took a deep breath. "I am sorry, Alana, for leaving you alone in the woods. But if I had stayed with you, they would have found you."

"I understand," she said. She wanted to tell him she forgave him, as upset as she was still that he had not warned her da or the other men what was to happen. Mayhap her da would not have listened, but Landon should have made the attempt.

She didn't have time to tell Landon she forgave him, because he melted into nothingness right before her eyes. It was different than when her brother left her alone to come and bother her at some other time. The spirit brightened a little right before he or she vanished all together. She knew he was gone, and she hoped after all these years he would find peace.

She stood staring at the spot for what seemed an eternity. Everyone was quiet that stood nearby her. Off in the distance, she heard men shouting, probably trying to find the man who attempted to shoot her. Had the man tried to kill her to keep her from telling what she learned from Landon? How would anyone know she could learn the truth from a ghost? That a ghost was standing here talking to her? Unless Hoel heard him speaking with her and thought she might learn the truth. That the MacDonalds had been involved in her da's murder.

Connell said, "I am sorry, Alana, that I hadna known."

She shook her head. "None of us did. You had naught to do with it."

"I might have."

She frowned at him. "How would you have known? You wouldna have risked all our lives."

"Nay, earlier, when we visited MacIverson and Da was making the marriage contract up. Someone who was about my age jested that you were special. He kept on and on and I finally said you were."

"Connell," she whispered.

"Aye. I think the lad was trying to learn the truth about you. He acted as though your being different was a good thing. He must have told MacIverson."

She shook her head. "I saw a ghost girl the one time we visited. I didna speak to her, but MacIverson and his people were always watching me. Mayhap I led him to believe I was distracted by something when I shouldna have been. I am sure they knew something about me and were trying to prove they were correct."

Dougald rubbed her arm, and then realizing he was waiting to hear what was being said, she turned to him. "Landon said MacIverson's men did it."

"A MacIverson didna loose that arrow," Cameron said, rejoining the party, her uncle furious and red-faced.

"How do you know it wasna MacIverson or one of

343

his men?" she asked, her heart pounding. She was afraid to hear who had.

"One of Dougald's men saw him. It was Gilleasbuig."

Her heart skipped a beat. And then she fumed. How many traitors were there among her people?

"I should have killed the mon, when I had the chance," Dougald growled, his arms wrapping securely around her again.

She felt chilled to the marrow of her bones. Her uncle had to decide Gilleasbuig's fate, but she knew if Dougald had any say in it, he'd kill him.

"They have caught him, my laird!" Bran shouted from the forest beyond.

She felt only a shadow of relief that they had him now. She didn't want to see what they would do to him. She only knew that she had to question him.

Dougald helped Alana mount, then they rode with the rest of his men to where they were holding Gilleasbuig. He was lying on his stomach, his black hair hiding his face as three arrows protruded from his back. His breathing was labored. Dougald helped Alana down, then they joined the men surrounding Gilleasbuig.

Before her uncle could question him, Alana said, "Why did you try to kill me?" She had it in mind that he wanted to silence her before she learned from the ghosts that he was involved.

He turned on his side and stared up at her. His blue eyes were glassy. "Nay ye, lass."

Did he think to win her uncle over if he lied? Angered that she'd saved his life and he repaid her by trying to take hers, but also infuriated that his arrow could have hit Dougald, she shook with outrage. "You aimed at me! Dinna tell me you saw a deer behind me and thought to hit it!"

Dougald slipped his arm around her shoulders in a comforting manner. Or mayhap he was worried she might use her dirk on the man to finish him off.

Gilleasbuig narrowed his eyes at Dougald. Her eyes widened. "You...you were trying to kill Dougald?"

"Ye had..." Gilleasbuig gritted his teeth and closed his eyes, then opened them. Pain reflected in them, like the time when she'd treated his sword wound. "...a marriage contract...with Hoel. Ye...belonged to...him."

"And MacIverson? Think you I didna belong with him, either?"

Gilleasbuig spat out blood and coughed. "Ye...saved...my...life, my lady," he managed with great difficulty to say. "He thought...ye a...witch. He would...have got ye...with child...and once the bairn was born...drowned ye."

She cringed when Gilleasbuig brought up the witch aspect in front of everyone here. She wished she could order everyone but Dougald away while she questioned the man. "So you helped the men who killed my da and our people?"

"I...didna. I...I dinna know...who did it."

She glanced at MacDonald. His face was strained. Was he worried Gilleasbuig might implicate him?

"The night in the tent. You came to kill me," she said.

"Nay, take ye to Hoel. Ye..." Gilleasbuig took a shuddering breath. "Ye belonged to him."

"I was married to Dougald!" She let out her breath and folded her arms. "Why did you want Odara for your wife?"

He raised his brows at her as if he needn't say as the reason was perfectly clear.

"She didna want you," Alana said. Surely that counted for something.

"She didna…know me." Gilleasbuig stared off for a moment, then frowned. "If ye could have been mine…"

Cameron snorted.

"I wouldna…have wanted Odara," Gilleasbuig said.

Her lips parted. He could not mean it, yet he sounded so sincere. A chill ran through Alana. In his odd way, had he really wanted her? And since he couldn't have Alana, he wanted to get as far away from her as he could by marrying Odara because she lived near the MacNeill border? Dougald had said their own healer, Tavia, had trouble with saving a man's life and then he thought she wanted him and she should be his.

"I saved your life because it needed saving," she said. "I would have done the same for any man."

"No' this…time…eh, lass?" Gilleasbuig asked. His gray-blue eyes were dimming. "No'…this…time."

She was certain she couldn't save him. He was too badly wounded. Even so, she glanced at her uncle to see what he wanted her to do. He shook his head at her, his expression dark and foreboding. She knew he would have the man killed for trying to murder her husband if he lived.

"You killed one of our kin at the camp. The man guarding us," she said.

"Nay."

She was so surprised, she just stared at him. Was he lying now? "If you didna, who did?"

His breathing was so labored now, she didn't think they'd learn much else. She was desperate to learn all she could. "Gilleasbuig, who killed the man on guard duty when we camped?"

He opened his mouth to speak.

Waiting in anticipation, she held her breath. "Gilleasbuig?"

But he was looking off into the woods. He appeared unable to focus any longer. She moved closer, though Dougald frowned down at her. "Alana."

"The man is dying. We must know." She crouched in front of him. "Gilleasbuig?"

His eyes stared at nothing. She touched his chest, but felt no heartbeat. "He is dead."

Her voice was hollow. She couldn't believe it. Someone else was involved with this vile business? Someone else who had come to the camp that night? Had Gilleasbuig known the man was going to kill the guard?

"Alana," Dougald said, pulling her away from Gilleasbuig's body.

Cameron said to a couple of his men, "Take care of him."

"Aye, my laird."

"Let us hunt, shall we?" Cameron asked the MacDonald men, then cast Alana a knowing look.

She realized her uncle wanted to leave her alone with her escort while he moved the MacDonalds away from there, mayhap so that if Gilleasbuig was still about, only in ghostly form now, she could speak with him further.

MacDonald narrowed his eyes at her. "Lady Alana looks distraught. Mayhap we should return to the keep after what has happened."

"Nay," she quickly said. "I will stay with Dougald and a couple of other men, and we will catch up. Enjoy the hunt, my laird."

MacDonald cast a quick look at Hoel. He nodded and turned to Alana. "I will stay with you and—"

"Nay," Dougald said so vehemently, Alana was afraid he'd unsheathe his sword to make the point more clear if Hoel did not get it. "My wife doesna need your assistance."

Hoel bowed his head to Dougald in the slightest manner possible, yet as the men began to mount to hunt, Hoel hung around, and she thought he must be able to see the ghosts. Or he truly believed *she* could.

Was he hoping to learn if Gilleasbuig said the MacDonalds took part in this sordid affair?

His fists on his hips, Connell stood with Seana some distance away, and he was glowering at Hoel as if he wanted to take the man to task for having ogled Seana's breasts. Or mayhap it was because Dougald was now Alana's husband, and he'd told the man to move along and Hoel wasn't doing so.

Connell said, "Hoel, you look at Seana's breasts like that again and you will be feeling my sword!"

# Chapter 28

Seana was so flushed, she appeared to want to crawl into the earth and hide. Or kill Connell.

Alana couldn't blame her, but she knew why Connell had taken Hoel to task for ogling Seana. Or at least she *thought* she knew the reason.

Hoel was just as red-faced, his eyes wide as he stared at Connell, finally dropping his gaze to Seana for a brief glance. He quickly turned and said to Alana, "I am off to join the others on the hunt. Please excuse me."

He mounted his horse and galloped off to join the men hunting.

Connell folded his arms and looked down at Seana. "I told you he could see you, and he was indeed—"

Not saying a word, Seana slugged Connell in the chest with her fist, knocking him backward a step, then vanished.

He grinned at Alana. "See? I was right." Then he vanished, too.

\*\*\*

Dougald thought he'd be used to Alana's conversations with the dead by now, but he couldn't get accustomed to seeing her like this. The emotions played across her face—the anxiety, the shock, the upset, and then the merest hint of a smile. He was dying to know what she was hearing and seeing. He wanted to be there for her, but he felt he could do naught but watch her.

He glanced at Angus and Niall, who were both observing her just as closely. Angus raised his brows at Dougald in question, but no one said a word. Gunnolf was watching also, and he was just as quiet, while the rest of Dougald's men provided a protective guard.

Alana didn't say anything for a moment, then once Hoel MacDonald was well out of range of hearing, she said, "Gilleasbuig, I must know who killed the guard at our camp. Did you draw the man away, and then another killed him?"

Bran, Cameron's military advisor, drew near and folded his arms as he whispered to Dougald, "Has she learned anything yet?"

Dougald shook his head. He wondered then if Cameron had sent Bran so he could ensure that all the MacDonalds left for the hunt and Alana could question Gilleasbuig further.

Alana kept listening, then looking around. Dougald suspected Gilleasbuig wasn't talking to her or she would have remained focused on one location.

"She was conversing with her brother before this, aye?" Bran asked, still speaking quietly so as not to disturb Alana's concentration.

Dougald nodded. He didn't want her to have to stay here for any longer than necessary, nor did he want to bring her here again unless she wished it.

She turned to Dougald. "I have dried flowers in my pouch I want to leave in the area where the men died."

"Aye, lass. As you wish." Dougald helped her onto his horse and once he was seated behind her, they rode in silence.

Angus and Niall flanked them whenever they could in the thickly treed forest.

"You look quite upset," Dougald whispered against her ear, not wishing anyone to hear who should not.

"Hoel can see the dead."

Dougald didn't say anything right away. What if the lass preferred a husband who had special talents like she did? They could discuss what was being talked about between ghosts and the like. Hoel would be able to understand what she was going through much better than Dougald could. Not that he had any intention of giving the lass up, but the notion did bother him that the man might have suited the lass well after all.

Alana cleared her throat.

Dougald waited expectantly to hear what she had to say.

She didn't say anything. She fidgeted in the saddle. He pulled her closer and kissed the top of her bonny head.

She still didn't speak.

"Alana," he said softly, meaning to tell her that she should feel free to speak to him about anything.

She blurted, "He was eying your sister's endowments."

Dougald was so taken aback by what his sweet lassie said, it took him a moment to recover. "Hoel?"

"Aye. Connell was incensed. Seana didna believe Hoel could see ghosts. But Connell proved her wrong when he told Hoel to quit ogling Seana or he would use his sword on him. That was when Hoel took off."

Fighting laughing out loud and possibly embarrassing his wife in front of the other men, Dougald grinned. He imagined Connell giving Hoel hell and his sister blushing furiously, if ghosts could do such a thing, and then seeing for himself that Hoel had become flustered. The way Hoel lighted out of there, Dougald knew someone had said something that had shaken him.

"I feared Gilleasbuig told Hoel something that scared him, and he rode off to warn his da and brother."

"Nay. Gilleasbuig appears to be gone. 'Twas my brother who scared off Hoel." She turned and looked up at Dougald. "I think my brother has finally found the woman for him. Although I canna say she feels the same about him."

Dougald smiled down at Alana and kissed her lips. "All that matters is that you want to be with me." He hoped he would see no doubt in her expression, still concerned that she might believe Hoel would have suited her better because of their unique abilities.

She studied Dougald for a moment. "You look worried."

He shook his head. If she hadn't considered the merits of being with someone like Hoel, he didn't want her thinking in that direction.

She narrowed her eyes at him. "You dinna believe I would be interested in Hoel, now do you?"

"Of course no'," Dougald said, frowning.

She smiled brightly. "Aye, you do. And nay, I am no' interested in him. But, Dougald, if we take a tumble from your horse in the future, next time I want to be on top."

"Do you now, lass?" He was certain his smile turned wicked.

She blushed furiously, and he laughed. How could he have gotten so lucky to find her all alone on their lands?

"You are as bad as my brother."

"You love me for it."

"Aye, I do," Alana said, smiling at him.

Dougald loved her. He glanced at his brother. "Are you going with us back to Braniff, Angus?"

"Aye. After I was to give you the news about Rob MacNeill, James wanted me to watch your back. He said he has plenty of men to take care of our lands. But he worries about you. What if you end up in a dungeon, or worse?"

Niall laughed. "He has already done so once. If you fancy ending up in the dungeon with him, be my guest."

Angus gaped at Dougald. "Already?" He shook his head. "All of us who were betting believed it would take you longer than that." He grinned. "Then the next question is, did a lassie free you?"

"Aye," Alana said.

Angus raised his brows at her, still smiling.

"Someone had to. If I had learned he had good reason to be in there, he would still be there." She tilted her chin up.

Angus laughed. "'Tis a shame you are already Dougald's wife, Lady Alana. 'Tis a shame."

Dougald's arms tightened around Alana. She was all his.

After she left flowers in the area that her kinsmen had died and said a prayer, they all mounted to join the others on the hunt.

Bran was riding in front of them and tossed back over his shoulder, "Laird Cameron said we could return Lady Alana to Braniff after her business here was finished if she preferred, rather than continue with the hunt."

He was speaking to Dougald but he knew she'd wish to have her say and so he remained quiet, waiting for her to speak.

When she didn't, he looked down at her and said, "Alana? What do you wish?"

She looked up at him. "Take me home."

"Aye, lass."

She quickly said to Bran. "Tell my uncle where we will be so he doesna worry about me."

Bran said, "Mayhap one of the lads can ride ahead and let him know."

"Nay," Alana said, surprising Dougald. "They are here for my protection."

He wondered why she would not agree with Bran if one of the boys wished to do as Bran suggested. Mayhap they wished to take part in the hunt. She had plenty of men protecting her.

Tavis immediately said, "Lady Alana is right. I will stay with her." He patted his sword and smiled. The lad would have a big head when he returned to Craigly Castle. *If* he ever returned.

Callum said, "Aye, me, too." He patted *his* sword, mimicking Tavis. His friend grinned at him.

"Would anyone else prefer to hunt?" Bran asked, brows raised, looking hopeful.

A number of men either said no, though Dougald knew they'd love to. Others shook their heads in the negative. Their allegiance was to him and Lady Alana.

Bran studied Alana and her resolve, then nodded. "I will tell Laird Cameron what you are doing." Then he rode off.

"Hurry back to the castle," Alana whispered to

Dougald.

He turned his horse and headed in that direction. "What is it, lass?"

"We return and question the staff."

"About?"

"Why Brighid went to see her sister before I was found and returned home. I have been giving it some thought and I dinna believe she would have done so."

"Brighid?"

"My maid. She said she was ill the morning I left to speak with Odara. I could see no symptoms of her being ill but had taken her word for it. I had no reason to doubt her at the time. But dinna you think it odd that Brighid couldna travel with me when I left the keep? Then we return home, both Pelly and Brighid are gone?"

He didn't see the significance. Brighid could have been ill, then recovered sufficiently to want to travel. "Did anyone say where Brighid had gone?"

"Aye, her father, Turi. My uncle's advisor. She was to have seen her sister. But the issue of Pelly bothers me as well. She was so nervous. I believed at the time that it was because she thought I would be upset that my uncle didna tell me that Odara was sick. Now I think she must have been concerned that I would catch her in a lie. No' that Odara wasna feeling poorly, but 'twas the man who had spoken with Odara who had passed along the word. And that no lad had told my uncle that Odara had been unwell."

Dougald turned to Gunnolf. "Have two men return to see Rob MacNeill and have him and Odara meet us at Braniff Castle. Rob can ask Laird Cameron's permission to move in with Odara at her shieling. Alana can learn if Odara recognizes the man who came to see her and would pay for her to convince Alana to cross into MacNeill lands. Ensure Odara knows she isna in trouble for any of what happened and neither is the man who wished Alana to leave."

"Aye, will do." Gunnolf rode back to speak with some of the men.

"Dougald, there is another odd matter," Alana said. "Apparently MacIverson didna wish to marry me, except to see a woman who promised herself to him if he agreed to wed me. But her husband learned of the affair and said he would kill both her and MacIverson if the two of them should meet. That was when MacIverson decided he didna want me. He couldna convince my da to end the marriage contract and so MacIverson had Da killed. But someone else wanted me that day. Someone who knew I had abilities and wished to wed me. The men that were searching for me said that they were to take me to him."

"Hoel MacDonald," Dougald guessed.

"I suspect so."

"Then were MacDonald's men also in on the killing?"

"Mayhap."

"Who was the woman who was seeing MacIverson?" Dougald asked.

"Landon wouldna say or he didna know. I couldna tell."

Dougald was quiet as they rode back to Braniff, then finally asked, "Was the woman with your clan?"

"I think so since MacIverson thought to see her further if he wed me. So it would be someone that would…" She paused, a cold sweat breaking out all over her skin.

"Someone that was close to you. Who was intimate with you?" Dougald asked, his voice dark.

"My maids, but none were married."

"No' a maid then. Who else was close to you who might have used that as an excuse to visit you at MacIverson's castle when she truly wished to see MacIverson and no' you?"

"I hadna sisters, nor cousins." Alana frowned, then glanced back at Dougald. "I only had my aunt, who was Cameron's wife. She died three years ago. But she is the only one who would have been close to me, the right age at the time, and married. She was ten years older than me. And I was nine."

"And your uncle is forty-nine now. So he would have been thirty years older than her. And MacIverson?"

Alana shook her head. "Younger. Mayhap ten years older than my aunt. That would have made MacIverson twenty-nine. Since I was so young at the time, my aunt would have looked a lot more appealing to him than I would." A cold chill spread through her. "I never knew. Never suspected."

She felt terrible for her uncle and glad he had tried to change her da's mind about a marriage to MacIverson. Had Alana wed MacIverson and he'd continued to see her aunt...

She shook her head, not even wanting to imagine such a horrible thing. She could envision her uncle flying into a rage and killing both her aunt and MacIverson. The thought of what he'd gone through if it were true, would most likely have made him unhappy about her brother, who had such a way with the lasses.

"But this is only conjecture. We canna know for certain unless my uncle tells us the truth," Alana said.

"Aye. 'Twould make sense though. He would tell James naught concerning his reasoning for no' wanting you married to MacIverson. Mayhap he hadna wished your da, his brother, to know the truth, either. A man learning of a wife's infidelity might cause him to feel inadequate, and he would hide the truth from others."

"If 'tis true, I am glad I knew naught about it growing up." Alana's mother had died when she was young, but Alana was six and ten when her aunt died. She had been much closer to her uncle than her aunt. She had always believed it was because her aunt had never had any children of her own and wasn't comfortable around children. Mayhap that wasn't the reason at all.

When they arrived at Braniff Castle, Alana had new concerns to deal with. Questioning the staff and learning who else might have seen or overheard something that would clue them in as to who had tried to protect her and from whom.

\*\*\*

Dougald noted MacDonald's men milling around the inner bailey, talking with each other. Dougald's own men and Cameron's were actually speaking to one other as if they had decided the MacNeills were here to stay. At least Dougald was. But they were making some headway as far as getting along, and Dougald was pleased to see it.

The MacDonald men scowled at him, but Dougald's men and Cameron's greeted him with well wishes. Dougald explained to everyone that Laird Cameron and Laird MacDonald and the others were still on the hunt.

He didn't say anything more than that, expecting Laird Cameron to speak about what happened to Gilleasbuig with his own men. As soon as Dougald escorted Alana inside the keep, he asked, "Would you like to wash up a bit before you question the kitchen staff?"

"Nay. I wish to do this before my uncle returns. I dinna want him to stop me."

Gunnolf, Angus, and Niall stayed close, ever protective as the lads followed behind them.

When they reached the kitchen, they found Cook supervising the making of a mutton stew and baking loaves of bread. The aroma of the bannocks cakes made from barley and oat, and cullen, the tastiest smoked fish soup Cook created at Craigly Castle and he wondered how it would compare. It made Dougald's stomach growl, to his chagrin.

Alana startled Cook and her assistants when she hurried inside the kitchen and asked, "Where is Pelly?"

Cook was a stout woman who appeared to sample much of the food before it was served, her blue eyes huge as she stared at Alana. Then Cook's lips thinned.

"Aye, I know she was convinced to tell me to leave our lands and she thought it was for my own good. I wish to reward her, no' punish her." Alana took Dougald's hand. "I am grateful to her."

Cook wiped the flour off her hands onto a cloth, looking away from Alana's inquisitive gaze.

Dougald sorely wanted to shake the truth from the woman. Her four assistants were quietly watching. They were young, mayhap five and ten or so, learning the trade.

"When Odara arrives, she will be able to identify the man who wished her to convince me to cross the MacNeill lands. I will learn the truth. Might as well be now, rather than later," Alana said. She spoke softly, but with an edge to her words.

Dougald folded his arms and gave the woman an imperious look, letting her know that if she didn't answer Alana to his satisfaction, he would take Cook to task in his own way.

"I canna say, my lady," Cook said, trying to ignore Dougald, but she glanced his way a couple of times, and she was still wiping off her now clean hands.

Alana frowned at her. "She isna with Brighid at her sister's place, is she?"

This time Cook visibly paled. Aye, Alana had the truth of the matter now.

"All right." She turned to Dougald. "I wish to go to Brighid's sister's manor. 'Tis only a half-day's ride from here. We should arrive by nightfall and…"

"Nay, my lady," Cook said. "You guessed right. She is there."

Alana frowned at her. "Who put her up to it?"

"I canna say."

"You mean you willna say."

"Nay, I mean, I canna say. I wasna privy to any of it. All I know is Brighid came for her, said that her sister needed Pelly to aid her sister's cook for a time, and they left."

Alana folded her arms. "How did they act?"

"Pelly had been dropping things constantly. She broke so many eggs, I had to give her another task. I had never seen her so clumsy in the year she has been with us. And Brighid? She was wringing her hands, could barely stand still, looking like she wanted to grab Pelly and drag her out of the kitchen as quickly as she could. I was glad she took her, mind ye. The girl was causing too much havoc. I did think it odd that Brighid was leaving before she learned if ye were all right or got yer permission. But then her da came and had Duff take them to her sister's place, and that was that."

"When was this?"

"As...as soon as..." Cook glanced at Dougald, then said to Alana, "...as soon as Pelly had shared word with ye that Odara was sick."

"And who told Pelly to speak with me?" When Cook didn't say, Alana added, "The person should be rewarded, for heaven's sakes. Come, who told Pelly to give me the message that Odara was sick?"

Before Cook could answer her, Turi hurried into the kitchen, looking troubled, his brow deeply furrowed, "Dougald, your men and the MacDonald are fighting. I canna order them to stop. Will you?"

Dougald asked, "What about your men?"

"Bran is in charge of them. He is still on the hunt, I take it."

"All right. Angus, escort Alana up to her chamber and stay with her. Niall, you and Gunnolf, come with me." Dougald kissed Alana briefly, then hurried out of the kitchen, saying to the lads, Callum and Tavis, "Remain outside Alana's chamber until I come for her."

"Aye," they said, and hurried off with Angus and Alana to her chamber.

"Do we kill the MacDonalds?" Niall asked.

# Chapter 29

As Dougald and the others headed for the door of the keep, he couldn't tell if his cousin sounded hopeful or not that they might have to fight the MacDonald clansmen to the death. "If they are trying to kill our men, what do you think, Niall? If they are just angry that Hoel MacDonald didna have Alana for his wife and are fighting without using their weapons, we will watch. 'Twill make our lads fight harder."

Though the MacDonald men should not have their weapons, and if they did, that was another matter altogether.

"The Cameron clansmen should be fighting alongside ours," Niall said, as they emerged from the keep.

"Och, we have been the Camerons' enemies for years," Dougald said. "That willna change overnight."

The Camerons were watching the melee as if observing a practice fight, their arms folded across their chests, only glancing in Dougald's direction as he, Gunnolf, and Niall approached. The MacNeills and the MacDonalds were fighting, using their fists. Dougald was relieved to see no one was wielding a weapon.

"Put your backs into it, lads," Dougald said to his men and several smiled as they fought even harder. "See, it helps to give a little encouragement." He turned to one of the Camerons and asked, "Who started it?"

"One of the MacDonalds said that one rake was easy to get rid of. The next would be a wee bit harder."

Which sounded a lot like the MacDonalds had something to do with Connell's death, or why else would one of the men have said such a thing?

Dougald narrowed his eyes. "Which man said it?"

"That one over there," the Cameron said, motioning to a red-haired and bearded man.

Dougald headed for the redhead, Gunnolf and Niall quickly joining him. When they reached him, Dougald grabbed hold of his arm, effectively allowing the MacNeill clansmen to slug the MacDonald in the jaw.

The MacDonald swore in Gaelic as Gunnolf and Niall grappled his arms as everyone else ceased fighting to see what was going on.

"Who killed Connell?" Dougald asked, grabbing the man by the throat, his dirk in his hand in an instant. Dougald was so angry, he had to fight injuring him before he learned the truth.

"Ward Cameron, as far as I know," the redhead said. "Husband of the woman Connell was tupping. Canna blame the mon for wanting Connell dead. If 'twas my woman, I would have felt the same. Any mon here would."

"Your name?"

"Gair."

"Well, Gair, who set Connell up to be murdered?"

"This has naught to do with us," Gair choked out.

"Niall, can you fetch Alana for me?" Dougald asked his cousin.

"Aye," Niall said, releasing hold on the man's arm, and stalking off to the keep.

Immediately, one of Cameron's men seized Gair's free arm. "My name is Kvist," the Cameron said, his blond hair and blue eyes reminding Dougald of Gunnolf. "If these men had anything to do with Connell's death, we want to know also. We thought 'twas strictly a case of a husband's revenge."

Dougald nodded to Kvist. Then he turned his attention to Gair. "Laird Cameron said that Ward and his wife ran off. Where did they go?"

"How would—"

Dougald poked the dirk at the man's chest. "'Twould be easy to make an example of you, and then take the next man to task."

"They were to meet a Cameron at a hovel south of here," one of the MacDonalds said, who was watching the affair.

Dougald glanced at the black-haired man. Both Dougald's men and the Cameron's had taken the MacDonalds in hand in case they thought to free Gair.

A Cameron's fist connected with the black-haired man's jaw. "Which one of us would have done such a thing? Speak, mon!"

The MacDonald spit out blood. "I dinna know!"

"How do you know the man was a Cameron then?" Dougald asked.

"A couple of us overheard someone—we didna recognize the voice—say that Connell Cameron was in the way and they knew how to get him out of the way."

"By setting him up with Ward's wife?" Dougald asked.

"Aye. 'Twould be easy to do since he was already seeing her," Gair said.

Which was what Dougald had suspected all along.

"Did she take part willingly?"

"I dinna know."

Alana strode out of the keep, her cheeks flushed as Niall and Angus flanked her, the lads beside them.

"What has happened?" she asked, seeing the MacDonald men in custody and Dougald with his dirk in hand.

"These men know something about your brother's murder. They say a Cameron was involved."

"Who?" she asked.

Dougald took her aside and said for her hearing only, "He said a man was to meet them at a hovel south of here. I would need some of your men to search this place as they would most likely know of it and if Ward and his wife are holed up there, they will recognize them."

"I will go also," Alana said.

"Nay. I wish you to stay here. I only wanted you to know I would be leaving and return as soon as I can. Angus and the lads will stay with you."

"What if my brother could help when you apprehend them?" she whispered.

Dougald frowned at her. "How?"

"Connell could tell me things that occurred when he was murdered. I could share what he says with Ward and Gwyn, mayhap frighten them into telling the truth."

"I dinna want you going." Dougald rubbed her arms in a soothing, but placating way.

"But you know I can help," she insisted.

Dougald took a deep breath. "If we find them there, we can bring them back for your questioning."

"It was a verra long time ago since they ran off. Are you certain they would still be there?" she asked.

"Mayhap not." Dougald spied Turi leaving the keep, his eyes wide as he saw the Cameron and MacNeill men had seized the MacDonalds.

Dougald said to the Cameron clansmen, "Lock the MacDonalds in the dungeon. All but this man, Gair. He will ride with us." Then he turned to Alana and took her hand and kissed it. "I still would prefer you stay here."

She whispered in Dougald's ear, "What if they are dead?"

Not having considered such a thing, he frowned. She had the right of it. If she saw them, mayhap she could extract whatever information she could from them.

She took a deep breath. "'Tis possible, you know."

"Aye. All right." That decided it for Dougald. If the couple were now ghosts, they might very well still be there. And it was true that Alana was the only one who could learn anything from them.

Turi was frowning at Dougald. "Laird Cameron may no' like that you have ordered the MacDonalds to be locked in the dungeon."

"A couple know something about Connell's death," Dougald said. "We ride to the hovel."

"Wait, you canna take Lady Alana," Turi said, his brow deeply furrowed.

"She will help me to question Ward and his wife."

"They are there?"

"As far as the MacDonald men say."

Several of the men who had taken the MacDonalds to the dungeon hurried back to join Dougald.

"We will go with you," a Cameron said.

"You are no' in charge of the clan, Dougald," another Cameron said. "We do this for Connell."

Dougald dipped his head in agreement. "As do I."

Alana suddenly turned away from the gathered men, and Dougald took her arm. "Alana, are you all right?"

"Aye," she whispered, tears in her eyes. "My brother is ready to go with us." She closed her eyes briefly.

"What is wrong now?"

"Seana wants to come, and he doesna want her to because of what might be said."

Loving Alana for caring about his sister and her brother and their trials, Dougald kissed the top of her head. "They will have to sort it out between themselves."

Someone had already ordered their horses saddled and they were brought to them.

As they mounted, Dougald asked the redheaded MacDonald, "They wanted Connell out of the way so that Alana would marry a man who would take Laird Cameron's place someday, aye?"

Gair said, "We guessed as much when we learned not only had Connell been murdered, but that Laird Cameron was arranging for the marriage of Lady Alana to Hoel."

"Why tell us?"

"'Tis too late. Once you married the lass, 'twas too late to rectify the situation. Whoever is behind this will most likely attempt to murder you next. With Connell's murder, some thought it justified. With yours, the situation would look too suspicious."

"If this is what your laird wishes, why tell us? Your enemy?"

"Too many would wish to avenge your death. Your

Viking bodyguard. Your brothers, cousin, clansmen. Even Lady Alana. As I said, Connell's death was expected—angered husband bent on avenging his honor. No one had considered it might be anything else. But with you? The clans could go to war over it. Many of us dinna like the idea."

As another rider drew close, Dougald glanced over his shoulder and was surprised to see Turi join them. Dougald thought Turi always remained at the keep to manage duties there while Laird Cameron was away.

He nodded at Dougald, greeting him, but not saying a word.

An hour later when they arrived at the croft where half of the peat roof had caved in, the stone walls still intact, Angus hurried to help Alana down from her mare.

Gunnolf came out of the shieling, shaking his head. "No one here."

"Here!" one of Cameron called out.

When Dougald and the others went to see what the man had found, he observed a pile of freshly mounded dirt the length and width of two bodies.

The men began digging and found the remains of a man and a woman in the shallow graves.

Alana stifled a cry of distress and quickly moved away from the site. Angus and Niall and the lads hurried after her.

Dougald examined the decomposing bodies. "Stabbed."

"Aye," Turi said, shaking his head.

"Are they…?"

"Aye," Turi said, frowning. "That is Ward and his wife, Gwyn. Laird Cameron isna going to like this."

\*\*\*

"You whore!" Seana shouted, making Alana turn quickly to see Seana screaming at Ward's dead wife.

Alana's stomach was still reeling with upset after seeing the decomposing bodies. But now that she could observe Gwyn—alive and well—in ghostly form, but to Alana she looked just like the last time she had seen the woman, she actually felt a little better. The woman was wearing a green *léine*, no brat, her red hair hanging loose about her shoulders, her green eyes flashing with anger. Seana was so outraged over the woman, her fists were planted on her hips and her cheeks rosy, her dark brown eyes nearly black.

"Who are you? Another one of his conquests?" Gwyn shrieked.

"I am his *friend*!"

Alana stared at Seana, shocked to hear her say it as much as she and Connell always argued. Though Alana knew her brother well enough to realize he teased Seana to get a rise out of her in a playful manner just as he'd always done with Alana.

Swords began clanking, signaling a fight, and Alana swung around, worried that Dougald was fighting the MacDonald, when she saw Connell battling Ward. "You were incensed I had been seeing Gwyn, but you had neglected her for years. And then? You got her killed! For what? Money? Power? Position? For what, you greedy bastard?"

"You didna deserve to live," Ward said, thrusting his sword at Connell.

"Neither did you!" Connell parried and then took a vicious swing at Ward, slicing through his torso, but not doing any damage. "*You* murdered me, but who killed *you*?"

"That bastard Duff," Ward said. "If I could, I would murder him."

"Duff," Alana said. "'Twas Duff who convinced Ward to kill Connell?"

"Duff?" Turi said, his eyes widening.

"Aye," Alana said.

"Why?" Turi asked, sounding as shocked as she felt.

Connell thrust his sword again at Ward. "Why would Duff want me dead?"

"Your da kept throwing his sons in the dungeon and after your da was murdered, your uncle kept putting them there. No' that they didna deserve it. Hoel promised he would release Duff's sons and they would never be imprisoned when he was in charge."

"Then Duff meant to have my uncle killed also?" Connell asked.

"Aye, Duff did," Ward said.

"Why would Duff want *you* dead, if you worked for him and did what he wished of you?" Alana asked Ward.

"To get rid of us so we couldna tell who was behind all this," Ward said, pausing in his fight with Connell, that earned him another stab, which didn't affect him either.

"What about my da's death? Who was at the site looking for me and wanted to turn me over to someone else? And who was the person who wanted me?" She frowned as Ward lowered his eyes, bowed his head, then looked back at her, appearing guilty as sin, and she knew then...she knew *he* had been there. "'Twas you!" She could barely get the words out, she was so shocked.

He was the one who had been standing so close to her, his boot brushing against her arm. She had looked up at him and the shock at seeing one of her own kin searching for her to turn her over to someone else had stolen the breath from her.

"I told you that you would remember, Alana. You had seen him all along when he was so close. You couldna have avoided looking," Connell said. "I knew it!"

"You were in on the murder of my da," Alana said to Ward, stricken.

"Nay. MacIverson wanted to talk to your da to stop the marriage contract."

"Why?" She had to know if her aunt was at the root of it.

Ward didn't say.

"My aunt? Was she the reason?"

Ward actually turned a little red. "Aye, Lady Alana." Ward frowned at her. "Ye saw me in the forest that day and said naught to yer uncle?"

"I dinna...I dinna remember. 'Twas your voice, though." She tilted her head and tried to recall the words. "Whispered. I didna recognize them. You didna see me?"

"Och, the devil take ye. Where were ye?"

"Hiding in the leaves at your feet."

He shook his head. "We thought ye would be running away. And then ye were too greatly guarded for anyone to make a move after that."

"Who were you supposed to turn me over to?"

"MacDonald. He intended to have rescued you, and then he would have offered to have his son wed you."

"Nay," she said, frowning. "Connell was still alive.

My uncle would have wanted me to be a laird's wife. It wouldna have worked if MacDonald had wanted Hoel to wed me with the intent of having him take over the clan as my brother was only five and ten and still very much alive."

"Aye, my lady. He intended for ye to wed his eldest."

"But an arrangement to marry me to Evnissyen was never initiated," Alana said, glancing at Turi to see his response.

"Nay, Lady Alana, you were never betrothed to his eldest son," Turi said.

Ward sheathed his sword. "Evnissyen didna like that ye were different. Hoel wanted ye. MacDonald only wanted ye wed to his son Evnissyen to tie the clans together. After yer da was murdered, Laird Cameron wouldna agree to another marriage arrangement. He canceled the one with MacIverson because of his dallying with Cameron's own wife, and mayhap he believed MacIverson arranged to have yer da murdered. Then when yer brother died so fortuitously, Laird MacDonald pushed to have ye married to his younger son."

"Did Laird MacDonald also push to have my brother murdered so that Hoel would rule the clan should my uncle die prematurely as well?" she asked.

"Nay," Gair said.

"Be quiet," Gunnolf told the MacDonald clansman.

"I dinna know for certain who planned yer brother's murder. Just that Duff paid me, but 'twas more than that. I would have killed Connell anyway when I learned what he was doing with my unfaithful wife," Ward said, giving Gwyn a scornful look.

Thinking that Duff had been so involved in all of this, Alana became alarmed about Turi's daughter and Pelly. "You had Duff take Brighid and Pelly to Brighid's sister's manor. If he was involved in my brother and da's death, did he take the women where you had ordered him to, or no'?" she asked Turi.

"I will ride at once to see," one of the Cameron said.

Turi looked ill. "Aye, and take three more men with you."

"Nay, wait," Dougald said. "We should return to the keep and question Duff there. We need to take him into custody now before he does any further damage."

"Aye," Turi said, sounding rattled. His face had lost all its color.

"Did you know about my aunt, Turi?" Alana asked, as Angus helped her into her saddle.

Turi said, "Nay—"

"I *know* she was having an affair with MacIverson. Dinna try to hide it from me," Alana said.

Turi frowned as he mounted his own horse. "I am sorry, Lady Alana. I never wished you to know."

"Dinna be sorry. The matter wasna your fault."

"You canna leave us out here like this," Ward said.

Connell helped Seana onto his horse and hurried to climb on behind her. "You made your bed," Connell said to Ward.

Gwyn folded her arms and scowled at Connell. "So this is the way 'tis. I am gone and ye find someone else?"

"You helped your husband to murder me. What did you expect? That I would return for you? Seana is the only one for me. I have finally found the lass I want..."

He paused and gave Alana a heart-warming smile. "...above all others."

Tears filled Alana's eyes. In death, had her brother finally settled down and found real love?

Seana was still scowling at Gwyn. Alana wasn't certain if Seana believed Connell yet or not.

Dougald urged them back to the castle in all haste. "If Duff is behind all this, what if he frees MacDonald's men?" He glanced at Gair. "Did you know of this?"

"Nay."

Alana didn't know whether to believe the man or not, though he had told them more than she thought they would learn.

Before they reached the outer bailey, they heard fighting taking place inside the inner bailey—the striking of swords, the clanking of metal ringing out, the yells of men, some angry, some in pain. Her heart was already pounding hard, but now she was terrified her uncle might be in the midst of it should he have returned from the hunt already.

Dougald immediately began issuing orders. "Take Alana to the stables and watch over her there," he told Angus, since she couldn't reach the keep with all the fighting going on.

Not only had the MacDonald men been freed, they had been armed as well.

Her uncle *was* in the middle of the fighting as she had feared.

"Alana, go with my brother."

"Aye, Dougald." She would not fight him on this. Her wee dagger would not keep her safe from a man armed with a sword. As soon as several lads hurried to take the horses to safety and Alana was with them in the stables, she urged Angus, "Go, help your brother. Tavis and Callum will stay with me."

Angus looked fraught with indecision, stay as his brother had commanded him and protect the lass, or leave her with the two lads and the stable hands while he helped his brother in the fight.

Two of the young men grabbed pitchforks. "Ye can go if ye wish," one of the lads said. "Ye fought in the Crusades. Ye can fight them out there better than we can, and we will protect the lass in here."

Alana was watching through the open stable doors as the men fought when Angus noticed and hurried to move her away from it. "My duty is to the lady," Angus said to the lads.

Then Connell stormed through the doorway. "Tell Seana she must join you in here!"

"She canna be hurt. What is she doing?" Alana asked.

"She is throwing things. That is what she is doing! She is giving me a near heart attack!"

Alana shook her head. "Angus willna let me leave. Tell her I told her I am afraid, and I need her to stay with me."

"All right." Connell stalked back outside.

Everyone in the stable cast small glances at each other, and Alana folded her arms. "Lady Seana, Dougald's sister, is throwing things at the MacDonalds. She is a ghost, for those of you who didna know it," she said for the benefit of the stable hands.

Everyone crowded around the door to watch.

"Look, there, a spear jabbed that mon in the arse," one of the stable hands said.

Angus cleared his throat and the lad looked a little

red-faced and bowed his head to Alana. "Sorry, my lady." But then he went back to watching the fight. "No one is wielding it!"

"Lady Seana is," Alana guessed. She couldn't get near enough the doors to watch.

"Oh!" Tavis said.

"What?" Alana asked, trying to get closer, but Angus turned and gave her a warning look to stay away from the doors.

"Well, what then?" she asked, annoyed.

"The MacDonald mon took the spear from the lady—I guess—and swung it…at naught but air. Then a rock lifted off the ground and was thrown at his head—only no one was doing the throwing—and after it smacked him in the forehead, making a nice bloody imprint, he ran away," Tavis said.

"I didna believe ghosts could throw things," Callum said.

"I am no' surprised," Angus said. "When my sister was angry at me once, she slapped me upside the head with a flopping fish."

Everyone looked at him, mouths agape.

Angus shrugged. "I said something to make her angry and probably deserved it."

\*\*\*

Dougald fought against a much heftier Laird MacDonald, who was trying his damnedest to kill Dougald—most likely because he'd ruined his plans to have his son, Hoel, take over the Cameron clan someday. Mayhap sooner than later if some *accident* had befallen Laird Cameron.

"What do you hope to gain by trying to kill me now?" Dougald asked MacDonald, feeling the same as

MacDonald's own man did that it was too late for MacDonald to win this game.

"The satisfaction in seeing you dead," the man said, his eyes black with hatred, his sword swinging with such power, Dougald tried not to falter under the impact, which might have given the impression he could not manage the onslaught. "I dinna believe that 'twas providence that you met Alana on your lands the way you did without you having been the instigator."

Dougald wasn't about to defend himself. He wanted the truth of what had happened. "You killed Alana's da."

"I had no need to. Duff and his sons, Ward, and Gilleasbuig, a couple of MacIverson's men—"

"And some of yours?"

MacDonald lowered his sword for a moment. Dougald did likewise and waited for him to answer.

"I might have suggested that the lass would be in the wrong hands should she wed MacIverson, which was true. One of my maids had a cousin who worked as a guard for MacIverson and had overheard him talking to his men about the lass being a witch. 'Twas why my eldest son didna want her. But we still wanted the affiliation with the Cameron clan, so he would wed the lass by my order. Then Laird Cameron refused to make any agreement for the lass's marriage, and we had to bide our time. When Connell died, my son Hoel made it clear he wanted to marry the lass."

Dougald didn't want to acknowledge why Hoel would wish Alana for his wife—the connection that Hoel and Alana had might still have pleased her.

MacDonald swung his sword again, barely connecting. He was tiring. He had the weight behind him, aye, but also he was older.

"So if some of my men had taken it upon themselves to change Laird Cameron's mind about having the lass wed to MacIverson, it wasna my doing," Laird MacDonald said.

As if MacDonald wouldn't have known. "And Connell's death?"

MacDonald shook his head. "An aggrieved husband."

As MacDonald lifted his sword to strike Dougald, a rock suddenly hit MacDonald in the side of the head. Dougald forced himself not to look to see where the missile had come from. MacDonald looked. Given the advantage, Dougald slashed at the man's sword arm, forcing him to release his weapon. As soon as MacDonald dropped his sword and yelled out in pain, grabbing his arm to stem the bleeding, Hoel dashed in to fight Dougald.

He was Dougald's age, and more his size, not big and bulky like his da. He also was not as practiced a fighter—his swings not as decisive, his thrusts shallow as if he was afraid to get too close. He was driven by rage, so he made mistake after mistake. When he fell back to avoid being cut, he dropped behind farther than necessary. Dougald felt he had to chase after the man to get a good fight out of him. He wanted to end this now, to let the MacDonald clan know neither he nor the Cameron clan would allow anything further to happen to their people.

Dougald must have moved halfway across the inner bailey, fighting Hoel as he kept parrying short, and falling back long.

"You had Connell murdered so that you could take

Alana as your wife and someday lead the clan," Dougald accused Hoel.

"Ward had every right to kill the man for sleeping with his wife."

"But you put him up to it!"

"I dinna know what you mean."

"If Connell had lived, your da wanted his eldest son to wed Alana. She was to be a laird's wife and married to you, she wouldna have been one. No' unless you had your brother murdered."

"Conjecture and untrue."

Dougald knew it was true, knew the man had been behind Connell's killing, but he couldn't prove it. He wanted to tell Hoel to hold still and fight like a man, but when Hoel tripped and fell onto his back on the grassy bailey, trying to catch his breath, Dougald stepped on Hoel's sword, planting it in place, his sword tip at the man's throat. "You were there, were you no', when Alana's da was murdered?"

Hoel shook his head, his eyes bulging.

"You are no' a strong fighter, so back then, you might no' have killed anyone, but you were there."

"Landon was supposed to watch over Alana," Hoel growled. "She could have died when she ran away and hid."

"You killed Landon."

"I didna say that."

"You didna have to."

"We leave in peace," MacDonald shouted. "Let my son live and we leave in peace."

Cameron said, "Let him go. This is done. Take your wounded and leave, MacDonald. This is over between us."

Mayhap it was over between them today, but they would fight again, Dougald was certain.

# Chapter 30

Angus stiffened as he watched the fighting from the stable. Alana didn't hear as many swords striking each other now. And horses were riding off.

"Are they leaving?" Alana asked, hating that they would not let her see what was happening.

"Aye," Angus said. "Dougald is headed this way."

"Let me see," Alana said, but none of the lads or Angus would move out of her way.

"Angus," Dougald said in greeting, and only then did the lads step back to let him in to see her. "Alana, lass, some of the injured men need your help."

"They are gone, the MacDonald men?" she asked, as Dougald escorted her out of the stable, the lads racing to help move men inside who had not been injured too severely.

"Aye, they have admitted defeat."

"And the man who went with us, Gair?"

"He wouldna fight us. He tried to convince his kin to leave well enough alone."

"Laird MacDonald?" she asked.

"If he could have killed me, he would have. And Hoel. He wanted you, you know," Dougald said.

"Hmph, 'tis trouble enough keeping after one husband."

Dougald smiled down at her. "Did I tell you how

much I love you, lass?"

"Aye, and I, you." Then she saw her uncle, his arm dripping with blood, and she rushed toward him. "Uncle, you are hurt."

"Naught but a scratch, Alana. See to the other men." Her uncle motioned to Turi. "A word with you, now. You sent Lady Alana away..." His words trailed off as he stalked with Turi toward the keep.

"My daughter..."

"She is here."

"You may see to the other men," Alana said to Dougald as a maid dashed to bring Alana her bag of herbs and strips of clothing and sewing materials.

Dougald crouched down in front of the man, one of the Cameron men—the one who looked like he had Norse blood, Kvist—and helped tear his tunic sleeve so Alana could take care of the cut on his arm.

"If you are to see to these men, I will stay with you and remind them that you do this only to keep them alive, naught more," Dougald said.

She knew her husband was referring to Gilleasbuig.

The injured man grinned at Dougald. "I dare say no one will fight you for the lass. Several of us had stopped—no' only our men and yours, but the MacDonald men as well—to watch you fight Laird MacDonald and then when he could fight no more, Hoel MacDonald. Everyone realized at once what a worthy adversary you are."

"I keep telling Lady Alana 'tis tough to kill me."

She hmpfed again.

The two men laughed.

\*\*\*

At a feast that night, where the deer meat and wild boar the men had caught on the hunt were served, Laird Cameron said to Dougald and Alana, "Duff was killed in the fighting. Had he lived, he would have been hanged for murdering Ward and his wife, for hiring Ward to kill my nephew, and for his involvement in the battle that ended my brother's and several other clansmen's lives."

"And his sons?" Dougald asked.

"Ran off. They didna even stop to fight. As soon as Duff released them from the dungeon, they tore off," Cameron said. "If they show themselves around here, they will know the price they will pay."

"You are no' going to punish Turi for sending Alana away, are you?" Dougald asked. He had nothing but respect for the man.

Cameron snorted. "He is one of the most loyal men I have. If I punished Turi, I would have to punish half of my clansmen and lasses who were involved in the plan."

"Half?" Dougald asked.

"Aye. Odara admitted that Bran had talked to her about sending Alana to see Rob MacNeill, and then Bran and a dozen men were waiting for her in the forest, quiet, watching her every move. Had she had any trouble, they would have taken care of it. When they were assured that you had taken the lass in hand, they followed from a safe distance, then returned home once you reached Craigly Castle."

Dougald was glad to know the lass had never been in harm's way. "MacDonald said MacIverson sent some men to kill your brother, and that some of his own men might have been there, too."

"I suspect it is so. I could never get the full truth from either man," Cameron said.

"Then later, MacIverson had an unfortunate accident."

"Aye," Cameron said. "Most unfortunate."

Dougald suspected Cameron had something to do with the "accident."

"As long as the men who were traitor to our kin are no longer able to do anything further, I am satisfied," Cameron said.

Dougald nodded, then glanced at Alana who was picking at her meat, but not eating it. She was watching one of the lower tables.

"Is there something wrong, Alana?" he asked, taking her hand in his and kissing it.

She looked up and smiled at Dougald with tears in her eyes. "My brother just proposed to Seana on one knee, and she smiled at him and said she would marry him."

Laird Cameron leaned around Dougald and said to Alana, "Connell did?"

Alana wiped away tears dribbling down her cheeks and nodded with a smile. "He did, Uncle. He did."

To Dougald's surprise, Cameron lifted his tankard and said, "To the end of strife for our clans. To Connell and Seana's happiness. To a new beginning between the MacNeill and the Cameron clans."

"Thank you, Uncle," Alana said. "Connell is beaming and saluted you back, though he did so with his sword. It appears he canna locate a ghostly tankard." Alana squeezed Dougald's hand. "I am tired and no' hungry. With my uncle's permission, I wish to retire to bed."

"Aye, lass. I will join you in a wee…"

She raised her brows.

Dougald smiled. "It seems I am tired also." He grinned down at his bonny lass. And she couldn't have offered him a brighter or more wicked smile in return. "With all due respect, Laird Cameron, I am taking my wife to her chamber."

"When you return…," Laird Cameron said.

"Aye, mayhap in the morn to break our fast."

Laird Cameron smiled. "You will do fine, Dougald MacNeill. I will have a hard time remaining laird of this clan for too many more years. The men are all talking about the way you fought out there today, and the way you led them—despite their telling you that you were no' their laird."

"That will be many years to come," Dougald said. "I still have much to learn from you." Then without another word, Dougald helped Alana from her seat and wrapped his arm around her waist as he walked her across the great hall.

The room grew silent as he knew it would. He glanced down to see how she was taking it. She was blushing furiously.

He leaned down and kissed her cheek. "We could have waited until the meal was done."

"Nay, we couldna. What if I retired to bed and you stayed to talk to my uncle, and he locked you in the dungeon again?"

"I have it on good authority, my bonny wife would rescue me."

"Aye, but I would rather have you in my bed tonight."

And with that, he scooped her up in his arms,

cheers went up in the great hall, and Dougald carried his wife off to another night of wedded bliss. He knew they wouldn't break their fast the next morning but rather much later that day. Mayhap not until later that eve.

###

## The Highlanders Series:

*Winning the Highlander's Heart,* Book 1
*The Accidental Highland Hero,* Book 2
*Highland Rake,* Book 3

## About the Author

*USA Today* bestselling and an award-winning author of urban fantasy and medieval romantic suspense, Terry Spear also writes true stories for adult and young adult audiences. She's a retired lieutenant colonel in the U.S. Army Reserves and has an MBA from Monmouth University. She also creates award-winning teddy bears, Wilde & Woolly Bears, that are personalized that have found homes all over the world. When she's not writing or making bears, she's teaching online writing courses or gardening. Her family has roots in the Highlands of Scotland where her love of all things Scottish came into being. Originally from California, she's lived in eight states and now resides in the heart of Texas. She is the author of the Heart of the Wolf series and the Heart of the Jaguar series, plus numerous other paranormal romance and historical romance novels.

For more information, please visit www.terryspear.com, or follow her on Twitter,

@TerrySpear. She is also on Facebook at http://www.facebook.com/terry.spear .